The Peter Pan Chronicles

The Peter Pan Chronicles

The Nearly 100 Year History of "The Boy Who Wouldn't Grow Up"

Bruce K. Hanson

BIRCH LANE PRESS

PUBLISHED BY CAROL PUBLISHING GROUP

A Birch Lane Press Book
Published by Carol Publishing Group
Birch Lane Press is a registered trademark of
Carol Communications, Inc.
Editorial Offices: 600 Madison Avenue, New York, N.Y. 10022
Sales & Distribution Offices: 120 Enterprise Avenue,
Secaucus, N.J. 07094
In Canada: Canadian Manda Group, P.O. Box 920 Station U,
Toronto, Ontario M8Z 5P9
Queries regarding rights and permissions should be addressed to Carol
Publishing Group, 600 Madison Avenue, New York, N.Y. 10022

Carol Publishing Group books are available at special discounts for bulk
purchases, for sales promotions, fund-raising, or educational purposes.
Special editions can be created to specifications. For details, contact:
Special Sales Department, Carol Publishing Group, 120 Enterprise
Avenue, Secaucus, N.J. 07094

Manufactured in the United States of America
10 9 8 7 6 5 4 3 2 1

Library of Congress Cataloging-in-Publication Data

Hanson, Bruce K.
The Peter Pan chronicles : the nearly 100-year history of the "boy
who wouldn't grow up" / by Bruce K. Hanson.
p. cm.
"A Birch Lane Press book."
ISBN 1–55972–160–X :
1. Barrie, J. M. (James Matthew), 1860–1937. Peter Pan.
2. Barrie, J. M. (James Matthew), 1860–1937—Adaptations.
3. Children's stories, English—History and criticism.
4. Children's stories, English—Adaptations.   5. Peter Pan
(Fictitious character)   I. Title.
PR4074.P33H36   1993
823'.912—dc20   93-37572
CIP

To
Drew Tobias,
Whose every phase of growing up
is an extraordinary adventure.

Contents

"TO DIE WILL BE AN AWFULLY BIG ADVENTURE!"

Preface

*L*et's end one misconception right now. James Barrie never wrote a book titled *Peter Pan*! He did, however, write a novel, published in 1902, called *The Little White Bird*, which introduced Peter as a baby who ran away seven days after he was born. This character was so unique the author was compelled to develop him further in a play, *Peter Pan, or The Boy Who Wouldn't Grow Up,* which had its world premiere in 1904. In 1906 the chapters featuring Peter in *The Little White Bird* were published in a separate illustrated text called *Peter Pan in Kensington Gardens,* and in 1911 Barrie novelized his play into *Peter and Wendy.* Each venture met with great popularity, but before long, with three different versions of the story available, the public was confused about Peter's origin. The author only added to the enigma with his whimsical yet elusive explanations of the birth of Peter Pan.

The character of Peter was developed from a group of stories that the author created to amuse the children of his friends, Sylvia and Arthur Llewelyn Davies. Influenced by the great commercial successes of English pantomime, he decided to write his own using Peter as the focal point. Intended for one season only, *Peter Pan, or The Boy Who Wouldn't Grow Up* was an unexpected success with the critics and audiences. Soon the popularity of the play was eclipsed by Peter himself.

"The difference between Peter Pan and his rivals," observed Roger Lancelyn Green, "is that, however hard it is to believe that they are mere characters of fiction, Peter alone has crossed the border-land of folklore. Even Alice is only three-dimensional: Peter Pan has broken into the fourth dimension of the imagination." There are many children who have not read the book or seen the play, but everyone is familiar with this remarkable boy. Movie mogul Steven Spielberg was banking on this with his film *Hook,* from which he departed greatly from Barrie's concept. No other piece of literature could be so drastically changed. Spielberg, like everyone else, approaches Peter Pan as an established myth that can be as relevant today as it was yesteryear.

Would Barrie have been pleased with the many alterations that have taken place with his favorite play? Certainly no one worked harder to nurture the concept of Peter Pan as a myth than the writer himself. As he wrote in *The Little White Bird,* "If you ask your mother whether she knew about Peter Pan when she was a little girl, she will say, 'Why, of course, I did, child.' And if you ask her whether he rode a goat in those days, she will say, 'What a foolish question to ask; certainly he did.' Then if you ask your grandmother whether she knew about Peter Pan when she was a girl, she also says, 'Why, of course, I did, child,' but if you ask her whether he rode on a goat in those days, she says she never heard of his having a goat. Perhaps she has forgotten, just as she sometimes forgets your name and calls you Mildred, which is your mother's name."

My fascination with *Peter Pan* began in 1960 when at the age of seven I was allowed to stay up late with my brothers, Wayne and Mark, to watch a musical version on television. That evening, we had our baths before supper as our mother set up TV trays with our rocking chairs. Amazingly, on this special occasion we were allowed to eat our meal in the living room while watching television. Our supper was also to be a treat, frozen chicken TV dinners! All the rules were broken that night so I knew that we were in store for something special. The tension mounted when the Darling children were put to bed while their mother asked the night lights to protect them. And then it happened! Peter Pan flew into the Darling nursery and into the hearts of another generation of children.

Of course I knew that Peter was really a woman. Mary-What's-Her-Name! After all, the "Baby Boom" generation was known for its sophistication. We had been brought up with Howdy Doody, Kukla, Fran and Ollie, Sky King, Roy Rogers and Dale Evans. Like most children of that seemingly innocent time, I was intelligent enough to allow myself to believe what the artists were trying to convey. So, when Roy and Dale sang "Happy Trails to You, Until We Meet Again" at the end of each program, I knew that they were sincere in their wishes, and more important, they knew that I knew. Likewise, when Peter flew into the Darling nursery and took the children to Never Never Land, I believed. Thirty years later I am wiser and older, but not old! And to my generation, Mary Martin never grew old. Neither did the other actresses who played Peter to nearly five generations of children before her.

It is difficult to watch other productions of *Peter Pan* after you have experienced that first encounter. How can any other Peter compete with sweet memories. Yet we are able to let go of our preconceived notions if we really want to. When I see a play by Shakespeare I want to see a fresh, new production. Similarly, when I see a musical that I have seen before I also do not view it as a "revival." I am there to experience the play for the first time. I want to see a singing King of Siam again for the first time, or a dancing man in the rain or a chorus girl who makes good. I want the magic. I want to believe.

For each generation the role of Peter and the actresses (or actors) playing him are inseparable; therefore, the chapters in this book are listed by who played Peter. Time has not been as important a factor for the changes in each production as have the performers playing the part. During the playwright's lifetime, changes constantly occurred, often at the whim of the actress performing that particular season. Even the 1928 published script was different than the acting versions used in England and at the Civic Repertory Theatre in New York. Many productions were adapted in one way or another to suit the talent of the stars. Consequently, when I hear that irritating statement that a musical of *Peter Pan* is not as good as the original, I ask, "Which original?" Unlike a *Show Boat* or *Oklahoma!* there is no definitive Pan. James Barrie could never leave the play alone, and, so it seems, neither can anyone else.

In an interview with Sondra Lee, Tiger Lily to Mary Martin's Pan, the actress made an interesting observation. She felt that during interviews, the media is too obsessed with the ages of actors, actresses, and celebrities in general. This struck a chord that is played back in this book. While the careers of stars of *Peter Pan* are examined to comprehend what they have brought to the role, their ages at that time are not discussed unless it is vital to the characterization. If the actors can make us believe, what does it matter if they are twenty or forty? The experience brought to the role is what matters. Hence you will only see photographs of the actors and actresses in their theatrical prime. If Peter is never to grow old, shouldn't the performers also remain young in our hearts?

July 27, 1992
Staten Island, New York

The Peter Pan Chronicles

The Peter Pan Statue by Sir George Frampton in
Kensington Gardens, London.

Peter Pan (I Love You)

Peter Pan, I love you
Loved you from the start
You have brought the sunshine
Back into my heart
In your land of fancy
Childhood dreams come true
Always after
Joy and laughter
Peter Pan, I love you

—Robert King and Ray Henderson as a dedication to Marilyn Miller in the 1924 production of *Peter Pan*. "Peter Pan (I Love You)" by Ray Henderson and Robert King.© September 22, 1924 by Shapiro Bernstein & Co., Inc. Renewed. Used By Permission

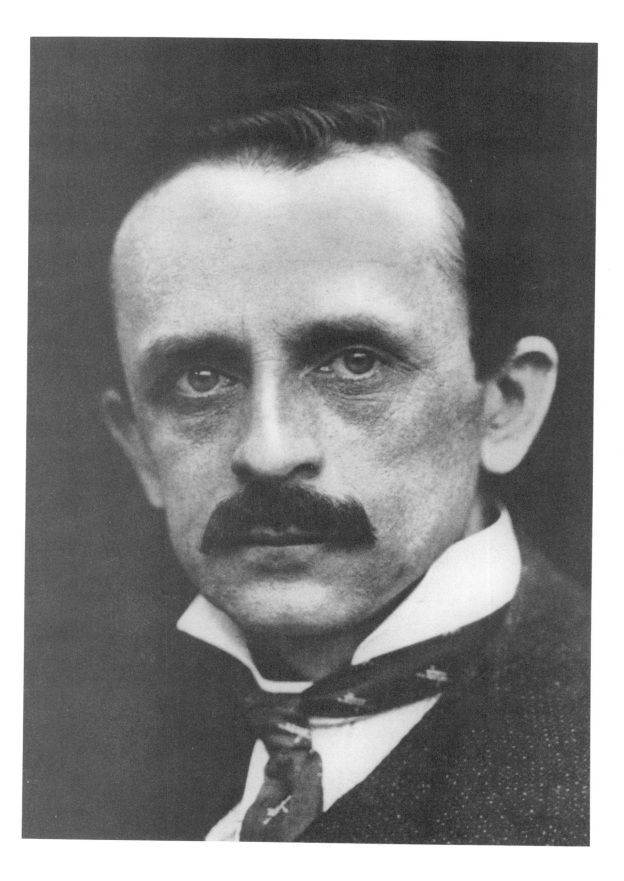

James Barrie

The Man Who Wouldn't Grow Up

I sometimes feel about Peter that there is a little inner circle who would know (as if it were a record of fact in which they had participated) the moment I went astray with him....

—J. M. Barrie, 1908

*T*his is not the "complete" history of *The Boy Who Wouldn't Grow Up*. Roger Lancelyn Green thoroughly analyzed the creation and endurance of this classic children's play in his *Fifty Years of Peter Pan*. Furthermore, there will undoubtedly be many more productions during the next fifty years. This is also not a biography of J. M. Barrie. There are volumes of words and photographs by writers like Andrew Birkin, Janet Dunbar, and Denis Mackall who are far more equipped to analyze the playwright's life through his art and to explain his writing by dissecting his life. Rather, this book is intended as a celebration of the individual productions of Barrie's most famous play that have remained so special to generations of children.

There are at least three reasons why people of all ages enjoy *Peter Pan*—the play, the flying, and Peter Pan himself. (Barrie provided another from a youngster sitting in his private box. "What I think I liked best," the boy said, "was tearing up the programme and dropping the bits on people's heads.") What always stands out is the personality and talent that each actress or actor brings to the part of Captain Hook, Wendy, or even Smee. Above all, though, we remember Peter.

After seeing the show for the first time, we are especially aware of who played Peter, and that performance usually remains the quintessential interpretation. But what of the past achievements of actors who played Peter and those who came after our first exposure to the play? With the exception of Hamlet, no other role has been as coveted by so many actors as has Peter. Therefore, we will take a trip to the beginning of this century to discover the earliest of Peter Pans and at a time when innocence was not confined to the young. We will continue to the present with the ever-growing affection for Peter at the end of a century where

PAGE 16: J. M. Barrie, age twenty-six. (Courtesy of Barrie's Birthplace—The National Trust for Scotland)

innocence and magic are deliberately shattered for the sake of "truth"—the truth of whoever happens to be profiting from an exposé book or realistic film. To bring back the magic let us dispel any suggestions of sexual misconduct by a writer who simply loved children. When Nicholas (Nico) Llewelyn Davies, the last surviving brother of the five Davies boys whose welfare was provided for by Barrie, was asked by Andrew Birkin, author of *J. M. Barrie and the Lost Boys,* if he ever noticed any inappropriate behavior by Barrie toward children, Nico replied, "He was an innocent—which is why he could write *Peter Pan."*

All children, except one, grow up. They soon know that they will grow up, and the way Wendy knew was this. One day when she was two years old she was playing in a garden, and she plucked another flower and ran with it to her mother. I suppose she must have looked rather delightful, for Mrs. Darling put her hand to her heart and cried, "Oh, why can't you remain like this forever!" This was all that passed between them on the subject, but henceforth Wendy knew that she must grow up. You always know after you are two. This is the beginning of the end.

In order to examine the theatrical performances of *Peter Pan* it is necessary to briefly discuss the man who invented it all, for despite the popularity of the folk hero, Peter comes from the mind of one man. The lighthearted passage above is the opening paragraph from James M. Barrie's 1911 novel, *Peter and Wendy.* It is a combination of the author's natural talents for writing sentiment with his tongue-in-cheek humor, but there is also a melancholy aspect that escapes many readers. Barrie's Peter Pan controls his own destiny. He chooses not to grow up. The author did not have this luxury. "It is as if, long after writing *Peter Pan,* its true meaning came to me," he inscribed in his notebook many years after he penned his most famous play. "Desperate attempts to grow up but can't." Cynthia Asquith, his secretary, friend, and confidante, made it a point to state that we should not be allowed to take this random confession too seriously, yet authors Janet Dunbar and Andrew Birkin have both illustrated in their comprehensive biographies that his statement is lucid and quite tragic.

"All Barrie's life led up to the creation of Peter Pan," wrote *Pan* historian Roger Lancelyn Green, "and everything he had written so far contained hints or foreshadowings of what was to come." Perhaps no one was more aware of this than Barrie himself. Born in Kirriemuir, Scotland, on May 9, 1860, he was one of the ten children of David Barrie, a linen weaver and his wife, Margaret Oglivy. Typical of even the poor inhabitants of that country, the education of the children was a major concern for both parents, although the primary focus for the mother was her second son,

TOP: James Barrie, age six. (Author's collection); ABOVE: James Barrie, age nine. (Courtesy of Andrew Birkin, author of *J. M. Barrie and the Lost Boys*)

David. He was an extremely intelligent boy for whom she had great expectations. The eldest son, Alexander, grown, educated, and teaching at Glasgow, sent for his thirteen-year-old brother in order to help him win a scholarship. Margaret had great reservations about letting David leave her and subsequently she was stunned for life when David was fatally injured in a skating accident.

Six-year-old Jamie sensed the deep loss that his mother was experiencing. He later wrote that once while his mother was sleeping, she heard him stir and called out, "'Is that you?' I think the tone hurt me, for I made no answer, and then the voice said more anxiously 'Is that you?' again. I thought it was the dead boy she was speaking to, and I said in a little lonely voice, 'No, it's no' him, it's just me.'" At his sisters' urging, Jamie tried to replace his brother by acting as much like David as he could. While the act helped his mother and also gave him the attention he craved, a deep wound was created that would have a significant impact on his writing and personal life. Margaret Oglivy would spend the rest of her life mourning David; Jamie would grow older and David would always remain a boy.

Jamie thrived on storytelling and drama and he would listen intensely for hours as his mother told him stories of her childhood. His friends at school would later remember how he would tell a

ABOVE LEFT: Margaret Ogilvy. (Courtesy of Andrew Birkin); ABOVE RIGHT: David Barrie. (Author's collection)

story "with sparkling eye, full of the minutest detail and entrancing to the listener. And I have no doubt that he heard it from the lips of some old body in Kirriemuir."

Family finances improved when his father accepted a managerial position for a commercial linen company and he could now afford to send James to Dumfries Academy. The boy already knew that he wanted to be a writer. While studying at the academy, he lived with Alexander, who was now inspector of the schools in the district of Dumfries. Here the boy discovered his love for cricket and the theatre. With a group of friends, he formed a pirate band that would meet by the river Nith. Their games of pretending led to the establishment of a small theatre group, the Dumfries Amateur Dramatic Club. The acting bug had bitten him. In an adaptation of a story by Fenimore Cooper, the boy played six parts. The group was highly criticized by a local clergyman as "grossly immoral," but the written support of prestigious patrons was sought out by the boys, which helped in the continuation of their productions.

James's social life was not as stimulating as his life on stage. The young man was painfully shy. Standing about five feet tall, he was described by a friend as a "sallow-faced, round-shouldered, slight, somewhat delicate-looking figure, who quietly went in and out amongst us, attracting but little observation." He as extremely uncomfortable with women, venerating them to a level that he could not possibly obtain. He particularly liked stage actresses.

Before long, the theatre group became the center of his life at school, and his work in other subjects suffered. It was obvious that James was not going to receive a scholarship to go to a university, so Alexander managed to make arrangements for him to attend Edinburgh University where renowned David Masson was professor of Rhetoric and Literature.

While at school Barrie became the drama and book reviewer for the *Edinburgh Courant*. After his graduation in 1882, he returned home where his sister, Jane Annie, implored him to apply for a "leader-writer" position with the *Nottingham Journal*. He worked in that capacity for a year while he also wrote a play and contributed stories to other journals. November 17, 1884, was to prove a turning point in his artistic career when the *St. James's Gazette* printed his short story, "An Auld Licht Community." Publisher Frederick Greenwood requested more sketches of the Auld Lichts.

Against Greenwood's advice, Barrie moved to London in March of the same year. During the next few struggling years he managed to write a book, *Better Dead*. Yet it was the Auld Licht sketches that brought him to the attention of the critics and the

ABOVE: Caricature artists had a field day with Barrie. (Author's collection); LEFT: Mary Ansell, c. 1894. (Courtesy of Barrie's Birthplace—The National Trust for Scotland)

public. In 1888 he revised and compiled these works to form a new book, *Auld Licht Idylls* (Old Light Ideals). This met with critical and financial success, but it was quickly overshadowed by *A Window in Thrums* (1889) and *The Little Minister* (1891). Each of these works was influenced not so much by Barrie's childhood observations as by his mother's stories.

The reason my books deal with the past instead of with the life I myself have known is simply this, that I soon grow tired of writing tales unless I can see a little girl, of whom my mother has told me, wandering confidently through the pages. Such a grip has her memory of her girlhood had upon me since I was a boy of six....

This passage is from Barrie's biography of his mother, *Margaret Ogilvy*, which was published in 1886. The story of a girl whose mother died when she was only eight, who raised her brothers and took care of the house, moved the critics and book buyers, adding more to Barrie's purse. Still obsessed with the theatre, he also wrote his first play, albeit a short one, *Ibsen's Ghost*, in 1891. Although it was hardly a success, its producer wanted a full-length play from Barrie. He delivered with *Walker, London,* which ran for 511 performances and served as an introduction to Mary Ansell, an actress who would become the second most important woman in his life.

Barrie working on *The Little Minister* at Strath View, Kirrie (Courtesy of Barrie's Birthplace—The National Trust for Scotland)

As he did with other beautiful actresses, the insecure little man placed Mary Ansell on a pedestal. A slow courtship followed and had it not been for a serious illness that put Barrie near his deathbed, it is probable that the marriage would never have taken place. Despite his badgering Mary to wed him, Barrie had his doubts about such a union. "Our love has brought me nothing but misery," he wrote in his notebook only a few days before the wedding. He was particularly insecure with the idea of physical intimacy, and Mary Ansell later confided to actress Pauline Chase that their honeymoon was a nightmare. In an article, "The Boy Who Couldn't Grow Up," writer Allison Lurie suggested that Barrie was afflicted with incomplete puberty. Whether this was a result of some physical deformation or if it was psychological, the couple remained childless. This remained a sore point with Barrie, who adored children, and for Mary, who wanted to be a mother. As if he could foresee their future together, Barrie bought his new bride a consolation, a Saint Bernard puppy, which they named Porthos after a dog in George du Maurier's popular novel, *Peter Ibbetson*. The Barrie marriage appeared secure and proper to outsiders but both husband and wife were unhappy. Ironically, it was during his marriage that Barrie wrote his most successful plays, *The Little Minister* (1897), *Quality Street* (1902), *The Admirable Crichton* (1902), *Peter Pan* (1904), and *What Every Woman Knows* (1908).

An inside look at their lives was provided by Barrie himself, in *Sentimental Tommy,* published in 1896, and its sequel, *Tommy and Grizel,* written four years later. Tommy Sandys is a boy who adores being a child and can never really grow up. His marriage to Grizel fails because he is incapable of mature emotions. "He was a boy only," wrote Barrie in the second volume. "She knew that, despite all he had gone through, he was still a boy. And boys cannot love. Oh, it is not cruel to ask a boy to love?" The tragedy of Tommy's inability to love his wife as a man was a reflection of the author's own life, yet from such sadness arose a work of art. In fact, Barrie gave his literary figure, Tommy, the foresight of creating Peter Pan. "It was but a reverie about a little boy who was lost. His parents find him in a wood singing joyfully to himself because he thinks he can now be a boy for ever; and he fears that if they catch him they will compel him to grow into a man, so he runs farther from them into the wood and is running still, singing to himself because he is always to be a boy."

TOP: Sylvia Llewelyn Davies (Courtesy of Andrew Birkin); ABOVE: Arthur Llewelyn Davies (Courtesy of Andrew Birkin)

The third most important woman in the author's life was Sylvia Llewelyn Davies, the daughter of George du Maurier. He met her at a dinner party where he watched as she secretly hid some desserts in her reticule. When confronted, Sylvia confessed that they were for her youngest child, Peter. Further conversation revealed that she was the mother of George and Jack, two small boys whom the Barries often encountered with their nanny during their daily walks through Kensington Park. He would entertain the boys by wiggling his ears, lifting one eyebrow, wrestling with Porthos, and making up stories with the boys as the heroes. He was immediately enchanted by the beauty and charm of Sylvia.

"There was never a simpler, happier family until the coming of Peter Pan," Barrie wrote in 1911. In *J. M. Barrie and the Lost Boys* Andrew Birkin borrowed Barrie's words to make an interesting analogy between Peter Pan and his creator. The Davies family was the prototype for the Darling family and like their literary counterparts, their lives changed greatly—with the visits of J. M. Barrie. In a short time, he began to show up frequently at the Davies home, much to the chagrin of Sylvia's husband, Arthur Llewelyn Davies, a young barrister. Barrie began writing to Sylvia, addressing her by her middle name, Jocelyn, which no one else used. This irritated her husband, as did Barrie's excessive generosity toward the boys. Arthur felt helpless as the successful writer burrowed his way into his family. Now Barrie could be part of a whole family, a surrogate father to the boys and confidant to Sylvia without any fear of intimacy. He knew she was very much in love with her husband. This could not have improved Barrie's relationship with his own wife, Mary.

Barrie was spending more time with the Davies boys, telling them many stories and taking them to the English pantomimes. In 1900, after seeing *The Babes in the Wood*, he wrote one of his own called "The Greedy Dwarf." It was acted out for the boys by Barrie and his wife; Gerald du Maurier, a popular actor and brother of Sylvia; Porthos; and Sylvia as the principal boy. Barrie carefully observed the children's reactions and recorded them.

The daily stories were continued, expanded, and embellished to include talking birds, fairies, and the boys themselves. At some point that no one could remember, Peter Pan became part of these adventures. Many of these stories were incorporated into a new novel, *The Little White Bird*, which was published in 1902. This book also served as a written introduction to Peter Pan, a story within the novel told by the narrator to a small boy, David, who in turn, was modeled after George Davies. Peter appeared as a seven-day-old baby who ran away from home to live among the fairies on the island in the Serpentine River, which is part of Kensington Gardens. In this new fairy tale the writer explained that all children started out as birds eventually forgetting how to fly. Peter was content to live among the birds, thinking that he was one of them, until he was informed by an old bird, Solomon Caw, that he was neither bird nor boy—he was "betwixt-and-between." He even-

tually flew home only to find that he had waited too long and that the window to the nursery was barred. Through his tears he spied on his mother holding a new baby.

The book also introduced a predecessor to Wendy in a little girl named Maimie who exchanged a thimble for a kiss with Peter. A special house was built for her by the fairies.

With *The Little White Bird* almost finished, Barrie published an unusual book in 1901 with a very limited pressing—two copies— one for Barrie and one for Arthur Llewelyn Davies, who immediately lost his copy on a railway carriage. *The Boy Castaways of Black Lake Island* was a photo essay of make-believe adventures that the Davies boys shared with Barrie's dog Porthos at Black Lake. It seems that Arthur Davies could not escape Barrie even in the summer, for his family spent six weeks vacationing near the Barrie cottage. Written as if narrated by Peter Davies, the adventure is a takeoff of classic shipwreck stories like *The Swiss Family Robinson* and *The Coral Island* and it consists of thirty-six photographs taken by Barrie of the boys playing at Pirates.

Making a brief appearance in this book was the newest member of the family, Michael, who, born the year before on June 16, 1900, was soon to become Barrie's favorite.

For Christmas of 1901, Barrie treated the Davies boys to another pantomime, *Bluebell in Fairyland,* written by Seymour Hicks, who also starred opposite his wife, Ellaline Terriss. The English pantomimes were presented as a holiday treat for children.

TOP: Jack, George, and Peter in 1901 from *The Boy Castaways*. Photo: J. M. Barrie. (The Beinecke Rare Book and Manuscript Library, Yale University); ABOVE: Michael, age four, the year of *Peter Pan*'s first season. (Courtesy of Andrew Birkin)

They included songs, comedy, a harlequin clown, magic, flying, and spectacular effects loosely tied together. The principal boy was played by a woman rather than a male child as she would be able to handle the many lines and also appear convincingly as a young male, *Bluebell* was different from the other theatrical fare for children as it was not derived from a literary source and it presented a solid plot in the form of a dream. Amazed as he was by the youngsters' delight, he was also impressed with how profitable a children's play could be. Surely he could also write a pantomime of some quality.

All of the pieces of Barrie's life and writings were now being fused for his future masterpiece. During the next two and a half years there were many changes that would take place during the development of the new children's play, but a few remained constant. Mrs. Darling, the essence of motherhood, was found in Sylvia Davies, while Arthur was unfairly modeled into a cruel caricature in Mr. Darling, a man who has no time or patience for his children. Their daughter was named Wendy Moira Angela Darling, in honor of Margaret Henley, the deceased daughter of Barrie's friend, W. E. Henley. The six-year-old, one of several of the author's favorite children, had a special nickname for Barrie: "my Friendy." Since her childish speech prevented her from pronouncing her *fr*'s properly, it came out as "my Fwendy" or "Wendy." In a few years this would become one of the most popular names for girls. Moira was the same name he used in a play the year before, *Little Mary*, and Angela was in honor of a cousin of the Davies boys who also just so happened to be one of the daughters of Gerald du Maurier, the first Captain Hook.

Barrie playing Captain Hook to Michael's Pan. (Courtesy of Andrew Birkin, author of *J. M. Barrie and the Lost Boys*)

The names of the Davies boys were also used, with George becoming Mr. Darling's first name, Jack becoming John Napoleon Darling, and Michael becoming Michael Alexander Darling. The middle name of Alexander was soon replaced with Nicholas, who was born to the Davies family on November 24, 1903. Peter Davies's name was given to the hero of the play, but he did not serve as the single model for Peter Pan. "...I made Peter by rubbing the five of you violently together, as savages with two sticks produce a flame," he wrote in his dedication to the published version of *Peter Pan, or The Boy Who Wouldn't Grow Up*. "That is all he is, the spark I got from you." Barrie states that he does not remember writing the play that is influenced by so many of the adventures and stories he shared with the Davies boys. "What was it that made us eventually give to the public in the thin form of a play that which had been woven for ourselves alone?" Poetic and sentimental as he sounds, Barrie always was able to separate feelings from the real-life events that he was writing about. When his sister Maggie's fiancé died from a fall from the horse that her brother gave as a wedding present, the writer within was always present and jotted down an idea for a novel:

After death, a character [a la Maggie] talks beautiful resignation, &c. Yet what is the feeling at heart? A kicking at the awfulness? A bitterness? Work this out in novel, showing how almost no one in these cir[cumstances] gets at other's real feelings. Each conceals from the other.

Barrie recorded many important events in his life. No one incident resulted in the birth of Peter Pan. He is a combination of many experiences, acquaintances, and the desire to tell a good tale. Barrie was shrewd enough to use life experiences to create art.

Captain Hook is a direct outgrowth from the Captain Swarthy of *The Boy Castaways* and one of the most famous and evil villains ever created for a children's play, with only the Wicked Witch of the West from *The Wizard of Oz* rivaling him. Interestingly, he was originally envisioned as a cruel schoolmaster, someone to whom many children could relate and love to hate. In fact, this idea was not discarded until the play was well into rehearsals. Below is a passage from an early script where Smee meets Hook outside the Darling house at the end of the play.

TOP: Sylvia and Nicholas, the fifth Davies boy. (Courtesy of Andrew Birkin); ABOVE: Margaret Henley, who died at age six, inspired Barrie to create Wendy. Many stage Wendys would wear a replica of her cloak. (Courtesy of Andrew Birkin)

HOOK

I'm a schoolmaster—to revenge myself on boys. I hook them so, and then lay on like this. When it was found what a useful hook I had every father in Merry England clamoured for my services.

Hook plans to watch Wendy until she meets again with Peter so that he can catch the boy truant.

With the exception of Noodler, the pirates' names were derived from literary figures or actual pirates. Noodler was given his name after John Kelt's amazing rubbery arms. Tinker Bell was called Tippy in the early drafts, and while most of the lost boys were given nicknames of the period, Slightly was the only boy given a last name, Slightly Soiled, from a note that his mother pinned on his clothing. As for the twins, they are a direct influence of twins used in *Bluebell* although they are given no names because Peter cannot tell them apart.

When Barrie completed the first script it was merely titled "Anon—A Play." He was sure it would be difficult to find anyone interested in a theatrical venture that required many set changes and special effects. He read the play to actor-producer Beerbohm Tree, who was renowned for his elaborate productions at His Majesty's Theatre. Not only was Barrie's play rejected, Tree went so far as to tell Charles Frohman, Barrie's American producer and friend, that Barrie had gone mad with his latest writing.

Wrote Daniel Frohman and Isaac Marcosson in their biography of impresario Frohman:

No two men could have been more opposite. Frohman was quick, nervous, impulsive, bubbling with optimism; Barrie was the quiet, canny Scot, reserved, regressed, and elusive. Yet they had two great traits in common—shyness and humor. As Barrie says:

"Because we were the two shyest men in the world, we got on so well and understood each other so perfectly."

Frohman was known for taking chances, a luxury he enjoyed and could afford. In addition to his lucrative theatre business in the States, Frohman also rented the Duke of York's Theatre in London, which reminded him more of a drawing room. It was only a matter of time before he was confronted by the Scotsman during his annual trip to England. According to Frohman's biography, the two met for dinner at the Garrick Club in London. Barrie seemed nervous and Frohman asked what was wrong.

"Simply this," said Barrie. "You know I have an agreement to deliver you the manuscript of a play?"

"Yes," said Frohman.

"Well, I have it, all right," said Barrie, "but I am sure it will not be a commercial success. But it is a dream-child of mine, and I am so anxious to see it on the stage that I have written another play which I will be glad to give you and which will compensate you for any loss on the one I am so eager to see produced."

"Don't bother about that," said Frohman. "I will produce both plays."

Barrie and his second dog, Luath, a Newfoundland. While Porthos was the model for Nana's character, Luath's coat was copied for the costume. (Courtesy of Andrew Birkin)

The Duke of York's Theatre, home of *Peter Pan* for ten years. (Author's collection)

The second play was *Alice-Sit-By-the-Fire* and despite the presence of Ellen Terry in the leading role in London and Ethel Barrymore in the American production, it played very short seasons and was quickly forgotten. Frohman was not too concerned for he was sure that the other play would be a perfect vehicle for an American actress under his contract: Maude Adams.

According to his biographers:

When Frohman first read *Peter Pan* he was so entranced that he could not resist telling all his friends about it. He would stop them in the street and act out the scenes. Yet it required the most stupendous courage and confidence to put on a play that, from the manuscript, sounded like a combination of circus and extravaganza: a play in which children flew in and out of rooms, crocodiles swallowed alarm-clocks, a man exchanged places with his dog in its kennel, and various other seemingly absurd and ridiculous things happened.

Charles Frohman looked forward to the London production not only for its own sake but also as a test for an American production with Maude Adams. Earlier, Barrie had written to Adams of the progress of his new play. Informally it was referred to as "Peter and Wendy" but Barrie was toying with the title "The Great White Father." Frohman suggested something snappier should be used, and Barrie quickly came up with another title. In the spring of 1904, *Peter Pan, or The Boy Who Wouldn't Grow Up* was finally on its way into production.

Nina Boucicault

And the First Peter Pan

To me Peter Pan *has always been much more than a fairy play for children. The fairy trappings are only a setting for the development of a serious idea. From beginning to end the story is a rather wistful commentary on human nature, taking as its theme the supreme selfishness of man and the supreme unselfishness of woman.*
                                                        —*Nina Boucicault, 1923*

*F*or years Nina Boucicault was remembered by London audiences as being the best of all Peter Pans. Barrie sustained this belief years later when he advised a young actress on her approach to the role. He told her that Peter should be a lovable tomboy, as his favorite actress, Pauline Chase, portrayed him, or "...he must be the whimsical, fairy creature that Nina Boucicault made him...." But memories last only as long as a lifetime and today, almost a hundred years later, we each have our own favorite Peter Pan. Only one thing remains constant—Nina Boucicault was the first actress to play Peter Pan.

We know the background that led to the writing of the play, but was Barrie thinking of Nina while he was writing? At one point he did correspond with Maude Adams stating that he wrote the play for her and with her in mind. Still, even then he was not sure which part he wanted her to play. Later he approached Ellaline Terriss to play Peter with Seymour Hicks as Captain Hook. The talent and popularity of the husband–wife acting team, not to mention their success with *Bluebell in Fairyland,* must have influenced him to some degree. Mrs. Hicks was pregnant, however, and her husband did not want to appear without her, although he did star as Captain Hook in 1938. Barrie was enamored with several other actresses and it would be difficult to access if he was thinking of one in particular to play Peter, least of all Nina Boucicault. No, if any other character from *Peter Pan* was inspired in any way by the performer who would eventually play him, it was probably Captain Hook. In 1964 Christopher Calthrop wrote to Nicholas Davies inquiring if his father, Donald Calthrop, a nephew of Dion Boucicault and an actor who had worked with Barrie on several occasions, was the original source of inspiration for Captain Hook. Nicholas responded:

I would say that J.M.B. only on the rarest occasions had an actor or actress definitely in mind while he was writing a play: Elisabeth Bergner certainly for *The Boy David:* Gaby Deslys certainly for *Rosy Rapture:* but nearly always the part came later, came, probably, at the rehearsal stages when J.M.B. took an unusually active part in moulding and rewriting and so on.

From what he told me—and it was frequently pretty difficult, if not impossible, to know what he really meant—it was highly desirable if not, indeed, essential that the man to play Captain Hook should also be Mr. Darling. Ideally, he would say, Mrs. Darling should be played by someone impossibly young to have children as old as John and Wendy and Mr. Darling should really not be all that much older. So that, although I remember well his affection for your father and high appreciation of his acting: and am, of course, aware of the connection with Dion Boucicault [producer of *Peter Pan*] on whom J.M.B. depended a great deal: I would, I'm afraid, be certain enough that if anyone at all was in J.M.B.'s mind for Mr. Darling as he created the story, it could have been in the shape of Gerald du Maurier, the original of course of Captain Hook and Mr. Darling, who was, as you probably know, my mother's brother. As you will also know, the story/stories evolved out of tales told to my brothers, and indeed, while the published version of the play is dedicated to my brothers and myself, the book of *Peter Pan in Kensington Gardens* is dedicated to my father and mother as well as to us. My mother was the real spur, so it would seem, possibly, most natural that her devoted brother, Gerald, should always have been somewhere in the mind of the author.

Gerald du Maurier had already achieved stardom in several plays, including Barrie's *The Admirable Crichton* and *Little Mary*, and was yet to create his greatest triumph in *Dear Brutus* when he was asked to play Captain Hook. In addition to being an excellent actor, he also had the distinction of being the uncle to the Davies boys and the youngest son of their grandfather, George du Maurier.

In the biography, *Gerald*, his daughter, Daphne du Maurier, wrote:

When Hook first paced his quarter-deck in the year of 1904, children were carried screaming from the stalls, and even big boys of twelve were known to reach for their mother's hand in the friendly shelter of the boxes. How he was hated, with his flourish, his poses, his dreaded diabolical smile! That ashen face, those blood-red lips, the long, dank, greasy curls; the sardonic laugh, the maniacal scream, the appalling courtesy of his gestures; and that above all most terrible of moments when he descended the stairs and with slow, most merciless cunning poured the poison into Peter's glass. There was no peace in those days until the monster was destroyed, and the fight upon the pirate ship was

Captain Hook's costume designed by William Nicholson. (©1984 Sotheby's, Inc.)

a fight to the death. Gerald was Hook: he was no dummy dressed from Simmons' in a Clarkson wig, ranting and roaring about the stage, a grotesque figure whom the modern child finds a little comic. He was a tragic and rather ghastly creation who knew no peace, and whose soul was in torment; a dark shadow; a sinister dream; a bogey of fear who lives perpetually in the grey recesses of every small boy's mind. All boys had their Hooks, as Barrie knew; he was the phantom who came by night and stole his way into their murky dreams. He was the spirit of Stevenson and of Dumas, and he was Father-but-for-the-grace-of-God; a lonely spirit that was terror and inspiration in one. And, because he had imagination and a spark of genius, Gerald made him alive.

Gerald du Maurier not only provided the new play with his talent but also with his attraction at the box office. The part of Peter was another story, demanding great sensitivity and athletic prowess. Ironically, Dion Boucicault did not have to look far. Continuing with pantomime tradition, Peter, the principal boy, would be played by an actress, but none other than the director's own sister, Nina Boucicault. Hardly a newcomer to the theatre, Nina, who was born

Original drawing for Peter Pan costume designed by William Nicholson (© 1984 Sotheby's, Inc.)

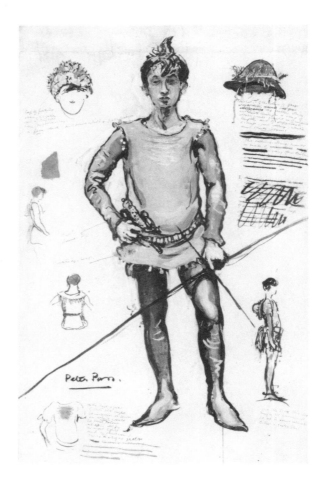

Peter Pan.

Nina Boucicault as Moira
Loney and Henry Vibart as
Terrence Reilly in Barrie's
Little Mary (1903). Photo:
Lizzie Caswell Smith.
(Author's collection)

on February 27, 1867, made her first stage appearance in 1883 in her
father's American production of *The Colleen Band*. Nine years later,
the Strand Theatre featured her London debut in *The New Wing*. In
1892 she played Kitty Verdun in *Charley's Aunt* and continued in
the role for two years. Except for a seven-year hiatus in the 1920s,
Nina was seen on the stage almost every season until she made her
last appearance in 1936. She died on August 2, 1950, at age eighty-
three.

Nina previously created another Barrie character, Moira
Loiney, in the minor success, *Little Mary*, which opened on September 24, 1903. Almost four decades later Denis Mackail wrote of her
performance as Moira:

Not beautiful. Or you don't think so for a minute or two. But then her
voice and movements do rather more than the trick. If Barrie writes
something that raises a slight shudder in print, Miss Boucicault only has
to say it and your heart turns over three times while tears trickle from
your eyes. This gift and others she will be bringing, in only a little over a
year now, to the creation of the first stage Peter Pan.

Everything about *Peter Pan* was unconventional—including
rehearsals. The actors were given only a few pages of the script at a
time and only those that pertained to their parts. The actress to play
Wendy did not know that she would be flying until she was asked to
take out a life insurance policy. The press as well as the cast were

kept in the dark. Barrie himself was of little help to Nina as she tried to figure out just who *was* Peter Pan. Nina wrote in 1924:

When first I began to study the part of Peter Pan, I remember going to Sir James Barrie and asking him, since I was to be the first Peter, if he would tell me something of his conception of the part and how it should be played. I thought that he would naturally have a great deal to say on the subject, that he might perhaps explain to me how he visualized Peter, and give me his ideas as to how the character should be developed. But I was doomed to disappointment. "Peter is a bird." he said to me in that quiet, level voice of his," and he is one day old." And that is all I had to go on. At rehearsals, it is true, he would drop an occasional hint, but if one wanted to ask him a question one could never be quite sure of finding him. At one moment he would be sitting in the stalls, and the next he had slipped out in his elusive way and disappeared.

The part of Wendy was of equal importance to Barrie and had to be played by an actress of equal stature to Nina Boucicault. Hilda Trevelyan, born on February 4, 1880, was an experienced actress who made her theatrical debut at age nine. She retired fifty years later after creating the original roles in *What Every Woman Knows* and *A Kiss for Cinderella*, as well as touring as Babbie in *The Little Minister* and Tweeny in *The Admirable Crichton*. As far as Barrie was concerned, she was the best. "You are Wendy," he wrote years later, "and there never will be another to touch you." For several years no one had the opportunity to challenge her, for she continued to play Wendy until the 1907 to 1908 season then came back to play her again in 1909, 1911, and 1914. Hilda died on November 10, 1959.

Dorothea Baird, the actress chosen for Mrs. Darling, was very popular in her day and she had appeared in Barrie's *The Wedding Guest* in 1900. Five years later she originated the part of Trilby opposite Beerbohm Tree's Svengall. Mrs. Darling's oldest son, John, was portrayed by George Hersee, who appeared not only in *Quality Street* but also in *Bluebell in Fairyland*.

For the part of Smee, George Shelton was selected. In addition to his many years of experience as a character actor, Shelton was also in Barrie's first produced play, *Ibsen's Ghost,* as well as *Walker, London* and *Quality Street*. The part of Smee would become his most famous role, one that he would continue to play until 1929, missing only two seasons. In his autobiography, *It's Smee,* Shelton explained:

There have been two great reasons for my long association with *Peter Pan.* The first of these is my love for the play and for the part of Smee. The second one I must keep to myself. Having been connected with the stage for over fifty years, one cannot expect to be much in demand.

Consequently, I welcome each revival of *Peter Pan* with great pleasure, looking upon it, as my old friend, Chance Newton, once said, as "my old age Peter Pansion."

Of the Lost Boys, two actresses went on to fame. First there was Pauline Chase, an American who earned popularity in New York as the "Pink Pajama Girl." It is more than likely that her success in that show prompted Barrie to include a special dance in *Peter Pan* which allowed her to demonstrate her terpsichorean talents with pillows. Christine Silver who played Nibs also continued acting for many years

Nina remembered,

I shall never forget the strenuous times we had during rehearsals. Fifteen to eighteen hours a day was nothing uncommon, and before they were over both Sir Gerald du Maurier and I lost our voices. It was the first production of the play, and there were so many points that needed constant rehearsing. Apart from the actual play, the flying, the lighting, the dancing had each to be rehearsed separately until it was perfect, and often there would be calls for three separate rehearsals at three different theatres in the course of the morning.

Hilda Trevelyan as Wendy.
Photo: Ellis and Walery.
(Author's collection)

Program from opening night. (Courtesy of Barrie's Birthplace—The National Trust for Scotland)

Duke of York's Theatre.
ST. MARTIN'S LANE, W.C.

Proprietors — Mr. & Mrs. FRANK WYATT.
Sole Lessee and Manager — CHARLES FROHMAN

EVERY AFTERNOON at 2, and EVERY EVENING at 8,
CHARLES FROHMAN
PRESENTS

PETER PAN
OR
THE BOY WHO WOULDN'T GROW UP.
A Play in Three Acts, by
J. M. BARRIE.

Peter Pan	Miss NINA BOUCICAULT
Mr. Darling	Mr. GERALD du MAURIER
Mrs. Darling	Miss DOROTHEA BAIRD
Wendy Moira Angela Darling	Miss HILDA TREVELYAN
John Napoleon Darling	Master GEORGE HERSEE
Michael Nicholas Darling	Miss WINIFRED GEOGHEGAN
Nana	Miss JANE WREN
Tinker Bell	Miss JOAN BURNETT
Tootles	Miss CHRISTINE SILVER
Nibs	Mr. A. W. BASKCOMB
Slightly	Miss ALICE DUBARRY
Curly	Miss PAULINE CHASE
1st Twin	Miss PHYLLIS BEADON
2nd Twin (Members of Peter's Band)	Mr. GERALD du MAURIER
Jas Hook (The Pirate Captain)	Mr. GEORGE SHELTON
Smee	Mr. SYDNEY HARCOURT
Gentleman Starkey	Mr. CHARLES TREVOR
Cookson	Mr. FREDERICK ANNERLEY
Cecco (Pirates)	Mr. HUBERT WILLIS
Mullins	Mr. JAMES ENGLISH
Jukes	Mr. JOHN KELT
Noodler	Mr. PHILIP DARWIN
Great Big Little Panther	Miss MIRIAM NESBITT
Tiger Lily	Miss ELA Q. MAY
Lisa (Author of the Play)	

Redskins, Pirates, Crocodile, Eagle, Ostrich, Cat, Pack of Wolves, by Misses Mary Mayfren, Victoria Addison, Moira Creegan, Gladys Stewart, Kitty Malone, Marie Park, Elsa Sinclair, Christine Lawrence, Mary Maddison, Gladys Carrington, Laura Beresfield, Daisy Meach, Messrs. E. Kirby, S. Spencer, G. Malvern, J. Grahame, Messrs S. Grain, A. Ganker, D. Doccone, C. Lawson, W. Scott, G. Henson, B. Franks, E. Marini, F. Gigardo, A. Biscega.

ACT I.—OUR EARLY DAYS.
Scene 1.—Outside the House.
Scene 2.—Inside the House.
ACT II.—THE NEVER, NEVER, NEVER LAND.
Scene 1.—The House we built for Wendy.

ACT II.—continued
Scene 2.—The Redskins' Camp.
Scene 3.—Our Home under the Ground.
ACT III.—WE RETURN TO OUR DISTRACTED MOTHERS.
Scene 1.—The Pirate Ship.
Scene 2.—A last glimpse of the Redskins.
Scene 3.—Home, Sweet Home.

The Play produced under the Direction of Mr. DION BOUCICAULT.

General Manager — For CHARLES FROHMAN — W. LESTOCQ

Stage Manager — DUNCAN McRAE | Musical Director — JOHN CROOK
Business Manager — JAMES W. MATTHEWS

ICES, TEA AND COFFEE can be had of the Attendants.

George Shelton credited Dion Boucicault's direction for much of the success of the play. He wrote:

> Those who have enjoyed *Peter Pan*—and they are legion—will remember the divisions of the stage, the flying feats of John Napoleon Darling and his family, and so on. I wonder if they can realize what each one of these scenes meant in the beginning, when ways and means had to be devised by which all should work smoothly, and the frequent change of picture be effected without waits interminable in length. Truly, this was a great piece of work for any man to undertake and carry through successfully. Nor did Dion Boucicault's task end here, for when the scenery was in train there were still the rehearsals of the play itself to organize. During that time Boucicault must have spoken every word of the text, sung every note of the music, and danced every step of the dances many times over. I think that in the whole of his long experiences as a producer—and he has had many successes in that field—Boucicault can never have surpassed this effort.

The play was to premiere on December 22, 1904, but major mechanical problems delayed the date. Even when it opened five days later, it was necessary to omit two and a half scenes. The following is based on a description given by Roger Lancelyn Green of that first evening's performance.

The first few moments of the play prepared the audience for an extraordinary evening at the theatre. A small girl in a maid's costume stepped in front of the curtain to cue the conductor to play the opening music.

The program has Act I of the play beginning scene 1.—Outside the House, although this is no more than a glimpse of a painting of a house, which quickly goes up revealing scene 2—Inside the House. In a nursery Mr. and Mrs. Darling are preparing to go out for the evening. Mrs. Darling is hesitant to leave her three children, Wendy, John and Michael this evening. She explains to her husband that a small boy has appeared at their window and that one evening he left his shadow. Her husband has no patience for his wife's story or for Nana, the dog that cares for the children. The dog is brought outside to her kennel. Before Mrs. Darling leaves she sings the "Lullaby" to her children, a 17th century song with music by John Crook, a staff composer and conductor for the Duke of York's Theatre who wrote most of the music for the play.

While all the children are asleep Peter Pan returns and with the aid of his fairy, Tinker Bell, a flickering stage light, he finds his shadow. He cannot make it stick and soon his sobbing awakens Wendy. After she sews it on for him, he does a shadow dance. Peter then tells her about Never Never Never Land (in later versions of the play the fairy land would be shortened to Never Never Land and finally to Never Land). Wendy is so pleased with the lovely things that Peter has to say about girls she offers him a kiss but gives him a thimble when he reveals his ignorance about kisses. Peter then gives Wendy an acorn button which she attaches to a chain around her neck. Peter convinces Wendy to go back with him but she asks that her brothers also be permitted to go. Peter teaches the children to fly around the nursery and then they fly out the window to Never Never Never Land.

Act II—The Never Never Never Land introduces the Lost Boys and their enemies, the pirates and Captain Hook, in the first scene called The House We Built for Wendy. The pirates sing "The Song of the

The Darling Nursery. Photo: Ellis and Walery. (Author's collection)

Pirates" and it is revealed that the Pirate king obtained his hook when a crocodile ate his hand. It has been following him ever since but the reptile also swallowed a ticking clock which serves as a warning to Hook.

Tinker Bell, jealous of Wendy, flies ahead of the children to warn the Lost Boys of the coming Wendy-Bird. They shoot her down only to find out from Peter that he intended her to be their mother. Luckily, the arrow hit the "kiss" Wendy is wearing and she is not dead. The boys build a house around their sleeping mother.

The curtain comes down while scene 2 and 3 are being set. Because of the time needed to move the elaborate sets, Captain Hook comes out in front of the curtain to offer his imitations of famous actors pretending to be pirates. The curtain goes up and reveals the Redskins' Camp in front of a drop cloth where we are introduced to Great Big Panther and his daughter, Tiger Lily, during an Indian dance.

Scene 3—Our Home Underground, shows the boys living underground, guarded above by the Indians. A lively pillow dance is followed by a story from Wendy as she puts the boys to sleep. Her story describes the joy that they will bring to their parents when they fly home. Peter groans and explains what happened to him.

> Peter:.... Wendy, you are wrong about mother. I thought like you about the windows, so I stayed away for moons and moons, and then flew back, but the window was barred, for my mother had forgotten all about me and there was another little boy sleeping in my bed.

Wendy realizes that it is time to go and Peter asks Tinker Bell to lead them home. As they leave they are kidnapped by the pirates who had driven the Indians away. Hook sneaks down to poison Peter's medicine

ABOVE: Gerald Du Maurier as Mr. Darling scolding Nana. Photo: Ellis and Walery. (Author's collection); RIGHT: The Pirates. George Shelton as Smee (right), Gerald Du Maurier, and "The crocodile!" Photo: Ellis and Walery. (Author's collection)

while the boy is sleeping. After he leaves, Tink tells Peter about the pirates and then drinks the medicine to save Peter who does not believe it was poisoned. Peter begs the audience to save her by clapping their hands, thus assuring her that they still believe in fairies. Then they leave to rescue Wendy.

Act III—We Return To Our Distracted Mothers, begins with Scene 1—The Pirate Ship where Wendy and the boys are in captivity. Hook orders all of the boys to walk the plank after Michael and John decline his offer to join his crew and swear, "Down with King George." Peter arrives just in time to save them. When all fails, Hook jumps off the ship to the waiting crocodile. The curtain falls and rises again to show Peter dressed as a triumphant Napoleon.

Scene 2—A Last Glimpse of the Redskins, shows a pirate, Starkey, as a prisoner of the Indians, tied up and forced to play a concertina. "Oh, miserable Starkey," he cries until the Indian Panther threatens him to change his tune to "Oh, happy Starkey." Then Smee, Hook's first mate, arrives followed by the crocodile. Starkey softly plays his instrument as the reptile falls asleep. Then Smee calls inside its mouth to see if his captain is really there.

ABOVE LEFT: "Lullaby," seventeenth-century words set to music by John Crook. (Author's collection). ABOVE RIGHT: "The Song of the Pirates." Words by J. M. Barrie and music by John Crook. (Author's collection)

SMEE
Avast, belay, inside! d'ye hear?
My Captain Hook, yo-ho!
Oh are you still a pirate bold,
Or have you gone below?

"The House We Built for Wendy." Hilda Trevelyan as Wendy, surrounded by (from left) Alice Dubarry (Curly), Christine Silver (Nibs), Joan Burnett (Tootles), George Hersee (John), Phyllis Beadon (Second Twin), A. Bascomb (Slightly), Nina W. Boucicault (Peter), Winifred Geoghegan (Michael) and Pauline Chase (First Twin), Photo: Ellis and Walery. (Author's collection)

(After Song, SMEE *finds hook in Crocodile's mouth. Takes it out. It gives two snaps.)*

Ah, it has got him! The gentle Captain is inside! Thus crime is punished and all villains die! Oh! Tempora! O mores! O cui bono? Cui!

Scene 3.—Home, Sweet Home.—The children return to their mother.

The omission of scenes and a delayed opening would not have been a good omen for a new play.
Nina Boucicault wrote:

But the first night brought us our reward. The gasp of surprise that greeted me as I flew in through the window and the enthusiasm at the end of the first act were well worth all the hard work. The audience were splendid; I don't think they missed a single point. I remember that I had been rather anxious about the scene where Peter appeals to the audience to clap if they believe in fairies. "Suppose they don't clap?" I had asked. "What do I do then?"

Nina was not the only one concerned about the clapping. Dion instructed the musicians in the orchestra to initiate the clapping if the audience was slow to take up their cue. Incredibly, the spectators, made up of mostly adults, including theatre critics, applauded wildly, bringing Nina to tears. She remembered:

But clap! I think everyone in the house believed in fairies. And I am sure the play took them by surprise...the play was so utterly different from any other play that the audience, I fancy, were swept off their feet.

"The Redskin's Camp." Philip Darwin (Great Big Little Panther) wearing inverted top hat and Miriam Nesbitt (Tiger Lily) pointing with other Indians. Photo: Ellis and Walery. (Author's collection)

Pauline Chase as First Twin doing the "Pillow Dance" in the underground home. Photo: Ellis and Walery. (Author's collection)

ABOVE: Hilda Trevelyan as Wendy wearing her cloak on the ship. Photo: Ellis and Walery. (Author's collection); BELOW: Peter Pan to the rescue! Photo: Ellis and Walery. (Author's collection)

Most of the critics were also swept off their feet. Said the *Illustrated Sporting and Dramatic News*:

Miss Nina Boucicault both acts and looks Peter Pan admirably, and Miss Hilda Trevelyan is simply marvelous as the very young heroine.

Du Maurier was also praised for playing Hook with "comedy and wit."

A critic from the *Morning Post* wrote:

In *Peter Pan* Mr. Barrie again relies not on any real dramatic interest but on his marvelous powers of keeping you amused in the theatre. Mr. Barrie is the only living writer, except perhaps, Mr. Bernard Shaw, who can build palaces of entertainment on an unsubstantial basis.

The critic also found that

The play is admirably acted. Miss Nina Boucicault is excellent as Peter, and preserves the half-human, half-fairy character with exquisite skill. Mr. Gerald du Maurier makes a spirited Mr. Darling, but the part, though requiring very delicate handling, is comparatively short. He has greater chances as Hook, of whom he gives a splendidly high-colored impersonation. It is not often that an actor catches his author's meaning so completely. Miss Hilda Trevelyan is most delightful and sympathetic

Peter as Napoleon. Photo: Ellis and Walery. (Author's collection)

as Wendy, and Master George Hersee and Miss Winifred Geoghehan are also excellent. All the other characters are well rendered, but we must specially mention the Smee of Mr. George Shelton and the First twin of Miss Pauline Chase, who performed a most remarkable dance with each foot in a pillow. Great pains have been taken with the mounting and with the stage management, while the crocodile and some of the other animals are immense.

The *Daily Telegraph* said:

The Peter Pan amalgam, as it is of the oddest and most contrary ingredients, is in its essential qualities, a play of such originality, of such tenderness, and of such daring, that not even a shadow of doubt regarding its complete success was to be discerned in the final fall of the curtain....It is so true, so natural, so touching, that it brought the audience to the writer's feet and held them captives there....We have unfortunately to endure a "front scene" as meaningless and as exasperating as it is paltry. The only excuse for its introduction, if excuse it can be considered, is that it affords Mr. Gerald du Maurier an opportunity of imitating the bearing and style of Sir Henry Irving, Mr. Tree, and Mr. Martin Harvey: but that Mr. Barrie should have fathered an interlude so unworthy of his brilliant talent is wholly and entirely incomprehensible. The sooner it is replaced by something of a fresher and more exhilarating character the better it will be for play and author.

One of the most famous reviews was quite negative. It was from Barrie's friend, Anthony Hope, who remarked, "Oh, for an hour of Herod!"

On December 31, four nights after the opening, the omitted scenes were put in their place. Scene three of the last act was changed from "Home, Sweet Home" to "How to Know Your Mother." This was an embarrassingly sweet scene where several

Wendy, John, and Michael reunited with their mother, played by Dorothea Baird. Photo: Ellis and Walery. (Author's collection)

beautiful women gather in the Darling nursery to claim their lost boys. Slightly is unable to find his mother until Liza reveals that he is her son because she can feel it in her bones. The actor playing Slightly, the only male of the Lost Boys, was a tall comedian named Archie Baskcomb who provided the last laugh of the evening as he reached out to hug his mother, Liza, played by the tiny Ela Q. May, and missed way above her head.

The mechanical problems being solved, a small house was now able to be lifted to provide the intended ending, scene five—The Tree Tops. Scene four—Outside the House, ends with Mrs. Darling agreeing to allow Wendy to visit Peter once a year to do his spring cleaning. The mother goes into her home as Wendy says good-bye to Peter.

WENDY
(Opens door and is going) You won't forget me, Peter, will you, before spring cleaning comes?

PETER
No.

WENDY
(Going again, then turns) Give me a thimble, Peter. *(They kiss)* Oh, Peter, how I wish you were littler so that I could take you up and squdge you. Good-bye. *(Kiss again)*

PETER

Good-bye.
(Wendy runs into house)
(Peter exists R.)
(Music Cue. No. 56)
(Eliza [LIZA] eners from L. with Harlequin Wand. Crosses to C. Shows Wand to audience, taps door, and exits L., dancing to Music)
(Segue Music)

S C E N E   V

The Scene changes to the Tree Tops. The tops of a great wood of fire are seen, the idea being that we look down on the wood from on high. Beyond is a great blue sky. Not seen at present, are nests which are really fairy houses, to be lit up presently inside by connection with unseen electric wires. Nightingales unseen, sing. House appears up trap when lights full up. LIGHTS appear in house, doors open. LIZA comes out, wire is fixed. WENDY stands L. of door. PETER sits R. of door.)

LIZA

Well, good-night, Miss Wendy.

WENDY

(At door) Tell mother the spring cleaning is getting on very nicely. You really do like the house?

LIZA

Of course it's small, Miss Wendy.

"The Beautiful Mothers" scene added four nights later. Photo: Ellis and Walery. (Author's collection)

WENDY

It is small. Peter, don't bite your nails. But, you see, it isn't as if we meant to entertain.

LIZA

Quite so, Miss. *(Getting on the broom, ready to fly)*

WENDY

And it's rather noisy in the evening. You see, those nests are the fairies' houses and they light up at bath time, and fairy children are so naughty in their baths that the row they make is positively deafening.

LIZA

One can't have everything

WENDY

That's just what I say. Most people of our size wouldn't have a house at all. Good-night.

WARNING FOR CURTAIN DITTO FOR CHIMNEY SMOKE TO DOLL'S HOUSE.

LIZA

Good-night, Miss. Home!

(Amid hand waving, she flies away on broom and disappears L.)

(WENDY and PETER sit on steps of house, PETER playing pipe. Clocks of fairy houses begin to be lit up. Chattering of bells increases. There can be hundreds of lights as there are many small ones among the trees on back cloth. Bells chatter is great—some fairies flit about. WENDY and PETER wave handkerchiefs to audience as:)

THE CURTAIN FALLS

"The Tree Tops." Photo: Ellis and Walery. (Author's collection)

The additions did not change the critics' opinion of the play, as seen in this review of January 14, 1904, from *The King*:

Dear Mr. Barrie,

There is only one word for your new play, and that is—Larks! All through it is a delightful spree.

You have the secret of making us grownup people feel like the children for whom you wrote Peter Pan or The Boy Who Wouldn't Grow Up. *It is true we enjoy your ingenious entertainment with a difference. To us it is a rollicking burlesque with dashes of tender sentiment.*

To them it is much more real, and, I expect, much more enthralling. They can believe, without any difficulty, in the activity of Peter Pan, the boy who ran away the day after he was born, because he heard his parents discussing what he should be when he grew up, and because he wanted to remain a little boy all his life.

...My advice to everyone who has children is to take them to the Duke of York's Theatre without delay. Those who have no children should immediately borrow some for the afternoon. They will find that they get a rare pleasure out of watching their little companions enjoy your quaint inventions, and there will be something wrong with them if they do not enjoy the piece on their own account as well.

...In spite of themselves they laugh at Mr. Gerald du Maurier, both when he is the fantastic parent of the three little children, and when he is enjoying himself immensely as the Pirate King. He certainly is very funny indeed, and funny in the most natural and artistic way.

...I do not suppose that children will be greatly entertained by Mr. du Maurier's imitations of Sir Henry Irving, Mr. Tree, and the rest. But there is no doubt about their instant appeal to the elder portion of the audience. Children, again, may find the talk between Peter and Wendy about playing at being the father and mother of the little family that lives underground rather beyond their comprehension. Even I could bear a little priming in this direction.

But, for the rest, I would not sacrifice one line or one gesture of Miss Hilda Trevelyan or of Miss Boucicault. Even now I can hardly believe that eleven year old Wendy in her long nightgown and short frocks was played by a grown-up girl. Even now I think there must be some mistake when I read on the programme that Peter Pan is in private life a young lady whom I know to have been married for several years.

They and all the rest play their parts in exactly the right spirit of dainty and amusing make-believe. The whole piece is the best lark I have had for a very long time. So believe me, dear Mr. Barrie, yours gratefully.

There was one review that was most disturbing. It was written by Max Beerbohm for the *Saturday Review* of January 7:

Undoubtedly, *Peter Pan* is the best thing he has done—the thing most directly from within himself. Here, at last, we see his talent in its full maturity; for here he has stripped off from himself the last flimsy remnants of a pretense to maturity. Time was when a tiny pair of trousers peeped from under his "short-coats," and his sunny curls were parted and plastered down, and he jauntily affected the absence of a lisp, and spelt out the novels of Mr. Meredith and said he liked them very much and even used a pipe for another purpose than blowing soap-bubbles. But all this while, bless his little heart, he was suffering. It would be pleasant enough to play at being grown up among children of his own age. It was a fearful strain to play at being grown up among grown-up persons....Now, at last, we see at the Duke of York's Theatre, Mr. Barrie in his quiddity undiluted—the child, as it were, in bath, splashing, and crowing as it splashes....

Mr. Barrie is not that rare creature, a man of genius. He is something even more rare—a child who, by some divine grace, can express through an artistic medium the childishness that is in him.

Our dreams are nearer to us than our childhood, and it is natural that *Peter Pan* should remind us more instantly of our dreams than of our childish fancies. One English dramatist, a man of genius, realised a dream for us: but the logic in him prevented him from indulging in that wildness and incoherence which are typical of all but the finest dreams. Credible and orderly are the doings of Puck in comparison with the doings of Peter Pan. Was ever, out of dreamland, such a riot of inconsequence and of exquisite futility?...

Mr. Barrie has never grown up. He is still a child, absolutely. But some fairy once waved a wand over him, and changed him from a dear little boy into a dear little girl. Some critics have wondered why among the characters in *Peter Pan* appeared a dear little girl, named in the programme "Liza (Author of the play)." Now they know. Mr. Barrie was just "playing at symbolists."

The parts of Peter and Captain Hook were very taxing on their stars. On January 29, 1905, Nina missed her first performance and her understudy, May Martin, took her place. By the end of the run Martin had replaced an exhausted Nina. *Peter Pan* closed on April 1, 1905, with notices that the production would return in December. Nina wrote in 1923:

Peter's conduct is typically masculine in its selfishness, its swagger, its sublime egotism. When he relates how he went back to his parents' house he utters no word of regret for all the anxiety his thoughtlessness has caused; what he resents, because it hurts his pride, is that another little boy has usurped his place and was lying in his cot. Again when he is going away, and Wendy, longing in her woman's heart for a word of love from him, asks him wistfully if he has anything to say to her, he can find nothing to say except that he has had a very jolly time. Human Peter! And when Wendy reminds him that if he goes to live in the tree-tops she may never see him again, he comforts her with the magnanimous assurance that she can visit him every year and do his spring cleaning. What delicious satire!

His treatment of Tinker Bell is just as callous—Tinker Bell, who is always at his elbow to serve him when he needs her help, always to

Cover of the score by John Crook. (Author's collection)

encourage him with her musical voice. When, woman-like, she grows jealous and pulls the children's hair, Peter tells them to take no notice of her; she is only the scullery-maid in the Never-Never Land who washes pots and pans! Yet it is Tinker Bell who drinks Peter's poisoned medicine, and it is only then, when he realizes that he is in danger of losing her, that he recognizes her true worth and, panic stricken, cries, "Save her!"

It is all so human. Yet Peter's fairy qualities redeem him, and we cannot help loving him, just as we love the selfish little boy because of his boyishness, though we may sigh over his selfishness.

With the exception of Nina Boucicault, the original cast members were brought back to repeat their roles in December 1905. For reasons known only to the author, Nina was not invited to participate in the 1905–06 revival. This came as a surprise to the actress as her personal reviews were so outstanding that it would have been deemed inconceivable not to use her. We can only speculate why Barrie wanted another actress for the part of Peter. It is possible that he was not happy that Nina had missed a few performances. Perhaps, Barrie sought to make the first *Peter Pan* as elusive and ethereal as lost childhood, with only memories that improve with age. Whatever the reason, Nina Boucicault's Pan now belonged to history and whoever took over the role of Peter would have to live up to her legendary performance.

Issued Monthly
$3.00 a Year.

FEBRUARY 1906

Vol. VI. No. 60.
25 c. a Copy.

THE THEATRE

ILLUSTRATED MAGAZINE
OF DRAMATIC AND MUSICAL ART.

3

Maude Adams

Peter Pan Lands in America

My Dear Maudie,

I have written a play for children, which I don't suppose would be much use in America. She is rather a dear of a girl with ever so many children long before her hair is up and the boy is Peter Pan in a new world. I should like you to be the boy and the girl and most of the children and the pirate captain. I hope you are coming here before the summer is ended and I also hope I may have something to read you and tell you about. I can't get along without an idea that really holds me, but if I can get it how glad I shall be to be at work for little Maudie again.

—J. M. Barrie, 1904

When Maude Adams received J. M. Barrie's letter of April 18 she believed that she would be playing the part of Wendy. However, Charles Frohman realized that Peter was the focal part of the play and suggested that the part of Peter be tailored for Maude and that the title be changed from *The Great White Father* to *Peter Pan*. In the *Boston Transcript* on October 20, 1906, Maude described her first encounter with Peter.

One afternoon last year while I was playing *The Little Minister* and *'Op o' Me Thumb* at the Empire Theatre, Mr. Frohman called to have a talk about plans for my coming season. He told me that he had *As You Like It* in mind for me, also another Shakespearean play and one of the old comedies. He said he would on the following afternoon show me some of the scenes in the Shakespearean plays and we could then decide upon the one in which I would appear. Meanwhile he gave me the manuscript of *Peter Pan* to read, because it was a play by Mr. Barrie.

I read the play after going home, and was so completely won by the character of dear Peter and so thoroughly interested and thrilled by his numerous adventures that I fell in love with him at once. In the evening, when I saw Mr. Frohman at the theatre, I said: "The Shakespearean plays and the old comedy that we spoke of are all right, but I would like to act *Peter Pan*." That is how I come to be acting another Barrie play this season, but that is not all of the story. The season before last, when I was in London, Mr. Barrie said to me one day: "A character which is in my mind I propose to make a play of, and that character has come to my mind through you."

I thought no more of the remark until I was reading *Peter Pan* that afternoon, when it came back to me, and I seemed at once to feel and understand its meaning. For while I read *Peter Pan* it seemed that nothing I had ever read before, nothing I had ever imagined and no play in which I had ever appeared had appealed to me so strongly or inspired me with such full and direct happiness and with such anxiety to appear in it. Every line of it thrilled me, and as I passed from scene to scene an affection for Peter grew and took hold of me, until I was perfectly wrapped in a spell of desire to be Peter Pan himself. Mr. Frohman, I believe, said nothing to Mr. Barrie about my eagerness to play Peter until he met him last spring in London. After that meeting he sent me word that Mr. Barrie had said:

"Whether or not Miss Adams was to play Peter Pan I did not know, but I am going to send her word that it was she who inspired the writing of the play." And so what was in my mind with regard to the play, the part and myself was really true.

Of course there is no doubt that James Barrie's own upbringing and the influence of the Davies boys germinated the seed of the play. However, it must also be noted that his artistic relationship with Maude Adams, not to mention his infatuation with her as one of the most popular stage actresses of her day, also played a role in the

development of *Peter Pan*. Even the master script was later given to her with a special written dedication. We cannot overestimate her unconscious influence on the writer.

Maude was already a respected actress under personal contract since 1890 to Charles Frohman when Barrie first met her in 1896. Yet, Frohman realized that his rising star needed a vehicle that would put her in the public's eye and establish a profitable stage personality. Luckily, Frohman also knew that Barrie had been trying to convert his novel, *The Little Minister*, into a stage play before the inevitable unauthorized stage adaptations appeared. What kept him from converting his novel to play form was his belief that no actress could possibly play the character of Babbie, the Minister's wife, as he envisioned her.

During a rare visit to the United States, Frohman arranged for Barrie to see his production of *Rosemary* at the Empire Theatre on Broadway. Ada Patterson, a contemporary biographer of Maude Adams, described that first eventful meeting. "'There,' said he, when the final curtain had fallen upon Maude Adams, to an accompaniment of 'bravos,' 'is the woman to play my Lady Babbie.'" Frohman was not exactly surprised. He had envisioned the teaming of his star with the Barrie heroine when he gave him the tickets to see the play. Barrie was enamored by the young actress but it still took a considerable amount of convincing from Frohman and his secretary, Elizabeth Marbury, for the writer to convert the play into a vehicle for Maude Adams. Finally, a contract was drawn up that guaranteed a dramatization of *The Little Minister* by the summer of 1897. Not only did the author adapt the play to suit Frohman's needs, he was also receptive to the producer's many suggestions during the rehearsal period.

The Little Minister opened as a moderately successful play but within a period of a few months it became a surefire hit. One critic from the *Herald Tribune* wrote,

Miss Adams will be a better Babbie in a week hence. She was clearly nervous. Her sudden alternations of seriousness and gaiety will gain ease and effect. That Miss Adams knows what should be done in such places no one doubts.

The *New York Times* stated that her "personal charm was never more potent and she was satisfying to the most exacting taste."

By the time the play opened in Boston, the reviews changed from lukewarm to ecstatic.

Nearly the whole triumph of the thing is due to Miss Adams. Her gay mischievousness, her sudden dashes and spurts of coquetry, her consciousness of her woman's power and the helplessness of the little

TOP: Maude as Babbie in *The Little Minister* by J. M. Barrie, 1897. Photo: Sarony. (Author's collection); ABOVE: "Little Miss Maude Adams" as Adrienne in *The Celebrated Case* (1879). (Author's collection)

minister, her gift at swift dryness of speech, and with and through all her quaint and taking personality which gives to every word and movement a pretty girlish piquancy and grace—these avail completely to turn the regard of her audiences.

Maude did not achieve overnight success in her climb toward stardom. Born as Maude Adams Kiskadden on November 11, 1872, she began her acting career at the age of nine months. She described her auspicious debut to writer Perriton Maxwell:

My mother was playing in a dramatic stock company in Salt Lake City, and one of the pieces put on was a farce called *The Lost Child*. The infant in the play got into bawling tantrums one night, and the manager was on the point of ringing down the curtain and "calling off" the performance, when he spied my precious self cooing in the arms of my nurse as we waited for my mother in the passage-way to the street. The child in the farce had to be brought in on a tray carried by a bewildered waiter, and without so much as "by your leave" to my astonished mother, the desperate stage-director whisked me from the hold of my nurse, plumped me on the waiter's tray and literally pushed the man, tray and child into view of the audience.

And that audience! A month-old infant had just been taken off the scene, only to reappear in a few minutes miraculously grown into a lusty nine-months-old child. The transformation was so sudden, so unexpected that the house rocked with laughter, while I sat comfortably on my tray crowing with glee at the cheerful noise and evidently pleased with the spectacle of so many merry faces. In the jargon of the press agent, I had made my "initial appearance in contemporaneous drama."

Her mother, Annie Adams, a distant kin to John Adams, and her father, James Kiskadden, decided that their daughter would not be further exposed to the stage. Yet the daughter, like her mother, was hooked on acting. At five she made her debut as "La Petite Maude" in *La Belle Russe*. Over the next decade she would appear in such productions as *Oliver Twist, A Celebrated Case, Pinafore* (as Little Midshipmite), and *Uncle Tom's Cabin* (as Little Eva), always billed as "Little Maude Adams." She auditioned for Frohman but he politely informed her to come back when she was older. In 1888 she was billed as Miss Maudie Adams for the first time in a production of *The Paymaster*.

"There's a charming little girl in Hoyt's new play," wrote one reviewer about *The Paymaster*. "I think her name is Adams, or something like it. She's so different." Manager Charles Hoyt realized what a prize he had in Maude and attempted to sign her to a five-year contract. Unfortunately for him, Maude's mother persuaded her to accept a small role from Charles Frohman instead. The pay was less than half of what Hoyt offered, yet the opportunity to remain in New York with the prestigious Frohman company was

LEFT: Maude as Nell in
The Lost Paradise (1891).
Photo: Sarony (Author's
collection); RIGHT: Maude
as the Duke of Reichstadt
in *L'Aiglon* (1901). Photo:
Byron. (Author's
collection)

too tempting to turn down. Maude was cast in the role of Dora
Prescott in *Men and Women* by David Belasco and H. C. DeMille.

After only two years in the Frohman Stock Company, Maude
was elevated to leading-lady status. From 1892 to 1896 she played
opposite John Drew in several popular theatre pieces, which led to
her first solo effort with *The Little Minister*. In his comprehensive
study, *The Story of J. M. Barrie,* Denis Mackall wrote:

"It was the riotous triumph of *The Little Minister* that made Barrie and
Miss Adams such allies. Which if either of them really felt indebted to
the other will probably never be known; for both had temperaments,
and both had good grounds for taking more credit than they might
openly admit. Yet here, with this staggering success to set it off, was the
beginning of another close friendship—and of a most profitable
association, too. Miss Adams became a private heroine, and another
object of sentimental devotion. It was eighteen years after that performance of *Rosemary* before Barrie next saw her on the stage, though in
the interval she had starred for him in America over and over again. But
whenever she took a holiday on this side of the Atlantic, there he was to
squire her, to flatter her, to employ his old and ingenious wiles again.
Very possessive, and rather mysterious about it all to others—perhaps
so as to heighten the romance. Always spoke of her as Miss Adams,
even to those who knew her better than himself. But if you were to
gather that she was royalty, you were also to gather that it was he who
stood nearest the throne.

Before she was to portray Peter, Maude had the opportunity to
act in *Romeo and Juliet, L'Aiglon,* Barrie's *Quality Street,* and *The
Pretty Sister of Jose.* It was during a December 1904 revival of *The*

Flyer put in each program for latecomers. (Author's collection)

FOR THE BENEFIT OF LATE COMERS,

THE FOLLOWING OUTLINE OF THE STORY OF PETER PAN IS GIVEN

MR. Barrie says in his instructions to the actors in Peter Pan: "The actors in a fairy play should feel that it was written by a child in all earnestness, and that they are children playing it in the same spirit." And so when little Liza, the supposed author of the play, appears before the curtain and tells the leader of the orchestra that he may proceed, we are prepared for all the strange things that follow.

Peter Pan is a boy who did not want to grow up. When he was a very little fellow he ran away from the human world and lived with the fairies in the Never Never Never Land. But he had a great fondness for stories, and so, now and then, he would fly to earth at Story Time and peep into nursery windows. One night, when Mrs. Darling was telling stories to her children, he crept into the room to listen. Mrs. Darling saw him and was frightened, and Peter tried to escape, but Nana, the faithful dog, who had always been the Darling children's nurse, closed the window so quickly that it cut off Peter's shadow, and he was forced to fly away without it.

Little Minister that Frohman was anxiously awaiting word from his London representative on the success of the opening of *Peter Pan*.

The London premiere of *Peter Pan* exceeded beyond all Frohman's hopes. As Barrie was writing revisions for a second season in London, an American version based on the script of the first season was planned. In his book, *Charles Frohman*, Isaac Marcosson described Maude's preparation.

The way she prepared for the part was characteristic of her attitude toward her work. She took the manuscript with her up to the Catskills. She isolated herself for a month; she walked, rode, communed with nature, but all the while she was studying and absorbing the character which was to mean so much to her career. In the great friendly open spaces in which little Peter himself delighted, and where he was king, she found her inspiration for interpretation of the wondrous boy.

If Charles Frohman was delighted with the London production, he was ecstatic with the American presentation. Not only did his gamble pay off with a financial success, he also had exclusive rights to a children's play of genuine artistic merit. The opening night was on November 6, 1905, and the reviews were generally enthusiastic.

The *New York Times* headlines on the theatre page read, "A Joyous Night With 'Peter Pan,'" "Maude Adams Triumphs as 'The

Boy Who Wouldn't Grow Up,'" and "An Exquisite Dream Play—The Fanciful Barrie at His Best."

The review continued:

Maude Adams is Peter. Most ingratiatingly simple and sympathetic. True to the fairy idea, true to the child nature, lovely, sweet and wholesome. She combines all the delicate sprightliness and the gentle, wistful pathos necessary to the role, and she is supremely in touch with the spirit of it all.

The *Times* critic concluded:

All New York may not believe in fairies, but there is no doubt last night, when Tinker Bell is dying, that the audience in the Empire, irrespective of age or condition, had gotten back very near to second childhood.

Maude was honored with a note from Mark Twain:

It is my belief that *Peter Pan* is a great and refining and uplifting benefaction to this sordid and money-mad age; and that the next play on the boards is a long way behind it as long as you play Peter.

Raved the *New York Herald Tribune*:

Miles away from the beaten paths of Broadway drama was the exquisite bit of fairyland which Miss Maude Adams unlocked in Mr. J. M. Barrie's phantasy [sic] play *Peter Pan*, before a brilliant audience in the Empire Theatre last night. To theatregoers surfeited with the stale dramatic conventionalities which pass for real life in the theatre, this invitation of Mr. Barrie's into a delightful corner of the unreal, was like a drought of fresh air, a sight for sore eyes.

The *Tribune* critic concluded:

What the play would be without Miss Adams it is difficult to say. She was the chief medium by which it was made alive last night. It seemed made for her and she for it. As Peter Pan...she was a Puck, an Ariel and a blithe child all in one.

If *Peter Pan* was the perfect vehicle for Maude Adams, it was not by Barrie's hand alone. A critic for the *Boston Transcript* disclosed in 1929 that

truth to tell, it was hardly Barrie's play...that Miss Adams acted. Rather she appeared in a version of her own in which speeches were shifted because she fancied them; characters, like Wendy, subordinated lest they should draw too close to the star-part; the whole piece conformed to her wishes or necessities. Within the frame of the script she wove a Peter quite as much out of her own fancy as off Barrie's

Program for *Peter Pan* at Empire Theatre, November 6, 1905. (Author's collection)

sheets—the player versus the playwright, with the victory where, in this land of "personality," it usually lies. The public applauded long and loud.

James Barrie certainly must have been aware of the "tinkering" with his play but he added his voice to the cheers:

22 March, 1906

My Dear Maudie:
. . . How splendid all the accounts of your Peter are. Even Babbie surely is getting jealous, and she could go to the Never, Never Land and make a row were it not (she says) that after all he is a boy, and she had always a weakness for boys herself. I feel sure you are the most entrancing little boy that ever was by sea or shore, and I hear of things you do in the part which are so absolutely what Peter did that it makes me gay. There never was such a girl as you for finding out what her author was up to. I must see you as Peter, and so, dear, Maudie, good-night.

Not all of the praise was awarded exclusively to Adams. Wrote a *New York Times* critic:

But though she is the centre of it all, there are several others in the cast who deserve more space for praise than can be spared just now. Especially Mildred Morris (Wendy), whose task to hers was perhaps the

"The Darling Family." From left: Charles Weston (Nana), Walter Robinson (John), Martha McCraw (Michael), Grace Henderson (Mrs. Darling), Ernest Lawford (Mr. Darling) and Mildred Morris (Wendy). (Author's collection)

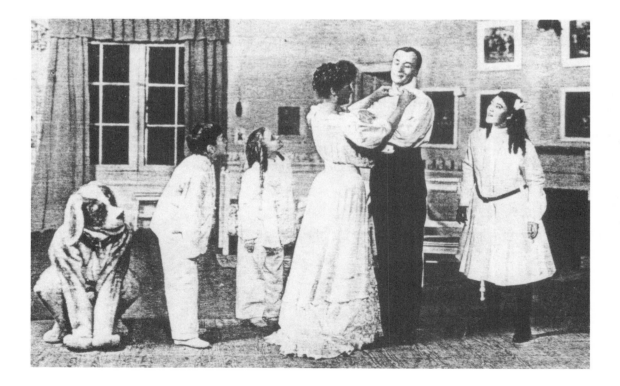

most difficult; Ernest Lawford, who in his dual role of Papa and Pirate developed the proper ferocity to suit the case, and his chief bloodthirsty assistant, Thomas McGrath, who was also most excellently ferocious, contributed a share to the generally sympathetic acting, while the dog, the crocodile, and the rest of the live stock were—well, they were very much like life.

Mildred Morris, the daughter of character actor Felix Morris, was born in 1887 and soon followed in her famous father's footsteps by becoming a competent juvenile performer. She appeared as a boy in *Two Little Sailor Boys* and as Becky in *The Little Princess*. The sixteen-year-old won enough praise for her portrayal as the scullery maid in this hit to be cast in Richard Mansfield's productions of *Prince Edward* and *Richard III*. Frohman caught her performance in the Shakespeare play and cast her as Wendy.

Besides Captain Hook, Ernest Lawford had the distinction of being the original Charley in *Charley's Aunt*. The English actor had been educated at Oxford for a career in law but changed professions at the age of twenty-four when he made his 1890 London stage debut in *As You Like It* with Lily Langtry. For several years he was cast in juvenile roles in Shakespeare's plays. He arrived in the United States in 1904 to play in *The Coronet of the Duchess*, which was quickly followed by *Peter Pan*.

A few reviewers managed to find fault with Barrie's play. One writer criticized the producer for not using all children in the boys' roles.

The four real children who act in the play are most satisfactory and delightful, but they serve to accentuate the painful shortcomings of the imitation boys....The haunting contralto notes of Miss Adams's rich voice sound damningly womanly when Peter Pan talks to Wendy, John Napoleon and Michael Nicholas.

Another reviewer for the New York *Daily Tribune* found Maude's presence

sprightly...indicative of sweetness and mirth, and graced by the allurement of pretty ways. As an actress, Miss Adams is incarnate mediocrity—for she possesses neither imagination, passion, power, depth of feeling, or formidable intellect, and her faculty of expressive impersonation is extremely limited; but as a person she is piquant, interesting and agreeable, and, in such a play as *Peter Pan*, which is an amiable fabric of whim and fancy, devised for the amusement of children, she is shown to advantage.

The *Evening Sun*'s critic wrote:

From the beginning of its second act, *Peter Pan* inevitably challenges comparisons with plays like *The Wizard of Oz* and *Babes in Toyland* and it fails to show either the spirit of fun or childhood which made both these pieces a delight to children of all ages. It will be very interesting to watch the effect of this play on its first audience of children. The one thing a child demands before all else in either a story or a play is a narrative clearly told. And that is one of the things which they will not find in *Peter Pan*.

He continued:

As a novelty *Peter Pan* may prove a "go." Certainly nothing quite like it has ever been seen here. But as a fairy story or as an embodiment of the lost delights of childhood it must rest for its artistic success entirely on its first act. For an artist of Miss Adams's standing this play seems like a waste of time.

There were several distinct differences between the American production and its British counterpart. References to England and its monarchy were substituted by the "Stars and Stripes" and the president of the United States. The first New York edition was revised by Barrie in the summer prior to its opening. The impersonation scene was cut. Maude Adams also wore a different costume that she designed, influencing the fashion industry with her "Peter Pan Collar."

Maude enjoyed singing, and this play presented a perfect excuse to showcase her musical talents in "Sally in Our Alley," a popular song of the period. The scene using this song is explained in a review from the *Boston Transcript*, dated October 23, 1906:

So they lived for a while in the Never, Never, Never Land. High up over the house underground, the Indians sat on guard, under the trees, and Tiger Lily sat with them and watched for Peter to come back from his hunting. And underneath was Wendy mothering the boys. She put Michael in a basket that hung from the wall, because if she was to be a mother, she must have one baby in the cradle, and he was the littlest. Seven though there were to care for, she gave them their supper, which was very noisy and let them meet their father, who had given Tiger Lily a thimble-kiss, and came down through the tree. When Peter, who was all in white now, found that the boys had been good, he let them rummage his pockets for sweets. And when they had eaten the sweet stuff, he sang them the old song of "Sally in Our Alley" because it was

The Never Never Never Land. (Author's collection)

A sulking Peter. (Author's collection)

Saturday night, when even the fathers and mothers are carefree. Then they danced, danced with pillows on their legs, while he talked sagely to Wendy of the care of seven, and she as sagely of his flannels and his medicine.

When the company went on tour the following year, other music was added between acts. However, Crook's contribution remained the most popular, as a critic from the *Cleveland Leader* reported during a 1913 visit to the Cleveland Opera House:

The incidental music written for the play is of uncommon excellence. It follows the action throughout with remarkable fidelity and harmonizes perfectly with the emotional key of the various scenes.

Peter Pan lasted thirty-one consecutive weeks or 237 performances. This was the longest continuous engagement that Maude Adams had ever played in New York. She closed the season on June 10, 1906.

The following autumn she toured with the play, and in Boston an announcement was made in the *Herald* on December 2, 1906:

The popularity of *Peter Pan* will undoubtedly be redoubled by the announcement that a new act is to be added to the play during the last two weeks of its Boston engagement, which begins tomorrow night. The new act, "Marooner's Rock, or the Mermaid's Lagoon," describes the exploits of Peter Pan, his friends and his enemies, in the open ocean. It is a recent composition by J. M. Barrie, and is written in his best characteristic vein—a delicate interweaving of the serious, the comic and the grotesque—such as only Barrie can conceive. Tomorrow night will be the first time the new act has ever been performed upon any American stage. It is only lately that sufficient time has been gained in the staging of *Peter Pan* to make possible any addition to an already lengthy evening's entertainment. Mr. Barrie's new act is placed between the second and third acts of *Peter Pan*—between the act called "The Never-Never Land" and the third act, "Our Home Under the Ground."

The play sailed into New York with the additional act in place and was welcomed back by audiences and critics alike with enthusiasm.

A Christmas Eve review in the *New York Telegram* found:

Ernest Lawford as James Hook. (Author's collection)

At the Empire Theatre last night a multitude of Peter Pan's old friends took "the first turn on into morning" to the Neverland. It was a fitting journey for Christmas Eve, and those who went upon it had some new adventures, as delightful as any surprises that ever came out of a Christmas stocking.

The new adventures took place in a scene called "Marooner's Rock," which will be described in Chapter Five.

Adams's *Pan* became one of the most successful touring companies in the United States. "It was on a road tour of *Peter Pan* that occurred one of those rare anecdotes in which Miss Adams figures," wrote Isaac Marcosson.

Frohman always had a curious prejudice against the playing of matinees by his stars, especially Maude Adams. A matinee was booked at Altoona, Pennsylvania. Frohman immediately had it marked off his contract. The advance-agent of the company, however, ordered the matinee played at the urgent request of the local manager, but he did not notify the office in New York. When Charles got the telegram announcing the receipts, he was most indignant. "I'll discharge the person responsible for this matinee," he said.

In answer to his telegraphed inquiry he received the following wire from Adams:

"The matinee was played at my request. I preferred to work rather than spend the whole day in a bad hotel...."

While on tour the actress commissioned a theatre car built to her specifications. The "Tinker Bell" was designed to include a stage and living quarters.

In 1908 Maude began one of her busiest seasons when she opened on January 12 at the Empire Theatre with *The Jesters*. In June she was off to Harvard University for two performances of

ABOVE: Maude Adams as Napoleon. (Author's collection); BELOW: Peter singing "Sally in Our Alley." (Author's collection)

Twelfth Night and was back at the Empire in December for a new Barrie play, *What Every Woman Knows*.

In 1907 a song by Jerome Kern and Paul West was added for Maude to sing in *Peter Pan*. It was customary for Frohman to insert American songs by up-and-coming songwriters in his shows of British origin. Kern first came to the attention of critics three years earlier when he wrote some material for Julian Eltinge, a female impersonator, in *Mr. Wix of Wickham*. "Who is this Jerome Kern," asked critic Alan Dale, "whose music towers in an Eiffel way above the average, hurdy-gurdy accompaniment of the present-day musical comedy?" Audiences did not find out because Kern spent the next few years doctoring other composers' musicals. Finally, in 1911, he was given credit for the first time as composer of "The Red Petticoat." His first hit show, *The Girl From Utah*, opened in 1914 and established Kern as a new force in the musical comedy world. While the Kern contribution to *Peter Pan*, "Won't You Have a Little Feather," is relatively small, his name would be associated with this play again in 1924.

The original sheet music indicates that the vocal part was followed by a dance, so it is quite probable that this music

accompanied the famous pillow dance that appears to have been performed by Maude. Here are Paul West's lyrics:

> Two little blue birds southward going
> Flew to a tree for a storm was blowing
> One found a nest all feathered and warm
> But one was left in the storm
> So he shivered and shook till the other bird
> His weak little trembling twittering heard
> And she cried "Poor Chap"
> My nest is warm
> You'll catch your death in that dreadful storm
>
> Won't you have a little feather from my little nest
> If your little nest is bare?
> It's a nice little feather for the wint'ry weather
> And I have feathers to spare
> It's a selfish little bird I've always heard
> Her feathers who will not share
> So please have a feather from my little nest
> If your little nest is bare?

Peter Pan joined Maude's repertoire with Barrie's *Quality Street, The Little Minister*, and *What Every Woman Knows*, making her association with the playwright extremely profitable for both. When Frohman developed the Theatre Syndicate, he was able to use the popular actress in these plays as a weapon against independent theatre owners. He sent the *Peter Pan* company to San Francisco to woo audiences away from other theatre companies, including the great Mrs. Fiske's. Ironically, a bigger "hit" attacked the area when the great earthquake of 1906 struck. All the profits from the *Peter Pan* engagement were donated by Maude to the relief fund.

Not all of the parts she played were by Barrie. Other Adams successes included an extravagant 1909 pageant of *Joan of Arc* at the Harvard University Stadium and *Chantecleer*.

Years later Maude would reflect:

Of all the plays that were trusted to my care, I loved *Chantecleer* best, and then came *Peter Pan*. It was not only that *Peter* was the most delightful of all the plays, but it opened a new world to me, the beautiful world of children. My childhood and girlhood had been spent with older people, and children had always been rather terrifying to me....Peter gave me an open sesame; for whether I understood children or not, they understood Peter.

Maude Adams in Barrie's *What Every Woman Knows* (1909). (Author's collection)

Peter Pan officially flew back to New York on December 23, 1912, meeting with just as much success as the first production. The *Morning Telegraph* announced:

There was a welcome homecoming at the Empire Theatre last night when *Peter Pan* was greeted by his adorers. The charm of this wonderful play never dies, and the popularity of Miss Maude Adams never can wane. Everyone loves the actress, and when she appeared coming through the window into the little children's sleeping room the applause stopped the play for minutes....Peter Pan surely can take its place in the dramatic Hall of Fame as one of the most popular plays ever produced in this country.

The play was brought to New York again on December 22, 1915, to mark Maude's farewell appearance as Peter. One member of this production was young Ruth Gordon, who played Nibs. In a letter written to her parents just after the opening, the newcomer described the exhilarating experience of sharing the stage with Maude Adams. Gordon was quite excited as she had even been praised by the *New York Times*, and wrote:

After my dance Miss Adams beckoned me to take three bows and our orchestra leader Henri Deering stood up and applauded. Gratifying after all I've been through. And Miss Adams has no jealousy like Alice Claire Elliot says many stars have. My cup runneth over and I guess when you read this, yours will, too.

Then came the final curtain with Miss Adams alone in the tree top house after having waved goodbye to Wendy who flew home and everybody including the cast in the wings were crying when down came the curtain to thunderous applause and we all took our rehearsed bows, then rushed back and stood in the wings. That means just out of sight in the scenery. Miss Adams took one of her calls alone then came over and said ''Nibs'' and led me on and while the audience applauded she broke off a rose from the immense bouquet that had been passed over the foot lights and handed me a long-stemmed American Beauty rose that must have cost I don't know how much and I will treasure and preserve forever.

A decade later, Ruth Gordon met Maude Adams quite by chance during a break in rehearsals. Remembered Gordon:

She recognized me instantly. Out of sheer nervousness, I think, I asked if she would like to see the rehearsal....She would. Whereupon, with such graciousness as only Miss Adams could have mustered, she turned to the lady who was with her and said: "We were together in *Peter Pan*."

In the years following the death of Charles Frohman, Maude Adams played other Barrie heroines in *The Legend of Leonora* and *A Kiss for Cinderella*. In 1919 a serious illness kept her off the stage, which had a strong effect on Barrie's purse, as stated in a letter dated February 13, 1919:

Miss Adams not well, hasn't been playing for months and won't before autumn. It makes a mighty difference in my income!

The classical beauty of Maude Adams is clearly seen in this 1909 photograph of the actress as *Joan of Arc*. (Author's collection)

Maude Adams with Pan's
pipes. (Author's collection)

In 1920 Maude Adams's contract with Frohman Company
terminated and she began negotiations with the Famous Players-
Lasky Company, which took over the Frohman enterprise. At the
same time she was anxiously anticipating the arrival of Barrie's last
play, *Mary Rose*. Written just for her, the play is a haunting ghost
story that is almost the female counterpart to *Peter Pan*. However,
there were clauses in the contract that she could not agree with,
primarily that she relinquish any rights to portray Peter or Lady
Babbie over a three-year period, giving them the freedom to film the
plays without competition from her potential stage revivals. Although Barrie had never sold the film rights of his stage success to
the company, it was obvious that they were hoping for that project
in the near future. Barrie's American representative, Mr. Delafield,
wrote a letter to the playwright concerning Adams's reverence for
the play.

September 2, 1920

As respects the contract filming of your plays between yourself and
the Famous Players Company (dated August 19, 1919) I have never seen
a copy of the instrument, nor did I have any reason to suppose...you
had given any sort of film right to *Peter Pan* to that corporation.
Apart from Miss Adams's curious feeling of reverence for the
play...she would be bitterly hurt and disappointed if that play should

be filmed by the Famous Players-Lasky Corporation while she is still upon the stage....

I am not by any means sure that Miss Adams's wish that you should reserve Peter for her is reasonable from an everyday standpoint. But none of us, I suppose, is altogether reasonable about the things that touch life most closely, and if it was in Miss Adams's nature to look at this sort of question as coolly and as impassively as I do, it is quite certain that she could never metamorphose herself into Peter or Lady Babbie, or Cinderella....

Over the years it has been written that Maude Adams was tired of *Peter Pan* and was happy to hand the role over to Marilyn Miller. It has also been said that she never cared to appear on film, yet letters of the day make it apparent that she desperately wanted to make a film of *Peter Pan*. In a letter to Barrie dated August 3, 1920, she wrote:

I have not liked being a dog-in-the-manger about the moving-pictures for *Peter*; especially during my illness it has seemed dreadful to me that you should be deprived of the large sums that *Peter* would bring you. For several months I have interested myself in a process which would make it possible to do pictures in color, which, of course, would give beauty and take away the monotony of black and white. In the meantime another process has been completed which would make it possible now to do *The Little Minister*. I should like more space for *Peter*, it is not absolutely necessary, but I am told that further adjustments will give more space. I have had some moving-pictures taken of myself and they are not quite bad as you think, but before the end of this month I hope to have some pictures done in color—then I shall know exactly what I can do. Perhaps you will let me know if you would care to have me do *The Minister* and *Peter*, provided that they be well done and beautiful....

Two months later she again wrote to Barrie:

As I wrote you I am very keen about pictures in color, but if nothing satisfactory should come in color I am quite willing to try one or two scenes in black and white to see what can be done with me. I should prefer to try at first in *Peter*'s own scenery, but if that should not be right, we could do some of the snow scenes this winter and wait for the other scenes until spring or summer. If the color schemes come to anything then I am sure the play will be better in its own theatre clothes and so far as I personally am concerned the sooner it can be done the better for me. I don't look so much older, but I *am* older. It would be the making of the play if you would come and direct it....I doubt very much that the Famous Players Company would care to do the play in colors because of the necessity of a different sort of projecting machine. The only pictures I have seen in black and white have been rather cheap—a cheap sensationalism or a cheap sentimentalism. Without color and sound there is little to appeal to the emotions and the

Portrait of Maude Adams.
(Author's collection)

repeated attempts to create sensations become rather monotonous. I don't know whether these pictures express the limitations of the medium or the lack of experience of the people who put the pictures together; it is probably the former but I shall know more about it within the next six weeks.

Love,
Maude

Maude Adams would never make a film of her beloved *Peter Pan*. What might have seemed like procrastination to Barrie was, according to Adams's biographer, Phyllis Robbins, simply a search for perfection. One can understand the reluctance of the actress to make a silent film of the Barrie classic. The dialogue, the core of his work, would be lost in a film without sound. The writer sold the film rights and bypassed her. The final irony was that Barrie never saw Maude Adams as Peter Pan. He wrote in October of 1920:

It is settled now between the Frohman Co. and Miss Adams that she does not play Mary Rose. Sad to me, but I can see they couldn't hit it off together.

Maude was heartbroken over the turn of events but more important, these series of misfortunes kept her off the stage until 1931.

The next few years were spent writing and doing some experimental work on camera lights for color film at the General Electric Plant in Schenectady, which paid off—at least for the company. She developed special lights that were strong enough for color film but she never patented her ideas so that the profits were absorbed by G.E. An out-of-court settlement of $500,000 was offered for this invention; however, Maude declined and only referred to it once, on paper, stating simply, "I was an idiot!"

A radio re-creation of *Peter Pan* with Maude Adams was scheduled in 1937 but Eva Le Gallienne replaced Maude when she became ill. On December 15, 1938, Maude was able to play the role on New York station WEAF. Earlier that same year she assumed a teaching position at Stephens College and accepted an invitation from David O. Selznick to test for a role in a film, *The Young in Heart*. While the screen test was successful, Maude felt that the role was not suited to her talents and suggested Minnie Dupree for the part, and she went back to her teaching duties. All that remains of her on film is that screen test.

Maude Adams's last years were spent in retirement from the stage. She died on July 17, 1953, while working to complete her autobiography. A review of one of her last performances demon-

Cover of the 1906 souvenir program. (Author's collection)

strates the effect this actress had on the public for almost four decades.

In his December 19, 1931, critique of *The Merchant of Venice*, Alexander Woollcott wrote:

...Sitting as one unresisting spectator in the largest audience I have seen in any theatre in many a season, I found myself yielding to the spell of a music familiar, dear, and ineffably touching. It was the music of a speaking voice I had not heard in years nor ever thought to hear once more. It was the voice—unchanged and changeless—of Maude Adams. And the sound of it filled me with an almost intolerable nostalgia for a day that is not now and never can be again.

Vivian Martin

The Unknown Peter Pan

It was while playing Peter Pan that I became fascinated with Barrie, and, oh, I think he is delightful, with his delicious humor and that pathos that grips me more than real tragedy.

—*Vivian Martin, 1919*

As far as the American public was concerned, Maude Adams was the only Peter Pan. Unfortunately, there was no way that she could possibly be seen in every city, so in 1907 Charles Frohman decided to send a juvenile company of the play to those other locales, with Vivian Martin in the leading role.

Vivian Martin was born on July 22, 1893, near Grand Rapids, Michigan. She was almost fifteen years old when she "came out of retirement" to play Peter. Previously she had attained great success as a child actress in Richard Mansfield's company. Her first stage role was in *Cyrano De Bergerac* and she made her Broadway debut in *Little Lord Fauntleroy* in 1903. Mansfield suggested she leave the stage to go to school and to come back to work for him in a few years. In 1907 she was about to leave her school in Greenville, Michigan, and return to Mansfield's company when she received word of his death. Devastated at the thought that her career was over, she was surprised when Charles Frohman asked her to come to his office for an interview. A second meeting was scheduled, this time without the presence of her parents. A newspaper article of the day detailed how she acquired the part of Peter.

"What do you want to do?" he [Frohman] asked.

"I used to think I wanted a dramatic part," replied the young girl, "but now I believe I would like to try musical comedy."

"Why musical comedy?" asked Frohman. "Your training has been dramatic."

"But I think the chances to rise fast are greater in musical comedy," replied the ambitious girl.

"Mr. Frohman thought this over and then said: "Come around tomorrow and I will see what I can do for you."

When she arrived on the scene next day at rehearsal hour he asked her: "How would you like to play in *Peter Pan*?"

"I would like it," she answered, "but how long would it be before I could hope for a leading role?"

"The part I have picked out for you is the part of Peter Pan himself, which Miss Adams is now playing," answered Mr. Frohman with a sly grin. The answer nearly took away the breath of little Miss Martin, but she promptly accepted the role and the astute Mr. Frohman has expressed himself as decidedly well satisfied with the result.

In a 1919 interview she later stated:

I had a wonderful season as Peter Pan. It was such a whimsical, fanciful thing and so popular that it was a joy to play it. I had met Maude Adams, for my father was in her company, but I did not see her as Peter until several seasons after I had played it, and what a treat it was! I shall never forget it.

While Frohman was pleased with her performances, she was no threat to Maude Adams's definitive portrait of Peter, thus never playing the part in New York. Vivian came back to Broadway in 1910 where she met with success in several plays and continued to do so through the twenties. She also signed with the Famous Players-

RIGHT: Despite Vivian Martin's youth, Maude Adams continued as the public's quintessential Peter Pan. In 1907 Oliver Herford created *The Peter Pan Alphabet* with illustrations of Maud as Peter. Here she is pictured with Teddy Roosevelt. (Author's collection)

Mon., Tues. & Wed., NOV. 11, 12 & 13
MATINEE WEDNESDAY.

CHARLES FROHMAN
Presents
J. M. BARRIE'S
Play, in Five Acts,

PETER PAN

Or, THE BOY WHO WOULDN'T GROW UP.

"Who are you, Pan?"

"I'm youth, eternal youth, I'm the sun rising, I'm poets singing, I'm the new world, I'm a little bird that has broken out of the egg, I'm joy, joy, joy!"

CAST.

Peter Pan	Vivian Martin
Mr. Darling	John MacFarlane
Mrs. Darling	Margery Taylor
Wendy Moira Angela Darling	Violet Hemming
John Napoleon Darling	Renee Grau
Michael Nicolas Darling	Carol Pullman
Nana	James Grant
Tinker Bell	Jane Wren
Tootles	Bell Whiteford

Lasky Company and was featured in a few silent films including *Unclaimed Goods* in 1918 and *Louisiana* in 1919. She died on March 16, 1987, at age ninety-four.

Playing opposite Martin was Violet Hemming, making her American stage debut as Wendy. Violet was born in England as a member of a theatre family. Only twelve when she played Wendy, she next had the lead in *Rebecca of Sunnybrook Farm.* Her first adult part was in *Disraeli* with George Arliss, which she repeated on the screen in 1932 with Arliss and Bette Davis. In the years following, Violet became known for her comedic talents. In 1945 she retired to marry Bennet Champ Clark, a federal judge, and did not return to the stage until nine years later, after which she continued to appear on Broadway and in stock. She died on July 5, 1981.

Another actress to play Peter Pan was Eva Lang. In 1910 "Eva Lang and Company" was found touring the West Coast in the play. Beverly West toured as Peter in 1912 with Isoldi Illian as Wendy. This company had Jane Tyrrell reading a Prologue as well as playing Mrs. Darling. While these performances, like those of Vivian Martin, are of historical note only and have no bearing on the development of or changes to Barrie's play, they disprove the claim that no one but Maude Adams played Peter Pan in America until Marilyn Miller decided to accept the challenge almost a decade after Adams's last stage appearance in the role.

5

Cecilia Loftus

And the Mermaids

I think it is in the combination in him of the mature knowledge of a man and the wonderful imagination of a child that the secret of Peter Pan's charm lies. But neither Peter nor his creator is really capable of explanation. Fairies were never meant to be explained.

Cecilia "Cissie" Loftus, 1923

Once *Peter Pan* proved himself in London, Charles Frohman made his plans for the play as a vehicle for Maude Adams in the States. At the same time, he was also preparing *Pan* for a second season at the Duke of York's Theatre, again during the Christmas holidays.

It appears that the decision to replace Boucicault came rather late, as Cecilia Loftus was not offered the role until November 1905. She recalled:

My first introduction to Peter Pan was when I went to see Maude Adams, the American Peter, play the part in New York. I thought what a glorious part it must be to play, with no idea that I should ever play it; but by an extraordinary coincidence I received a cable from Mr. Charles Frohman the very next morning, asking if I could sail immediately and play Peter Pan in London. I rushed to the cable office, cabled that I was sailing at once, left America within a couple of days, crossed the Atlantic in a state of dreadful anxiety lest something go wrong at the last moment and, still hardly able to believe in my good fortune, found myself interviewing Sir James Barrie and Mr. Boucicault at the Duke of York's Theatre. I was rather frightened at meeting Sir James, but I soon discovered that he was as shy and as timid of me as I was of him.

Cecilia (Cissie) Loftus, a young actress from Glasgow, Scotland, was an extremely popular music hall entertainer with a remarkable talent for mimicry. The product of theatrical parents, Ben and Marie Loftus, Cissie was on vacation from her convent school in 1891 when she served as a temporary replacement for her mother's backstage maid at the Oxford Music Hall. Only fourteen at the time, the girl stood in the wings watching the different variety acts with great interest. She was particularly intrigued with the imitations of some of the performers. Convinced that she could do better, she persuaded the theatre manager to give her a chance mimicking famous entertainers. A year later she was earning two thousand dollars a week for her clever imitations of popular performers like Henry Irving, Ada Rehan, and Sarah Bernhardt.

She said in an interview years later:

I had a trick voice. I couldn't do anything with it as myself, but I could make it accurately copy the speech or singing of anyone else. When Sir Arthur Sullivan asked me to sing for Marchesi I wasn't able to produce a note, so I imitated a celebrated singer, and Marchesi wanted to train me for opera.

Enrico Caruso was amused at her takeoff of his singing, as were Eleanor Duse, Maude Adams, and Ethel Barrymore of her imitations of them in their famous stage roles. Despite her success, Loftus was anxious to act on the legitimate stage and decided to give up her enormous salary to appear in Justin Huntly McCarthy's *If I Were King*. Henry Irving caught her performance and asked her to appear opposite him in *Faust* as Marguerite at the Lyceum in 1903. That same year she played Ophelia to E. H. Southern's Hamlet.

At the age of seventeen, Cissie eloped with Justin Huntly McCarthy and continued to grow artistically but not only on the stage. She also enjoyed writing verse and was good that she was often seen in the company of Aubrey Beardsley, Max Beerbohm, and E. W. Mason. Ironically, with all of her impressive credits,

Cissie Loftus is best remembered as the "second" Peter Pan on the London stage. Like all who followed her, Cissie had her *Peter Pan* stories.

Of the play I particularly remember one incident which might have had a tragic end. When Peter flies he must always take off from exactly the right spot or he will fly in the wrong direction. There are marks on the stage to guide him, but on one occasion I missed the mark and was swung right out over the stalls. It seemed that on the backward swing I must crash into the scenery, but so skillfully were the wires manipulated that I swung, without touching anything, straight through the window at the back of the stage through which I entered.

Like many other actresses before and after her, Cissie was charmed by Peter Pan's creator.

I realized...during my visit, how much of a boy he is at heart. During meals he would have his big dog—very much like Nana in the play—in the room, and often between the courses he would leave the table and lie on the floor with his arm round the dog's neck....

But with grown-ups he never seems quite at home; it is only children that can get really close to him and share his fairy kingdom.

During the second season, audiences that came back for another dose of Barrie were surprised with the addition of Act Three. "There are Mermaids, Wendy, with long tails," he now promises in Act One. In place of the Indian scene, a new act was added where Peter takes Wendy and the boys to Marooner's Rock. It is a fantastic place with mermaids and a pelican protecting her eggs in her floating nest. Barrie edited some of Hook's lines from Act Two and snugly fit them in the new act.

"The game's up: those boys have found a mother," he moans.

"What is a mother?" asks Smee.

Hook points to the floating nest to explain. "The nest must have fallen into the water, but would the mother desert her eggs? No. No!" The boys delight in teasing the mermaids and share a humorous song with a baby mermaid and her mother.

The tranquility is broken by an encounter with the pirates. The fight leaves Peter wounded and he and Wendy are stranded on the rock with the threat of the rising tide. Too tired to fly, Wendy is saved by Michael's kite, but Peter remains with no hope of being rescued. "To die will be an awfully big adventure," he says.

Of course Peter cannot die. Barrie steals from himself by adding a scene similar to one in *Little White Bird*. He takes the nest from the bird and uses his jacket as a sail, floating away from danger.

Several reviewers were very critical of the new addition. They were disappointed with Peter's lack of compassion for the mother

Portrait of Cecilia Loftus. (Author's collection)

ABOVE: Rosamund Bury and Geraldine Wilson as the Mermaid and the Baby Mermaid in the new Lagoon Scene. (From the collections of the Theatre Museum. By courtesy of the Board of Trustees of the Victoria and Albert Museum); BELOW RIGHT: "The Song of the Mermaids." (Author's collection)

and her eggs. The following year Barrie revised the scene further, depicting a more sensitive Peter. Now he carefully places the eggs into a pirate's hat before sailing off. The contented mother sits again protecting her eggs.

Another change takes place on the pirate ship. The few lines Hook had at the opening of the scene have become a soliloquy, stuffed with those now memorable phrases; "How still the night is....Nothing sounds alive....All mortals envy me, yet better perhaps for Hook to have had less ambition....Oh, fame, fame! Thou glittering bauble...."

Like Nina Boucicault, Cissie Loftus starred in *Peter Pan* for only one season but her career spanned more than fifty years. She appeared in the *Ziegfeld Follies* and made her motion picture debut in 1913, but a year later she was not working and wouldn't for the next decade. In 1923, she was charged with possession of illegal drugs, which she explained she needed for relief from the pain caused by the premature birth of her child. She was given one year's probation. That same year she enjoyed the personal success of appearing at the Palace Theatre on Broadway. Her imitations of Mrs. Fiske, Harry Lauder, and Nora Bayes delighted her audiences and brought her standing ovations. The Loftus career once again bloomed and Cissie was featured in many plays such as *Becky Sharp, Uncle Tom's Cabin, Merrily We Roll Along, The Holmes of Baker Street,* and *The Wooden Slipper.* She

also appeared in several motion pictures, including *East Lynne, The Old Maid,* and *The Blue Bird.*

Cissie brought her great imitations to the stage again in 1938 during a series of Sunday concerts at the Little Theatre. At first the public was shocked by the appearance of the actress, who looked even older with her shocking white hair, but her imitations of popular artists of the day, Gertrude Lawrence, Fanny Brice, Beatrice Lillie, and even Noël Coward, were wickedly funny.

During an interview a few years before her death in 1943, Cissie Loftus replied to a question about the state of American theatre.

For the sake of the future artists, I wish the American theatre were not so exclusively committed to realism. The romantic drama, the poetic drama, the theater of magnificent illusion should form a part of every actor's experience. They discipline that tiny spark of immortal soul which is indispensable to the interpretive artist. Without such discipline, he will be the poorer.

May it be added that the actor will also miss having a great deal of fun, as Cissie Loftus did playing *Peter Pan.*

Roger Lancelyn Green—who had the good fortune of seeing almost every English actress to appear as Pan (from 1904 to 1953), as well as acting in the 1943 *Peter Pan* touring company as Noodler—wrote that

Cecilia Loftus as Peter Pan. (Author's collection)

Cecilia Loftus, the second Peter, lacked her predecessor's uncanny, eerie qualities, but was more boyish and elfin—characteristics even more apparent in her understudy Pauline Chase, who played for a few performances at the end of the tour before tackling the part in earnest the following Christmas. `

6

Pauline Chase

And an Afterthought

Dear Peter Pan thank you very much for the Post Card you Gave me I am Longing For some more of them and I have sent you A picture of the Little House For you And Nik-o thinks he can fly But he Only tumbles about ~~his~~ he sends his Love. From Michael

—*A letter from Michael Llewelyn Davies to Pauline Chase, 1906*

Of all the actresses selected by James M. Barrie to play *Peter Pan*, his favorite was Pauline Chase, an American who appeared as Peter in England fourteen hundred times. Born in Washington, Chase made her stage debut in 1898 at the age of thirteen in *The Rounders* at the Casino Theatre in New York. Two years later she was playing boys' parts in *The Belle of New York* and *The Lady Slavey*. Fame arrived with her dancing role as the Pink Pajama Girl in *The Liberty Belles* in 1903. Charles Frohman was impressed with the audience reaction to the vivacious blond and hired her to appear in a London production of *The School Girl*. With the exception of an occasional visit to New York, Pauline Chase enjoyed a successful career on the London stage.

It came as no surprise that Dion Boucicault added a pajama-costumed dance for Pauline in *Peter Pan,* but even he could not have foreseen the success with which the "Pillow Dance" was greeted. The audience was as delighted as Barrie and Frohman. Pauline was cast as the First Twin again for the 1905–06 season, but she replaced Loftus for the last week of the tour. Years later she wrote:

I was appearing as Peter Pan at Liverpool, and it had been suggested that the following Christmas I should take the part in the London production. There was some doubt as to whether my voice was strong enough, and Sir James Barrie and Mr. Charles Frohman journeyed to Liverpool to see me play and to come to their decision. I saw them before the performance, and they told me that they were going to watch me from the circle, that they might have no time to see me afterwards, and that, as I should naturally be very anxious to know what had been decided, they would send a note after the last act to my dressing-room. But it was to be no ordinary, prosaic, unromantic letter of

business. If I received a note at all it would bring me good news—that I was to be Peter in London—and would be a slip of paper simply marked with a cross.

It was an anxious Peter that flew on to the mantelpiece that evening, but the anxiety did not last long. The slip of paper with its fateful cross was waiting for me at the end of the first act, and Sir James and Mr. Frohman had left to catch their train back to London.

Pauline took over the role of Peter Pan for the 1906–07 Christmas season and continued playing the part up to and including the 1913–14 season. During her tenure a few important changes took place. Gerald du Maurier's schedule could no longer permit him the luxury of playing a short season in the perennial favorite. His part was divided between two actors with A. E. Matthews given Mr. Darling and Robb Harwood as Hook. While Harwood received excellent notices (Mackail called him "the next-best of all Hooks"), the fascinating parallels between the parts of the father and the villain were lost.

Another change occurred from the inquiries of Barrie's friends and colleagues who were always asking him whatever became of Peter and Wendy as she grew older. In a letter dated December 10, 1957, Hilda Trevelyan explained how he responded:

Whenever Mr. Barrie entered the Duke of York's Theatre stage door during the first Christmas season of *Peter Pan* he was ambushed and made prisoner by Michael, John, the Lost Boys, the Wolves and even the front legs as well as the back ones of the Crocodile. Having been made quite secure by entwining arms, he was conducted to a dressing-room and an ultimatum was presented to him. It was always the same. "A Story please" that is how it ran. Mr. Barrie would sit down solemnly & told his captives [sic] a story, that generally was made up on the spur of the moment. These ultimatums for stories I believe was the birth of a one act play that he wrote called *An Afterthought* which is the epilogue to the immortal *Peter Pan*. It was produced at the Duke of York's Theatre, and enjoyed a run of exactly one night. It was secretly rehearsed by J. M. Barrie as its production was to be a surprise for his great friend and manager, Charles Frohman, who was present at the performance. There was only one manuscript, the original one as written by the Author. This was the Prompt copy & Production copy all in one. The production of the *Afterthought* took place on the last night of the 3rd Christmas Season at the Duke of York's Theatre.

When the curtain fell on *Peter Pan* for the last time that season, the Tree Tops were quickly swept away and Mr. and Mrs. Darlings' nursery took their place. In the prompt-corner with manuscript in hand stood the author and producer, ready to help should anyone forget what they had to say. The curtain rose and "discovered" were a grown-up Wendy with her hair done on top of her head, and dressed in a

fashionable ball gown. In a bed nearby snored rather feebly a dog, who was very tired and fast asleep. It was Nana who was so old and feeble that she had really got beyond being a nurse anymore. On another bed was a child called "Jane," daughter of Wendy. That was the glimpse the audience got when the curtain rose.

As the play proceeded the nursery window opened itself unaided and in flew Peter Pan, in his usual manner. He had called to fetch Wendy to do his spring cleaning. Time to Peter Pan means nothing; it is something he cannot understand. It seemed to bewilder him to find Wendy grown up and with a little girl of her own. Wendy told him all that had happened since they had met last and it was quite a shock to him when he heard that "Slightly Soiled" had married a Lady and become a Lord. When the curtain fell on that first and last night of the *Afterthought* Mr. Barrie walked on to the stage and thanked the cast for playing so well and as he thanked Wendy for her performance, he slipped the original manuscript into her hand and pressed it.

The addition was unveiled on February 22, 1907, and introduced by Tessie Parke, earlier seen as the mermaid and now playing Jane. Hilda Trevelyan played the grown-up Wendy. The scene was met with a fifteen-minute period of applause.

ABOVE: "Peter Pan is the fairies' orchestra." Reprinted with permission of Charles Scribner's Sons, an imprint of Macmillan Publishing Company, from *Peter Pan in Kensington Gardens* by James M. Barrie, illustrated by Arthur Rackham. Copyright 1906 Charles Scribner's Sons; copyright renewed 1934 James M. Barrie. RIGHT: Program cover. (Author's collection)

PETER AND JANE.

The company gave a special performance of *Peter Pan* in Paris at the Theatre du Vaudeville in June of 1908 and was so well received that an encore was presented the following year. The reason: Barrie wanted to go to Paris.

Over the years each actress playing Peter has received a large volume of fan mail from children as well as adults. In 1909, Pauline Chase compiled just a few of these for a publication, *Peter Pan's Postbag*. Barrie even gave her permission to have it sold at the theatre.

Sharply contrasting the success of *Peter Pan* was the disintegration of the Davies family and Barrie's marriage. First, Arthur Llewelyn Davies died of cancer on April 18, 1908, leaving his young wife and her five boys financially vulnerable. Barrie assured the dying father that he would take care of the family.

While he furnished the financial needs of the Davies family, he was unable to fill his wife's needs. He discovered that she was having an affair. Although James basically wanted to forget the whole thing, Mary Barrie could not continue living a lie. She wanted a normal marriage and perhaps, even, children. Against her husband's wishes, she filed for a divorce, which went to court in October 1908. Barrie was asked by his lawyer to refrain from seeing Sylvia Llewelyn Davies until after the divorce was complete. Of course, Mary Barrie knew her husband too well and never brought up his relationship with Sylvia. In his book, *J. M. Barrie and the Lost Boys,*

ABOVE: An enterprising Pauline Chase received Barrie's permission to have her book sold at the Duke of York's Theatre. (Author's collection); TOP: "Peter and Jane." Reprinted with permission of Charles Scribner's Sons, an imprint of Macmillan Publishing Company, from *Peter and Wendy* by James M. Barrie, illustrated by F. D. Bedford. Copyright 1911 Charles Scribner's Sons; copyright renewed 1939 Lady Cynthia Asquith and Peter Llewelyn Davies.

Andrew Birkin published a letter Mary Barrie had written to Peter Davies years later. "J. M.'s tragedy was that he knew that as a man he was a failure and that love in its fullest sense could never be felt by him or experienced, and it was this knowledge that led to his sentimental philanderings." She continued, "One could almost hear him, like Peter Pan, crowing triumphantly, but his heart was sick all the time." True to his character, Barrie also helped his ex-wife years later when she was in financial trouble.

Just two days after a divorce was granted it was discovered that Sylvia, still mourning the loss of her husband, also had cancer. She succumbed to the disease on August 27, 1910, with the secure knowledge that Barrie would take charge of her boys. George was now seventeen years old, Jack was sixteen, Peter was thirteen, Michael, ten and Nico, six. While the boys, particularly George and Michael, loved Barrie, the three older ones were reluctant to call him Uncle Jim. They continued to go to boarding school while Jack joined the navy, and they spent their summers with their guardian in the country.

In 1912 Barrie published the book *Peter and Wendy,* which included the ending used in *An Afterthought.* That same year Barrie commissioned Sir George Frampton to sculpt a statue of Peter Pan for Kensington Gardens. He gave the artist some photographs that he had taken of Michael Davies at the age of six for inspiration, but ultimately they were not used. Although Barrie was unhappy with the results, the statue was still placed in the garden where it remains today.

During her long tenure as Peter Pan, Pauline Chase did other plays, too. In 1910 she returned to New York as a star and appeared in *Our Miss Gibbs*. Back in London she starred in *The Little Japanese Girl* in 1911 and in *Man and Superman* in 1912. Pauline became a very close friend of Barrie's and he, in fact, became her godfather. He gave her away when she wed Captain A. V. Drummond in 1914, the year she also retired from the stage.

Pauline remained fixed in the public's eye as Peter Pan for many years after she retired. Even with three children of her own she would be asked to wear Peter's costume for charity events. On June 16, 1928, she appeared again in that role for *The Pageant of Peter Pan,* a celebration at Sefton Park in Liverpool in honor of the presentation of a duplicate of the statue by Frampton for that park. The elaborate pageant included small children dancing around the statue as fairies, but the highlight of the day occurred when Pauline accidentally fell into the lake. Her fondness for the role never waned. She christened her country cottage "Tree Tops" and had a small replica of Peter's stage house built for the birds, placing it high in a treetop.

Pauline Chase died on March 3, 1962, at the age of seventy-six. Almost fifty years since she had appeared on the stage as Peter, she was remembered by the press with fondness as Barrie's favorite Peter Pan.

ABOVE: Michael Davies dressed as Peter Pan, July 1906. Barrie later gave this photograph to sculptor Sir George Frampton as a model for the statue in Kensington Gardens. Frampton chose another model instead. Photo: J. M. Barrie. (Courtesy of Andrew Birkin, author of *J. M. Barrie and the Lost Boys*); LEFT: In May 1928, Pauline Chase once more donned her Peter Pan costume for a special celebration in honor of Barrie's famous character in Sefton Park, Liverpool. The statue she is seen with is a duplicate of the Kensington Gardens original. (From the collections of the Theatre Museum. By courtesy of the Board of Trustees of the Victoria and Albert Museum)

Jean Forbes-Robertson

And the Other English Lasses

She has only to appear in any character and before she has crossed the stage you feel that you are in the presence of a spirit whose excess of fineness cannot escape the world's pain, of a soul importunate for things not of this earth, and in Herbert's phrase, something "divinely loose" about her.
    —*James Agate of the* Sunday Times *writing about experiencing a play starring*
Jean Forbes-Robertson, 1926

*E*ach actress to play Peter Pan naturally had her own idea of how the part should be played. Often Barrie would allow them to carry it to the extreme. Noël Coward, who played the role of Slightly in 1913 and 1914, gave his biographer, Cole Lesley, a humorous account of Madge Titheradge's performance as Peter. Madge was the first actress to play the role in London after Pauline Chase vacated the part. Wrote Lesley:

Miss Titheradge was a dramatic actress of enormous power, and in the scene when Tinker Bell will die unless we all applaud and help to save her, she asked, "Do you believe in fairies?" and commanded, "Say quick that you believe!" so ferociously that little children whimpered and clung to their mothers instead of clapping their hands, and Miss Titheradge never played Peter Pan again.

On June 13, 1913, Barrie was honored with the Baronet title and became Sir James. In 1915 he suffered a severe loss when Charles Frohman went down with the *Lusitania*. The producer was on his way to London to help Barrie with a new theatre project that involved extensive use of motion picture film. Subsequently, the Daniel Mayer Company produced the play on a yearly basis starting in 1915 at the new Theatre. In 1919, George M. Cohan's daughter, Georgette, played the part. Edna Best took over in 1920, receiving very good notices. During the rehearsals Barrie added some charming dialogue for Michael and Mrs. Darling:

MICHAEL
(as he is put between the sheets). Mother, how did you get to know me?

PAGE 92: Jean Forbes-Robertson played Peter in the Gaiety Theatre in 1927, moved to the Garrick for 1928 and to the St. James for 1929, and finished at the Palladium, 1930–34 and 1938. (Author's collection) BELOW: Noel Coward as Slightly, 1913. (Author's collection); BOTTOM: Impresario Charles Frohman on board the ill-fated *Lusitania* on May 1, 1915. It was reported by a survivor that his last words were, "Why fear death? It is the greatest adventure in life." (Author's collection); BOTTOM RIGHT: Georgette Cohan, daughter of the great George M. (Author's collection)

MR. DARLING

A little less noise there.

MICHAEL

(growing solemn). At what time was I born, mother?

MRS. DARLING

At two o'clock in the night-time, dearest.

MICHAEL

Oh, mother, I hope I didn't awaken you.

Gladys Cooper was cast in the play in 1923 and immediately confronted Barrie with alternatives. She wrote in her autobiography,

"I wonder where Peter got his high boots from. Did he go to Clarkson?" I said at one lunch. Barrie pondered for some time, and then said: "Well, what do you propose?" Result: I got my own way and played Peter in a pair of old shoes of John's (her son). The same with shorts. I asked Sir James where he got them—result, I was allowed to wear an old pair of flannel shorts belonging to Gerald du Maurier. By taking thought—and Barrie out to lunch—I even managed to get the fight between Peter and Hook changed. I said it was "silly" for them to fight with wooden swords, and so it came about that when Franklyn Dyall [Captain Hook] and I had our fight we used real sabres.

It is doubtful that Barrie, a man who loved tradition, would have even considered such changes if he had not himself become a different person. It was a terrible shock when he was informed that George, the oldest of the Davies boys, had been killed in action during World War I. The boys were like his own. Just four days

Henry Ainley and Edna Best, 1920. (Author's collection)

earlier, March 11, 1915, in his last letter to George, Barrie tried to comfort the young man who first influenced him to write of Peter Pan's adventures in Kensington Gardens:

It was terrible that man being killed next to you, but don't be afraid to tell me of such things. You see it at night I fear with painful vividness. I have lost all sense I ever had of war being glorious, it is just unspeakably monstrous to me now.

Among George's possessions was a copy of *The Little White Bird,* which he had bought before going back to the front.

Six years later Barrie lost his other favorite, twenty-year-old Michael, who drowned in the river Thames at Sandford Pool at Oxford on May 19, 1921. It was more than he could take. Just six months earlier Barrie had convinced him to go back to school at Oxford rather than quit and study painting in Paris. Barrie would spend the rest of his life mourning "the lad that will never be old." He recorded a hauntingly pathetic dream that expressed his underlying guilt:

On 7th Nov 1922 I dreamt that he came back to me, not knowing that he was drowned and that I kept this knowledge from him, and we went on for another year in old way till the fatal 19th approached again & he became very sad not knowing why, and I feared what was to happen but never let on—and as day drew nearer he understood more & thought I didn't—and gradually each knew the other knew but still we didn't speak of it—and when the day came I had devised schemes to make it impossible for him to leave me yet doubted they could help—

Lila Maravan and Gladys
Cooper, 1923. Photo:
Sasha. (Author's collection)

and he rose in the night and put on the old clothes and came to look at
me as he thought asleep. I tried to prevent him going but he had to go
and I knew it and he said he thought it would be harder if I didn't let
him go alone, but I went with him, holding his hand and he liked it and
when we came to the place—that pool—he said goodbye to me and
went into it and sank just as before. At this point I think I woke but
feeling that he had walked cheerily into my room as if another year had
again begun for us.

How ironic that Barrie was experiencing the same pain his
mother went through when she lost his brother, David. Despite the
void in his heart, *Peter Pan* continued to visit London every
Christmas season. The scenery and costumes, the same as when the
show opened, were getting old and musty, and the performances
were beginning to follow suit. In 1924 Gladys Cooper again played
Peter with Angela du Maurier as Wendy. In her autobiography, *It's
Only the Sister,* Gerald's daughter complained:

Another thing that horrified me was the exceedingly dirty (or so I
thought) old clothes I had to wear! No new wardrobe for a hardy

annual like *Peter Pan*! My diary quotes that my senses revolted at "clothes dreadfully shabby, ghastly old shoes."

During one performance Angela crashed during the flying scene right into the footlights and off the stage. She wrote in her book:

A more uncomfortable, nerve-shattering and painful experience I have never had. There was a hush throughout the whole house, quite obviously it was thought I was seriously injured, if not killed. The next few moments are hazy because I do not know just what did happen, but I recovered my "wind" which had been knocked out of me, and when I came to I realized from the orchestra pit that my understudy had been hurriedly pushed on.... When I felt certain I was going to be neither sick nor faint I gave the signal that I'd go on again.... The ovation which greeted me was almost frightening. The audience stood and clapped and yelled, and with tears running down my face by then (from emotion not pain), I blew them all a kiss, and then the play went on.

A breath of fresh air arrived with Jean Forbes-Robertson, the daughter of the famous actor, Sir Johnston Forbes-Robertson, and actress Gertrude Elliott. Jean was born in London on March 16, 1905, and she made her stage debut using another name, Anne McEwen, in her mother's production of *Paddy the Next Best Thing* in South Africa in 1921. After touring New Zealand and Australia she returned in 1925 to make her London debut in *Dancing Mothers*. The critics started to take notice of her when she played

ABOVE: Jean Forbes-Robertson, 1927. The first Peter to be put on records. (From the collections of the Theatre Museum. By courtesy of the Board of Trustees of the Victoria and Albert Museum); LEFT: Dinah Sheridan toured as Wendy in 1934 and 1936. She is featured on the 1939 recording. (Author's collection)

Helen Pettigrew in *Berkeley Square* and Juliet in *Romeo and Juliet* in 1926. St. John Ervine wrote in *The Observer:*

For my part, I have never in a long course of playgoing, during which I have seen many Juliets, witnessed anything so beautiful as Miss Jean Forbes-Robertson's performance in the Balcony scene. She gave us here the young girl newly acquainted with affection, opening out to high and lovely passion, the very "bud of love" proving itself to be "a beauteous flower." Her expression is extraordinarily mobile; she has a singular ability to illuminate her slightly somber face with fleeting smiles, and with the least movements she betrays a medley of emotions. When Romeo first kisses this Juliet she shyly draws back as his lips touch hers, not because the importunate youth is displeasing to her, but because some delicate apprehension fills her mind. But when she resolves her doubts and has allayed her fears, she pours her affection out, not unmaidenly, but with young and innocent ardor. This was Juliet on her balcony, for me at all events: my imagination was here fulfilled.

The following year Jean Forbes-Robertson became Peter Pan and continued until 1934–35, vying with Pauline Chase for longevity in the part. Wrote a critic for the *Era:*

Personally, I think she is the best Peter I have seen. She is a boy with youth and vigor and fun, and yet she is fey. Her wings are those of the imagination, and she is at home in the Never-Never-Land.

The critic for the *Times* found:

This Peter is full of fiery beauty; he sparkles with vitality; he gives a magic to Wendy's house that we have not known it to possess. Here is a Peter who is at the farthest possible remove from a principal boy in a pantomime, whose vitality is something altogether different from rollicking high spirits, who hovers most brilliantly between the joy and melancholy of boyhood, and the different joy and melancholy of the immortals.

Jean suggested the addition of a line to further suggest Peter's fairy quality. When Wendy hears that Peter has no mother she jumps to hug him.

PETER

You mustn't touch me. No one must ever touch me.

WENDY

Why?

PETER

I don't know but I think if you were to touch me I shouldn't be here.

WENDY

No wonder you were crying.

The record jacket cover of the first recording of the play *Peter Pan*. (Author's collection)

Barrie liked her suggestion so much he also modified it in the published version of the play.

For eight seasons the critics continued to find new phrases to describe the experience of seeing this gifted actress play Peter. In 1928, Charles Morgan wrote in a review:

It has lately been thought enough for Peter to be boyish and sprightly and full of "go"; it has been forgotten that, in spite of his human parentage, he has, by long association with fairies, become more than half fairy himself. It has been forgotten that he is an immortal with more of the powers of the immortals in him than an ability to fly in the air. Now Miss Forbes-Robertson has restored him to his own kingdom.

In 1929 Peter turned twenty-five and audiences were treated with the original Captain Hook, Gerald du Maurier. Also back was the mermaids scene which had been cut a few years before. And in 1930 Zena Dare played Mrs. Darling, twenty-three years after she toured as Peter.

In 1933 a critic for the *Times* continued with the flow of praises that Jean Forbes-Robertson had been receiving:

Tall, slender, and agile, with quick turns of the head that could disconcert a whole shipload of unsusceptible pirates as easily as they bewildered poor Wendy, and with wide-set eyes that look through and beyond them all, Miss Forbes-Robinson is Puck's own Scottish cousin, in whom sentiment and heartlessness play see-saw with each other until the steely heart (which the Freudians would call the Pleasure Principle) rises in final triumph to abide in the tree-tops.

TOP: Charles Laughton as Hook with his wife, Elsa Lanchester, who played Peter in 1936. (Photofest); ABOVE: Seymour Hicks finally got an opportunity to play Hook at the London Palladium in 1938. (Author's collection)

Jean was again scheduled to play Peter in 1935, but illness prevented this and Nova Pilbeam filled in, also receiving excellent reviews. The next year saw a teaming that suggested tremendous possibilities—Elsa Lanchester and Charles Laughton. The famous husband and wife actors took a break from their busy film schedule to appear in the play. The response to the play with this unique casting was mild at best.

Noted the *London Times:*

Those who fear that Mr. Charles Laughton's Hook might be too terrifying, too macabre, may be reassured. Mr. Laughton has approached the part in a fresh and generous spirit, erring, where he errs at all, on the side of the benign. This is a portly, rounded pirate with whom it would be pleasant to dine at ease after a morning's murder and a little plank-walking with afternoon tea....Peter, too, is freshly interpreted and, whatever else may be thought of Miss Elsa Lanchester's treatment of the part, it is certainly not sticky or mawkish. What she appears to be seeking is an emphasis on Peter's fiery, Pan-like quality, and to attain this she has stylized her performance, phrasing it with a hard, clipped precision, varying her facial expression so seldom that she gives almost the effect of a mask with highly coloured cheeks and staring eyes, and regulating her movement as though she were describing the pattern of a dance.

On June 19, 1937, Sir James M. Barrie died at age seventy-seven. It was only six years earlier that he made his most generous gift to the Great Ormond Street Children's Hospital—perpetual rights of the books and plays of *Peter Pan*. His last play, *The Boy David*, with Elisabeth Bergner, proved a disappointment only six months before his death.

That same year Anna Neagle came to the Palladium to play Peter and then Jean Forbes-Robertson returned for the ninth time, outdistancing Pauline Chase's record. Seymour Hicks played Hook. Because of the war, there was no London production in 1939, but there was a tour.

In 1940 most of the props and scenery were destroyed in the Blitz and this time both productions ceased. An original cast album of sorts was recorded with Jean Forbes-Robertson, preserving her last performance as *Peter Pan*. She continued to add her magical qualities to many plays, though her final years saw her in failing health. The actress died on December 24, 1962, only fifty-seven years old.

The 1940s and 1950s saw changing styles and attitudes, atomic weapons, and instant or concentrated food products. Still *Peter Pan* came back for his yearly visit. As welcome as he was, Peter was merely being dusted off rather than given fresh interpretations. In

1958 Julia Lockwood played Wendy opposite Sarah Churchill, Sir Winston's actress daughter. Apparently, one evening Sarah was performing while "under the influence" and during her first flight to the fireplace mantel, grabbed the attached monkey's tail to gain balance only to have it fall off. She blurted out a curse for all to hear. A horrified Lockwood finished the scene through her tears. Later, in the Mermaids Lagoon, Sarah removed from under her knees the pillow used to glide across the stage through the dry ice lagoon and began to have a pillow fight with Lockwood.

Julia Lockwood had also played Wendy opposite her mother, Margaret Lockwood, the year before. In 1959, 1960, 1963, and again in 1966 Julia was able to play Peter. Wrote Patrick Gibbs for the *Daily Telegraph* on December 18, 1959:

There is much to be said for a youthful Peter Pan. It was said very eloquently by Julia Lockwood in the annual revival of Barrie's play at the Scala last night. . . . It is a part in which appearance is half the battle, and this Miss Lockwood won immediately and easily by looking with her cropped hair and clean-cut features very much the boy of phantasy.

Gibbs continued:

To this impression her grace of movement contributed much—no Peter that I recall has flown so gracefully or with less apparent anxiety. I only hope, though, that her operator steers her more accurately in future

ABOVE: Alastair Sim played Captain Hook in London at the Adelphi Theatre in 1941, the Winter Garden Theatre in 1942, and the Scala Theatre in 1946. (Author's collection); LEFT: Margaret Lockwood flies to the rescue in the Scala Theatre in 1949. The pirate pointing in the middle is Cecco who was played by William Luff for forty-five years between 1906 and 1953. (Author's collection)

through the nursery window in her first act exit—it's no part of the magic for Peter to fly through a wall!

On April 5, 1960, tragedy struck the Llewelyn Davies family again. Peter Davies, now a sixty-three-year-old publisher, committed suicide by throwing himself in front of a train. Always moody, Peter had been troubled for some time. His brother Jack had died the year before. Earlier he had compiled letters of correspondence between his brothers and Barrie, adding editorial comments as he went along. The depressing task finally became too much for him and he stopped, burning much of the documents. While Barrie's creation of *Pan* delighted millions, Peter Davis referred to it as "that terrible masterpiece," something from which he could not escape. Even his death was reported as PETER PAN'S DEATH LEAP.

Meanwhile, *Peter Pan* continued his yearly visits to the London stage with actresses like Anne Heywood (1961); Millicent Martin (1967); Hayley Mills (1969); Maggie Smith (1973); pop singer, Lulu (1975); and Susannah York (1977) in the lead role. An interesting assortment.

On October 14, 1980, Nico, the last surviving Davies brother, died. Still, the play goes on....

In 1985, the Broadway musical version of *Peter Pan* came to London with Bonnie Langford in the title role. Surprisingly, the critics were more receptive than one would have thought. Jack Tinker wrote in the *Daily Mall:*

Of course, the story is virtually foolproof. The boy who would not grow up lies buried deep inside the crustiest adult. And over the years I must have seen some of the finest talents rekindle his elusive

ABOVE: Pat Kirkwood on the Jolly Roger at the Scala Theatre in 1953. (Author's collection); BELOW RIGHT: Sarah Churchill at the Scala Theatre in 1958. (The Billy Rose Theatre Collection of the New York Public Library); FAR RIGHT: Maggie Smith at the London Coliseum in 1973. (From the collections of the Theatre Museum. By courtesy of the Board of Trustees of the Victoria and Albert Museum)

spirit...Maggie Smith and Dorothy Tutin, to name but two. Yet it has to be said that if you have seen Miss Bonnie Langford orbit ecstatically across this star-decked stage, radiant with youth and joy and a wistful longing, you have seen Peter Pan personified.

Lulu again played the part of Peter in 1988, only this time, the musical one. The *Daily Telegraph*'s Charles Osborne wrote:

Lulu makes an appealing and credible Peter. She puts her numbers across with confidence, flies like a kite, and deals robustly with the dialogue.

Osborne found the musical

something else: something quite delightful, in fact. With as little of Barrie retained as is feasible, it proves entertaining to adults and, if the first-night audience can be used as a gauge, a treat for the adults-to-be.

The year before Lulu was playing Peter, the terms of the *Peter Pan* legacy ran out for the Great Ormand Street Hospital for Sick Children. Copyright ownership of stage and book rights expired. In the United States the novel had already entered the public domain in 1986 while the play would continue to pay royalties until the year 2003. Peter had earned millions of pounds for the then 146-year-old hospital. Not affected was the 1954 musical, which would continue to collect royalties for the hospital.

On March 10, 1988, the House of Lords voted almost unanimously to amend the copyright law for *Peter Pan* which in essence allows the hospital to receive perpetual royalties from English productions of the play. Barrie would have been pleased to know that his favorite play would continue to aid children.

Marilyn Miller

The Ziegfeld Treatment

It may sound strange, but I never want to grow old. I never want to see the day when I cannot sing and dance as I can now. I cannot bear to think of being middle-aged, with all my success behind me. The picture of a dear, gray-haired old lady by the fireside doesn't appeal to me.

—Marilyn Miller, 1922

She was the darling of the 1920s American musical. She possessed youth, beauty, a sparkling personality, and a talent for dancing, and while her singing voice was merely adequate, her great charm pushed her songs over the footlights and into the hearts of her audiences. For more than a decade she was the ultimate "Ziegfeld Star," the toast of Broadway. Though she is fondly remembered by those fortunate enough to have witnessed her on stage, the rest of us must rely on her three film appearances, which barely reflect the talent about which so many critics raved. Perhaps no one was more aware of this than Marilyn Miller herself, who refused to record the songs she made famous or to appear in any silent films. Although there were plenty of offers, it was as if she knew that these mediums could not offer the "whole" Marilyn. It was not until the advent of "talkies" that she allowed herself to be recorded for posterity.

Marilyn Miller was born on September 1, 1898, and given the name Marilynn Reynolds. The name "Marilynn" was derived from her grandparents' names, "Mary and Lynn" Thompson. Her mother, Ada Reynolds, married a second time shortly after her first husband deserted her and their four children. Her new spouse, Caro Miller, was a well-rounded vaudeville entertainer who eventually added Ada, Marilyn, and her two older sisters to his act, the Columbians. Much of Marilyn Miller's training and discipline came from her stepfather, whom she detested. He was extremely short-tempered and strict in his rehearsals, yet despite his corporal punishments for unsatisfactory performances, Marilyn's happiest memories of childhood were those moments on the stage. As her dancing improved, the little girl developed her unique talent for impersonations that included Nora Bayes, Lillian Russell, Eva Tanguay, and even Bert Williams! When she was five years old her name was legally changed to Marilyn Miller.

PAGE 104: Lobby card photograph. Photo: Art Edeson. (The Billy Rose Theatre Collection of the New York Public Library at Lincoln Center)

In order to enable young Marilyn to perform with the family, Caro Miller booked their act abroad, thus avoiding the strict child labor laws in the top cities of the United States. While Marilyn was performing in London, impresario Lee Shubert of the Shubert Brothers spotted her and signed her for *The Passing Show of 1914.* This was one in a series of revues that poked fun at fads and personalities of the day. Marilyn's impersonations were well suited for such productions. As Caro Miller's Columbians were breaking up anyway (Marilyn's sisters were getting married), he signed his fifteen-year-old stepdaughter to a Shubert contract for seventy-five dollars a week, neglecting to mention that she was underage.

During this period, Marilyn trained extensively in ballet, acrobatic dancing, and tap. When *The Passing Show of 1914* opened on Broadway at the Winter Garden, a star was born. "The real hit of the entire performance was little Miss Marilyn Miller," raved the *Telegram,* "who is youthful and pretty, who dances as if she enjoyed it, and who as an imitator approaches very closely to Miss Elsie Janis." Three months after the opening, the new star turned sixteen, the legal age for a minor to perform at night.

The following year Marilyn appeared in another *Passing Show* to even more ecstatic reviews that cited her as "one of the daintiest, prettiest, and cleverest girls on the American stage. She is a vision of delight at all times." The next showcase was a much more sumptuous production, *The Show of Wonders,* with even greater personal reviews for Marilyn. Unfortunately, it was during a rehearsal for this production that she suffered a nose injury, a splintered bone, that would cause great pain for the rest of her life.

Marilyn came to the attention of Florenz Ziegfeld, through, of all people, his wife Billie Burke. Ziegfeld was notorious as a womanizer but Burke seemed to look the other way during his many brief affairs. This tolerance was not in the least due to her assurance that she always held the trump card in the form of their daughter, Patricia. As a businesswoman, Burke immediately recognized the charm and youthful vitality of Marilyn Miller as a possible asset for her husband's famous *Follies.* Unknown to Billie Burke, Flo Ziegfeld had been watching Marilyn's progress for some time. He was in need of a beautiful headliner to replace Olive Thomas, who left the stage for the movies. During the run of her show, *Fancy Free,* in 1918, Marilyn was approached by the Ziegfeld organization. It seems that her original contract with the Shuberts was invalid since she was not yet sixteen when it was signed. Despite generally poor reviews for her singing and acting abilities in *Fancy Free,* Marilyn Miller left the company to become a Ziegfeld star.

In the *Ziegfeld Follies of 1918,* Marilyn performed a "Yankee Doodle" dance and shared the bill with Eddie Cantor, Will Rogers, and W. C. Fields, but it was a young and handsome featured performer, Frank Carter, who received most of Marilyn's attention. They fell in love and received excellent notices for their *Follies* contribution. In particular, Marilyn received howls of laughter for her impersonation of Billie Burke in a number entitled, "Mine Was a Marriage of Convenience."

Ziegfeld was not too happy with the prospect of a marriage between his two young stars; he had professional (and perhaps personal) plans for Marilyn. In addition, her parents disapproved of Carter and refused to allow him in their home, where Marilyn was still living. Promoting the sale of war bonds was one of the few ways the couple could have solitude during their time off from the theatre. And at one of these rallies, Marilyn sold $1.25 million of Liberty Bonds.

During a break in rehearsals for the 1919 entry of *Follies,* Marilyn and Carter tied the knot. Ziegfeld, furious, promptly fired Carter, but the young man was quickly signed up by the Shuberts for a new musical, *See Saw.* Both husband and wife received excellent reviews for their respective shows and set up housekeeping. After

TOP PAGE 106: A valentine from Marilyn Miller, age seven, two years after her professional debut. (Courtesy of Robert Gable); BOTTOM PAGE 106: Marilyn dancing, c. 1915. (Courtesy of Robert Gable); TOP: Marilyn in *Ziegfeld Follies of 1918.* (Courtesy of Robert Gable); ABOVE: Dressed to sell war bonds in 1918. (Courtesy of Robert Gable)

the initial Broadway engagements, their shows went on tour, eventually meeting in Chicago. During their reunion, Carter secretly bought an expensive Packard automobile that his wife admired. Following the rest of his tour he planned to drive it home to her with his friends. He never made it. He was killed instantly when his car flipped over negotiating a sharp turn.

Marilyn was devastated. After the funeral she continued with her *Follies* performances but was miserable when not on the stage. Following the tour she went to Europe to rest and, at Ziegfeld's request, to study voice and acting seriously. Her next project was going to be something special.

Sally opened in 1920 to the best reviews Marilyn Miller had ever received. This was important since the entire show, a book musical, revolved around her. No expense was spared in the Cinderella story of a young waif who is raised by waiters to eventually become a "Ziegfeld girl." The music was composed by Flo Ziegfeld's favorite songwriter, Jerome Kern. Everyone expected fine dancing from Marilyn, but they were pleasantly surprised by her singing voice. According to her biographer, Warren C. Harris, when she sang "Look for the Silver Lining":

There was a hush for a moment as the last note died away, followed by a storm of applause. Again and again, Marilyn had to repeat the chorus, and each time she sang it there was that awed silence before the ovation.

The plea for practical optimism was obviously the kind of sermon audiences wanted to hear in that time of postwar depression. Performance after performance, the response was always the same.

Marilyn was rewarded for her success with the best contract ever given to a musical-comedy ingenue: 10 percent of the gross receipts against a guarantee of $2,500 weekly. The Ziegfeld–Miller teaming spelled magic in the box office but not offstage. Marilyn was seeing a movie star, Jack Pickford, the legendary Mary's brother. Ziegfeld was worried, and with good reason. One of his "girls," Olive Thomas, left the *Follies* in 1917 for a successful career in Hollywood where she met and married Jack Pickford. As far as Ziegfeld was concerned, Pickford was responsible for Thomas's mysterious death. According to the French police, she died in Paris as a result of an accident, having mistaken bichloride tablets for sleeping pills. It was rumored that Pickford and Thomas were taking illegal drugs and Thomas had died of an overdose. Ziegfeld was not only worried about losing Marilyn, he also believed that Pickford was all wrong for her. Ironically, his interference only strengthened the relationship and Marilyn and Jack married at Jack's famous sister's Hollywood estate, Pickfair, in 1922.

Marilyn and Jack Pickford, her second husband. (Courtesy of Robert Gable)

Producer Charles
Dillingham was a former
associate of Charles
Frohman, the first
producer of *Peter Pan.*

During the first few months of the marriage, Ziegfeld, Jack, and Marilyn provided the press with a field day as they publicly hurled insults and accusations until finally Jack suggested that Marilyn not renew her contract with the showman. According to Marjorie Farnsworth's book, *The Ziegfeld Follies,* another reason for the split was that Marilyn wanted to play Peter Pan and Ziegfeld felt she couldn't do it. In *The Other Marilyn,* Warren Harris cites the personal conflict as the end of her professional relationship with Ziegfeld.

A contract was drawn up with producer Charles Dillingham, who offered an attractive salary and a beautiful and extravagant musical spectacular to be built around her talents. However, since that would take almost a year to plan, he suggested starring her in a revival of *Peter Pan.* No one had attempted to take the part to Broadway after Maude Adams put her stamp on it.

Negotiations were begun with Barrie in 1923. Basil Dean, a close friend of the playwright who also directed several productions of *Peter Pan* in England, was asked by Barrie his opinion of Marilyn Miller. Dean had seen her in *Sally* and reported back that her great talents and pixie quality were perfect for the part.

During the negotiations it was learned that a film version was also being prepared, but Dillingham decided to proceed with his plans, reasoning that most people would rather see a live and colorful performance of the play than a silent black-and-white film. Furthermore, the publicity generated by the film could only improve business for all. It was a mistake he would regret.

Everything about the 1924 production of *Peter Pan* suggested a Ziegfeld extravaganza. Over $300,000 were spent in recreating the lavish sets and costumes originally used in the Maude Adams version. The original score by John Crook was played by a full-sized orchestra under the direction of Milan Roder, and Marilyn's numbers, "The Pillow Dance" and "The Indian Dance," were arranged by Alexis Kosloff of the Metropolitan Opera House. Jerome Kern supplied several songs including "The Sweetest Thing in Life" with lyrics by B. G. DeSylva and "Won't You Have a Little Feather," the song Kern had written with Paul West for the Maude Adams touring company.

"Just think of me following Maude Adams in that wonderful play," Marilyn told the press. "I honestly get the shivers when I think of opening night. But it's something I've dreamed of doing since childhood—and, if work and study count for anything, I know I'm going to make good."

Rehearsals did not run smoothly, as Marilyn's conception of the show conflicted greatly with Basil Dean's more traditional approach. Dillingham backed Marilyn. Charles Eaton, who played

John, remembered that almost 50 percent of the actors were English, brought in an attempt to legitimize the Broadway production. Eventually what emerged was a production that was not a musical and not the *Peter Pan* Barrie had envisioned. Yet when *Peter Pan* opened out of town in Buffalo it garnered excellent reviews.

According to the *Buffalo News:*

She won completely an audience that filled every seat of the Majestic....Miss Miller brings us a new *Peter Pan* and wins triumph in a new friend.

Echoed the *Buffalo Express:*

A performance that was a sheer delight.

When it opened on Broadway at the Knickerbocker Theater on November 6, 1924, the critics were not as impressed. The *New York Post* noted:

In writing about *Peter Pan* it is necessary, perhaps, to put on several pairs of gloves as a precaution against hurting either present feelings or older memories.

It was not that she made you remember Maude Adams—at least, not after the first few minutes. It became, soon after it began, simply a test

TOP: Lobby card photograph of Marilyn as Peter Pan from the Knickerbocker Theatre. Photo: Art Edeson. (Harvard Theatre Collection); ABOVE: Sheet music from *Peter Pan.*

ABOVE LEFT: Lobby card photograph. Photo: Art Edeson. (The Billy Rose Theatre Collection of the New York Public Library at Lincoln Center); RIGHT: Guarding Wendy's house. Dorothy Hope (Wendy) is in the center of the entrance with John Grattan (Michael) at the bottom and Charles Eaton (John) to the right. Photo: White Studio. (Courtesy of Charles Eaton)

of Miss Miller's powers as an actress; it became a struggle between her and the part, not a three-cornered affair with Miss Adams included.

The *Post* critic concluded:

Here is again merely the old matter of interest. Miss Miller doesn't interest you in herself, so she can't very well interest you in *Peter Pan*. It appears of slight importance whether or not she is on the stage.

And *Peter Pan* without Peter was exactly what it turned out, with the help of the critics, to be—Peter Panned.

And there was this from columnist Heywood Broun:

There are few in all the world who can dance like Marilyn Miller, and Peter Pan should not be one of them. He dances because he is happy and gay and not because he has been to ballet school.

The critics were also not pleased with the added songs, finding Marilyn's performance of them "brittle and sharp" and stating that they belonged instead in a musical review.

In *Life* magazine, Robert Benchley summarized what many felt.

The fact that a script like that of *Peter Pan* could fall into the hands of people who didn't know last January that Marilyn Miller could never be Peter Pan, beautiful and graceful as she is, any more than Mary

Eaton or Julia Sanderson or seven hundred other beautiful and graceful ladies could ever be Peter Pan, shows exactly what is wrong with the commercial theatre to-day and what will probably be wrong with it to-morrow. The fact that people should be allowed to present this play who would interpolate a Broadway song-hit into it, shows exactly what is wrong with the world.

The song Benchley was referring to was "The Sweetest Thing in Life."

> Picture a happy home
> When suppertime is near:
> The kettle gaily singing
> Children's laughter ringing:
> Through it the tender grace of
> The lovely face of your wife,
> That is the sweetest thing
> The sweetest thing in life.

Benchley continued:

That song hit was particularly revolting...when Peter sang it to Wendy as they sat by the fireplace, a tawdry affair on the order of "Look for the Silver Lining," about Home being the best little thing after all.

Perhaps the fault was not entirely Miss Miller's, or Barrie's, or Mr. Basil Dean's. The trouble probably lay in our having once been fifteen and, being fifteen, having seen Maude Adams.

None of the new songs were listed in the program; only John Crook's name appeared. However, Dillingham was determined to have a hit song in the play. Much ado was made when Wanamaker's

Cartoon from *Daily Mirror*, November 8, 1924. (Courtesy of Charles Eaton)

department store decided to have Marilyn sing "The Sweetest Thing in Life" in a live radio broadcast that would be transmitted to London on December 10, 1924, but a sudden cold caused her to back out at the last minute.

"Won't You Have a Little Feather" was probably performed in the same spot in the show as Maude Adams had sung it but it was apparently built up to showcase Marilyn's dancing.

If Marilyn's Peter was not embraced by the critics, she was not alone. Most also agreed that "Wendy scarcely emerged per Dorothy Hope."

Heywood Broun wrote:

I do not mean to be severe about the actress who does Wendy for she is probably an excellent player, but this is not her role. With the possible exception of Mrs. Fiske I can think of no one less appropriate. Here the fault is not that of the actress, but of Basil Dean. It is silly and unfair to ask anybody who is not distinctly childlike in quality to play the part.

Broun felt that

the present Hook is not the unctuous ruffian created by Ernest Lawford. Edward Rigby is fine as Smee and Violet Kemble Cooper has

Wendy (Dorothy Hope) sewing on Peter's shadow. Photo: White Studio. (The Billy Rose Theatre Collection of the New York Public Library at Lincoln Center)

no trouble with Mrs. Darling, but on the whole, *Peter Pan* has been badly cast for the revival.

Dorothy Hope disappeared from the entertainment scene, but not the same can be said of British actor Leslie Banks, who played Captain Hook. Banks made his English stage debut in *The Merchant of Venice* in 1911 and his first New York appearance was in *Eliza Comes to Stay* at the Garrick Theatre in 1914. For forty years the actor starred on the British and American stages. In London he appeared in *Goodbye, Mr. Chips* and *Life With Father* but his biggest hit was *Springtime for Henry.* Banks made his film debut in 1932 in *The Most Dangerous Game* and immediately became one of the busiest actors on the screen, appearing in almost seventy-five movies, including *Fire Over England, The Man Who Knew Too Much, 21 Days, Jamaica Inn,* and *Henry V,* and also serving as president of British Equity.

The last time Broadway witnessed a Banks performance was in the musical *Lost in the Stars,* which opened in 1949. Leslie Banks died on April 21, 1952, at age sixty-one.

One other actor in *Peter Pan* who bears mentioning is Charles Eaton, who was the younger brother of another famous Ziegfeld star, Mary Eaton. He was thirteen by the time he appeared with Marilyn Miller, but he was already a veteran of the stage and screen.

TOP: Captain Hook (Leslie Banks) and Peter fight it out. (Photo courtesy of Warren Harris, author of *The Other Marilyn*); ABOVE: Peter and Slightly (Donald Searle). Photo: White Studio. (The Billy Rose Theatre Collection of the New York Public Library at Lincoln Center)

Liza (Carol Chase), Peter and Wendy. Photo: White Studio. (The Billy Rose Theatre Collection of the New York Public Library at Lincoln Center)

At the age of three he was cast by the Shuberts in *Blackbirds,* and at ten he was a cast member of the *Ziegfeld Follies of 1921.* That same year he made his first film, *Peter Ibbetson,* with Wallace Reid and Elsie Ferguson. Then he returned to a Broadway revue to play Romeo opposite one Miriam Battista in the balcony scene; he was only twelve, but the critics were amazed at the depth of his understanding of Shakespeare's tragic figure.

Four years after *Peter Pan* Charles Eaton had his biggest success as Andy Hardy in the Broadway play, *Skidding.* During the late twenties, Eaton was one of the busiest juveniles on Broadway.

Only one performer was able to captivate the reviewers: Carol Chase, who portrayed Liza. Broun said she "played superbly," and Alan Dale, distinguished critic of the *New York American,* felt she "made a hit as Liza with her tiny voice, and her cunning presence." Still, the success of *Peter Pan* could not depend on the excellent reviews gathered by as minor a character as Liza.

Only one critic enjoyed this production more than the original, and he was Alan Dale, who wrote:

Those who had memories of Maude Adams missed from the latest Barrie heroine, the wistfulness, the sweet aloofness, and dainty un-selfconsciousness and the irresistible charm that Miss Adams gave to the role. Last night they saw a delightful young woman known as

Marilyn Miller, who had her own ideas and her own figure....She was a nice, jolly, material girl, with no nonsense about her—an ice-cream-dosed Peter Pan—well nourished.

Dale also felt that

Miss Miller, moreover, had it one over Miss Adams with her dancing. She gyrated and she cavorted deliciously. She looked like an elongated Ariel, as she flitted about. Then she sang with a voice—a real voice, a voice that had quality and tone. Oh, such a different Peter Pan...towards the close of the third act, you began to like her for herself, and Barrie and Maudie go hang! She was so very healthy, so beautifully plump, so well molded, so gracefully agile and so lissomely alert.

Dale was usually a very perceptive critic, but his enthusiasm for Marilyn's "charms" only made the other critics seem more objective. Despite the poor reviews, the show did surprisingly well during its short run, breaking all kinds of attendance records.

It is a shame that Marilyn or any other popular artist of the day did not record the songs from the play. Ironically, a song, "Peter Pan (I Love You)," was written in honor of her Broadway show and was recorded by many musical groups of the twenties (see Appendix A— A Selected Discography).

To counter the generally negative reviews, Dillingham came up with several gimmicks to attract audiences, including contests, puzzles in the newspapers, and charity benefits. Marilyn frequently gave interviews on the subject of her latest play. She told several reporters:

I will show Peter grown up and making real love to Wendy. And of course they will marry in the last act. The second act shows Peter as a young man living in a big city—London or New York, as you please, though the name of the city is not given. The act shows how difficult he finds it to adapt himself to modern life, but he is made to realize that the only way he can win Wendy is to settle down like any other human being.

Peter Pan ran for ninety-six performances before going on the road. Dillingham hoped to at least break even with his investment, but the film version was hurting the touring play's receipts and the tour was cut short.

Had Marilyn's career ended with *Peter Pan* she would not be remembered today. However, the next vehicle, *Sunny,* was carefully tailored to show her at her best—a simple story, a great score by Jerome Kern (including "Who?"), fantastic sets, a circus background, and a short title similar to *Sally.* A hit, *Sunny* put Marilyn back on top. And while her marriage to Jack Pickford was over, her

Sheet music of "Peter Pan (I Love You)," a popular song of 1924. (Author's collection)

career continued to flourish. In 1928 she appeared in *Rosalie* and in 1930 she filmed *Sally* for $100,000 and *Sunny* at $50,000 more. It was the highest salary ever given to a Broadway star making a film.

Her marriage to Pickford was clearly a mistake. Marilyn was basically a hard worker while her husband was very laid back. However, the couple were not divorced until 1927. Jack Pickford died in 1932 of multiple neuritis, but before he departed, he was to marry one more Ziegfeld girl, Mary Mulhern, who also divorced him.

Marilyn watched her money carefully and she was one of the few who were not hurt by the Depression. This was a double blessing as she was unable to work during the last few years of her life. Her chronic sinus condition worsened to a point that her last show, *As Thousands Cheer,* despite being a hit, had very little Marilyn in it. She met her last husband, Chet O'Brien, in this show. He was eleven years younger than Marilyn, and the press was not kind about the age difference.

In 1935 an operation was performed to alleviate some of the pain from her ailment. Apparently, the doctor cut into her skull to relieve the pressure but he had cut too deep, subjecting Marilyn to many infections. She grew progressively weaker and tired easily, causing her to reject the lead role of the ballerina in *On Your Toes.* Insulin injections were given by her doctor in the belief that they could rid her of emotional stress. Neither her husband nor her sisters had any idea of the seriousness of her illness, but according to writer Marjorie Farnsworth, Marilyn knew the end was near. On a cold

Marilyn singing the song she made famous, "Look for the Silver Lining," with Alexander Gray in the film *Sally*. (Courtesy of Robert Gable)

The sculpture of Marilyn Miller is still there. (Author's collection)

March day in 1936 Marilyn was shopping with a friend when she spotted a blue silk dress.

"I must have it," she said clutching her companion's arm.

"For a special occasion?" her friend inquired.

"Very special. I'm going into the hospital tomorrow."

"And you want to wear the dress when you leave? I don't blame you. It's lovely."

"Yes. When I leave. I want to be buried in it. I am certain I won't leave the hospital alive."

Her sisters accompanied her to Doctors Hospital in New York on March 12. Marilyn was alert and in good spirits so they felt it safe to go on a small trip to visit their parents. Her doctor told the press that she only needed rest, but she slipped into a coma on March 20 and died on April 7. There was no autopsy, but the probable cause of death was from a toxic condition that was a result of the operation for her sinusitus the year before.

Marilyn was buried in Woodlawn Cemetery, next to her first husband, Frank Carter. While the image of Marilyn will remain as she wished, young and beautiful, her mausoleum has aged, with a roof that is caving in. The other reminders of the legend are three films, a few RCA recordings of nursery rhymes, and the memories of those who witnessed her magic on stage. In 1927, a poll was taken for the most popular performers in the United States. The four winners were sculpted by A. Stirling Calder and the statues were placed on the new I. Miller Building on Broadway and Forty-sixth Street. Amidst the noise of taxis, construction machines, and the steam emerging from the manhole covers remain the four sculptures: stage actress Ethel Barrymore; opera singer Rosa Ponselle; film star Mary Pickford; and the musical-comedy beauty who never wanted to grow old, Marilyn Miller.

The National Guide to Motion Pictures

N.S.E.

PHOTOPLAY

January   25 cents

BETTY BRONSON

MEN I LOVE!   *Who Gets The $5,000?*
By Harriette Underhill   Title Contest Prize Winners on Page 32

9

Betty Bronson

The Silent Treatment

I loved Peter. I am a lot of Peter myself. But I am at least a little different. It isn't fair. They look for Peter, not for me. I am grateful to Peter. But he's like a poor relation—he hangs around so!

—Betty Bronson, early 1930s

When the Lasky Company took over controlling interest of the Frohman empire, one of the first thoughts was to put *Peter Pan* on screen. While several other companies had tried in vain to convince its author to sell, Barrie finally gave in to the Famous Players in 1921. The public's anticipation over the project was heightened when it was announced that Barrie himself would be staying in Hollywood during the filming. He also wrote a film scenario that biographer Denis Mackail called

twenty thousand words of the most carefully rewritten scenario, with all the subtitles, and a mass of fresh visual detail which to anyone but a film producer and his attendant experts must surely have seemed like a gift from heaven. It's authentic, it comes from the one and only source of the saga, who took enormous trouble over it, and never forgot for one moment the special medium for which it was meant.

The first picture we see is of Peter riding gaily on a goat through a wood, playing on his pipes (a reproduction of the painting in my possession). He suddenly flies on to a tree in the inconsequential way of birds. From this he flies over a romantic river, circling it with the careless loveliness of a sea-gull. He as suddenly re-lights on his goat and rides away playing his pipes, his legs sticking out cockily.

This incident should show at once that the film can do things for *Peter Pan* which the ordinary stage cannot do. It should strike a note of wonder in the first picture, and whet the appetite for marvels.

From the first frame of Barrie's treatment, Peter was to be portrayed as a long-established myth, as in the book *Peter and Wendy*.

Barrie follows this with the Darling nursery scene, but he uses portions of his book to open the scene up for film. Mr. and Mrs. Darling walk down a snow-filled street to a business

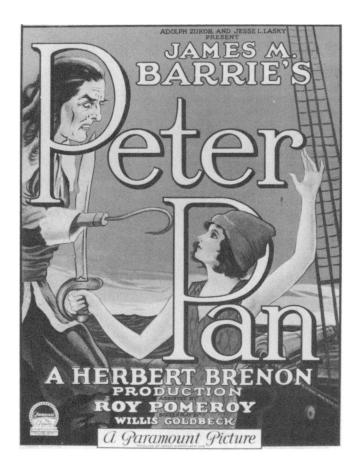

supper. Later, they are convinced by Nana, who has broken loose from her rope, to hurry home as the children are in danger.

The parents and Nana burst into nursery just in time to see them disappear. From the window they watch the children flying over the house-tops.

Here Barrie outdoes himself with an exhilarating flight scene:

The flight to the Never, Never Land has now begun. We see the truants flying over the Thames and the Houses of Parliament. Then an ordinary sitting of the House of Commons, faithfully reproduced. A policeman rushes in to the august Chamber and interrupts proceedings with startling news of what is happening in the air. All rush out to see, the Speaker, who is easily identified by his wig, being first. They get to the Terrace of the House and excitedly watch the flying group disappear.

Then the children flying over the Atlantic. The moon comes out. Wendy tires, Peter supports her.

Then they near New York. The Statue of Liberty becomes prominent. They are so tired that they all alight on it. It is slippery, and they can't find a resting-place. At first we should think it a real statue. Then we should get the effect of the statue mothering them by coming to life, to the extent of making them comfortable in her arms for the night.

This should be one of the most striking pictures.

Next we see them resume their journey. They cross America, with Niagara seen.

Then they are over the Pacific, where the Never, Never Land is.

We see the island all glorious and peaceful in a warm sun. We see the whole of it as in a map, not a modern map but the old-fashioned pictorial kind with quaintly exaggerated details.

BELOW: Peter was a popular fellow in 1924. Mary Hay appeared in a Peter Pan costume in her film *New Toys* with her husband, Richard Barthelmess. (Author's collection); BOTTOM: Viola Dana also dressed as Peter. (Author's collection)

We can clearly see the love that went into this adaptation of his play. It is rich in visual details that could never be seen on stage and even more Barrie charm and wit have been added for the celluloid version.

While Barrie's screen treatment was taking shape, Famous Players launched a well-publicized search for the actress to play Peter, announcing that the author would have the final choice. Many photographs and screen tests were supposedly sent to London for his consideration. Filming, however, was not to begin until 1924.

Despite the fact that she had appeared only as an extra in a few films, seventeen-year-old Betty Bronson knew from the start that she was the only person to play Peter Pan on the screen. Born Elizabeth Ada Bronson in Trenton, New Jersey, on November 17, 1907, she left East Orange High School and convinced her parents to let her move to California to aid her career in films. Her father decided that the whole family would go too.

Before she moved to California, she appeared in a few films made in New York. In a 1930s manuscript for an aborted auto-biography, Betty elaborated on her first attempt to get into the movies:

I went over to the Paramount studio in Long Island for an interview with the casting director. When I appeared at the studio I pinned my hair up and tried to look as old as possible. And it was quite discouraging to me when the casting director said he had a part that would suit me perfectly, that of a twelve-year-old in a picture, *Java Head*. Although this was not exactly what I had visualized myself playing, I was delighted that I was actually to have a part in a picture. It meant that my career as an actress was really to have a beginning.

After the move to California, she heard that *Peter Pan* was to be made into a movie. Betty relentlessly campaigned for the part to any Lasky official who would listen. Director Herbert Brenon finally permitted the youngster to be tested.

...I felt very sad and tearful as I returned to the wardrobe to change from my costume and felt that I had made a failure of it.

Brenon went to London to show the best screen tests to Barrie and he was still there when Betty was offered a contract.

I felt when that took place that I had probably been chosen for Peter Pan or at least that I was to play Wendy. The contract was for a hundred and fifty dollars a week for a year and then two hundred and fifty for the second year or so, for five years.

Jesse L. Lasky, the head of Paramount, was cabled by the author:

BETTY BRONSON CHOSEN TO PLAY THE ROLE OF PETER PAN—REGARDS—BARRIE

When the picture was completed, the studio realized that it had a hit and a new star on its hands and Betty was rewarded with a five-thousand-dollar bonus.

In a *Films in Review* article on Betty Bronson, DeWitt Bodeen wrote that Lasky later confessed: "We had decided on a pert kid named Mary Brian, when along came another unknown, even better

Peter (Betty Bronson) finds his shadow. (Quality First Photos)

suited to the part. Betty Bronson was given the lead and Mary Brian shifted to the role of Wendy."

In an interview for this book Mary Brien stated:

No, no, I was never considered for Peter. Betty had already been chosen for Peter. They wanted me to be the little house mother. I was much more that type than Peter. Everyone else had been set for their parts and they made a screen test and signed me immediately and we went to work almost immediately.

This is confirmed by Esther Ralston, who played Mrs. Darling. Coincidentally, she only met her costar the day before their first rehearsal.

I was judge for a beauty contest for Miss Los Angeles or something.... I kept looking at this little dark-haired girl with long curls. She was about fourteen years old and I kept saying to the other judges, "I like that little girl down at the end. She's got personality. She's beautiful." They said, "She's too young." I said, "She may not be Miss Los Angeles but she certainly can be Miss Personality." And that's the title we gave her.

The next day I was called on the set to meet the cast of *Peter Pan* and who did I meet, Louise Dancelor, only she had a new name now. She was Mary Brian.

Mary elaborated,

We had come out from Texas; my mother's sister was living out here. Through people that she met, they said that they were looking for little people for the fairies. You would never see their faces but they would

Wendy (Mary Brian) sews
on Peter's shadow.
(Quality First Photos)

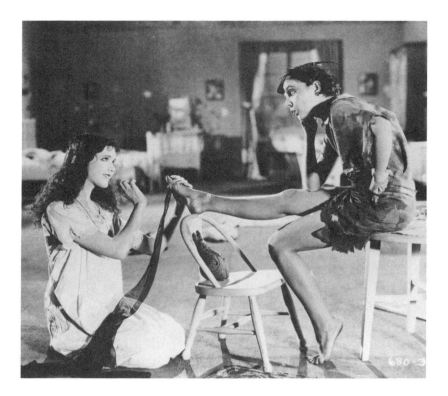

just be flying about. So they asked me if I would come over. That was Al Kaufman who was Mr. Lasky's brother-in-law and an executive at the studio, but that's what I went in for. When Herbert Brenon saw me and talked to me, he was recovering from an eye operation. I walked into this dark room because he could only have a light on the person he was interviewing. I didn't know that I was up for Wendy. After we talked, he said "Is that your own hair?" I said, "Yes and you can pull it if you want to." They called me back and I made another test with Betty and then it was decided right after that.

Of course, this was the first thing that I had ever done. I had nothing to compare. They had decided to go with unknowns. Betty Bronson had done a few things but as long as she was playing Peter, they thought that if Wendy and the little lost boys were all unknowns to the audience it would seem more like a fairy tale. That was the reason I got the break. Herbert Brenon, who picked me, was one of the better directors at that time. It was wonderful for me because I was his choice to play Wendy.

The casting of Esther Ralston as Mrs. Darling surprised no one more than Esther herself. She was only twenty-four, much too young to be the mother of Wendy! Sixty-seven years later she still remembered the day that she was cast.

I was working with Tom Mix wearing a Stetson hat with a gun on each hip when my agent called me about a part at Paramount as a mother. I said, "Who me, a mother?" He said, "No, no, the director, Herbert

Brenon, feels every child thinks of his mother as a young girl. And they want a young girl to play the part." So I went over to Paramount on my noon hour and met Walter Wyman and Jesse Lasky.

I heard Jesse Lasky say, "Walter, you don't think of this cowgirl as Mrs. Darling?" He said, "Wait a minute," and called the wardrobe department. "I have a Miss Ralston down here and we want to test her for the part of Mrs. Darling. Do you think you can make a lady of her in fifteen minutes?" So, of course they made a lady out of me in fifteen minutes and I got the part.

Ernest Torrence took the role of Captain Hook. He had costarred in several prestigious films, including *The Hunchback of Notre Dame* and *Ruggles of Red Gap*, before this important assignment and he would go right on into talkies with *The Cuban Love Song* and *Sherlock Holmes*. The screen's foremost Oriental actress, Anna May Wong, Tiger Lily, had a long career in films that ended in 1960.

Animal actor George Ali was Nana and the crocodile. By the use of strings running from the head of the dog costume through the whole body, Ali was able to move the eyes, mouth, ears, and tail. This was particularly effective as Nana looks sad at the loss of the children. Just as we are able to sense a dog's emotions in real life, Nana's half-closed eyes and drooping ears convey mourning.

Wendy gives Peter a "kiss." (Quality First Photos)

For the first time, Tinker Bell would actually be played by a human, Virginia Brown Faire. Her few scenes were shot with giant sets that brought a pixie touch to the film.

With an excellent cast and a handsome budget, *Peter Pan* began filming in September 1924 and was completed and edited in time for the Christmas holiday season, opening at the Rivoli Theatre in New York where it was accompanied by a prologue, *The Storm*, and an animated short, *Out of the Inkwell*. The reviews were some of the best that Peter ever received. The *New York Times* led the praise:

That wonderful, ecstatic laughter, tinkling and beautiful, just the laughter that Barrie loves to hear, greeted Herbert Brenon's picturized version of *Peter Pan* yesterday afternoon in the Rivoli. Again and again the silence of the audience was snapped by the ringing laugh of a single boy which was quickly followed by an outburst from dozens of others, some of whom shook in their seats in sheer joy at what they saw upon the screen....Obviously inspired by his discussions with Sir James Barrie, Mr. Brenon has fashioned a brilliant and entrancing production of this fantasy....It is not a movie, but a pictorial masterpiece which we venture to say will meet the approval of the author.

The *Times* critic found Betty Bronson to be

ABOVE: The audience was allowed to see Tinker Bell for a few moments. She was played by Virginia Brown Faire. (Author's collection); RIGHT: "I must blow the fairy dust on you first." (Quality First Photos)

a graceful, vivacious and alert Peter Pan. She is youth and joy, and one appreciates that she revels in the role. Her large eyes are wide with

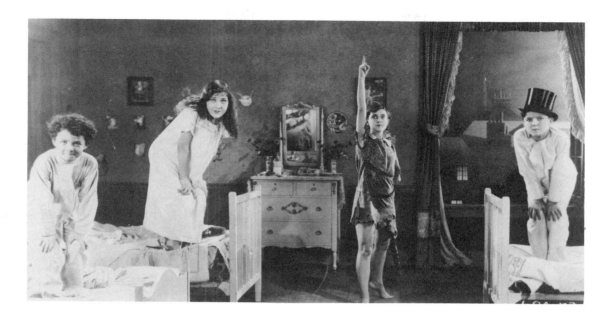

wonder when she first greets Wendy and she is lithe, erect and straight of limb when she fearlessly fights the horrible Captain Hook on his pirate craft.

He also observed:

Captain Hook is impersonated by Ernest Torrence, who is as effective as he can be as a gruff pirate whose voice is not heard....Esther Ralston is comely as Mrs. Darling, whose mouth is "full of thimbles." Mary Brian makes a charming Wendy, and Phillippe de Lacey and Jack Murphy are effective in their respective roles of Michael and John.

Peter Pan was part of the *New York Times*'s Best Ten Films list of 1924.

Bronson was cited by almost every critic as the chief asset of the film. Wrote James R. Quirk of *Photoplay:*

The more we think of Betty Bronson, the more we marvel at her perfect performance. Not only the expression in her face but the way she stood and walked, and the grace that she showed every instant caused us to feel that she was truly an ethereal child who never could grow up. And anybody who can do that is, in reality, Peter Pan.

James Barrie was also quite impressed with the young actress and told her so two years later when she paid him a visit in London.

Seen today, the 1924 *Peter Pan* stands as a testimony to the silent-film era, yet it was not the film that its author had envisioned. For some incomprehensible reason the producers discarded Barrie's scenario! To give them credit, they did take a few of his ideas and

"I can not strike. There's something stays my hand." Peter, the Lost Boys, and Wendy. (Quality First Photos)

these are shining moments in an otherwise conventional screen translation of the play. As for the rest, it is merely a retelling of the stage play with an unusually rigid camera. Except for the location footage of the pirate ship and the mermaids on the beach, the movie takes on the look of a filmed stage play. Director Herbert Brenon decided not to shoot the famous "To die would be an awfully big adventure" lagoon scene, therefore relegating the mermaids to little more than scenery. However, they do find the crocodile to help save the children from Captain Hook.

Peter's first entrance, on film, into the nursery becomes uneventful as he steps into the window rather than making a greater impact by flying. The nursery scene seems much too long and claustrophobic, but the actors had to suffer more as they waited considerable amounts of time between takes. Esther Ralston remembered a humorous incident on one of these occasions.

We were standing; I had my daughter, Wendy, on one arm, my son, John, on another arm, and Michael, who came to about my waistline. We were standing close together with our arms around each other and we were waiting for the camera man to focus and get the correct lighting. Well it was a little long, at least five or ten minutes. All of a sudden Mr. Brenon said, "Lights, camera, action!"

I let out a scream. And he said, "Cut, cut! for heaven's sake, Esther, what's the matter? What happened?"

I said, "Michael, he bit me in the stomach!" And the director said to young Michael, "No matter how long you have to wait, or how bored you get, you are not to bite Miss Ralston again!"

* * *

It is the charm and youth of the young actors that save the nursery scene from being completely maudlin. By sticking to the stage directions Brenon prolonged the scene with actions that are not necessary to the screen. For example, onstage Nana's barking alarms the children to hide behind the curtains, which was necessary for the attachment of their flying wires. However, this same routine in the film is just not needed. Rather than editing in the flying, Brenon seems to have shot a continuous scene, therefore using this same curtain device to no avail.

Mary Brian defended:

It was done according to tradition. I think that so many people are familiar with the play that they would miss certain things if it had been done quite differently. It's like people with opera. They don't want anything left out....It wasn't usual at that time, but Herbert Brenon...really wanted us to speak the lines from the script and from the book. And that we tried to do.

As for the assumption that the movie was filmed in the order of the narrative, Mary assured me that this was not the case.

At that time the wiring wasn't perfected as it is now. They had planks across the cross beams up above the set. Men with piano wires would run across these tracks and we would fly from one place to another. But they were so complicated that they would have to change the tracks up there for each of us. So we were put to bed there on the set in the

Tiger Lily (Anna May Wong) and the Indians. (Photofest)

ABOVE: Michael is forced to walk the plank by Captain Hook (Ernest Torrence). (Cinemabilia); RIGHT: Esther Ralston as Mrs. Darling reunited with her children. (Film Favorites)

nursery until they changed the flying direction. I would almost finish with that and I'd get a certain amount of sleep there, my mother was with me. Then we would just go home and clean up to be ready to go out to San Pedro.

She went on:

The Pirate ship was down in San Pedro, and we had to go down very early in the morning so that we would be shooting by the time the sun came up. So we had hours that people would never think about doing anymore. Because this was my first I thought, "Well this is the way they make pictures!"

Mary Brian continued to make pictures until the early forties. She also did some work on Broadway, including *Three After Three* with Mitzi Green, Simone Simon, and Jack Whiting. When *Peter Pan* was being adapted for Mary Martin some thirty years later, Mary Brian was approached by the producers.

They wanted me to open the second act, Wendy Grown Up. The only thing was I was doing television at the time and I couldn't do it. I'm sorry now that I couldn't have made arrangements, that would have been great fun.

Peter Pan retains a special place in Mary Brian's memories.

I hadn't seen it for years. I knew that it was *Peter Pan* but I didn't know it was going to be a classic all through the ages. I had never seen the stage play. Everything was like a fairy tale to me when you have never been before a camera before. About five or six years ago, I guess it was, Eastman showed it in one of the Century City Theatres with a full orchestra. They asked me to come. It was really quite a thrill to see this beautiful hand tinted film. I was quite impressed.

Esther Ralston continued to work for many years in film, radio, and television. She also made another movie with Betty Bronson, Barrie's *A Kiss for Cinderella*. In 1985 the eighty-three-year-old actress published her very candid autobiography.

As for the lead in the silent-film version of *Peter Pan*, Betty Bronson enjoyed the immediate but terribly brief stardom that it brought to her. After several films she starred again for Herbert Brenon in *A Kiss for Cinderella*. Both she and the movie were lauded by the critics. The *New York Times* wrote:

Hers is a truly wistful characterization, in which there comes a smile in daring to hope and trust, a tear creeping to the eye in pity for something, a dread of the hour of midnight, the gratification expressed at the sight of the Prince, whose face is not that of a stranger, after all.

She is captivating in every scene, pathetic to the point of making one look at her through a mist of tears.

Her portrayal of Mary in *Ben-Hur* was also praised despite the part being not much more than a cameo appearance. Again quoting the *New York Times*:

A most astounding performance happens in the initial chapter of this picture. It is that of a girl who was practically unknown on the screen eighteen months ago. She here delivers a portrayal of the Madonna that is gloriously beautiful. At first you may wonder who this young actress is, for her appearance is completely changed in the brief performance she gives here. She is none other than Betty Bronson, the girl who was selected to play the title role of *Peter Pan* a little more than a year ago, and who won further laurels by her impersonation of the slavey in Barrie's *A Kiss for Cinderella*. In both those films she was a pert, lively, skittish little creature, fantastic, impudent, or impish.

Another good film that Betty made was *Are Parents People?*, but the quality of the scripts offered to her soon diminished. In *Classics of the Silent Screen*, Joe Franklin gives a perceptive analysis of her:

The real tragedy of Betty Bronson's career is that she arrived on the screen just a few years too late. *Peter Pan* should have been the zenith of one phase of her career, not the beginning of it. Had she arrived on the

Peter and Wendy as paper dolls. (Author's collection)

Betty Bronson as
Cinderella in the 1926
film, *A Kiss for Cinderella.*
(Photofest)

scene just ten years earlier, in that age of innocence when honest
sentiment, whimsy, fantasy, and Cinderella themes were not deemed
old-fashioned and out of touch with the times, what a star she could
have become.

Betty appeared in a few talkies, including *The Singing Fool* and
Sonny Boy with Al Jolson, and stayed in films until 1932, making
one more feature in 1937, *The Yodelin' Kid From Pine Ridge,* which
starred Gene Autry. She then decided to become a full-time wife and
mother. During the sixties, Betty returned to make cameo appearances in films like *The Naked Kiss* and *Evel Knievel.*

Upon reading several reviews of the films that she made after
Peter Pan, one finds that the critics unintentionally helped to destroy
her career with their insensitive typecasting. PETER PAN IN CIN-
DERELLA or PETER PAN AS THE VIRGIN MARY were among the headings
of the film reviews. It is no wonder that Betty complained to
reporter Myrtle Gebhart of their unfairness, yet the latter ironically
chose to title her story, "Peter Pan's Rebellion."

Betty Bronson died on October 21, 1971. Earlier that year she
made an appearance on the "Merv Griffin Show" along with other
stars from the silent-film era. DeWitt Bodeen remembered that last
appearance: "Betty was so alive when I saw her that evening," he
wrote, "laughing and clapping her hands in delight, just as she did
when Lasky informed her that J. M. Barrie had selected her to play
Peter Pan, and she danced around the room, repeating, 'I'm the
luckiest girl in the world.'"

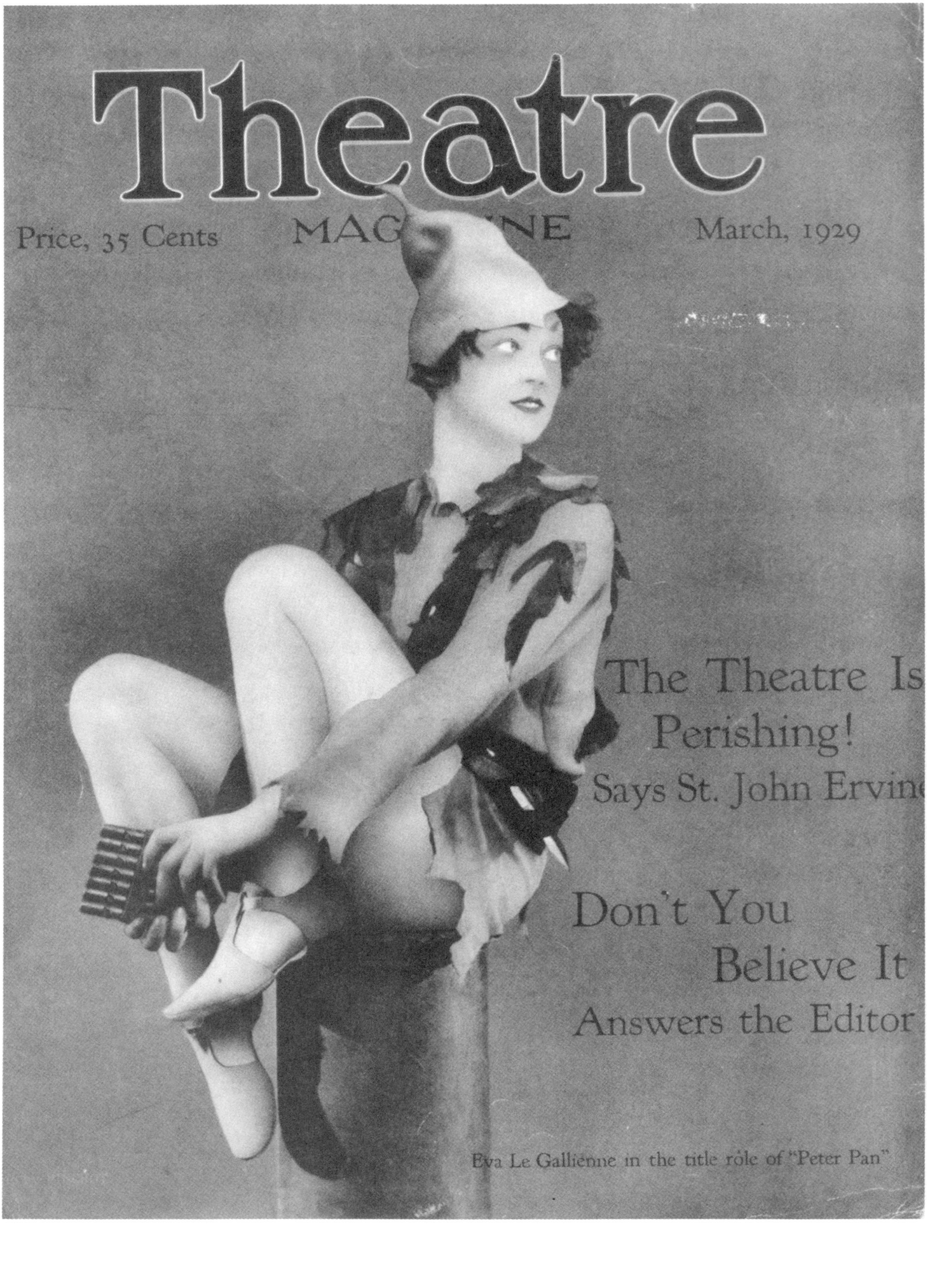

Theatre

MAGAZINE

Price, 35 Cents

March, 1929

The Theatre Is Perishing!
Says St. John Ervine

Don't You Believe It
Answers the Editor

Eva Le Gallienne in the title rôle of "Peter Pan"

Eva Le Gallienne

The Civic Repertory Theatre

How Barrie would have hated my Peter Pan. It's always puzzled me that he should have written a character all boy *(the braggadocio, the cockcrows, the fear of being trapped and held—all traits which, rightly or wrongly, we associate with* boy) *and yet the performances of the part he most enjoyed were unfailingly "Girlie-Girlie"— a cross between the customary Viola of the '90s and the Principal-Boy in an English pantomime. One can scarcely imagine anything less like Peter.*

—Eva Le Gallienne, 1970

*E*va Le Gallienne anticipated playing *Peter Pan* ever since childhood. In fact, at the age of thirteen, this remarkable creature made a list of characters that she hoped to portray by her thirty-fifth birthday. It included Juliet, Hedda Gabler, Marguerite Gautier, and, of course, Peter. Amazingly, she fulfilled her aspiration! From an early exposure to the histrionics of Sarah Bernhardt the youngster realized that her life was to revolve around this art form. In her first autobiography, *At 33*, she wrote:

One ultimate goal from which I never again wavered for an instant: the Theatre—the power to spread beauty out into life.

Eva Le Gallienne was born in London on January 11, 1899, but was raised in France after her father, poet Richard Le Gallienne, and mother, Danish journalist Julie Norregard, were divorced. She did not see her father while she was growing up but a tight bond evolved nevertheless. Her superior education was carefully planned by her resourceful mother to include six languages (which she would use to translate Ibsen and others) and physical education.

In an unpublished essay many years later, she wrote:

I'd had a great deal of physical training in my childhood and was quite a gymnast. Since the school I went to in Paris made no provision for exercise of any sort, mother arranged that I should attend a gymnasium, the Gymnase Georges on the rue de Vaugirard—twice a week. Monsieur Georges was so pleased with my progress he asked mother to let me take a course in professional acrobatic training; he felt I had a natural aptitude for it. But the idea of her daughter becoming an acrobat had no appeal for mother and she firmly refused. However I managed to persuade Monsieur Georges to give me some advanced ring and trapeze work all the same. This gave me a control and flexibility invaluable to any actor. It came in very handy in *Peter Pan*.

Her nanny stopped her from exercising her athletic abilities in her very first attempt at Peter Pan. After seeing Pauline Chase in the English production, the child went home and attempted to "fly" right out of her bedroom window! "If she can do it I can," she muttered as her nurse caught her just in time. Yet this episode clearly illustrates the high regard that she had for an actor's ability to paint a portrait of a character effectively, for when she said "if she can..." she was also criticizing Miss Chase's performance. To Eva "she" was never believable as a "he." This thought would remain with her until she was at last able to try her hand at Peter.

Before Eva was in a position to pick the kind of roles she wanted to play, she paid her dues. Her first stage appearance was at fifteen, a walk-on in *Mona Vanna* which was arranged by actress Constance Collier, a close friend of the family. Two decades later, Eva recalled her first opening night in *At 33*:

Five minutes before "Overture" was called, I rushed down to Constance Collier's room, and with the most perfect disregard of her nerves, and of the fact that after all it was she and not I that was to carry the brunt of the performance, I invaded her dressing-room and taking possession of her mirror proceeded to put a few last touches to my wig, which would not seem right to me. Instead of throwing me out, she helped me with the utmost patience, and watched me in smiling amazement. Utter thoughtlessness, utter selfishness of extreme youth!

After the run of the play, Julie Le Gallienne enrolled her daughter in Beerbohm Tree's Academy. While she was appearing in a school play as a cockney, producer Lyall Swete happened to be in the audience and offered her the part of a cockney servant in *The Laughter of Fools*. Eva unintentionally left her audiences in stitches and in return received radiant reviews. When the play closed, England was entering the Great War, so Eva and her mother decided to try her luck in the United States.

Her first part in New York was that of a black maid. Later she was turned down for a cockney part as being not authentic. A series of disappointments and so-so parts followed until she appeared in *Not So Long Ago*. Her excellent notices resulted in her winning the role of Julie in the Theatre Guild production of Molnar's *Liliom* (the

play from which Rodgers and Hammerstein's *Carousel* was derived). The play was the biggest artistic and commercial success for the Guild to that time, and Eva received more than her share of the laudatory reviews.

Her next starring role, in *The Swan*, clearly established her as one of the foremost actresses of her generation. Richard Le Gallienne wrote to his ex-wife at this time:

How often I have thought of that time when you took her to Drury Lane, and she was almost heartbroken because she couldn't be a pantomime fairy. And now her name is in big letters on the billboards of New York! I stood, one day, a full quarter of an hour, looking at it, with tears in my eyes.

Five years later, Eva would be codirecting and starring in England's most famous pantomime. Her father's letter would remain with her then and for the next sixty-three years. As happy as she was with *The Swan*, Eva did not relish acting in long-running plays. At this point she could have had her pick of the roles available on Broadway, yet instead of opting for commercial success she chose to work in an area that required someone of her skills and ideals. In 1926, Eva Le Gallienne, or LeG, as she liked to be called by her friends, founded the Civic Repertory Theatre and made the Fourteenth Street Theatre their home.

The purpose of the Civic Repertory was to allow the average-income person the opportunity to see classic plays at affordable prices and to give the actors a chance to work in several plays in a

TOP: Eva Le Gallienne in Molnar's *The Swan*, 1923 (Courtesy of Joseph T. McMahon); ABOVE: As Juliet. Photo: White Studio. (Courtesy of Joseph T. McMahon)

As Peter Pan. Photo:
White Studio. (Author's
collection)

short period of time. Orchestra and box seats went for $1.50 and the second balcony was only 50 cents. The repertory would consist of works by Ibsen, Shakespeare, Molière, Dumas, and Barrie, giving LeG a chance to exercise her other theatrical talents. She believed that distinguished theatre did not require a Broadway house. From 1926 to 1932, thirty-four plays were produced at the Fourteenth Street Theatre as LeG assumed the triple task of managing while also directing and acting. Wisely, she chose not to take the leading roles in every play. In the dramatization of *Alice in Wonderland,* she played the White Queen, leaving Alice's chores to Josephine Hutchinson, who also played Wendy in *Peter Pan.*

Hutchinson became an important member of the company quite by chance. Her mother, Leona Roberts, a character actress best known for her screen portrayal of Mrs. Meade in *Gone With the Wind,* was a member of the group. Josephine, also acting for some time, was in town to see her mother in one of the plays in repertory. Coincidentally, an actress who was usually cast as the ingenue left the company rather suddenly after artistic differences with the director, and Roberts suggested her daughter as a replacement. While she had recently received excellent Broadway notices in *A Man's Man*, this chance meeting with LeG provided Hutchinson a unique opportunity. More than sixty years later the actress reflected, "That was the best training you could imagine. And for me, those years in the repertory was the luckiest thing that could ever happen." One week could find the company performing and rehearsing six or seven different plays.

Peter Pan was the most ambitious undertaking for the Civic Repertory, for it not only required elaborate sets and costumes, it also boasted music, dancing, fencing, and of course, flying. In addition, the new production would have to live up to Maude Adams's legendary performances.

LeG wrote:

I never saw her act. She left the stage shortly after I came to America; but I soon discovered that "Peter Pan" meant "Maude Adams" to most Americans.

I had been puzzled when asking various people about the Adams performance, why none of them seemed to have much recollection of Wendy; they remembered her only in the vaguest terms. Now Wendy is a tremendously important part, second only in importance to Peter. Was the Adams magic so overwhelming that it could successfully blot out all memory of Wendy? I couldn't understand it—but I did, as soon as I studied the Adams's acting version sent me by the Frohman Company from whom I leased the rights. At least two-thirds of Wendy's lines were either cut or else, incredibly enough, transferred to Peter! Even the bedtime story Wendy tells the Lost Boys before she tucks them in, the story they loved best, the sort Peter hated (with all its typical little-English-girl Victorianisms: "Let us now take a peep into the future..." "this elegant lady of uncertain age alighting at London station...", "...and the two noble portly figures accompanying her..." etc.)—even this story was spoken by Peter Adams Pan! It's hard to believe that Barrie knew of this and condoned it, and one wonders who thought of it in the first place: Charles Frohman? The director? Maude Adams herself? Almost certainly not the director, for directors in those days had very little importance, especially when a star of Maude Adams's brilliance was involved. Charles Frohman, who was Czar of all his enterprises, might have insisted on it as "better Box-Office"; or Miss Adams might have found the actress cast as Wendy weak in the part and decided to play most of it herself along with Peter. We shall never know.

In a gesture of respect, LeG introduced herself to Maude Adams to tell her about the plans for *Peter Pan*. The meeting ended with Adams saying that she would attend one of the performances, which to LeG's knowledge she never did.

The Civic Repertory Theatre program of *Peter Pan*. (Author's collection)

The new director had many ideas about her first children's production, one primarily being the flying effects:

That flying entrance of Peter's is of the first importance. It immediately sets him apart from ordinary pedestrian folk. Most Peters simply climb in through the window—but any boy could do that, and Peter is far from being any boy: his last name being Pan.

Aerial expert Fred Schultz and his family were hired to rig the machinery at the theatre and to teach the principals how to fly. At 110 feet, the grid was unusually high, perfect for flexibility in planning and executing the flying effects. The actors were taught by a daughter-in-law of the family. Before long, Josephine Hutchinson was able to copy every gesture of the instructor. Eva reminded the young actress that since the scene called for this to be Wendy's first attempt at flying she should be a bit clumsy during flight. At the same time, LeG herself had to resist the temptation for a graceful flight in order to maintain her vision of Peter as "all boy."

During our conversation over tea it quickly became apparent that the part of Wendy has remained a favorite of Josephine Hutchinson's.

We had the Schultzes. We were called on stage and Mrs. Schultz was a typical German hausfrau type and there seemed to be either her husband or son who was there, I don't remember. And Gus, who had a great mustache. He was like a character who would be cast by a casting department. And we had to have our lessons. Now the lessons…the main thing was that it is like ballet. You must have control from here [pointing to abdomen]. And the position is arabesque, like in ballet. If you saw that show of Jerome Robbins…a potpourri of all his work.…The girl goes by flying as Peter, she is directed, absolutely only one position…she is flying to be beautiful. The way that we were taught to fly was to be in every position. To fly as if we were a bird because we flew all the time. This girl flies because she is showing that she can fly.

The way they do it is with two ropes. They pull you up on one and release the other and you shoot like an arrow. Let me tell you about one of the funny things that happened.…Naturally we fly out the first time…that's not too difficult although a danger, always a danger with her [LeG] and everybody else because that window was about that high and if Gus didn't raise you high enough you were going right into it, which was something you didn't look forward to. All right, this time they flew me quite high, too high for the proscenium, and my dress went by like that…and a kid in the aisles yelled out, "He shot her head off," when Slightly Soiled shot his arrow—which of course blew everybody. But it was fun to fly.

The Civic Repertory productions of *Peter Pan* included flights that were labeled by many as near impossible, but that word was

just not in LeG's vocabulary. Peter's last impression was to be even greater than his first magnificent entrance into the Darling nursery, so important that LeG insisted that a special flight be inserted at the end of the play. Recalled Hutchinson:

Now the fly that she loved of course was the audience fly. Eventually someone went on after Schultz and perfected it where it wasn't so dangerous. I always thought with Schultz on those wires that it was pretty tricky, that flight. But she loved doing it and the children loved it.

In an essay on *Peter Pan*, LeG wrote:

I took to flying like the proverbial duck to water. I'll never forget the first time I flew to the balcony and back—it was a marvelous feeling. My mother was not so happy though. She was always scared of that flight though the Schultzes repeatedly assured her that there was no danger. This was not quite true, as I discovered at a matinee a couple of years later when mother luckily was back in England. Just as I started the return from the balcony I felt the wire drop slightly and heard a gasp from the audience. Instinctively I drew my legs up as high as I could under my chin and in this way just managed to glide onto the stage; if I hadn't drawn my legs up they would have been smashed to pieces against the apron. It was the audience's warning and split-second response to it that saved me.

And how could I ever forget the look on the faces of the children sitting on the first rows of the balcony as I flew above them. Even now I

The Darling Family, 1931–32 cast—Burgess Meredith (John), Jackie Jordan (Michael), Beatrice Terry (Mrs. Darling), Donald Cameron (Mr. Darling), Josephine Hutchinson (Wendy), and Nana. Photo: White Studio. (The Beinecke Rare Book and Manuscript Library, Yale University)

"The Wendy House." Josephine Hutchinson as Wendy in center with Burgess Meredith and Jackie Jordan to her right. Eva Le Gallienne is at extreme right standing on a mushroom. Photo: White Studio. (The Beinecke Rare Book and Manuscript Library, Yale University)

quite often meet people who tell me they were one of those children, and how the memory of the thrill that "audience fly" gave them has remained vivid through the years.

LeG was the first Peter to fly into the audience, an innovation that recently has been the only highlight of stock productions of the play.

Another effective flying bit was the so-called barrel fly, a difficult piece of business that took place at the end of Act Four. After fighting Captain Hook on the ship, Peter sits on a barrel with his legs crossed, playing his pipes. Hook sneaks up and knocks the barrel from under the boy, but he remains floating in the air in the same position. Suddenly Peter turns and flies toward the captain, causing his nemesis to fall overboard to the waiting choppers of the crocodile. LeG described how this was accomplished:

For this flight two wires were needed—the usual one from the back of the flying harness, the other fastened to a metal ring on a strap buckled around my leg. I put on this strap during the few seconds I was below in the hold and when I came back on deck I dashed over the rail of the ship where my Schultz attendant was concealed, and he attached both wires to me; speed and meticulous timing were needed on both our parts. Then, by putting my free leg over the leg supported by the wire, I was able to sit in the air quite comfortably.

To attain a smooth flight there were three points for the actors to remember: to stand on the designated spot—a small metal disk nailed to the stage floor; for a smooth takeoff—to sit down on the wire to keep it taut; and not to "help" by jumping in anticipation. LeG wrote:

We had difficulty in persuading little Michael to feel the "mark" with his foot, instead of peering at the floor in search of it. And he also had to be deterred from jumping in the air at the moment the wire picked him up, which made for a very jerky, bumpy, "turbulent" flight!

Even if the actors were properly set for flight, the technicians often spoiled the smoothness.

Josephine Hutchinson had an amusing flying anecdote to share:

When we came back from flying—it didn't matter before when we didn't know how to fly—but when we came back, Gus sometimes didn't sit you on the lift. You came back and you were in the nursery and you were supposed to be yourself, yet you were far off the ground. And you have no way of getting down unless he drops you. And you

Peter and Wendy. Photo: White Studio. (The Beinecke Rare Book and Manuscript Library, Yale University)

had to pretend that you were meant to be there. Horrifying! And when he did drop you, you came down like that and you just had to pretend that was the right moment, but you never knew when he was going to do it.

Aline Bernstein, who designed the costumes, went to the F. D. Bedford illustrations in the first edition of *Peter and Wendy*. Peter's tunic was made of leaves loosely hung. One of the most clever aspects of the costumes came from LeG after studying the Bedford drawings.

...In studying these drawings one thing troubled me: the pirates looked like giants and Peter and the rest of the children looked tiny in comparison. I wished there were some way we could create a similar illusion. I had cast the tallest men in the company as pirates—they were all at least six feet—but this wasn't enough. I decided to have special boots made for them with soles literally twelve inches thick; our smallest pirate would then be seven feet tall. The bootmaker assured me no actor could walk in such boots—no actor would even try to. I told

Peter and Wendy. Photo: White Studio. (The Beinecke Rare Book and Manuscript Library, Yale University)

him he didn't know the actors of the Civic Repertory! Our valiant actors even climbed ladders and danced a Hornpipe in them.

The great care and large budget spent on *Pan* did not go unnoticed by the critics. The play opened on November 26, 1928. A critic from the *Morning Telegraph* wrote:

Somehow, you may feel a sort of reluctance about seeing this play in other hands than those of Miss Adams, but this idea is dispelled shortly after the rise of the curtain on the first act when Miss Le Gallienne makes her entrance, and you leave the theatre crowing with *Peter Pan.*

The reviewer felt:

Miss Le Gallienne, perhaps a little more hoydenish than boyish, brings to the Barrie character an elfin charm, an eerie wistfulness, an imaginative understanding and a graceful sprightliness. It is not the Peter Pan of Maude Adams—neither is it the Peter Pan of Marilyn Miller—it is one that Miss Le Gallienne has fashioned after her own ideas, and perhaps you will find, as we did, the Barrie humor a little differently conveyed by Miss Le Gallienne's interpretation.

And he concluded:

It is doubtful if a more perfect or more tasteful production has ever been given *Peter Pan.* The cast is flawless with Egon Brecher as Captain Hook, Josephine Hutchinson as Wendy and John Eldredge as Smee.

The *Herald Tribune* declared the production "Brilliant!" and found:

Through it all there was evident in the production intelligent appreciation, clear understanding and tender regard for the author's fancies, and Miss Gallienne [sic] shared with him the plaudits of the audience....Josephine Hutchinson gave to Wendy just the right sense of budding motherliness the part demanded.

He further felt:

Lithe and graceful in every move, whether walking, running, leaping or flying, Miss Le Gallienne was an alluring picture to which her attire lent not a little. If, perhaps, there was not altogether that whimsical, elfish element in her characterization it must be remembered that the labor and strain involved in directing such a production make severe demands that even the most courageous spirit and physical strength must be affected.

In the *New York Times,* there was this notice:

Nothing was left undone and everything was well done, from the stage settings to the wag of Nana's tail. If Eva Le Gallienne lacked something

Le Gallienne's Civic Repertory Theatre, circa 1933. (Author's collection)

of the sweet, keen wistfulness which Maude Adams gave the part of the boy who would not grow up, she was a gallant, buoyant, clean-cut figure, and gave Peter plenty of elan and boyish grace. She even expressed something of the aloofness of Peter—the boy who would not be mothered to the ruin of his boyhood—which was not within the compass of Miss Adams herself.

And this from the *American:*

Miss Le Gallienne was splendid in her part. No doubt about it. Throughout, though, persisted the thought of those listening and watching that here was a very emotional Peter Pan, rather than the whimsical "sweet" boy of the original Barrie story. Peter Pan seemed just a bit too filled with pep and vigor. An interesting figure though.

This review is interesting as well for the critic unintentionally compared Eva with Maude Adams. Barrie's Peter is many things, but "sweet" and "whimsical" are not his characteristics—they are characteristics that Maude Adams brought to the play.

Other critics openly compared this new Peter with their memories of old. Some were disappointed with the liberties that they mistakenly believed the Civic Repertory production took. Unknowingly, they were referring to the newly published edition of the play as their source. It was different in many ways from the acting version. For instance, in the published format Liza is no longer the writer of the play and does not introduce it. The Lagoon Scene of Act Three was omitted in the Civic version as it was in the Marilyn Miller edition, but the published edition included it. One critic for the *Boston Tribune* aptly appraised the situation when he wrote, "before long, we friends of Peter and lovers of his play will be disputing over the text as scholars do when a page of Shakespeare or a speech in Sophocles is in question."

The most important critics were still the children and they loved this Peter as the previous generations loved him.

Josephine Hutchinson recalled:

Those children that came to the matinees with their parents were one thing, but the children she [LeG] "gave a performance for" came with only a teacher. They came from various schools, various convents, and they were in groups. I could see them [from the stage]. When it got to the fights and things, I was on the upper deck and I could be above the footlights so I could see all of them. The minute the fight started the boys jumped out of their seats, came forward, and tried to get over the orchestra to get into the fight. And the poor musicians had some problems. The teachers had to grab them and get them back in their seats. But it was all very exciting.

At these particular parties, some big concern gave us candy and in our costumes we went out to the lobby and when the children went out we gave them the candy. And we just felt good about that. "Oh aren't we cute and oh so nice we are to be giving these children candy!" So this little boy came up to me and I gave him his candy and he looked at it and he said, "Hell! Hard candy!" It really blew my ego.

LeG was always concerned about the response of the children to Peter's plea to save Tinker Bell. What if they didn't clap? She wrote:

I half expected some child to shout "No!" to the famous question, but for years none of them ever did. Then—it was at a matinee in Boston, of all places—from the front row to my left it came. "Do you believe in fairies?"—"No!" I don't think anyone heard it but me—the shouts of "Yes!" were too loud and the clapping too vigorous; I stole a quick look at the child—a little girl of about eight, I judged—before carrying on with my rescue of Tinker Bell, which was successfully accomplished. But I did not forget that little girl! Now and then I went down to the footlights, stood directly above her seat and stared at her—stared right into her eyes, and gravely shook my head.

Towards the end of the play I went to give her a farewell look, but her seat was empty. Then I saw that she was hiding underneath it. Peter's reproachful gaze had been too much for her!

During the next four seasons, the Civic Repertory's *Pan* played for 129 performances, becoming a Christmas holiday tradition for many theatre lovers in New York. One performance was cancelled in December 1932 when after rehearsing all day for their new production of *Alice in Wonderland* an exhausted staff and director found there was not enough time to change the elaborate sets. Eva apologized to the audience and asked them if they wouldn't mind seeing a sneak preview of their newest play. The audience responded positively and enjoyed the substitution. On November 7, 1932, the *World Telegram* reviewed the revival with an accustomed note:

Miss Le Gallienne's *Peter Pan* is just about what he was, yesteryear. He is the same lovely, wistful elf that he's always been and flies about with grace. But this time, dear children, Peter flies high. Almost as high as the second balcony, to be sure, and that should be reason enough for a revisit to the play.... Heaven, Eva Le Gallienne and the Civic Repertory be praised, Sir James Barrie's whimsical tale will never grow old.

The critic from the *Boston Tribune* shared an interesting analysis of Maude Adams's Pan and LeG's Pan:

The best that the player may do with Peter is to express him in terms of herself—no man has yet acted him—and in the terms of her time for its pleasure.... Miss Le Gallienne's Peter springs from another temperament in another time. Both are harder, more energetic, rational, and realistic.... At this outset her generation and the next younger are quick with response. The times change and we change with them. Even a creature of fantasy may not escape. The classic figures of the theatre

Eva Le Gallienne: Photo: Albert Peterson. (Author's collection)

From left: Mary Layne, Rosemary Harris, Eva Le Gallienne and Ellis Rabb portray three generations of the Cavendish royal family in Edna Ferber and George Kaufman's *The Royal Family*, 1977. (Photofest)

remain such only so long as each new period may find itself somehow alive and reflected in them. Therefore a Peter Pan for the late nineteen-twenties.

In 1933, the Civic Repertory Theatre came to an end. The year before, LeG barely escaped with her life from an accidental explosion in her Connecticut home, but her hands were horribly burned. After a brief interlude she resumed her career and continued trying to find backers to help subsidize her theatre. But the Great Depression was taking its toll and they were difficult to find. A plea to Eleanor Roosevelt for government assistance looked as if it would have promising results, but the president had different ideas and Eva finally had to give up her dream. The Fourteenth Street Theatre was rented out while a smaller version of her troupe toured with five plays, including *Alice in Wonderland* (which became the Civic's biggest financial hit), *Romeo and Juliet,* and three of Ibsen's plays. Finally the company folded.

Josephine Hutchinson went out to Hollywood where she became a respected screen actress with films like *Oil for the Lamps of China, The Story of Louis Pasteur, Son of Frankenstein,* and others going into the 1980s. LeG, on the other hand, rarely allowed herself to "go commercial." She did make three screen appearances: first in 1955, in *Prince of Players* (as the Queen in a scene from *Hamlet*), and Shaw's *The Devil's Disciple* in 1959, and *Resurrection* in 1980. Every few years the actress was involved in some noble

An informal portrait of a
great lady of the theatre,
Miss LeG. (Photofest)

cause for bringing theatre to the masses. Unfortunately, much of her time on these idealistic ventures was at the expense of popularity. The theatre world seemed to be reflecting Hollywood's philosophy of being as good as your last success. This is not to say that Eva Le Gallienne did not work. Quite the contrary, she continued acting until she was no longer able to. In 1942, she appeared in the highly successful *Uncle Harry* opposite Joseph Schildkraut, who had starred with her in the original *Liliom*.

In 1957 LeG played opposite Irene Worth in *Mary Stuart*, staged by Tyrone Guthrie. Eighteen years later she scored with another commercial success in *The Royal Family*. She almost was not cast, as the producers felt no one would remember her. Of course, her performance was brilliant and she proved them wrong. The play was also filmed for television, which gained the actress an Emmy Award. Typical of her character, she was not impressed with awards. She returned to Broadway again in 1981 for *To Grand-*

mother's House We Go and directed and acted (as the White Queen) her third Broadway edition of *Alice in Wonderland*. Both were received poorly. Fans of "St. Elsewhere," the popular television series of the eighties, saw several LeG guest appearances. Still, the actress complained to her lifelong friend, Josephine Hutchinson, that "there's just not enough work." Somehow, between her many projects, she was able to write a second autobiography, *With a Quiet Heart,* in which she revealed herself to be as feisty at "plus twenty" as she was two decades before in *At 33*. She also wrote a popular children's book, *Flossie and Bossie,* a biography of Eleonora Duse, and translated many plays.

One of the great artists of the twentieth century, LeG died in her Connecticut home on June 3, 1991. Despite her many roles and the sixty-odd years that have passed since she flew across the Fourteenth Street Theatre, a generation of children lives on to remember her as Peter Pan.

She wrote many years later:

I once made a nostalgic visit to the old manor-house in Chiddingfold, a small village in Surrey. My father had discovered it on one of his frequent bicycle tours and rashly decided to take it. We lived there until I was nearly three and the money gave out—as it had a way of doing sooner or later! Our friends, the William Favershams, took it over from us and mother and I subsequently spent many happy summers there, so it continued to be an important part of my childhood. As I walked across the village green towards the stableyard gate, I heard a boy's voice declaim "Proud and insolent youth, prepare to meet thy doom!" Hearing my cue I was through the gate in a flash, crying out in Peter's voice, "Dark and sinister man, have at thee!"

"The dark and sinister man"—a small boy of about ten, dressed in a Captain Hook outfit of scarlet flannel, wearing a black cocked-hat with a skull and crossbones painted on it, his round, baby face adorned with a beard and moustache of burned cork—gazed open-mouthed at this "lady of uncertain age" invading his stable yard.

"You...you know the words?" he stuttered.

"Yes—I know the words."

"But those are *Peter's* words," he said severely.

"I know," I humbly answered. Then I went on to ask his permission to look over the old garden—his parents were away for the day it seemed.

Every now and then as I wandered through the well-remembered paths, stroked the old sun dial, stood under the Monkey-puzzle tree, or peered under the yew hedges where the Faversham boys and I used to hide, I caught sight of a flash of scarlet in the distance. The "dark and sinister man" was keeping an eye on me. He was evidently puzzled. How *could* that lady say Peter's words and *sound* like Peter, too?

I naturally didn't tell him I had been Peter. He would never have believed it. How could he? There are times when I find it hard to believe too!

Jean Arthur

A Touch of Bernstein

Real maturity comes only when you have learned to hang on to your youth. If you can hang on to your individuality, hold tight to your freedom, and not get squigged out as you grow older, then and only then are you mature. Years have nothing to do with it.

—*Jean Arthur, 1950*

For movie fans the name Jean Arthur immediately evokes a bubbly yet sharp sophisticate. Her distinctive crackly voice and infectious laugh were combined with a well-groomed look that personified the emerging confidence of the American woman in the work force. Films such as *Mr. Deeds Goes to Town, Mr. Smith Goes to Washington, You Can't Take It with You, The Devil and Miss Jones*, and *The More the Merrier*, for which she was nominated for an Oscar, made her one of the more familiar faces on the screen in the thirties and forties. Yet, next to Garbo, Jean Arthur was also probably the most reclusive star of Hollywood. She honestly believed that audiences were more interested in her movies than her life. "How can anyone in an interview, really understand your thoughts, your ideas, when even people who know each other often can't really tell?" she asked a reporter in 1950.

Jean Arthur was born Gladys Georgianna Greenein in Plattsburg, New York, on October 17, 1900. Her family moved to Manhattan where she attended George Washington High School and worked as a model. Inevitably, she signed a contract for films and moved to California, appearing in many silent two-reel comedies. But Jean was determined to become a good actress, so she returned to New York to work on the stage. Although she did not appear in a major play, the experience matured her talents and she signed with Columbia Pictures, where she made many of her classic films.

When the relatively reticent Jean Arthur read about Peter Lawrence's plans to produce Peter Pan on Broadway, she called him: "Hello, this is Jean Arthur—you want to speak to me?" The actress had been looking for a show to take to Broadway. That Lawrence opted to star her is interesting, for although a great talent, she was also a quiet, moody woman who was sometimes unreliable when she let her emotions take over.

Lawrence decided to produce a musical version of *Peter Pan* initially. He called his friend, Leonard Bernstein, to see if he would be interested in writing the score. Bernstein quickly accepted. The success of *On the Town* in 1944 and his recognition as one of the world's major symphonic composers and conductors had typecast him with audiences as the sophisticated "wonderkid" of the music world. "First time in five years someone hasn't called me to say he has a wonderful show for me to do—all about subways, sky-scrapers, and New York's crowds," he said at the time. "I'm very flattered to be thought of for this kind of play."

Ironically, Bernstein's contribution to the American stage is best exemplified by three musicals that utilize New York as an important setting. *Wonderful Town*, a 1953 musical version of *My Sister Eileen*, with lyrics by Betty Comden and Adolph Green, was a glorious glimpse of Manhattan's Village scene in the thirties. Its cousin, *On the Town*, also created with Comden and Green, was a bubbly salute to the virtues of the Big Apple. His third musical about life in the city was a departure from the other two. *West Side Story* was a landmark stage event depicting the rivalry of two street gangs and its effect on the lives of two young lovers. Bernstein's music and the lyrics of Stephen Sondheim are just as exciting today as in 1957 when the show opened.

PAGE 154: Jean's enjoyed dressing as Peter Pan. This photo was taken in the mid thirties. (Photofest); TOP: Leonard Bernstein, composer, conductor and personality. (Photofest); RIGHT: Jean Arthur and James Stewart in *You Can't Take It With You*, 1938. (Author's collection)

One of Bernstein's least successful musicals is now recognized as one of his most brilliant works—*Candide*. Transforming the satirical Voltaire novel into a musical was described by him as "three years of agony, trying to make an impossible situation possible." Although it lasted for only seventy-three performances initially, it was totally revised seventeen years later and played for 740 performances.

Peter Lawrence also asked Bernstein's friend and colleague, Jerome Robbins, to direct his production. On December 25, 1950, an announcement was made that Jean Arthur would star in *Peter Pan*, "a fantasy with music."

A lot had transpired since Peter Lawrence's initial plans to make a musical of the play. Jean was at first attracted to the idea of appearing in a musical treatment of Barrie's beloved work. Bernstein had already written several new songs and revised a few of his other tunes that were taken out of past shows. One in particular was "Dream With Me," which he penned with Comden and Green. The beautiful ballad spoke of an unrequited love, a closeness that could be shared between two people worlds or oceans apart. The song was written for *On the Town*, but it could easily be sung by Peter to Wendy at the end of the play. There was just one problem: Jean Arthur was no singer!

Jean quickly realized that she did not want to appear in a musical where everyone but the star would be singing. It was decided that *Peter Pan* would not be a musical after all, but it would retain some of Leonard Bernstein's songs and suites. Therefore, Jerome Robbins's specialized skills were no longer necessary and Jean asked for English director John Burrell to be given the task of staging the production. Wendy Toye was assigned as his associate director. Another song omitted from the score was "Hallapalooza," a reworked song dropped from *Wonderful Town*. The six that remained were "Who Am I?," "My House," and "Peter, Peter," all sung by Wendy; "Never Land," sung by two mermaids; and two songs for Hook and his pirates, "Pirate Song" and "Plank Round."

The part of Wendy was given to Marcia Henderson, a young ingenue from Massachusetts who was advised at the age of fifteen by Sinclair Lewis to seek a career on the stage. Marcia followed his advice and enrolled in the American Academy of Dramatic Arts, where she graduated in 1949. There were several seasons of summer stock during her formal education, but *Peter Pan* marked her New York debut. Marcia appeared in a few films, including *All I Desire* and *The Glass Web*.

The most interesting piece of casting for this production was the veteran Boris Karloff as Captain Hook. Karloff was equally comfortable on stage and screen. In fact, after he left his native

Jean Arthur as Peter Pan,
1950. (Author's collection)

England where he was educated for the British diplomatic service, he spent twenty years with various acting companies in the United States and Canada. He appeared in several silent films but it was not until *Frankenstein* in 1931 that audiences became aware of the actor. Other horror films followed, including *The Mummy, The Black Cat,* and *The Bride of Frankenstein* in 1935 with Elsa Lanchester, who would play Peter a year later.

On the stage, Karloff enjoyed the delicious irony of playing cousin Jonathan, the character in *Arsenic and Old Lace* who has his face altered to resemble Boris Karloff.

Mrs. Darling was played by Peg Hillias and Joe E. Marks played Smee. Marks, an excellent character actor, previously appeared in *The Man Who Came to Dinner* with Alexander Woollcott and the musical *Bloomer Girl.*

Norman Shelly, who was cast as Nana and the crocodile, shared the amusing details of his audition:

I knew the producer, I knew the stage manager. I did not know the director, so I came to audition and they gave me a script to read. The description was kind of charming. The stage manager came out, Mortimer Halpern, who is now considered the dean of stage managers, and I said, "Where's the dialogue?" And he said, "No dialogue."

I kept reading… "dog comes in with a child on his back, puts him in bed, tucks him in, comes out…" Again I said, "Where's the song? Any songs?"

"No songs."

So then they asked me to come in, they wanted to know if I was in good shape and physical condition. I said yes.

"Do you think you could play the dog?"

"Yes."

Then they said, "Can you bark?"

"I don't know, but I'll try." I barked and that was it….I did not audition for the crocodile.

During the opening-night curtain call, Jean Arthur spontaneously walked over to Shelly and removed the dog's head from his costume. The actor was grateful for her acknowledgment, but he was satisfied to remain in his costume during the future curtain calls. He did not want the illusion of the show to be broken for the children.

Peter Pan was one of the most eagerly awaited entries of the 1949–50 Broadway season. Except for a charity benefit of six performances in 1946, it had been almost seventeen years since Broadway offered Peter's flight to Never Never Land, and while LeG's Peter was a critical and commercial success, the budget

ABOVE: Boris Karloff as Captain Hook. (Author's collection); LEFT: Peter flying into the Darling Nursery. (Photofest)

allocated for this Broadway venture seemed to promise a sumptuous production. There are many who consider it to be the best *Peter Pan* ever done on Broadway. The play opened on April 24, 1950.

John Chapman of the *Daily News* wrote:

To a time and town which badly needed it, J. M. Barrie's *Peter Pan* has brought the sweet, sentimental and complete enchantment of Never Never Land. This whimsical comedy about the only boy who ever licked the world—he licks it by simply refusing to grow up—has been given a lovely production at the Imperial Theatre, and last evening it cast its unworldly spell over one of the most worldly of groups, the regular first-nighters.

I'm an old Maude Adams man—or was until last night, now I'm an old Jean Arthur man and I feel much younger than I did three hours ago. Miss Arthur's Peter Pan is in all ways splendid—boyish and cocky, yet one to tug at the heartstrings. And Boris Karloff's dual roles of Mr. Darling and Captain Hook are a triumph of comedy—a performance of high style and sly humor.

Critic Chapman went on to observe:

But it may come as a surprise to many modern theatregoers, as it does to me, that *Peter Pan* is still a thoroughly disarming stage entertainment, even for adults who imagine they have no time for anything except important things. Since it was a genuinely imaginative creation when it was new—as genuine in its way as *Alice in Wonderland*—it is still fresh and enchanting today.

Like his fellow critics, the *Herald Tribune*'s Howard Barnes raved about Jean Arthur:

It is a bravura performance, but that is exactly what the Barrie script called for. That she manages to give the piece a great deal of feelings as well as fairy tale high jinks is the greatest index to the quality of this first revival of *Peter Pan* in some twenty-two years [sic]....Karloff, in the doubly bombastic role of Mr. Darling...and the evil Captain Hook...is captivating. And Marcia Henderson, Peg Hillias and Joe E. Marks add to the excitement and make-believe.

Barnes also felt that

Leonard Bernstein has written an excellent musical accompaniment for the action. It heightens the fantastical mood of the drama at every point and contributes such enchanting songs as "Who Am I," "My House," and "The Plank."

The *New York Post*'s Richard Watts, Jr., was not entirely won over:

As a production, it has considerable charm and beauty. Mr. Bernstein's music doesn't seem to me to add much to it....In the title role, Jean

Arthur, looking and sounding pleasantly like Mary Martin, is boyish and engaging, even though she hardly makes the part as impressive as theatrical legend makes it out to be....But the most charming performance is contributed by young Marcia Henderson, who is fresh and delightful as Wendy. She and the manipulators of the wires for the flying children are the triumphs of *Peter Pan.*

Eva Le Gallienne attended one of the performances but did not share Watt's enthusiasm for Henderson nor was she impressed with the direction, which she thought was too stiff. She was, however, very pleased with Jean Arthur's Peter and told her so after the production when she also made a few suggestions to Jean about loosening up and adding a bit more of the magical Pan to her successfully boyish Peter. LeG later wrote an entry in her diary lamenting that she had not been asked to direct the play. This American production had the flying effects supervised by Kirby's Flying Ballet.

During the run, the play moved to the St. James Theatre with [Miss] Jackson Perkins taking over the role of Mrs. Darling. The "modern" version play was the longest run yet for "The Boy Who Wouldn't Grow Up," at 320 performances.

According to Norman Shelly, Jean Arthur was painfully shy and particularly preoccupied near the end of the run. One evening she received a telephone call before curtain time and abruptly left

Peter Pan to the rescue.
(Photofest)

the theatre. Understudy Anne Jackson had to go on that evening. Jean returned and started to tour the play with most of the original cast (Jennifer Bunker replaced Henderson and two actors took over for Shelly), but her tour was mysteriously cut short when Jean again suddenly left the show. Joan McCracken was called to replace her for the last three weeks of the tour. Another touring company was formed with Veronica Lake and Boris Karloff, who was eventually replaced by Lawrence Tibbett. Despite the behind-the-scenes shuffling, the tour played very successfully for almost a year.

English *Pan* historian, Roger Lancelyn Green, was not able to see this production but he was not pleased with the musical changes. He wrote in *Fifty Years of Peter Pan:*

By this time the craze for "musicals" had fallen like a blight upon the America stage, and therefore *Peter Pan* must be shorn of Crook's music, Leonard Bernstein must write a new score and interpolate five songs, while a ballet sequence must be devised for the Redskins, and the Pirates become a chorus.

Wendy Toye, the associate director, wrote him a most reassuring letter:

I truly don't think you could have been appalled with the New York production; it was done with great, great respect and love. For my part, I love the play so and am such an admirer of Barrie, that if anyone was going to be shocked by it, then it would have been me. I must say I have been shocked sometimes going to the London productions—there seemed little enough love or money spent on it.

We hardly altered a word of the script, and the music came in exactly the same places as always—the Indian ballet is always in, and I did the whole of the fight very musically, although extremely realistically: the music had great youth and joy about it. There were two extra songs for

Wendy, and that's a matter of opinion if it was an improvement or not. All I can say is that America loved it—and it introduced Barrie's *Peter* before Disney's arrived on the scene.

After *Peter Pan* her growing insecurity brought Jean to seek help through psychoanalysis with Dr. Erich Fromm, whereupon she confessed, "I guess I became an actress because I didn't want to be myself." Her intensity and self-doubts caused her to withdraw from Garson Kanin's *Born Yesterday* before it hit Broadway, and made a star of her replacement, Judy Holliday. In 1954, she again withdrew from a show, George Bernard Shaw's *Saint Joan*, during the tour prior to a New York opening. After that disappointment she retired to her home, "Driftwood," on the beautifully scenic Monterey Bay, but she came out of retirement to do a guest stint on the long-running western series, *Gunsmoke*. Director Joe Lewis thought that her work was "delightful, harmonious," with a sense of professionalism that he hadn't experienced since "the days of the great, great luminaries."

Jean looked forward to starring in her own television series, but *The Jean Arthur Show*, a poorly conceived comedy that starred the actress as a lawyer, was cancelled after only twelve episodes. After another artistic disaster, *The Freaking Out of Stephanie Black* on Broadway, Jean retreated permanently to the privacy of her Carmel home. Once, when a reporter tried to interview her he was told, "I don't mean to be impolite to you personally, but I'm out of the business and all I want to do is read and be let alone." This time she was determined never to go back to the business in which she had worked so hard to become successful. The twice-divorced actress died in 1991 in Carmel where she had lived for thirty-five years. She was ninety years old.

ABOVE: Advertisement for the original cast album; BELOW, LEFT: Jean Arthur and Marcia Henderson. Peter whistles to avoid showing pain as Wendy sews on his shadow. (Photofest)

The Greatest Campaign
in Showmanship History!

Walt Disney's
PETER PAN
color by *TECHNICOLOR*

Distributed by RKO Radio Pictures, Inc.

The Disney Touch

The greatest challenge I have ever faced is the task—the very pleasurable task—of bringing Peter Pan to life in a dream world which only he and his friends can see—and only the animated cartoon can reveal to us in all its magic.

—Walt Disney, 1953

*T*he Walt Disney film of *Peter Pan* might not seem to belong in a book that traces the history of an entertainment performed by live actors. Neither, for that matter, does the 1924 film nor the 1991 *Hook*. Yet how can an art form that has been responsible for introducing this famous literary character to so many children be ignored? The 1953 feature-length animated film with depictions of Peter, Wendy, John, Michael, Captain Hook, and even Smee are recognizable to children all over the world. The only name on the film more famous than Peter is Disney, a name which connotates magic, music, color, and fun.

Born in Chicago in 1901, Walt Disney was one of five children. He was always interested in art and enrolled in an art school at the age of fourteen. He formed his own commercial art studio four years later. But Disney was intrigued by animation and gave up his firm to work at the Kansas City Film Ad Company. He was moonlighting cartoons on his own and soon was able to finance his own company, Laugh-O-Gram, which he moved to Los Angeles. There he created fifty-seven "Alice" films, a successful series of shorts that featured a live child actress in animated adventures.

His next creation was a cartoon character named "Oswald," a rabbit. This too became popular, but Disney lost his rights to the series during a contract dispute with Universal Pictures. It was then that he decided to first create the product and then offer it for distribution, keeping the titles in his name. His first creation under these new conditions is still his most famous, Mickey Mouse. In 1928 Mickey made his debut in a silent cartoon, *Plane Crazy*, but didn't really make news until his third film, *Steamboat Willie*, which had a musical soundtrack. The cartoon premiered on November 18, 1928.

In 1929, Disney began creating a series of shorts called "The Silly Symphonies." One of the most successful entries was *The Three Little Pigs* with Frank Churchill's deceivingly

ABOVE: Walt Disney. (Copyright © The Walt Disney Company); BELOW: Wendy stitches a runaway shadow back onto Peter Pan. (Copyright © Walt Disney Productions)

simple nursery-rhyme tune providing the structure for the plot and the dialogue as well as the lyrics of Pinto Colvig. When Hal Roach asked Disney a few years later if he could use the now standard song for his own classic film, *Babes in Toyland*, with Laurel and Hardy, Disney consented, which was typical of his generosity. He recognized the musical content of any film as an important asset. Despite the critical acclaim for his work, these cartoon shorts were prohibitively expensive and did not make much of a profit. Disney needed to create a full-length animated film that would cure his financial troubles while fulfilling his artistic dreams.

Even before he released his landmark *Snow White and the Seven Dwarfs* in 1937, Disney planned to animate *Peter Pan*. He bought the film rights in 1939, but with films like *Pinocchio*, *Fantasia*, *Dumbo*, and *Bambi* (all four also considered masterpieces of animation), he was not able to begin work on *Pan* until 1949. Four years and $4 million later, the film was released. While not quite in the same league as the other films mentioned, it, too, is recognized as a Disney classic.

Amazingly, the general structure of the screenplay does not deviate much from the book, *Peter and Wendy*. What is added, slapstick humor and a mad chase between the crocodile and Captain Hook, leaves children in stitches. A new ending unnecessarily reveals that Wendy has been dreaming about the adventures in Never Never Land. While a dramatic switch from the real world to a dream world

LEFT: Peter, Wendy, John and Michael fly by Big Ben on their way to Never Never Land. (Copyright © Walt Disney Productions); BELOW: Bobby Driscoll dressed as *Peter Pan*. (Copyright © Walt Disney Productions)

aided a live-action film like *The Wizard of Oz*, the animated *Pan* did not need to remind audiences that this was not the real world. The very nature of the genre succeeds in that area.

The original songs by Sammy Cahn and Sammy Fain are delightfully integrated into the dialogue. One of the most exciting numbers is "You Can Fly, You Can Fly, You Can Fly" which begins in the nursery, continues over London, and finishes as the children near Never Never Land.

"The Second Star to the Right" is beautifully sung over the opening credits by a heavenly chorus to an arrangement by Jud Conlon. Other Cahn-Fain songs include "The Elegant Captain Hook," "What Makes the Red Man Red?," and a sweet lullaby for Wendy, "Your Mother and Mine." Oliver Wallace and Erdmann Penner, two Disney staff composers, wrote "A Pirate's Life," and Wallace penned "Following the Leader" ("Tee-Dum Tee-Dee") with Ted Sears and Winston Hibler. Frank Churchill, who also wrote the *Snow White* songs with Larry Morey, contributed the humorous "Never Smile at a Crocodile" with Jack Lawrence, but the song was deleted from the release print.

Disney child star Bobby Driscoll's voice was perfectly matched to the artists' renderings of Peter, whose movements were copied from the studio-made live-action test film that featured dancer Roland Dupree as Peter. Driscoll also posed for the artists for the more impish qualities of the character. The lad made his first film

Peter and Wendy at
Mermaid's Lagoon.
(Copyright © Walt Disney
Productions)

appearance in *The Sullivans* in 1944. Two years and five films later
he was cast by Disney in *Song of the South*, then in *So Dear to My
Heart* and Disney's remake of *Treasure Island*, as well as a film noir
thriller, *The Window*. Like many child actors, as Driscoll matured,
his film offers grew fewer. Then tragedy—Bobby Driscoll became
addicted to drugs and died in obscurity from an overdose. It was
only through the Disney company that he did not remain a John Doe
in a pauper's grave.

The voice of Wendy was supplied by Kathryn Beaumont, who
three years earlier did the same for *Alice in Wonderland*. The
dialogue written for her in *Pan* is especially humorous as she never
seems to stop talking.

For Captain Hook, the studio decided to use Hans Conried as
a model in their live film and his voice in the animated film. In
Leonard Maltin's *The Disney Films*, Conried remembered his work
on the film:

Usually they had pantomimists and/or dancers, but they felt that I could
play the part. Now when I say I worked two and a half years, I don't say
that I worked constantly, but over that period they would say, "Have you
got two weeks?" "Have you got four days?" "Have you got a week?" I
was in costume, and they had an elemental set, and I would go through
the business making my physical action coincide with the soundtrack,

which was already finished. Usually, in dubbing, which I've done a lot of for foreign actors, you have to make your sound coincident with his latent action, but here you make your physical action coincident with the soundtrack. That was lots of fun; it was a very friendly, familiar surroundings at Disney, particularly in those days.

Another big change in this *Peter Pan* was the new look for Tinker Bell. The fairy was presented as a sexy little nymph hopelessly in love with Peter. The cartoon character had so much appeal that she became a sort of trademark for the popular Disney show on television.

The critics apprehensively approached this new version of the stage play. The *New York Times*'s Bosley Crowther suggested that the characters were not too original, with Wendy being a close cousin to Snow White, Smee a kin to the dwarf Happy, and Michael derived from Dopey. Crowther wrote in his review:

Mr. Disney's picture…has the story but not the spirit of *Peter Pan* as it was plainly conceived by its author and is usually played on the stage.

However, that's not to say it isn't a wholly amusing and engaging piece of work within the defined limitations of the aforementioned "Disney style." The Disney inventions are as skillful and clever as they have ever been—perhaps even more so, in some cases, as in the encounter of Captain Hook with the Crocodile. This episode in the

Tinker Bell, jealous of Peter's affection for Wendy, listens to a scheme proposed by Captain Hook. (Copyright © Walt Disney Productions)

story has been worked out in a burst of violent farce, with Hook struggling frantically to stay out of the ferocious old Crocodile's pink maw. The colors, too, are more exciting and the technical features of the job, such as the synchronization of lips, are very good.

Barrie biographer Roger Lancelyn Green observed:

There is, of necessity, no place in this kind of film for the delicacy of the play and the story. The magic must be purely visual and rather heavily underlined—just as the sentiment tends to be, and the excitement also.

The film has been reissued several times, most recently in 1989. An interesting review appeared in *USA Today*:

Peter Pan wasn't regarded as "A" Disney even in 1953; despite this, it has transcendent value for boomers eventually rewarded with Peter's face on a tie-in brand of peanut butter.
    Sometimes timing is all. Only the most precocious immediate-postwar tykes saw *Cinderella* in 1950; only for the movie-deprived was *Lady and the Tramp* ('55) an intro to full-length animation. Thus, a

Scenes like this provided plenty of laughs. (Copyright © Walt Disney Productions)

'53-vintage cartoon hits a sentimental bull's-eye—even given NBC's recent revival of Mary Martin's perennial.

The critic, who saw the film eleven hours after experiencing a reunion by the rock group, The Who, went on to explain the durability of its appeal.

One is that the talents of Captain Hook (and to some extent, the crocodile) hold up almost as well as Pete Townshend's and Roger Daltrey's. Another is that Tinker Bell shakes her booty with all the pizza-joint vigor of a notorious high school tart. Another is that, by contrast, Wendy is ooooh so straight. Is it possible that Uncle Walt's universe too conveniently divided girls into "fast" and insipid?...Besides, this Hook is super, and the songs aren't bad—even if "Never Smile at a Crocodile," a mild-or-more hit in '53, is inexplicably used only as background music....Yet how many tunes—now or then—offer advice upon which to construct a life?

On September 9, 1990, the film became available on home video and did phenomenally well in retail as well as rental. Kids still love Disney's film and they still want to play at being Peter, with the smallest child reluctantly assigned to be Captain Hook.

Mary Martin

A Musical Peter Pan

My honest desire is to have something that will stand up so it can be put on year after year, all over the country with lots of people playing Peter Pan, like the English pantomimes, because generation after generation have never seen Peter Pan.
—Mary Martin, 1954

*E*ven if Mary Martin never appeared in the musical *Peter Pan*, she would still be regarded as the consummate musical star, one of the best ever to grace the Broadway stage. Her portrayals of Nellie Forbush, Maria Von Trapp, Venus (as in *One Touch of...*), and even Dolly Levi placed her in the "legend in her own time" status. Most of the Martin roles were real, likable women. The characters in *Annie Get Your Gun* and *The Sound of Music* actually existed, while the heroines of *South Pacific* and *I Do! I Do!* are very much like women we might encounter. Yet the one character totally outside the realistic realm is the one that audiences found most believable. It is still incomprehensible not to believe that Mary Martin was Peter Pan.

The native Texan's first Broadway appearance was little more than a featured solo in the 1938 Cole Porter musical, *Leave It to Me*. By introducing "My Heart Belongs to Daddy" while warming up some native Eskimos (including an unknown Gene Kelly) with a mock striptease, Mary Martin became a sensation. Her picture was put on the cover of *Life* Magazine and before long, Paramount Pictures took notice of this saucy new Broadway star and offered her a contract. Never mind that just a few years earlier she had tried to break into pictures. Before she left for Hollywood, Mary did one more show, probably her least known, *Nice Goin'*, with a score by Ralph Rainger and Leo Robin. It closed out of town, but what did that matter? Mary Martin was about to become a movie star.

Ironically, the lackluster film roles offered reflected none of the qualities that first brought the actress to Paramount's attention. Although she was teamed with some of the studio's top stars, from Bing Crosby on down, it was clear that as with Ethel Merman earlier, Paramount was not quite sure what to do with the Texas bombshell. Each picture had her being groomed in the image of someone else. In her autobiography, *My Heart Belongs*,

PAGE 172: "I Gotta Crow." Publicity shot taken in California and eventually used on cover of the original cast album. (Courtesy of Robert Gable); ABOVE: On tour in *Annie Get Your Gun*, 1948. (Courtesy of Robert Gable)

Martin remembers that "...for months the makeup men had a field day. Using my same face they made me up to look exactly like Jean Parker...and Jean Arthur...Claudette Colbert...and Rosalind Russell...kinda. They even tried to make me look sexy. But most of the time, I just looked sick."

Despite Mary Martin's lack of screen identity and the so-so parts in *Rhythm on the Range, The Great Victor Herbert*, and *Star-Spangled Rhythm*, a story editor for Paramount named Richard Halliday recognized great talent in the musical star.

When Mary Martin was first introduced to him, she had no idea of the impact that he would have on her career. Their relationship transformed into one of those rare show-business phenomena—a marriage of mutual love and respect. Soon, Halliday gave up editing to manage his young wife's career. Under his nurturing and guidance, a new Mary Martin emerged. Confident, beautifully coiffured, handsomely dressed, and of course, still brimming with talent, the actress was treated like a queen by her new husband. He chose her wardrobe, her hairstyles, and roles in plays that suggested star quality. Her arrivals and departures from the theatre were always to be in grand fashion with a limousine. As dresser, hairstylist, confidant, and husband, Halliday was the perfect manager because his wife was his only client. With her new partner she accepted a role in a Broadway show that she never before would have considered—Venus!

Martin thought that audiences would never buy her as the beautiful goddess of love, a role originally intended for Marlene Dietrich! Little did she realize that her ability to handle this exciting role was actually helped by Hollywood's indecisiveness. There was no problem with typecasting as Mary Martin was not identified as any type. With a score by Kurt Weill, and libretto by Ogden Nash and S. J. Perelman, *One Touch of Venus* was directed by Elia Kazan and choreographed by Agnes de Mille, became a hit of the 1943 season, and put Mary Martin on her second *Life* cover.

After her next show, the lovely *Lute Song*, Mary had clearly established herself as a notable Broadway musical-comedy actress. Unfortunately, the following year marked a personal disappointment when she appeared in the eagerly anticipated London production of Noël Coward's *Pacific 1860*. Its failure created a rift between the star and writer that would take years to mend. Mary, though, still had to prove to producers Rodgers and Hammerstein that she could play the lead in *Annie Get Your Gun*. She desperately wanted the part on the road after seeing Ethel Merman on Broadway. It is interesting that she would take a chance on a part so closely associated with the great Merman, but Mary was not intimidated. An impromptu audition at Richard Rodgers's home proved that she

could belt a song when needed and she was given the role in the national touring company. This eventually led to his and Hammerstein's casting her as Nellie Forbush in *South Pacific*.

    Mary charmed audiences and critics with her lovely voice and down-to-earth characterization of a small-town Arkansas nurse in love with a worldly older man in the South Pacific during World War II. Her hair was permed so that it could withstand the nightly onstage shampooing in the thoroughly delightful "I'm Gonna Wash That Man Right Out of My Hair." With her picture on yet another *Life* cover, she was now clearly established as the toast of Broadway. Yet she was soon to attain a celestial level in the theatre seldom reached by actors. Playing the boy who never wanted to grow old placed Mary Martin in a realm that many envy but few can match. She never grew old in the hearts of her audience. She will always be Peter Pan.

    In her book, *My Heart Belongs*, Mary Martin wrote that "Peter Pan is perhaps the most important thing to me that I have ever done in the theatre." She often discussed her desire to play the part with her good friend, Jean Arthur. In fact the two had to keep track of whose turn it was to wear Peter Pan costumes to masquerade parties. After Arthur played the part in 1950, Martin assumed that she would never get a crack at it. She had coveted the role for several years when Edwin Lester, director of the San Francisco and Los Angeles Light Opera Company, approached her with this prize.

    Lester wrote in the program for the show:

My first invitation was extended in 1951 in the hope that she would do *Peter Pan* for us between the close of her *South Pacific* engagement in

LEFT: Mary with her husband, Richard Halliday, in 1942. Photo: Bob Beerman. (Courtesy of Robert Gable); RIGHT: At a Hollywood costume party with her good friend Jean Arthur who is dressed as Peter Pan, long before they ever thought that they would play the part. (Courtesy of Robert Gable)

Rehearsing with director
Jerome Robbins. (Courtesy
of Robert Gable)

New York and her London opening of the same play. It could not be arranged at that time. But neither of us forgot. And in the fall of 1953, knowing that her commitment to *Kind Sir* was limited to that season only, I proposed again that she come to California and that we make *Peter Pan* a festive event of our 1954 Civic Light Opera season.

When he assured Mary that this could be a wonderful musical version of the play with her choice of director and composer, she immediately accepted, telling Lester that she wanted Peter to fly further than he had ever flown before and that the children should share a flying song with him. Leland Hayward and Richard Halliday, who eventually replaced a convalescing Hayward as coproducer, carefully laid out their plans for the new musical. The idea was to take the beloved Barrie classic and create a whole new theatrical form for the play. The director-choreographer who had first been asked to direct *Peter Pan* with Jean Arthur was again beckoned to create a new version for Mary Martin.

"Jerome Robbins was our director," Martin wrote to this author. "And actually as far as I was concerned, he was another Peter Pan. Working with him was one of the most exciting experiences I have ever known in the theatre." Robbins first made a splash in the theatre world with his choreography of *On the Town* in 1944. Prior to this he had astounded the dance world with his ballet, "Fancy Free." He also was responsible for staging the memorable twelve-minute Mary Martin–Ethel Merman duet on the Ford 50th Anniversary television show in 1953, with the two stars merely sitting on a couple of chairs as they belted out one song after another. This convinced the Hallidays that Robbins should direct their play. The following decades would find him as one of the major creative forces in ballet and musical theatre, making dance an integral part of the story of several Broadway musicals. It is difficult to imagine *West Side Story* or *Fiddler on the Roof* without his touch. Musical theatre matured significantly under his direction. To that distinguished list we must add the musical adaptation of *Peter Pan*, which he created with the help of his associate director, Mary Hunter.

The flying sequences have always been the most memorable aspect of Barrie's play and there was a real challenge to bring a fresh approach to it. All of Robbins's shows are noted for the excitement ignited by the movement and dances that he devises. If anyone could choreograph the flying ballet it was Jerome Robbins. Just as necessary, however, was a specialist who could fly Peter farther than he'd ever flown. Even today, Peter Foy is the man you call when you need someone to fly in a play or television show. His patented method is responsible for scores of shows that include television's *The Flying Nun*, and productions of *Ice Follies*. He was trained by Joseph Kirby to supply the flying magic in *Peter Pan*.

The most important consideration and immediate concern was to commission a score that would serve the book in a memorable way. The text of *Peter Pan* had proven the test of time, but could a musical score live up to the expectations generated by such a venture? Martin recalled that "Richard and I discovered Carolyn Leigh one night while driving home and listening to the radio. We heard a beautiful song called 'Young At Heart' and I said, 'That's the person to be a part of *Peter Pan*'." Johnny Richards wrote the

Moose Charlap and Carolyn Leigh in Los Angeles while working on the score of *Peter Pan*. Photo: Bob Willoughby.

music but it was the optimistic Leigh lyrics that most interested the Hallidays. Through ASCAP, Halliday located Leigh, who was under contract to write lyrics for a music publisher. During the two decades following *Peter Pan*, she would become one of the busiest lyricists in the business, with many of her songs being recognized as standards. "Witchcraft," "Pass Me By," and "Hey, Look Me Over" were just a few of her hits, written with Cy Coleman. Not all of the shows were overwhelming successes, yet popular songs from the likes of *Wildcat* and *How Now Dow Jones* were able to live beyond the run of the plays due to the optimistic words of this young woman. Despite her untimely death in 1983, Carolyn Leigh remains one of the most talented lyric writers for the Broadway musical. "I never get tired of writing songs that make me want to jump out of bed in the mornings!" she said in a 1979 interview. Back in 1953, that same enthusiasm was displayed when Leigh signed to work on *Peter Pan*, her first Broadway musical.

A year before her death, Carolyn Leigh told an audience at the Society of Stage Directors and Choreographers symposium on *Peter Pan*:

"It might interest you to know that, very briefly, Leonard Bernstein was supposed to have done the music. Leonard at that time was busy with about five other things, and he and Mary didn't

"I'm Flying!"
(Courtesy of Robert Gable)

quite see eye to eye about which should take place first." Leigh continued, "Also, he wanted to incorporate a score he had done for *Peter Pan* a few years earlier, which had starred Jean Arthur, and Mary felt she couldn't sing that. So that all passed in a hurry."

By the time she signed with the Hallidays, Leigh was working with a young composer, Morris (aka Mark) Charlap, or, as he was affectionately called, "Moose." Moose was only five foot two, considerably shorter than the more statuesque Leigh. In fact, the nickname "Moose" was self-delegated during childhood to suggest an imposing figure. It worked! Overwhelming in his openness, Moose enjoyed meeting people and he would think nothing of walking up to strangers to initiate a conversation. Yet he was also troubled by diabetes and a weak heart. His widow, singer Sandy Stuart, summed up his presence. "Moose was like a low-yield atomic weapon, ready to go off. He was fresh, young, and new! He did not sleep much. He knew that he wouldn't live to be an old man."

Like Leigh, Moose was almost childlike in his optimistic approach to life, but more important, he was able to convey innocence in his music. While he was capable of composing sophisticated symphonies and jazz pieces, he loved writing material for children. Sadly, Moose Charlap did not attain the status in the music world that he so richly deserved. A later musical, *Whoop-Up*, closed after only fifty-six performances, while another musical, *Clown Around*, closed before reaching Broadway, despite the direction of Gene Kelly. It was during rehearsals for this production that Moose suffered three heart attacks. yet he continued to work on other projects. At his death at forty-five in 1974, he was working on a musical play based on the life of Paul Gauguin.

In 1953, when Mary Martin was first introduced to Moose Charlap, he was the youngest member of ASCAP. She immediately liked this brash young man and the feeling was mutual. Despite the fact that established teams such as Rodgers and Hammerstein were interested in writing the score to *Peter Pan*, Martin committed herself to her new discoveries. Later, during one of the *Pan* rehearsals, Richard Rodgers sat behind Moose and quipped, "My boy, you have not written a show, you've written an annuity!"

The team's first three songs, "I've Gotta Crow," "I'm Flying," and "I Won't Grow Up," were characteristic of the innocence and magic that Robbins wanted. "I remember playing some things in my stocking feet for Mr. Robbins," said Leigh. "It was my very, very first venture. I had only been to see a musical once in my life prior to that. I was frightened out of my wits. Moose had no idea of what was happening either, although I think that he was braver than I was." Leigh went on, "I remember singing a line to Jerry, 'If I can lead a life of crime, and still be home by dinnertime,' and we got a nod of approval from him.... We had no idea what we were doing; we were only praying to get through it alive, and I didn't quite know what my function was. I wrote lyrics quite blindly, quite desperately."

In the 1979 interview Leigh also admitted that in 1954 she had "too much awe" for Jerome Robbins, a director who could be quite intimidating. She recalled her difficulty in writing an Indian song for the show:

"Robbins explained that the song should show that while noisy Indians are usually at peace, when they turn quiet they go on the warpath. I couldn't make any sense of the idea as it related to the show, so I wrote a song that was simply pleasant nonsense. Later it finally occurred to me that Robbins was making a metaphor about children, that when children become quiet you have trouble. But our

Peter and Tiger Lily,
played by Sondra Lee.
(Courtesy of Robert Gable)

Mary rehearsing the "I Gotta Crow" reprise in New York City with her daughter, Heller Halliday, who played Liza. Photo: Bob Willoughby.

communication problem was so bad that I missed the point completely." This is clearly reflected in the lyrics to "Wild Indians," which was removed from the show.

> Wild Indians Home In Wigwam
> Heap Noisy, Beat On The Tom-Tom
> But When We're Out On The War-Path
> Wild Indians Make Big Hush-Hush
>
> When All Is Still In The Bushes
> When Come No Sound Of A Foot-Fall
> You'll Know, That's Us, Take Care
>
> When All Is Still In The Bushes
> When All Is Calm In The Forest
> We Come, Get You, Be-Ware.

During this creative process Robbins began to recruit actors for the play. Actually, besides Mary Martin, there was one other performer cast from the conception of the project. "Long before we went in rehearsal for the show here on the coast [L.A.] I was preparing for my part at home in Norwalk....I learned the part of Wendy because at that time I thought I was going to play Wendy. But we all decided it would be a big responsibility for me and I am very happy with my part of Liza. Some day I would like to play the part of Wendy." Heller Halliday, Martin's daughter, was twelve years old when she wrote this passage for a magazine article.

"My daughter Heller playing Wendy was something we always talked about," Martin told this author, "but she was only twelve or thirteen. She did play the part of the little maid and performed a toe dance in the second act. Later on, when I was doing *Peter Pan* for

---

"Wild Indians" by Moose Charlap and Carolyn Leigh. Copyright 1954, Lyrics Used by Permission of June Silver.

Mrs. Darling (Margalo
Gillmore) and Nana.
(Photofest)

the last time on television and Heller was away at college, we called
and asked if she'd like to come back and finally play Wendy. But she
thought it best that she stay in school."

The decision not to cast Heller as Wendy did not come easily.
Mary Martin was the star of the show and the star wanted her
daughter in the play! That was that. Robbins argued that the
audience did not need to be reminded that Mary was a mother. A
compromise to cast Heller as Liza didn't meet with Robbins's
approval either. This was the one time during this production that
his associate director disagreed with him. "We need to do this to
have a happy company," reasoned Mary Hunter. Robbins conceded
and Hunter was assigned to direct the scenes with Heller, which
would be written to include a duet with her mother and a ballet.

Mrs. Darling was assigned to veteran Margalo Gillmore,
actress and author. Gillmore's prestigious appearance with Kath-
arine Cornell's *No Time for Comedy* and a series of grande dame
roles in films would bring a certain legitimacy to a musical of *Peter
Pan*. "For the villainous Captain Hook, Peter's sworn enemy, we
had only one choice—the great Australian actor, Cyril Ritchard." In
her autobiography, Mary Martin recalled, "I had seen him perform
only once, in a Restoration comedy with his wife, Madge Elliot, and
with John Gielgud, who also directed, but I had never forgotten his
perfect timing, his presence, He would be the ultimate Hook, and he
was."

Ritchard's career was quite diversified. He began as a chorus
boy in Australia, coming to the United States to appear in a musical
revue, *Puzzles of 1925*, as a song-and-dance juvenile. While usually
thought to be associated with Restoration classics, he had appeared

in many contemporary musicals and comedies, including *Daddy Long Legs* and later *Visit to a Small Planet*. Ironically, the San Francisco program on *Peter Pan*'s 1954 premiere treated the actor as a newcomer with the billing, "introducing Cyril Ritchard."

Cyril Ritchard off stage was nothing like Captain Hook. He was a loving father whose infant son's death made him sensitive to the needs of other children. Three years after *Peter Pan*, David Bean, the boy who portrayed Slightly, would become his protégé. The youngster's father was a dresser for Ritchard.

The casting of *Peter Pan* could now be officially announced...almost.

May 15, 1954

To New York Times
Sam Zolotow

Dear Sam:

You can now make official the announcement that Cyril Ritchard will play the roles of Captain Hook and Mr. Darling with Mary Martin in my production of Peter Pan. Please include in the announcement that Jerome Robbins is staging, also Margalo Gillmore as Mrs. Darling. No final decision yet on Heller's role so would prefer that you do not mention her in this story. Will give you that within a few days.

Best Regards,
Edwin Lester

On June 21, the actress who was to play Wendy entered her first rehearsal. The important role was awarded to a young woman whose life would make an interesting book. Starting her acting career at only thirteen months old, Kathleen Nolan spent most of her early childhood on the stage with her family, including a stint on a Mississippi riverboat. After graduating high school in 1951, she came to New York to attend the Neighborhood Playhouse School of the Drama. She paid for her classes by working as an usherette at the Palace Theatre, where Judy Garland was making her first comeback. What happened next is the stuff of show-business legend.

Nolan, who has a beautiful singing voice, learned all of Garland's act and would perform it to the amazement of the other usherettes. It was only a matter of time before word reached the headliner about this talented young lady. One evening after the show, Garland asked Nolan if she could remain at the theatre for a while and perform her (Garland's) entire act. As Nolan performed the "Palace Medley" and other songs, the star situated herself in different locations of the theatre so she could see how effective the staging was to all parts of the audience. "You can imagine how I felt," mused Nolan, "singing 'Over The Rainbow' to Judy Garland." Apparently, Garland was impressed enough to arrange an introduction to Richard Rodgers, who a few years later was instrumental in arranging Nolan's audition for Wendy at the old Theatre Guild. Meanwhile, Nolan was busy in "live" television dramas and a series entitled *Jamie*.

Ironically, Nolan was the first actress to try out for the part of Wendy and impressed the producers so that they could not believe their luck. In fact, they brought in other actresses for the part with the belief that if they were this fortunate on the first audition there must be other prospects. "They kept bringing me back," remembered Nolan. "They would audition somebody else and then they would bring me back.

"On one occasion Barbara Cook auditioned before I did. I heard Barbara sing and I left. I never heard a beautiful sound like that. How could I possibly compete? And the stage manager...Bob Linden, came running after me. And I said, 'I'm not going to follow her!' And he said 'It's not about just what your voice is. You don't have to hit that high C.' So I went in and I auditioned again."

Nolan continued, "There were some of us that were hired in New York...Billy Sumner and Sondra Lee, I think that there were about five dancers...Bobby Tucker, Jerome Robbins's assistant, auditioned the rest of the dancers in Los Angeles. We started rehearsing at the Union Hall on Vine Street. So being the energetic young lady that I was I wanted to do the bar with the dancers. I

Peter and Wendy, played by Kathleen Nolan. (Courtesy of Robert Gable)

Peter and Wendy in the
Darling nursery with
sleeping John (Joseph
Stafford). (Courtesy of
Robert Gable)

wanted to get right in there. So Jerry came in and Bobby Tucker was sitting next to him. The dancers were doing their morning bar and I was at the bar. Obviously I wasn't hired as a dancer although I could dance, but not very well. Jerry was always trying to get me to point my toes in the flying. So Bobby was sitting on a chair and finally he fell off the chair laughing. We found out later that Jerry said, 'Did you hire her? Did I hire her?' I had my hair pulled back and he didn't recognize me as the girl he hired for Wendy even though he had seen me fifteen times."

Playing Wendy is one of Nolan's most cherished experiences. A few years later she became Kate on the long-running television series, *The Real McCoys*. Ironically, the success of that program cost her the opportunity to reprise the role of Wendy in the 1960 videotape of *Peter Pan*. Nolan has continued to act on many television shows, including her own series, *Broadside*, as well as on the stage, and has had the distinction of being the first woman to become national president of the Screen Actors Guild.

Some of the casting required no search at all. From the Jean Arthur revival, Joe E. Marks was to repeat his role of the lovable Smee, while Norman Shelly would be on all fours again as Nana and the crocodile. "There was nothing deep here," Shelly has pointed out. "I needed the job." Tiger Lily was not immediately cast, as there was no conception of her character, but as time went on one of the Lost Boys took the part. This boy was played by the only female of the group, dancer Sondra Lee. Jerome Robbins had directed her in *High Button Shoes* and brought her along for *Peter Pan* even though he was not sure at the time how he was going to use her. The small pert blonde has since graced other Broadway musicals such as *Hello, Dolly!* while she also danced with Les Ballets de Paris and Robbins's

Ballets U.S.A. Years later, Sondra Lee is still best remembered for her captivating performance as Tiger Lily.

Robbins was trying to convey the innocence of childhood by directing the actors to portray children, who in turn, pretend to be Indians, pirates, and, of course, Peter Pan. Like real children, Sondra Lee recalls that their games were quite serious. "When you're playing fantasy you have to believe it every second. Children play to win. They play it total. When they are a cowboy, they are a cowboy. And the bad guys *are* bad guys! You have to play with that kind of conviction. When Tiger Lily says that Peter Pan is the sun, the moon, and the stars, she means it!" Lee's philosophy about acting in a fantasy play is very close to Barrie's own thoughts on how to produce a Fairy Play.

Barrie wrote:

The difference between a Fairy Play and a realistic one is that in the former all the characters are really children with a child's outlook on life. This applies to the so-called adults of the story as well as to the young people. Pull the beard off the fairy king, and you would find the face of a child.

The actors in a fairy play should feel that it is written by a child in deadly earnestness and that they are children playing it in the same spirit. The scenic artist is another child in league with them.

Robbins had the difficult task of maintaining the innocence of the source while also creating a production that was a proper vehicle for his star. Audiences would not buy just another Peter Pan so soon after the Jean Arthur success. Rather, they would be paying to see Mary Martin as a singing Peter Pan. Contrary to popular belief, the vehicle was always to be a full-scale musical. Below is an outline of the musical sequences of *Peter Pan* before it opened in San Francisco.

ACT ONE

Scene One

Dressing Up—Wendy and John (Introduction and Pantomime)
Lazy Shepherd [sic]—Mrs. Darling, Wendy, John, and Michael
I've Got to Crow [sic]—Peter (Shadow Dance)
I'm Flying—Peter, Wendy, John, and Michael

Scene Two

I'm Flying (Development)—Peter, Wendy, John, and Michael

Scene Three

Introduction to Never Land—Animals and Lost Boys
Indians Are About—Tiger Lily and Indians
Pirate Song—Hook and Pirates
Princely Scheme #1—Hook and Musicians

Be Our Parents—The Lost Boys to Wendy and Peter
Princely Scheme #2—Hook and Musicians

Scene Four

The Parade (Pantomime)—Animals, Indians, and Pirates
I Won't Grow Up—Peter and Lost Boys
Who Are You?—Peter and Hook
The Storm—Indians and Peter

ACT TWO

Scene One

Adventuring—Peter and Children
When I Went Home—Peter
The Battle (Pantomime)—Indians and Pirates
Capturing the Boys and Wendy—Pirates and Children
Poisoning Peter's Medicine—Hook and Peter
Death of Tinker Bell—Peter

Scene Two

Now It's Hook or Me—Peter, Animals, and Indians

Scene Three

Soliloquy and Song—Hook and Musicians
The Big Battle—Company

Scene Four

Reprise: I've Got to Crow—Peter and Liza

Scene Five

Reprise: Lazy Shepherd—Wendy, John, and Michael

Scene Six

Remember Me—Peter

Program for *Peter Pan* in San Francisco at the Curran Theatre.

During the rehearsals it was decided that the production would be featured on NBC's *Producers' Showcase*. However, Martin reserved the right to cancel this, as well as any plans for a Broadway run if she felt the musical was not up to her level of expectation.

By the time the new musical of *Peter Pan* opened at the Curran Theatre in San Francisco on July 19, 1954, scenes were cut and reshuffled and new songs were added. The program illustrates the changes that occurred in order to make a musical of the play. The five acts were condensed to two acts with eight scene changes—five in the first and three in the second. Essentially the original play was abridged to allow time for the musical numbers. One of Robbins's regrets was the loss of Peter's "To die would be an awfully big adventure" scene, but material had to be deleted to make room for the songs.

The basic text of the play remains in the first act with but a few alterations. This time, Michael walks into the nursery rather than

Peter and Nana, played by
Norman Shelley. Photo:
John Engstead.

riding on Nana, which saved some wear and tear on Norman Shelly. There was also some extended dialogue for Liza, who can not be much older than the Darling children. They bid her to take part in their playacting of being Mother and Father, but Liza remains adamant that she has more important housekeeping duties to keep her busy. While Mrs. Darling tucks the children into their beds, they sing "Lazy Shepherd," a rather insecure lullaby about a shepherd who loses his sheep. By the time the show was moved to New York, the title was changed to "Tender Shepherd."

Later, after Wendy has successfully attached Peter's shadow to him, he sings, "I've Got to Crow." Here is a fine example of the songwriters' ability to write a song that is an extension of the dialogue. In the original book, Peter announces his cleverness after Wendy accomplished the task of attaching his shadow. It should be noted here that the title and lyrics of this song eventually were altered to "I've Gotta Crow," which is used in this passage.

PETER

Wendy, look, look; oh the cleverness of me!

WENDY

You conceit, of course I did nothing!

PETER

You did a little.

WENDY

A little! If I am no use I can at least withdraw.

PETER

Wendy, don't withdraw. I can't help crowing, Wendy, when I'm pleased with myself. Wendy, one girl is worth more than twenty boys.

The dialogue has been revised a bit so that it reads as follows:

PETER

Look, Wendy, look! My very own shadow. Oh, I'm clever. Oh, the cleverness of me.

WENDY

Of course I did nothing. You're conceited.

PETER

Conceited? Not me.

> It's just that I am what I am and I'm me.
> When I look at myself and I see in myself
> All the wonderful things that I see
> If I'm pleased with myself
> I have every good reason to be...
> I've gotta crow
> I'm just the cleverest fellow
> Twas ever my fortune to know.
> I taught a trick
> To my shadow to stick
> To the tip of my toe
> I've gotta crow.

Charlap and Leigh wrote a buoyant number that not only served to show Peter's conceit but also gave the audience a taste of Mary Martin's total abandonment. The performance of this song had to be a key moment as Peter must convince Wendy and the audience of what a wonderful time he has in store for them.

The biggest change in scene one and certainly the most exciting is the flying ballet, whose clever lyrics and joyful sequence of ascending notes was beautifully wed to Robbins's memorable and at times humorous choreography. Peter rapturously soars and sings "I'm Flying" as the children are entranced to a near frenzy. Soon, they join Peter in flight all about the nursery, and the excitement is expanded with a new scene, En route to the Never Land. Liza is sprinkled with some fairy dust by a departing Michael and as she spins about the nursery, suggesting her eventual flight, the set moves apart, displaying a starlit sky for Peter and the Darling children to frolic through. Even John Crook's excellent flying music paled by comparison to this exhilarating experience. For the first time, the sheer joy of watching the flying performers was enhanced by Peter's song. An unforgettable piece of musical theatre, it is a small wonder

---

that Jerome Robbins included it as a part of an ensemble of key musical moments that he choreographed in *Jerome Robbins's Broadway* in 1989. After thirty-five years this number lost none of its magic.

Scene three took us to Never Land and included the soon-to-be- aborted "Wild Indians." (This song was also called "Indians Are About" and "Beware.") Then Captain Hook and the pirates planned a "Princely Scheme" for the death of Peter Pan and all of the Lost Boys. Captain Hook was also to sing a song entitled, "The Croc."

> And then to my horror and wild alarm,
> It swallowed my hand and my strong right arm
> And it liked the taste; so it started to look
> To find the remainder of Captain Hook!

Wendy is shot down by the Lost Boys and remains semi-conscious until Peter pulls the arrow from her "kiss," the acorn he gave her earlier in the nursery scene. When it is announced that she will be staying with the Lost Boys to tell them stories and act as their mother to Peter's pretense of being their father, they all perform "Be Our Parents." This song also went through several title changes ("Be Our Mother" and "Happy Is the Boy").

Boys: Happy is the boy who has a mother
All: Happy we would be with one like you
       Wendy Lady, say you'll be our mother
       Do, please do

Boys: But Don't be one who dear-oh-dears
(Big Boys): Dreadful manners, dirty ears
       Don't be one who interferes, but be our mother
       Do, Please Do

WENDY
(Spoken) All right! (Boys cheer) Provided Peter will be father.

BOYS
(Spoken) Peter, please be our father, please.

PETER
(Spoken) Alright.

Boys: Happy is the boy who has a father
        Happy we would be with one like you
        Peter, say that you will be our father
        Do, please do
        But don't be one who'll make us each
        Practice all the things you preach

"The Croc" by Moose Charlap and Carolyn Leigh. Lyrics Used by Permission of June Silver.

> Never make an angry speech, but be our father
> Do, please do

Peter: Happy I would be to be your father
> Even though I'm just pretending to

Wendy: Now do I agree to be your mother
> Yes I do

Boys: Be our parents
> Loving parents
> What a happy family
> We'd be
> And once we are a family
> Perfect children we will be
> Peter, Wendy Please agree to
> Be our parents (P & W: Be your parents)
> Say you love us (P & W: Yes we love you)
> Do, please do.

Scene three ends with another "Princely Scheme." "I Won't Grow Up" is featured in scene four as Peter's lesson for the children. This is a particularly effective song, one that most children remember and enjoy. It has the same nursery-rhyme quality as "Following the Leader" from the Disney film, but it is infinitely more interesting and memorable.

Scene four contains the essence of Act Three in the original play when Peter rescues Tiger Lily, although it takes place in the woods rather than Mermaids Lagoon, which does not appear in the musical. Upon his return to his crew, Hook realizes that someone has been impersonating his voice in order to save the Indian princess. This leads to "Spirited Conversation" or "Who Are You?" as Hook asks and finally emerges with the title, "I'm Hook." The

Program from Los Angeles
Civic Light Opera.

"Happy Is the Boy" by Moose Charlap and Carolyn Leigh. Lyrics Used by Permission of June Silver.

music for Carolyn Leigh's short duet between Peter and Captain Hook was written by another composer, Roger Adams.

Later, when the boys and Indians are safely home in the underground hideout, they share a peace pipe and perform "The Pow Wow." After this large production number, Wendy, pretending to be the Lost Boys' mother, asks their father if he knows a lullaby. In a most pensive moment Peter sings:

When I went home I thought that certainly
Someone would leave the door or window open wide for me
And surely there would be a welcome light.

When I went home I counted so upon
Somebody waiting up to ask me questions on and on
To ask me where I'd gone
Was I alright.

But the door was barred
And the window barred
And I knew with an awful dread
That somebody else
Was sleeping in my bed.

When I went home I found that sad to say,
You must expect to be forgotten
Once you've gone away.

And so I couldn't stay that lonely night
When I went home.

Mary and Shadow.
(Courtesy of Robert Gable)

Act Two opens on the pirate ship with "The Old Gavotte," a grotesque soliloquy by Captain Hook. Written by Nancy Hamilton to the music of William Morgan Lewis, Jr., it explains the origin of the pirate captain with lyrics full of gore.

Hook—A gently born mother, she could have been mine
Pirates—Or mine or mine...
Hook—Not quite. Was sitting at dinner, the flowers, the wine, the
      children, the cloth all white.
She glanced at her first born, It could have been me....
Pirates—Or me or me...
Hook—You think. His jacket was velvet, her lace filligree
      His collar and cuffs were mink.
      Her thoughts were most sad for this delicate lad
      The world would distress him no doubt
      When in came a footman with duck on a tree
      And the lad began to shout:
      Rip up his anchor and down his hatch
      And nip his nibs in the bud
      Then pass the fingerbowl Charlie
      We'll all dip our hands in the blood.

Interestingly, Jerome Robbins does not remember Hamilton or Lewis working on the show and Mary Hunter does not even recall the song. Hamilton was a good friend of Mary Martin's, so it's possible that she or her husband asked her to write the song as a favor. Hamilton and Lewis had been working in the business for many years. One of the many songs that they cowrote was "How High the Moon."

The scene ends with the reprise of "I've Got to Crow" sung by Peter and Liza.

"Lazy Shepherd" is reprised in scene two, The Nursery, by the Darling Children when they are greeting their mourning mother. Once Mr. Darling has agreed to adopt all the Lost Boys, the family sings "Happy Is the Boy." Here begins the major departure from Barrie's play, and as Mary Martin has told this writer, one of her favorite moments. "It's when Peter returns from Never Land to fetch Wendy. Peter discovers that Wendy now has a daughter named Jane who has been waiting for Peter to teach her 'how to fly' and take her with him to Never Land. Wendy asks if she can come too and Peter answers, 'No, you see, Wendy, you're too grown up.' I think, for me, that's the most touching dialogue in the show." When interviewed in 1989, Mary Martin was asked if Peter was being a little cruel in his statement to the now grown-up Wendy. She pointed out that Peter can be cruel, but this is part of his character as well as that of any child. Children can be brutally honest, not necessarily to hurt anyone but just because they say things as they see them.

A prerequisite for a conventional musical comedy is a happy ending, which could have been problematic as there are so many tragic overtones in *Peter Pan*. Furthermore, Peter's adventures with Wendy has a decidedly unhappy ending when the audience realizes that there will be tragic encounters in the future as Peter comes to bring Wendy back to the Never Land for spring cleaning. The girl must age!

Fortunately, Barrie himself supplied the alternate ending in *An Afterthought* which was also incorporated into *Peter and Wendy*, the novelization of the play. In the last scene Peter flies into the Darling nursery many years later only to discover that Wendy (without an aged Nana) has grown up. She is now too old to fly. But, she has a daughter, Jane, who begs her mother to let her do his spring cleaning. The text of the novel states:

Of course in the end Wendy lets them fly away together. Our last glimpse of her shows her at the window, watching them receding into the sky until they were as small as stars.

The act ends here with a subtle understanding that this sort of thing will continue so that Peter will never be too lonely. The book is more blatant.

As you look at Wendy you may see her hair becoming white, and her figure little again, for all this happened long ago. Jane is now a common grown-up, with a daughter called Margaret; and every spring-cleaning time, except when he forgets, Peter comes for Margaret and takes her to the Neverland, where she tells him stories about himself, to which he listens eagerly. When Margaret grows up she will have a daughter, who is to be Peter's mother in turn; and thus it will go on, so long as children are gay and innocent and heartless.

The tragedy of Peter's future is just as powerful as in the original. In fact, it seems almost more tragic than Peter's first meeting with Wendy as the grown-up version of the character reminds the boy of what he is missing. Jane does not realize the tragedy and irony in her line to her mother, "...he wants me always to do his spring cleaning." The innocence of childhood blinds her to the fact that she, like all children, will grow older.

The show was to end with another song for Peter, "Remember Me." Early rehearsals found Kathleen Nolan playing the grown-up Wendy. She was very excited over the prospect of aging in a play. Unfortunately, it soon became apparent that there was not enough time for a costume change, so the part was temporarily given to Sally Brophie.

While the initial prospects for the show seemed to be promising, the critics were polite at best and the general consensus was that

Publicity shot. Clockwise from top left: Cyril Ritchard (Captain Hook), Mary Martin, Sondra Lee, Kathleen Nolan, and Ian "Inky" Tucker (Tootles). Photo: Bob Willoughby

the show was in trouble. In its review of August 25, 1954, *Variety* said:

Peter Pan, in a musical version, got away to a flying social start tonight at the Curran Theatre, San Francisco, thanks to the presence of Mary Martin in the title role and the enthusiasm of the Civic Light Opera subscribers. But whether it will be material for New York is debatable.

Miss Martin, as Peter, is in one of her best moods, charming, lively, lithe and understanding. Cyril Ritchard is excellent as the troubled father and ominous Captain Hook. Sondra Lee is delightful as the whimsical Tiger Lily and Joe E. Marks is very amusing as the pirate Smee.

Variety's critic went on to criticize Jerome Robbins's direction, citing that he spent more time in the staging of musical numbers at the expense of the story. "In its present form it would be a little difficult for anyone unfamiliar with the Barrie story to understand just what it is all about." The reviewer labeled the music simply "indifferent," although "When I Went Home" was recognized as "the second act socko number...a plaintive refrain." Ritchard's rendition of "The Old Gavotte" was applauded.

Perhaps the most important *Variety* comments were the two on Sondra Lee and Cyril Ritchard.

The entertainment lies chiefly in the handling of the ensembles and choruses and the occasional ballets. As a consequence, the point of interest is Captain Hook, rather than Peter Pan, and Miss Martin is in

Kathleen Nolan as Wendy
singing "Distant Melody"
to Peter. Photo: Bob
Willoughby. (Courtesy of
Kathleen Nolan)

the rather curious position of functioning as a subordinate player, while
Ritchard emerges as the star of the performance....In the dance
department, Miss Lee has no difficulty establishing herself as an
important factor. She has a keen sense of timing and a shrewd method
of establishing audience relationships.

According to Kathleen Nolan, the problem was easy to identify. The show was in trouble "because the role of Peter Pan was not
as clearly defined or wasn't working. If you have a vehicle for Mary
Martin and Mary Martin is not getting all the reviews, then
something is wrong and it has to be fixed."

Each day a song was substituted and restaged. Among the
several numbers dropped were "Happy Is the Boy," "I'm Hook,"
"When I Went Home," Sondra Lee's "Wild Indians," and
Ritchard's "Gavotte." Lee was devastated when she arrived at the
theatre after an opening night of glowing personal reviews only to
be informed by Robbins that her number was cut. "The number was
struck because it stopped the show. I thought that you were
rewarded for that." Yet Miss Lee wisely reflected: "The show
revolves around a star. You have to face the nitty gritty. And the
nitty gritty has to do with reality. It may be tipping the show.
Unfortunately for me, the show is about Peter Pan. On the other
hand, fortunately for me, a wonderful character emerged unscathed,

finally, in the end. Is it a matter of creating a character that is memorable or getting another number?"

Often it was Richard Halliday who would inform members of the cast that a piece of their material or stage business was being cut. The tension was further heightened when the next rehearsal required the star to perform the song that had just been taken from another. Yet how could they be angry with Mary, who was so sympathetic to their loss. The character of Wendy, in particular, lost important lines and songs. "It was very painful at the time," remembers Kathleen Nolan. "I was very young and it was my first Broadway show....In retrospect now I can be a little bit more gracious about it, but I'm afraid I wasn't as gracious as I would have liked to have been at the time...but now having had the experience of carrying a show, I guess I have a little bit more understanding." In spite of her dwindling part, Nolan continued to be singled out by critics for her treatment of Wendy.

Only Cyril Ritchard seemed to be calm throughout all the deletions and additions. His contract specified that he was to sing a set amount of songs in the show. During all of these cuts the cast not only managed to continue performing, they were able to maintain a sense of humor as well. Nolan shares an amusing anecdote:

"It became so prevalent in San Francisco of things being taken from other people that the little boy (David Bean) who had the lines, 'Slightly Soiled, that's my name,' kept hearing all of the adults talking about what was being taken away and he was learning all of

At rehearsal when Mary Martin was given "Distant Melody." Photo: Bob Willoughby

Adolph Green and Betty Comden in Los Angeles in 1954, working on new songs for *Peter Pan*. Photo: Bob Willoughby.

this show-business jargon.... [At a rehearsal] I remember Jerry saying 'Aren't you going to say your line?' He said, 'I'm holding back 'til opening night!'"

Interestingly, one number that was cut was one of the few that the critics really liked. The beautiful yet simple lyrics of "When I Went Home" paired with a lovely melody produced a haunting effect on its listeners. When Mary Martin caressed the song she was greeted with a deafening silence. It was a tender, moving moment that caught the audience off guard. Sondra Lee remembered "When I Went Home" as "one of the most beautiful songs I have ever heard in my life. The reason that it was withdrawn was that they [the audience] didn't even applaud. They didn't applaud for the Gettysburg Address either. I believe that it was so deeply wounding that people would not want to applaud. It is the story of Peter Pan."

Norman Shelly echoed Lee's adulation for the song. Jerome Robbins remembered the song and liked it, but he did not recall why it was removed.

Kathleen Nolan stated: "It's a wonderful song. I remember hearing ["When I Went Home"] for the first time in the lobby of the Curran Theatre when Mary sang the song with Moose Charlap when they were down in the bowels of the theatre, mysteriously working away. And it was just incredible. It was so right for her voice.... I remember all of the words!"

Surprisingly, most of the performers interviewed not only remembered the words, but they sang them too. Mary Martin told Moose Charlap that the song was just too sad. It fits the story of *The*

Boy Who Wouldn't Grow Up so well that one would think that Barrie had written all of it, but Mary's point remains valid. For a musical of the 1950s that was being aimed specifically for children at an age when their chief anxiety is over separation from their parents, the song was not appropriate. It was removed before the play went to Los Angeles and, sadly, has remained in oblivion ever since. Perhaps someday all of the songs written for the play will be recorded and listeners will have a chance to hear what Sandy Stuart calls "a perfect marriage of music and lyrics. It is what *Peter Pan* is all about!"

Carolyn Leigh and Moose Charlap had attempted to create a score that was close to the heart of Barrie's Pan, but it was not working as a musical comedy. Furthermore, Mary Hunter remembered the great pressure placed on the inexperienced Leigh and Charlap. "It is very difficult to write and produce fast enough late at night in a hotel room with an arranger at your elbow and someone to write copy." As if things were not tense enough, Robbins had to leave for a few days when his mother died, and Mary Martin was under tremendous pressure from Rodgers and Hammerstein to abort the show to star in something that *they* were working on. This period was described by Mary Hunter as "very difficult and very painful." At the *Peter Pan* symposium, she related to the audience what followed:

"There was a change in the middle of the production in regard to the music and the kind of help needed for the design of the show. But what I remember so well is that at no point was there any question that there were great songs done by Mark Charlap and Carolyn Leigh that set in the public imagination the character for Mary as Peter, songs that were right for her voice, and also a springboard for the whole play. It's valuable to think about that because there was a consensus among all the people who worked on the play that that was the case."

What remained unknown to most of the creative staff, however, was that Halliday and Lester were toying with the possibility of having a completely new score written by a different team.

Recalled Betty Comden: "We were working in Hollywood on a movie, *It's Always Fair Weather,* when we got a call from San Francisco, from Jerry Robbins and Leland Hayward. The show was in trouble and they thought that they were going to close it. They asked if we would come up with Jule Styne and take a look at the show." The "we" that Miss Comden is referring to is, of course, her lifelong partner, Adolph Green.

Green remembered, "They wanted to see if we had any ideas and we all told Jerry afterward that the show could be saved. He got very excited and so did Mary Martin and we went to work on it."

"And actually at that point, we could have had the whole score," continued Comden. "I mean we would have said we will start from scratch with the whole score, but Carolyn Leigh and Moose Charlap had written some very nice things and they were young people with their first show. We certainly didn't want to come in and push them out. But what they had was the play with some songs, they didn't have a musical yet. I remember we talked to Jerry and he said we'll go back and tell Mary, and we told her that this could be the greatest role of your life. She got very excited."

"Before this she was desolate," said Green. "The show wasn't working...they were playing already, the show looked weak and they thought they would close it. That's why they called us."

Composer Jule Styne was also asked to look at the ailing musical. "I produced *Anything Goes* for Leland on television and he liked my kind of thinking and working so he came to me with Comden and Green." Styne is a producer's dream. If there is a song needed, he will have it the next day and if that song is no good, no problem; he will write another just as quickly. Yet speed is not at the expense of quality. Built with a strong, confident personality, the man has worked with the best to create the best.

Styne elaborated, "Mary Martin wanted to leave the show because she felt she needed more material and Cyril Ritchard the same. So we went up there and saw the show. We weren't going to do it because there was so much to do. We only had eight days to do it because she was going to L.A. from San Francisco."

"We had a free hand in whatever we felt should stay and what should go," remembered Green.

Styne recalled, "We were good friends with Carolyn Leigh and Moose Charlap. We didn't want to destroy everything. I told Mary that we can't improve on 'I'm Flying.' It's damn good....We didn't have the time to finish...we did eight songs in eight days. That's about as much as we could have done."

Theatre historian Stanley Green called Styne "one of the most successful musical comedy composers of all time." His music is known around the world. At eight Styne was playing with symphonies. Later, as a young man, he worked with a dance band, eventually drifting to Hollywood as a vocal coach and songwriter. And what songs! "Three Coins in the Fountain," "It's Magic," and "Let It Snow, Let It Snow, Let It Snow." As successful as he was in films, he was even better on Broadway, writing the music for the likes of *Gentlemen Prefer Blondes, Bells Are Ringing, Funny Girl,* and *Gypsy.*

Comden and Green met at New York University in the late thirties and soon began writing a series of skits for themselves. Then, with young Judy Holliday, Alvin Hammer, and John Frank, they

formed an act called the Revuers and performed material satirizing current events. Betty's piano talents were limited to a few notes yet those notes were incorporated into the songs they wrote. Their act caught on at the Village Vanguard and soon they became "the act" to see. The group moved uptown to the Rainbow Room, and even made a film where the Revuers appeared as themselves, but their footage ended up on the cutting-room floor, leaving Betty with one line and Adolph in the background reading a book.

Conferences: Adolph Green (left), Betty Comden, Jerome Robbins (center), Mary Martin, and Jule Styne. Photo: Bob Willoughby.

One of their friends was Leonard Bernstein, who enjoyed being a member of their audience and on occasion, part of the show. A bond developed among the three that professionally and personally spanned nearly five decades. When Bernstein was asked to derive a musical comedy after his success with his 1944 *Fancy Free* ballet score, he immediately suggested Comden and Green as the writers and lyricists. *On the Town,* the adventures of three sailors on a twenty-four-hour leave in New York, was packed with youthful freshness, fast dialogue and action, and a beautiful score. It was the perfect entertainment for 1944 wartime audiences. There were so many good songs—"A Lonely Town," "New York, New York," "I Can Cook Too," "I Get Carried Away," and "Some Other Time"— all from one show! Another show, *Billion Dollar Baby,* followed in 1945 (written with Morton Gould), and before long, Hollywood was calling.

Under the tutelage of producer Arthur Freed at Metro-Gold-wyn-Mayer, Comden and Green quickly became the screenwriters

Los Angeles rehearsal. Left: Sondra Lee listens to Jerome Robbins. Center: Jule Styne. Leaning against the stage is composer Elmer Bernstein (who provided incidental music) with Adolph Green sitting next to him. Photo: Bob Willoughby.

for some of his best musicals, musicals that always show up on someone's "ten best" list. Their screenplays include *Singin' in the Rain, On the Town,* and *The Band Wagon,* while their stage credits are just as impressive with *Wonderful Town, Bells Are Ringing, On the Twentieth Century,* and *The Will Rogers Follies.* Their satirical sharp wit and understanding of human nature, combined with their ability to reflect changing attitudes of the times, has kept them working into their sixth decade. In 1991, Comden and Green were among the recipients of the Kennedy Center Awards.

Speaking with the lyricists was truly memorable as they conversed "in harmony," interjecting and completing each other's thoughts throughout the interview.

Betty Comden explained how they began to "doctor" the play. "We approached this thing on an overall basis to try to make a musical out of it, and the first thing we said was it needs an overall theme, a big song that expresses Barrie and expresses the feeling of *Peter Pan....*

"And," added Green, "expresses Mary Martin, the star in *Peter Pan.*"

Comden continued, "So we wrote 'Never Never Land' and that was the kind of thing that pulled the whole thing together...."

"When she got 'Never, Never Land,' she decided that she was in good shape," stated Styne nonchalantly. "And then she gave the okay to do New York when she had the eight songs."

Comden said that "Cyril was a terrific musical performer and we wanted to combine those elements with his character of Captain Hook."

"So we wrote 'Captain Hook's Waltz,' a crazy musical comedy." Green continued, "The [songs] that we took out were all wrong. We had to write a whole new thought, a whole new character and a whole new theme."

"We had to go back to L.A. where we were working on the film," Comden continued, "so we spent some time there and we also went over the book with Jerry and we had some suggestions for condensing and putting it together and organizing it. Then they came to the play in L.A...."

"...and we got permission from the studio," interjected Green.

"Oh yes, we got permission to take some time and work on it."

"We were almost finished with the picture."

"Deadlines are wonderful," said Comden, who is used to writing under pressure. A few years later the team would come to the rescue of producer George Abbott when his songwriters backed out of the show *Wonderful Town.* The musical was to star Rosalind Russell, but her contract stipulated an opening that was now only six weeks away. In just four weeks an entirely new score was written by Bernstein, Comden, and Green!

"Yes, it moves along and it's either gonna happen or it isn't but there it is," Green concluded. "That's a good way to work!"

In addition to the lyrics, Comden and Green wrote additional dialogue to lighten up the play. "The book was there but Jerry was quite worried about the book being too long or too wordy. So we did some work with it, more or less cutting, trimming, or rearranging it.... There's a speech when Wendy is telling the story that Hamlet and everybody gets killed and we don't know if that's in the original play or if we made it up," mused Comden about their changes. The dialogue she referred to was indeed written by them and is typical of the two's delicious wit.

CURLY

Tell us the end of *Cinderella.*

WENDY

Well, the Prince found her, and...

BOYS

And?

WENDY

And they all lived happily ever after. (Boys cheer)

#2 TWIN

Tell us the end of *Sleeping Beauty.*

WENDY

Well, the Prince woke her up, and...

BOYS

And?

WENDY
And they all lived happily ever after! (Boys cheer)

TOOTLES
Tell us the end of *Hamlet!*

WENDY
Hamlet! Well the Prince Hamlet died, and the king died, and the Queen died, and Ophelia died, and Polonius died, and Laertes died, and…

BOYS
And?

WENDY
Well the rest of them lived happily ever after!

Barrie's text was perfect for the kind of humor that Comden and Green instilled in the musical.

Perhaps the most controversial change was the new song, "Oh My Mysterious Lady." Styne reflected, "They missed the boat you know. They didn't have a duet for the two stars or a number for 'Hook's Waltz.' We did our own thing." Early rehearsal scripts and programs indicate there was a song for Mary Martin to share with Cyril Ritchard, "I'm Hook," but it is probable that this song was deleted in San Francisco long before Styne ever had a chance to see it.

"Oh My Mysterious Lady" extends naturally from Barrie's dialogue. Disguising his voice as Hook's, Peter tricks the pirate crew into freeing the captured Tiger Lily. Hook arrives moments later only to be fooled by the boy as well. The forest appears to be bewitched with the unknown voice of Peter.

HOOK
Have you another name?

PETER
Ay, ay.

HOOK
Vegetable?

PETER
No.

HOOK
Mineral?

PETER
No.

HOOK
Animal?

PETER
Yes.

HOOK
Man?

PETER
No.

HOOK
Boy?

PETER
Yes.

HOOK
Ordinary Boy?

PETER
No.

HOOK
Wonderful boy?

PETER
Yes.

HOOK
Do you have another voice.

PETER
Yes. (Peter sings a few high notes.)

HOOK
A lady!

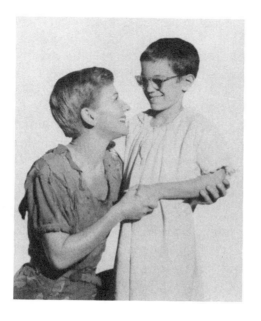

Mary Martin with Ian
Tucker (as Tootles).
(Courtesy Robert Gable)

"Oh, My Mysterious Lady" Cyril Ritchard and Mary Martin on opening night. Photo: Bob Willoughby

At this point, Peter sings in a beautiful voice as he tricks Hook into believing that he is a mysterious lady. The staging is every bit as clever as the lyrics, and children still roar with laughter during revivals of the play. Betty Comden remembers, "That was a risky thing. She plays a boy and we took a chance having her play this role, singing in her coloratura voice. It worked and it was very exciting."

"I liked the additional songs very much," said Carolyn Leigh many years later, "but I felt a little nervous around Betty and Adolph for some time. What finally set me at ease was a sight gag that Betty performed while Robbins was complaining about having one too many Indians on stage. Suddenly Betty pointed at one of the Indians and said, 'Bang.' That broke the ice."

While Comden, Green, and Styne were writing new material for the play, Charlap and Leigh continued with their own revisions as well. Added was their version of "Never Land" in Act One, a change in title from "Happy Is the Boy" to "Be Our Mother," and "Saturday Night Polka" in Act Two, which deleted "The Pow Wow." This last change reminds one of the scene in the Maude Adams production where Peter and the boys are curious about what their parents would be doing on a Saturday night. It could be possible that Charlap and Leigh made this change in an attempt to emulate "Sally in Our Alley." "Never Land" was also reprised at the end of the play, taking out the reprise of "I'm Flying." Another reprise, "Lazy Shepherd" replaced "When I Went Home." Charlap and Leigh's new material was included during the first few Los Angeles performances at the Philharmonic Auditorium.

"Moose Charlap was just such a wonderful human being," recalled Kathy Nolan. "And he had this incredible vitality, a little fireball. I suppose there was an initial resentment at the time…you are kind of on the road and you want to give them a chance. I'm not sure that Moose Charlap and Carolyn Leigh ever got the real credit that they deserved for *Peter Pan*."

Each night during the Los Angeles run the cast performed a variation of the show. With all the changes, it was sometimes quite hectic. Yet, Mary Martin said, "We just did it. Everyone helped each other. We were all having such a good time."

When the play opened in Los Angeles the new reviews were certainly better than those of San Francisco; the star was finally emerging as the focal point of the show. According to *Los Angeles Times* critic Milton Luban, the high points of the show were:

Mary rehearsing "Wendy."
Photo: Bob Willoughby.

...a direct tribute to the magic of Mary Martin, whose versatile and exuberant talents override a mediocre score by Carolyn Leigh and Mark Charlap and a second act that sags woefully, although it is soon forgotten through the spell of a moving and entrancing final act that holds one enthralled....Miss Martin's Peter Pan is one of the great events of theatredom and, as such, should be seen. She creates an elfin atmosphere of childlike gaiety that is contagious and is almost certain to make a box office hit of the show both here and in New York.

Kathleen Nolan, Sondra Lee, Cyril Ritchard, Norman Shelly, and Heller Halliday were also significantly praised for their support. With the score still in trouble, Comden, Green, and Styne exercised their right to remove material by eliminating all of Charlap and Leigh's new songs. Five of Moose and Carolyn's original songs were to remain. Their new "Never, Never Land" replaced "Never Land."

Comden and Green were not familiar with the original John Crook score, but they placed several of their new songs in the same spots as he did and as Leonard Bernstein also did in 1950 and Charlap and Leigh four years later. For instance, "Wendy" replaced "Be Our Mother." Bernstein's "Build My House," also in the same spot, merely replaced Barrie's original "I Wish I Had a House."

Peter and the Lost Boys sing "Wendy" on opening night. Photo: Bob Willoughby.

The lost boys listen to Peter's plan for building Wendy's house. (Photofest)

"Wendy" is a delightful piece of fluff that could quite conceivably be sung by children. It is cleverly choreographed with Peter and the Lost Boys building and painting a small house around their new mother.

> Peter—Bring lots of wood
> Bring lots of leaves
> Bring lots of paint
> But hush, hush, hush, hush, hush.
>
> Let's be quiet as a mouse
> and build a lovely little house
> For Wendy, all for Wendy
> She's come to stay,
> Boys— And be our mother,
> At last we have a mother
>
> Peter—Home sweet home upon the wall,
> A welcome mat down in the hall
> For Wendy, so that Wendy won't go away,
> Boys— We have a mother,
> At last we have a mother.

When construction was finished, Wendy emerged and sang:

> I'll be your mother
> Gentle and sweet
> I'll fill your pockets with good things to eat
> Tell you of Cinderella too
> Boys—Do, please do, do, please do.

Traditionally, Wendy always sang the song about the house she wanted. In this version Wendy did have a small vocal part, but it was eventually taken away so that only Peter is singing it with the Lost Boys. Jule Styne said, "We did that on purpose because Mary Martin is the star and you don't want anything to interfere with it."

An important substitution was the lullaby replacing "When I Went Home." An early draft shows the development of this song:

> I can hear a distant melody
> Somewhere from the past it comes to me
> Faintly as the whisper of a sigh
> I can hear this tender lullaby
>
> My child, my very own...

In a short time, "Distant Melody" emerged as a lullaby within a lullaby with a nostalgic sweetness suggesting a song that was sung to all of us when we were children. Comden and Green's ability to create diverse styles aided them in writing lyrics that were very much in keeping with Barrie's own genius at creating familiarity with original material.

> Once upon a time and long ago
> I heard someone singing soft and low.
> Now when day is done and night is near
> I recall this song I used to hear.
>
> My child my very own
> Don't be afraid you're not alone
> Sleep until the dawn for all is well
>
> Long ago this song was sung to me
> Now it's just a distant melody.
> Somewhere from the past I used to know
> Once upon a time and long ago.

Advertisement for *Peter Pan*. (Courtesy of Robert Gable)

In a noble gesture, the veteran songwriters refused equal credit, delegating themselves instead to the status of "additional music and lyrics by" Jule Styne, Betty Comden, and Adolph Green. Their contribution included six wonderful songs and numerous changes in the script that gave a new comic flavor to the proceedings.

Along with the ever-changing score, the play suffered other mishaps, one which always amused Mary Martin. In a 1989 interview with the *Washington Post,* she remembered a matinee performance where she flew too high and ended up being caught in the rafters. It was too dark up there beyond the lights for the stage crew to help unhook her, so the fire department was called in.

"They looked for me and couldn't find me. I was saying, 'I'm up here!' So finally they got the lights up and I was at the very top of the building, hooked on something. No one had prepared for that. They brought me down and I said, 'Let's start from where we left off.'"

Mary Martin finally gave the approval to move the musical to New York where it opened on October 20, 1954.

Under the headline PETER PAN PLAIN WONDERFUL; MARTIN, RITCHARD ARE SUPERB, critic Whiney Boulton of the *Morning Telegraph* led the praise.

Miss Martin is a smashing Peter Pan, boyish, eager, touching, her hair blonde as gold and short as caterpillar fur. She swings through the air with a pleased grin, plays her scenes with Wendy with a charm that is enormous and at times and under all conditions may be put down in theatre history as one of the truly great Peter Pans of all time. She has the voice, the figure, the air and the spirit....

The reviewer felt that

Whatever troubles may have beset the production in California, and it was only hearsay that there were such troubles, have all vanished now and from first curtain to last, *Peter Pan* at the Winter Garden is a show

The "Tarantella" performed by Cyril Ritchard and the Pirates on opening night. Photo: Bob Willoughby.

Sondra Lee dancing to "Indians" on opening night at the Winter Garden, October 20, 1954. Photo: Bob Willoughby.

of tremendous and hypnotic magic. There is no place in which it is weak or faltering, there is no moment but what it is a thoroughly lovely moment.

Variety wrote:

With Mary Martin as the personification of perennial boyhood, and a brilliantly inspired production, *Peter* seems the perfect vehicle for musicalization. How could it have been overlooked so long?

Miss Martin is so completely right, so believable and infectious as the eternal boy that it seems incredible that Barrie didn't write the original play for her. From her first, electrifying entrance through the Darling children's bedroom window to the curtain, when Peter and the three kids fly away to Neverland, soaring breathtakingly back and forth across the stage, it is one of the thrilling first acts in memory.

Other critics echoed these accolades. In the *New York Times*, Brooks Atkinson called it "A vastly amusing show." He found:

Miss Martin is the liveliest *Peter Pan* in the record book....She has more appetite for flying and swinging than any of her more demure predecessors, and she performs as actor, dancer and singer with skill and enjoyment. Peter Pan may have been a proper Victorian originally. He is a healthy, fun-loving American now.

As the bloodthirsty Captain Hook, Cyril Ritchard gives a superb performance in the grand manner, with just a touch of burlesque. Among the other stars of the production, put Jerome Robbins' name high on the list...he has directed this phantasmagoria with inventiveness and delight....

The taste in performance is impeccable. Kathy Nolan's round-faced beaming Wendy is perfect—girlish without sentimentality. As the mother of the Darling children, Margalo Gillmore gives a beautiful performance. Sondra Lee, as Tiger Lily, the Indian Maid, is uproarious. She dances and acts a sort of gutter Indian with a city accent that is mocking and comical. Altogether it is a bountiful, good-natured show.

In the *Herald-Tribune*, Walter Kerr said of Mary Martin:

She has tumbled into the role, like an eight-year-old hurling himself over and over in the best mud he can find, and as she darts, skips, and soars, she is the happiest truant in New York.

John Chapman of the *Daily News* found:

The musical version of this most endearing of all theatrical fantasies is a captivating show....Mary Martin and Cyril Ritchard win over another audience.

Wrote the *Post*'s Richard Watts:

A gay, lavish and colorful musical extravaganza....A resounding hit.

Strangely, the score was generally not credited as an element for the success of the musical. *Variety* reported the songs as "generally undistinguished" and Atkinson agreed, adding that the score "has no audible fondness for Barrie." Yet the most disturbing criticism was that the tunes were not memorable, or as one reviewer put it, the writers have not "come up with the type of songs that can be hummed at will from the recording of one's memory." While Stephen Sondheim has proven that a well-integrated score need not be "hit parade" material, most of the songs in *Peter Pan* are direct outgrowths of the dialogue and are indeed memorable. It is inconceivable that one can not hum the beautiful "Never, Never Land" or even be able to sing a line or two of "I Won't Grow Up" after the first hearing. In fact, this musical version of the play is performed more often than Barrie's published version, making it for many people, the quintessential *Peter Pan*. The wonderful new material by Styne, Comden, and Green is so well woven into the fabric of the play that it remains difficult to label each songwriting team's efforts. What started on shaky grounds was transformed into a sturdy musical comedy.

Peter Pan was scheduled for a limited Broadway engagement as NBC bought the rights to broadcast the musical on *Producers' Showcase* for $500,000, entire cast intact. It is most probable that the play would have had no problem playing to packed houses, but it would have taken a considerable amount of time to pay back its investors and net a profit. The television deal was extremely lucrative for its time and quickly brought the play out of the red.

After 152 performances at the Winter Garden Theatre, the five sets were transported to a studio in Brooklyn where they were adapted for the camera by NBC's set builders. Although there were only fifteen thousand color television sets in the United States at the time, the program was broadcast live and in color on March 7,

Peter Pan

(As of Dec. 11, 1954)

Original Investment	$125,000
Production Cost	99,841
(excludes $20,000 allowance from San Francisco Civic Opera)	
Gross last four weeks	205,853
Operating profit last four weeks	16,866
Cost still to be recouped	69,621
Bonds and deposits	31,420
Balance available for distribution	23,959

Weekly Operating Cost

Theatre share...30% of first $20,000 gross and 25% of balance	
Cast and chorus payroll (approx.)	13,600
(includes 10% of the gross to Mary Martin and flat $1,500 plus 5% of the gross over $40,000 to Cyril Ritchard)	
Company Crew (approx.)	2,500
Company musicians	583
Company and general manager	400
Stage managers	575
Press agents	300
Wardrobe and dressers	642
Extra stagehands	600
Extra musicians	1,588
Crew expense	1,089
Author royalty (book)	5%
Composer and lyricist royalty (includes $100 for dance music arrangements)	4.5%
Director royalty (includes $100 for asst. dir.)	2%
Designer (costumes and sets)	175
Assistant to producer	125
Ad-publicity expense (approx.)	2,300
Departmental rentals, expense (approx.)	1,285
Miscellaneous expense (approx.)	1,600
Gross necessary to break even (approx.)	37,500
Theatre stop limit	37,500

Mary applying makeup.
(Courtesy of Robert Gable)

1955. On that single evening, more people experienced Barrie's play than all the previous performances in its impressive history. Audiences and critics were charmed as the actors moved from set to set in the stadium-sized studio. Larry Elikann, later a prolific TV director, was technical director of this live television production. "It was opening night," he remembered, "flowers and telegrams. When the clock went straight up, you went straight through, and you didn't stop, except for commercial breaks. It was a tremendous strain on everybody, but it was wonderfully satisfying when things went right."

Since Walt Disney controlled the motion picture rights to the play, the production could not be filmed. Luckily, a record of this performance was preserved in the crude form of a black-and-white kinescope, which enabled this writer to critique the performance firsthand. In order to accommodate the commercials in the two-hour time slot, the play was trimmed just a bit. Among the deleted portions were the "Hamlet" story, a dance, and some dialogue from "Never Never Land," which was incorporated into an introduction for each act narrated by Patricia Wheel. Otherwise, this is a recorded document of a legendary Broadway show.

I expected Mary Martin to be excellent, but her performance is a revelation. Impish, bold, and boastful, she portrays all the qualities of a little boy on a great adventure. Add to this her distinctively beautiful voice, pulsating with vitality. One of the many highlights is her song, "I've Gotta Crow," which finds her showing off for Wendy. "Never Never Land" is equally memorable with its simple staging and Mary singing Jule Styne's beautiful melody and Comden and Green's lovely lyrics of childhood dreams. She believes the words and so do we.

Most of the coverage of the show concentrated on the mother-and-daughter aspect of casting, which understandably hurt Kathleen Nolan. Here she was Wendy to Peter and had received glowing reviews. "And I would constantly be having to tell people, 'No, I'm playing Wendy,' because there was so much press of Mary and Heller."

Personal feelings aside, the mother-daughter duet is all wrong for this show. Peter and Wendy never get to share a song. The few times that Wendy was to sing alone or with Peter were taken away. "Distant Melody" was originally sung by Wendy. From a dramatic point of view, it makes sense. The song tells of a yearning for home and ultimately convinces Wendy that she must return to her parents.

A duet for Peter and Wendy would also suit the structure of the play. Unfortunately, the most obvious place for a duet was lost when Heller Halliday was given the "Crow" reprise with her

The "I've Gotta Crow" reprise with Mary and Heller. (Photofest)

mother. While the part of Wendy was not as complete as it should have been, Nolan played it for all it was worth. Author Ken Mandelbaum reviewed the kinescope in 1991 for *Show Music* magazine and concluded that "the original Wendy, Kathleen Nolan, is quite marvelous, and definitely superior to her 1960 counterpart, Maureen Bally."

Nolan reminisced:

"Years ago, I guess it was in 1979 or whenever [Mary] was doing *Legends* or maybe before that when I was at the Screen Actors Guild...I was driving down Wilshire Boulevard in Los Angeles and I saw this big, huge window filled with a picture of Mary Martin flying. It was a promotion for the sale of linens of which she had designed patterns. There was supposed to be a reception for Miss Martin, so I pulled into the parking lot and I called the Screen Actors Guild and I said, 'Just cancel my appointments. I'll be there in a couple of hours.'

Nolan continued, "I went in and I got in the middle of one of the big beds with her sheets and towels on it and she was out to lunch. When she came back from lunch she screamed across the J. Robinson, 'Wendy!' And there I was sitting crossed-legged on the bed and sheets." Whenever Nolan would see Martin in a new show she would give her a "kiss" with a symbolic thimble.

Although the part of Liza is superfluous, Heller Halliday had an opportunity to show her dancing talent in a charming ballet with the animals. Sweet and lovely, but, again, not necessary.

Despite the major changes in Tiger Lily's part, Sondra Lee still managed to be as animated and humorous as those early California reviews indicated. Her dancing, her delightful mugging, and her look seemed to belong to a bygone era that was taken for granted and will never be repeated. Any show would have to benefit from her presence.

A beautifully controlled comic portrayal came from Joe E. Marks as the lovable Smee. His reactions to Hook's antics are priceless. In fact, all the performers are so good in their parts and at creating a true ensemble, it is difficult to pick individual accomplishments.

Peter Pan also succeeds from the ingenious casting of Cyril Ritchard and the revisions to the text to suit his style. The script indicates that Hook asks Wendy to say a few last words to her "sons" before they walk the plank. Her speech is long and noble. Yet, in the actual performances, Hook cuts her speech as she says, "These are my last words..." with a simple "Thank you!" His Captain Hook was unlike anything done before. He was hilariously theatrical in his operatic approach to the villain, and his solo moments in song were truly funny. "Oh My Mysterious Lady" and

TV advertisement for second *Peter Pan* airing. (Courtesy of Robert Gable)

"Hook's Waltz" were exuberantly performed, as were the tidbits of the song "Princely Scheme," which presents Hook finding any excuse to perform in front of an audience.

The actors who were interviewed for this book were all quick to identify Jerome Robbins as the major force behind the success of the show. But like all good theatre, it's teamwork. "Everyone in the cast was perfect," stated Mary.

At the end of the two-hour program, RCA, one of the sponsors, presented a commercial for the original cast album of *Peter Pan*. Peter and Captain Hook were represented in the form of marionettes moving to the music of the show. Finally, in full costume, Mary Martin came back on to bid farewell to the children:

"Thank you, all you grown-up children, all you little children, and all you middle-sized children for being with us tonight and believing with us in Never Land," she said. "I can't tell you how happy we are to share this lovely land with you. And I can't think how to say thank you to the Ford Motor Company, RCA, and NBC for making it possible for us to be with you. And remember this: always keep youth and joy and freedom of spirit within you. Think lovely, wonderful thoughts and don't forget to learn to crow a little…with fairy dust on you. Good night."

As she rose to fly among the credits, the Overture swept in for the finale. And a television tradition was born.

Dear Mary Martin. I am wirteing you because I like your Peter Pan show so much. I would like to see it again if you are not too busy. If you can not show it again please write and tell me. If you can show it again please wirte me anyhow. I will be 10 July the nineth and all I want is to see you in Peter Pan again. Please do not tell anyone about this.

Love,
Doris MacDonald

P.S. I ware glass's now and have short hare.

Despite her spelling errors, the little girl who wrote this letter was voicing the opinion of thousands. NBC was overwhelmed with mail requesting that *Peter Pan* be shown again, and they immediately announced plans for a repeat presentation the following year. On January 9, 1956, the entire original cast gathered for a rare television event—an encore performance. It is still incredible to believe that a musical of such proportion could be telecast "live" at all but a second time is astonishing. As was the first, the musical was treated with great enthusiasm.

Four years were to pass before television audiences would be treated to the musical again. In the meantime, Mary won a Tony Award as best actress in a musical, with a supporting actor Tony going to Cyril Ritchard. They also won the Donaldson Awards.

Mary continued to visit the small screen on several other occasions, each time with outstanding success. Between the telecasts of the first two *Pans* she joined Noël Coward for an hour-and-a-half of "live" entertainment, *Together With Music,* that won unanimous praise from the critics as a "tour de force accomplishment." Another successful tour of *Annie Get Your Gun* in 1957 also culminated with a television production of it, and while it was difficult for many to forget Ethel Merman, Mary's broad comic portrayal of Annie Oakley was a total delight. She then spent 1958 touring forty-seven cities with a delightful concert that was transformed into two "live" television specials on the same day, Easter Sunday! The afternoon program was entitled *Magic with Mary Martin,* a show derived for children. The evening show was called *Music with Mary Martin,* which was highlighted by a retrospective revue of songs from her career, ending with "I'm Flying." As she swayed across the stage, you could hear her exclaiming, "I love it!" This was not Peter flying on the stage, it was Mary Martin expressing her love for the part. These brilliant concerts and television specials were merely meant to be fillers in her professional life as *The Sound of Music* was being prepared for Broadway. Some time during these projects the idea of another television production of *Peter Pan* was germinating.

In a *New York Times* interview in 1960 Mary said, "Since we last did *Peter Pan* on television in 1956, the mail has never stopped coming in asking that we do it again. Now that it is being put on tape, it will be a permanent treasure and I hope it will be shown every year."

Mary with Noel Coward swing through the "Charleston" during a dress rehearsal for the "Ford Star Jubilee" special, *Together With Music.* (Courtesy of Robert Gable)

Peter is off to Never Never Land with a new cast. Maureen Bailey, Kent Fletcher and Joey Trent in the 1960 videotaped performance. (Photofest)

"The talk around NBC is that they intend to put this *Pan* in a vault," said director Vincent J. Donehue, "and it will last for years and years. Magnetic tape, they tell me, will stand the test of time better than film." It is interesting that for this permanent recording, Mary Martin chose a director other than Robbins to stage it, yet Donehue was no stranger to Mary Martin showcases. He directed her in the West Coast revival of *Annie Get Your Gun* as well as *The Skin of Our Teeth, Music with Mary Martin, Magic with Mary Martin,* and Broadway's *The Sound of Music.* It was during the run of this last that *Peter Pan* was taped. For convenience, Richard Halliday rented the Helen Hayes Theatre across the street from *The Sound of Music* for early rehearsals.

Due to the matinee performances of *The Sound of Music,* the two weeks of rehearsal days were limited to Mondays, Tuesdays, and Fridays. During the taping at the NBC studios in Brooklyn, the Hallidays took a nearby apartment. Taping began very early in the morning, yet the actress was able to give stunning performances as both Peter Pan and Maria von Trapp. "This role for some strange reason doesn't make me tired," she insisted. "It's mostly fun when I'm doing the most physically taxing part—the flying."

A flying accident almost ended the production when Mary suffered a serious injury to her elbow upon hitting a wall during a practice routine. "I nearly killed myself," she recalled in an interview many years later. "I started really fast and suddenly I'm out of sight, and I don't feel anything pulling me back. I'm heading for the wall, and like a shot, hit it. The man who was supposed to pull me back was new, and he got so thrilled he forgot. I said, 'I have to fly again, or those children never will.' The next time out, there was a mattress at the top of the theatre with a sign, MARY MARTIN CRASHED HERE." Not only were rehearsals continued, but she also performed nightly in *The Sound of Music* with her arm in a cast!

Mary wanted the same supporting cast as in the previous productions. Of course, the children had outgrown their parts, but NBC was able to get Sondra Lee, Joe Marks, and Norman Shelly without too much difficulty. Cyril Ritchard, though, was another story. He had to be bought out of his contract with an Australian touring company of *The Pleasure of His Company* and in addition, NBC had to pay any losses to the theatre company incurred by the absence of the actor. Ritchard resumed that tour after finishing the musical. After the taping, Donehue remarked to Cyril Ritchard that he was funnier than ever in this new production. "Why, I've lived four more years and ought to be!" quipped Ritchard. The part of Wendy went to a young actress, Maureen Bally, who had considerable experience on stage and television. She was eventually also featured in *The Sound of Music*.

Under Donehue's direction, the choreography of Jerome Robbins remained intact with just a few subtle changes. "This *Pan* is more visual," said Donehue. "The sets are prettier."

There were a few technical problems with the new format of videotape. Donehue commented at the time that "we still can't do dissolves with TV tape. The audio follows the picture." The major technical problem was "zeroing in each camera every day to match the day before." There was also the pending threat of a strike by the American Federation of Television and Radio Artists (AFTRA), which cut time available for taping. While the projected schedule for taping was four-and-one-half weeks, the possible strike accelerated the whole thing. "So in three days we did what had been projected for twelve days. That last Sunday was quite a fateful day," Donehue recalled. "...Mary still flying through the air at 3:00 A.M. We had doctors there to keep her and Cyril Ritchard in top form. If we had not gotten through and the strike had come at 12:00 midnight that Sunday as scheduled, *Peter Pan* might not have been."

The taped edition proved to be a worthy successor to its predecessors. *Variety* exclaimed:

In spirit, verve, performance and total execution, it was the best of the *Pan*s, and, thanks to the wonders of tape, a residual-happy bonanza for years to come....Miss Martin, perhaps the genuine reincarnation of the Pan who refused to grow up, was radiant. There is an incomparable iridescence in her never-never-never land behavior, and "the sound of Mary" was never more compelling or inviting. To say she's irresistible is almost to minimize a great talent.

The *Times* wrote:

In a third revival with many of the same principals, there might have been a danger that a little of the sharp edge of *Peter Pan* might have been lost. But it certainly did not seem so last night under the brisk and perceptive direction of Vincent J. Donehue. When Miss Martin soars through the window and whisks Wendy, John and Michael to the island of perpetual play and fun, all thoughts of age and years miraculously vanish. And she sang those lovely tunes, "I've Got to Crow," [sic] "Neverland" [sic] and "I'm Flying" with a special charm.

Sondra Lee and Cyril Ritchard received their due share of praise. Lee was referred to as "the nicest Indian ever to roam from the Broadway reservation."

Variety reported:

To watch Miss Lee and Miss Martin ugg-a wugg through the "Pow-Wow Polka" remained a high point....Ritchard was again superb as he hatched his nefarious plots to tangos and tarantellas and otherwise cavorted with delightful zestfulness.

Maureen Bally was also recognized for bringing the proper "enchantment" to the role of Wendy.

Even more important than the praise that the players were receiving was the realization that the underrated score was a major contributor to the success of the show. *Variety* observed:

In the few years since Moose Charlap and Carolyn Leigh, Betty Comden, Adolph Green, and Jule Styne penned the music and lyrics, the score seems to have taken on a new dimension and glow. The haunting "Never Land" [sic], the bouncy "Wendy" and equally infectious "I Won't Grow Up," the delightful "I'm Flying" and "I've Got to Crow," [sic], the beautiful "Tender Shepherd"—here was the musicalized Barrie fantasy treated to a merry romp, both in front and behind (and above) the cameras showing a fine qualitative skill.

There were only a few negative votes. Ben Gross of the New York *Daily News* wrote that

...those who saw the Barrie play in its original version could not but regret that it was not offered in its pure form. I had the good fortune as a child to have seen Maude Adams in *Peter Pan.*

Peter and Hook. This photo was taken in San Francisco. (Photofest)

Amazing! Critics were still comparing other Peters with Maude Adams, who clearly did not perform in the play as Barrie had written it. By now it should have been obvious that there never was a "pure" *Peter Pan*. Each production brings forth a Pan that a new generation can appreciate but that still contains the core of the legend that the fictional character has become. The musical may not be Barrie's *Pan,* but Peter does not belong exclusively to his author. He is a little boy that lives in the hearts of children of any age.

Mr. Gross reprieved himself when he said in the same review:

In this cynical, scoffing world of 1960, most of us believe in jet planes, spacemen and giant computers rather than in fairy tales. But for the benefit of those who still succumb to fantasy, Mary Martin came to television in *Peter Pan* again last night. It was an eye-filling spectacle....Mary can still fly better than any jet and Cyril is the most dastardly pirate of all.

Another Musical

≈≈≈≈≈≈≈

Flying has come into my dreams ever since I can remember. No wings or anything like that. In the dream I find myself flying completely naturally but the extraordinary thing is that I so often find I can't put the brakes on and I go faster and faster. This seems to wake me up without my ever having landed.

—Mia Farrow, 1976

On December 12, 1976, NBC telecast a new musical of *Peter Pan* as one of the prestigious *Hallmark Hall of Fame* specials. Perhaps a week before its airing, I discovered that this was not to be the Mary Martin musical but a new one starring Mia Farrow and Danny Kaye. Although disappointed that it was not the version with which I grew up, I was still excited that my favorite children's character would be visiting the small tube. My wife, Donna, and I stocked up on all sorts of goodies to snack on as we watched the program.

As Julie Andrews sang a beautiful song, "Once Upon a Bedtime," over the program's opening credits, we had no idea that we were witnessing the musical highlight of the evening. Halfway through the show Donna fell asleep, but I remained adamantly faithful, thinking, It has to get better!

The teleplay, produced by Gary Smith and directed by Dwight Hemion, was a beautiful presentation that had one problem—the songs! For reasons unknown, an intelligent script by Jack Burns was allowed to be cluttered with an undistinguished score that just got in the way. Even when Andrew Birkin was called in to doctor the script it was too late, for what the musical needed was a new score. Leslie Bricusse and Anthony Newley may not have been the giants of the musical comedy world, but they were no slouches either. Together they had written the music, lyrics, and books for *Stop the World—I Want to Get Off* and *The Roar of the Greasepaint—The Smell of the Crowd*, in both of which Newley also starred. Alone, Bricusse wrote songs for the films *Goodbye, Mr. Chips* and *Doctor Doolittle,* including the charming "Talk to the Animals."

With syrupy songs like "Love Is a House," "If I Could Build a World of My Own," "Mothers," and "Friendly Light, Burning Bright," it was no wonder that this *Peter Pan* was

PAGE 224: Mia Farrow as Peter. (Photofest); RIGHT: Mia Farrow and Danny Kaye. (Photofest)

never shown again. Only Danny Kaye's performances saved "By Hook or By Crook" and "The Rotter's Hall of Fame," which strongly resembled the delightful tongue-twisting specialty numbers that Kaye's wife, Sylvia Fine, used to write for him, and this definitely was not Kaye at his best. Though he lit up the stage in *Lady in the Dark* and *Let's Face It* in the early 1940s, it is his film work that continues to demonstrate his genius. *The Inspector General, Hans Christian Andersen,* and *The Court Jester,* among others, simply would not have been as memorable if not for Kaye's talent and personality. Captain Hook should have capped an outstanding career, but instead it remains a dismal outing.

Despite her vocal limitations, Mia Farrow played and sang a dark and melancholy Peter with a conviction that resembled the English critics' early-day descriptions of Jean Forbes-Robertson's portrait. The several songs given to Mia, though, are not worth the bother. "I'm Better With You," a song Peter sings once he has regained his shadow, was fun but only because of the animated shadow that would not stay attached. Her other songs were simply boring and only prolonged the action. It is interesting that just a few years later Mia's untrained voice sounded terrific when she sang and spoke for *The Last Unicorn,* an animated film with songs by Jimmy Webb.

Mia Farrow is remembered by television audiences for her role as Alison MacKenzie in "Peyton Place." The daughter of actress Maureen O'Sullivan and director John Farrow, she made her stage debut in *The Importance of Being Earnest* in 1963. Her fragile beauty is almost fawnlike and was used to great advantage on-screen in *Rosemary's Baby,* which brought her international acclaim. A list of her films indicates her diversity: *Secret Ceremony, The Great Gatsby, A Wedding,* and *Death on the Nile.*

In 1981 the actress began a professional and personal association with Woody Allen. Among the dozen or so films she appeared in under his direction were *Zelig, Hannah and Her Sisters, Broadway Danny Rose, The Purple Rose of Cairo,* and *Alice.*

Mia's stage credits are just as impressive, with *The Three Sisters, The Seagull, A Doll's House,* and *Twelfth Night.* Offstage Mia provided the news media with headlines of her marriages and divorces with Frank Sinatra and André Previn, not to mention her relationship with Woody Allen, lately proven to be stormy, but she continues to nurture her talent.

At one time Mia came very close to portraying Peter in another film project that never came to fruition. "I was relieved," stated the actress in a 1976 interview, "because I still hadn't brought myself around completely to thinking of Peter Pan as a girl."

The actors playing the Lost Boys were excellent, but they were also too old and in the costumes Sue Lucash designed for them, they looked like they belonged in Central Park during the hippie movement of the late sixties.

Talented Paula Kelly's dancing was great, but in the way, and her costume was much too sexy for this play.

Others involved in the telecast included John Gielgud as the Narrator and Virginia McKenna as Mrs. Darling. Whether McKenna did her own singing is not clear, but the entire show was poorly dubbed, which is inexcusable for a musical. On the other hand, the play had a definite English atmosphere and it even included an opening scene at the site of the Peter Pan statue in Kensington Gardens. It also restored Peter's "To die..." scene.

My favorite bit takes place in the nursery when Mr. Darling can not fix his tie. In a moment of frustration he loudly commands Nana to sit down, which of course she ignores. While helping him with his tie a second later, Mrs. Darling softly tells her husband to sit, and he obeys like a well-trained dog. Such light moments were surprisingly few and far between in a production filled with so much talent and effort. Watching the program fourteen years later I did not find it as bad as I first thought, but it is still one of the weakest *Peter Pan* versions. Too bad. It would have been a much better play if the creators had cut the songs.

The lack of audience response to the new musical fogged any interest by NBC of repeating the Mary Martin tape. However, writer Andrew Birkin must have learned a thing or two, for just a few years later the Royal Shakespeare Company would benefit from his contribution to their version of *Peter Pan.*

Sandy Duncan

When I was doing it there was a lot of encouragement to be Sandy Duncan doing Peter Pan. I said if I'm going to do it I'd like to do it as much as possible like a boy.
—Sandy Duncan, 1991

*I*n the theatre it is always difficult for an actor to play a part that another created and received universal recognition for, and while too many years have passed for comparison to Maude Adams's performances, the preservation of Mary Martin's *Peter Pan* on video continues to allow critics and audiences to indulge. Not since Marilyn Miller bravely fought and lost her battle against the memory of Adams has there been a more difficult challenge for an actress playing Peter. In 1978, Sandy Duncan decided to take the plunge in a production that was specifically planned as her first starring vehicle on Broadway.

"I was doing a nightclub act when I met with producer Zev Bufman," explained Sandy. When he asked her if there was a musical that she would like to star in on Broadway she responded, "There is really nothing that I want to revive."

"Why don't you do *Peter Pan?*" he suggested.

Now Sandy had enjoyed playing Peter in summer stock in Dallas and Ohio and was even Wendy opposite Betsy Palmer in a 1966 Bufman production, but she confessed that his suggestion did not generate much enthusiasm with her. "Oh, the rights were so complicated. Someone always held on to them. Michael Bennett had them at one point. He was going to do a new musical version of it. They just went from hands to hands to hands in those days. So Zev said, ' Well, let me get on it and see if we can get them.' So Michael released them to him."

No one could have predicted that this new Pan would meet with success, but Sandy was used to such challenges. In fact her career seems to consist of excellent performances in roles created by other actresses. From the age of twelve when she made her first stage appearance in a stock company of *The King and I* in Dallas, Sandy continued to impress her audiences with her acting, singing, and dancing talents. At New York's City Center she appeared in several shows, including *The Music Man, Carousel,* and *Finian's Rainbow.* An appearance in the Off-Broadway musical *Your Own Thing* led to Broadway's *Canterbury Tales,* for which she was nominated for a Tony Award. This was followed by another Off-Broadway show and then back to Broadway again for a second Tony nomination for her work in *The Boy Friend* in 1970. Judy Carnes may have been the star of the show, but it was Sandy who stole all of the excellent reviews.

Fred Silverman, then an executive with CBS, spotted her in *The Boy Friend* and offered her her own television series, *Funny Face*, a bubbly title derived from the Audrey Hepburn–Fred Astaire film. Her new success was dampened with a divorce from her first husband and severe headaches and dizziness. X rays showed nothing, but in fact a tumor was growing in her brain, pressed against the optic nerve of an eye. The operation to remove it was successful, but it cost her the sight in that eye. "It was an ordeal, but I refused to deal with it," she told *TV Guide*. "There I was, eighty-six pounds with my head in a big white bandage—I looked like a Q-Tip—running up and down the hospital halls checking on everyone else and signing autographs and being cheerful. I was locked into that perky, cheerful persona I had created for myself over the years." She went on, "I remember a psychologist saying to me, 'You think you're being brave, but you really haven't dealt with this at all.' He was right. It took me years—until after I married Don [Correia]. One month after the operation, still bald, I was guesting on *The Sonny and Cher Show*."

PAGE 228: "I've Gotta Crow." Sandy Duncan as Peter Pan. (Photofest); RIGHT: "Flying" Sandy with Jonathan Ward (Michael) and Marsha Kramer (Wendy). Photo: Martha Swope.

Following the operation, Sandy married a doctor whom she had met during her stay in the hospital. He convinced her to give up her career and settle down as a doctor's wife. Sandy's blood was too infected with greasepaint, however, and the marriage eventually ended. In 1977 she had one of her best parts in one of the most important miniseries ever derived for television, *Roots*. Critics were impressed with another facet of her talents as she aged from twenty to seventy years in a startling performance, which earned an Emmy nomination. In 1980 she married Don Correia, a talented song-and-dance man, who starred in the Broadway adaptation of *Singin' In the Rain*. He and Sandy succeeded Tommy Tune and Twiggy in *My One and Only*, proving themselves to be just as good as the original stars.

In 1987 Sandy Duncan was asked to replace Valerie Harper in the television series *Valerie* when, after its second season, legal entanglements caused Harper to withdraw as star. Based on a recently completed pilot that Sandy had done, it was agreed that she would be perfect as the aunt of the three boys on the show. Her warmth and natural comic abilities were ideal for the program, which was first retitled *Valerie's Family* and finally became *The Hogan Family*.

With all of the success that Sandy has deservedly acquired, her biggest challenge was encountered on September 6, 1979, at the Lunt-Fontanne Theatre when she stepped into the shoes of a Broadway legend and proved that she was the right size. Wrote Marilyn Stasio of the *New York Post*:

From the moment she flies into the Darling nursery and throws a tantrum because she can't get her wayward shadow back on, Duncan alerts us that her Peter will be all boy. An adorable boy, to be sure, with her grincracked face and graceful bounds in mid-air; but a boy, for all that, with ants in his pants and a nose that runs and a downright willful disdain for authority. Without losing any of the fun of the role, she avoids even the most tempting moments to be cute, or to signal a flash of grownup femininity. Her Peter is, at all times, a tough little guy who literally dances with the itchy joy of boyhood.

WCBS-TV (New York) critic Dennis Cunningham raved:

Sandy Duncan is the complete Peter Pan, which is to say Sandy Duncan is delightful perfection.

Reported ABC's Joel Siegel:

Yes she flies. All that energy from all those Wheat Thins [referring to a product she was endorsing on commercials]...I've never been a fan of Sandy Duncan's. She's always come across so sugary, I was afraid if I watched her I'd get cavities. But she is absolutely superb. At *least* Mary Martin's equal.

The show was directed and choreographed by Rob Iscove, who had guided her nightclub act. He was replaced near the end of the rehearsal period by Ron Field. In addition to the exciting new orchestrations by Ralph Burns, "I've Gotta Crow" was also improved with a clever bit of magic. The shadow takes on a life of its own thanks to another dancer behind a scrim. The idea may have been lifted from the Mia Farrow television version, but the execution is far better, not the least due to a superior song.

Another song, "Happily Ever After," written by Jule Styne, Betty Comden, and Adolph Green, was added to replace the reprise of "I've Gotta Crow," but it really wasn't needed, and besides, the staging left something to be desired. Sandy remembers the one time she performed it: "We had some weird song that I did one night. They sort of just threw it in the show during previews. It had nothing to do with the character of Peter Pan. It was a real kind of vaudeville thing. I

A sexy Tiger Lily (Maria Pogee) and her Braves. (Photofest)

was hysterical with embarrassment and I came off the stage and said, 'That's it! I'm never singing that again! I'm sorry!'"

There were two very important changes that affected the characters of Liza and Wendy. "In our version Liza doesn't get to Never Land," Sandy told this writer. "There's no reason for her to be there, so we leave her home." The other change was that Wendy now sang "Distant Melody." "I just felt it was more appropriate and more poignant for Peter to be excluded from that," Sandy said. "I thought it made more of a statement of his loneliness. It was an important step in Wendy's character."

Bright-eyed Marsha Kramer was given additional material and offered an effective performance as Wendy, but Sandy exerted so much verve and energy as Peter that almost everyone in the cast paled by comparison.

Walter Kerr of the *New York Times* wrote:

Sandy Duncan has convinced me of one thing at least. Flying is the only way to go. From the time of her moonburst entrance through the suddenly parted rooftop windows of the Darling nursery right through to her second curtain call—in which she soars rather farther than most performers care to chance—Miss Duncan is a Peter Pan who is at her most exhilarating when dizzyingly airborne.

Peter Pan, for all that Mary Martin and television were able to make of it, was never a landmark musical in Broadway history. It was a patch job—be nice and call it a patchwork quilt—originally put together by Mark Charlap and Carolyn Leigh, then hurriedly supplied with seven new songs on the road by Jule Styne, Betty Comden, and Adolph Green.

Douglas Watt wrote in the *Daily News:*

Though some of the songs—"Neverland" [sic] and "I've Got to Crow" [sic], to cite two of the best—are enjoyable enough, this is hardly a topnotch musical effort, a fact attested to by the realization, 25 years ago, that a second team [Comden-Green-Styne] was needed to bolster the show's musical elements.

Countered *Newsweek*'s Jack Kroll:

The 1954 score holds up surprisingly well. It's an amiable potpourri of songs by Mark Charlap and Carolyn Leigh like the exultant "I'm Flying" and Peter's anthem of eternal infantilism, "I Won't Grow Up," with additional numbers by Jule Styne with Betty Comden and Adolph Green

Twenty-five years later and the critics were still picking on a classic score in the same fashion critics have been putting down Barrie's classic play. Generally, though, they presented a positive attitude about the show. Not so, however, for George Rose's Captain Hook or "Oh My Mysterious Lady."

Said critic Walter Kerr:

Miss Duncan, with her slight, lithe build and her close-cropped hair, is much more nearly a boy than Miss Martin was, which makes it rather preposterous for her to drape herself in a veil, waggle a rose above her head, and prove instantly enticing to Captain Hook ("Mysterious Lady"). And dear old Hook, in this case George Rose, fares rather more poorly. Mr. Rose is a master of understatement, an exemplary deadpan farceur; the need to contort his evil countenance, complete with penciled-in-mustache, in the broad Restoration-Comedy style of his predecessor is enough of a strain to push him over into camp.

Peter, Captain Hook (George Rose), and the Croc! (Photofest)

Other critics including Howard Kissel of *Women's Wear Daily* agreed that Rose was too campy in the role. He wrote:

Most of the supporting cast is colorless. George Rose, one of my favorite actors, does not seem completely at ease as a Captain Hook—though he too is occasionally given bits that make the role more campy than necessary. Arnold Soboloff seems embarrassingly uncomfortable as Smee. Maria Pogee, who has a thick Latin accent, makes a very puzzling Tiger Lily.

Audiences flocked to the theatre with their children to share Sandy Duncan's *Peter Pan,* which ran for 551 performances, making it the longest-running *Pan* ever to fly on a Broadway stage.

The only negative criticism the star received was for her participation in the duet with Hook. Wrote Kissel:

Sandy Duncan, an immensely winning performer, really plays Peter as a little boy—impish, energetic and peevish. She does not mess with the Grand Tradition of alternating between boyishness and arch femininity, so the "Mysterious Lady" number, a focal point of the original production, just seems silly and dumb.

One of the disappointments for Sandy was that the show was never videotaped. "I've always wanted to do it," she lamented. "And the other thing that's been a real heartbreaker for me is never having our production and the arrangements that we did recorded. And the reason that's never happened is once again, there are so many people with a piece of the pie." Sandy confessed in our 1991 interview that her *Pan* almost made it to NBC:

"About two years ago Brandon Tartikoff called and asked if I would do that production as a television special for Easter. I said, 'I would love to. I can just make it—energy-wise. Another year goes by and I don't think that I will have the stamina to do it. I'll be too old and too tired. I'd be happy to do it!'"

Sandy continued, "At that point in time a man named Jerry Winthrop owned the rights and he said [to Tartikoff], 'I want to do a big expensive film of the musical and I would ask as a personal favor that you wouldn't do this as it would hurt my production.' So Brandon called me and said, 'I'm really sorry we can't get the rights together.' That was the Easter they ran Mary's version."

Mary Martin attended one of Sandy's performances as Peter, an event that scared the new Peter more than opening night. Mary was delighted with Sandy, as were the thousands of children who will always think of Sandy Duncan as *Peter Pan*. Now, why doesn't someone offer this lady a damn good original musical into which to sink her teeth?

16

A Change of Gender

~~~

Why does it always have to be a peterless Pan?
—*Silent film actor Gareth Hughes, 1924*

...let us never see a gal as Peter again.
—*Giles Gordon of* Spectator *on Peter Pan, 1984*

On December 16, 1982, British audiences were buzzing as they once again flocked to the theatre to treat themselves to Barrie's Christmas treat. The cause of the excitement was that *Peter Pan* would be performed at the Barbican Theatre by the Royal Shakespeare Company and Peter would be played for the first time by a man. As previously seen, the tradition of Barrie's time mandated that an actress play the role of the principal boy in a pantomime. Barrie had no idea that his play was beyond the level of that kind of theatre. This is not to say that he never wanted a boy to play Peter, for one of his letters reveals that he was more than interested.

29 September ['20]
Ainley has found a boy whom he thinks highly of as a possible Peter. I have sometimes hankered after that, and as the photographs he sent me are promising I've agreed to wait a fortnight until I can see the boy. Of course if he is decided on, it would affect Wendy and the other boys—mean their all being children, so nothing definite can be done at present about such parts. Ainley also says he would like to play Mr. Darling as well as Hook—as du Maurier used to do....

In 1920 Henry Ainley temporarily restored the tradition of one actor doubling in the parts of Hook and Mr. Darling, but the part of Peter was again played by an actress, this time Edna Best.

Barrie also expressed interest in silent film star Charlie Chaplin playing the part and it has been suggested by some that he wrote his film scenario with that thought. Yet by 1924, he was insisting that a girl must play Peter in the Famous Players' silent film, causing actor

Gareth Hughes, an excellent Tommy in the screen treatment of Barrie's *Sentimental Tommy,* to lament publicly his displeasure of the casting of a female Peter.

Not counting the Davies boys, the first male Pan was probably played in 1910 in a special performance put on by the juvenile members of the *Peter Pan* company at the Duke of York's Theatre in London. This merry masquerade was performed at least four other times by the various children who were then in the production, but this was a first for a male Peter. Young Herbert Hollom followed his older brother Ernest's footsteps into the part of Michael when Ernest left the company at the end of the 1906–07 season. For three years Herbert played the part, and when he outgrew it in 1909, he simply went on to play John. In between his transition he was able to play Peter for that one performance on February 8, 1910.

The first commercial venture that saw Peter being played by an actor was not on stage or, for that matter, in England. On February 24, 1936, Freddie Bartholomew took the part on a radio program. British-born Bartholomew was at the height of his career as a child movie star in *David Copperfield, Little Lord Fauntleroy,* and *Captains Courageous.* Although usually cast as the ideal English youngster, this attractive, curly-headed child demonstrated that he could also play a real, rough-and-tumble boy, but his performance as Peter never went beyond radio, and for that he was only mildly received for his pleasant vocal performance. Aaron Stein for the *New York Post* wrote:

Unfortunately, the production can boast the dubious distinction of being that very rare thing, a *Peter Pan* with a masculine star. The all important illusion faltered and died.

PAGE 236: Jewel Morse (Wendy) and Leslie C. Gorall (Peter). (The Billy Rose Collection, New York Public Library at Lincoln Center); ABOVE: Rare program of 1910 Juvenile performance of *Peter Pan.* (Author's collection); BELOW: Freddie Bartholomew as Peter Pan? He wasn't always the little gentleman as seen in this photograph from *Little Lord Fauntleroy.*

Miles Anderson as Peter in the Royal Shakespeare Company's 1982 production. Photo: Sophie Baker.

Two years later the Clare Tree Majors Children's Theatre of New York presented the first major production of the play since the demise of the Civic Repertory Company. John Ireland played Captain Hook with Jewel Morse as Wendy and Leslie C. Gorall as Peter. This Leslie was not a woman but rather a sturdily built young man whom audiences must have liked, as the play toured the United States for a year! Except for the voice in the Disney film, Peter would not be played by a boy again until the Royal Shakespeare Company decided to add *Peter Pan* to its 1982 season.

The RSC is well known as one of the best theatre companies in the world. The classical training of the actors and actresses and their dedication to Shakespearean drama is combined with repertory experience that adds to the distinction of each play, even those that are not by Shakespeare. The company's origins trace back to 1875 in Stratford when it was incorporated as the Shakespeare Memorial Theatre. A fire destroyed the building in 1926 and the company was housed in a movie theatre for six years. In 1932, a new Royal Shakespeare Theatre was built. In addition to that one, the Aldwych in London was used from 1960 until 1982, when the company, under the artistic direction of Trevor Nunn, moved to the Barbican. It is here *Peter Pan* was blessed with its finest production in many years.

The core of the creative talent responsible for the look of the new production was the same group that created *Nicholas Nickleby*—directors Nunn and John Caird, designer John Napier, and composer Stephen Oliver. For *Nickleby* the directors used Charles Dickens's narrative as part of Nicholas's dialogue. They decided to approach *Peter Pan* in a similar way. Andrew Birkin, author, film director, and Barrie authority was asked to help create a version of the play that was as close to the author's intentions as possible. The sources for the "new script" included the 1904 version, the novel, the silent-film scenario, and the original unpublished manuscript. During the meshing of this material, new elements were also added to give a Barriesque touch. Much of the charm of the 1928 published play is the insightful stage direction, the only way that the author could include himself as part of the text. The dialogue may belong to the characters, but the comments belong to Barrie. Normally, when a company chooses to use this script, Barrie's thoughts are left unheard. Birkin, Nunn, and Caird cleverly allowed Barrie to take his rightful place as one of the characters. A delightful narration was added for a Story Teller, not Liza, but an actor dressed to look like Barrie. This loving and respectful tribute allowed the audience to see the author deeply entrenched in his Never Never Land.

From the original manuscript was added the ending of the Lost Boys grown up to be stockbrokers and judges, while an adult Wendy was incorporated from *An Afterthought*. Peter, no longer the wholesome boy he had become in recent productions, regained his original selfish character, culminating with a threat to stab Jane when he bitterly discovers that she is Wendy's daughter.

With so many wonderful innovations added to the play, the casting of an adult male as Peter did not become a gimmicky attraction of the play or an issue with the critics when it opened on December 16, 1982.

David Roper wrote in the *Daily Express:*

Whether or not the Royal Shakespeare Company had chosen to defy tradition by casting a full-grown man as the boy who never grew up, their *Peter Pan* would be a noteworthy production. Wendy herself is infinitely more fascinating than Peter now as Jane Carr is playing her as a purse-lipped, clever little madam determined to get her man, Tinker Bell or no damned Tinker Bell.

Sadly, the 35-year-old Miles Anderson as Peter is not the revelation everybody expected. Despite some spectacular flying and antics in the magic lagoon created from billowing blue satin, he makes a stubborn and sulky child, though doubtless closer to the unlikeable monster Barrie intended.

In his *Guardian* review, Michael Billington echoed the raves for Jane Carr's Wendy but also admired Anderson's performance.

Miles Anderson also treats Peter as a tough, rough, cocky, tattered urchin whose pathos comes from his plight rather than from any signalled winsomeness. And there is a gem of a Wendy from Jane Carr, full of precocious maternal briskness and a genuine sexual jealousy towards the possessive Tinkerbell.

The revision in text was also approved by Billington:

Jane Carr as Wendy in
1982. Photo: Sophie Baker.

Just occasionally, the narrative-line gets a little clogged by the spectacle. But this is my only cavil against a production that gets right to the heart of what Peter Llewellyn Davies called this 'terrible masterpiece.'

The *Daily Telegraph*'s John Barber thought that the grownups playing the children were weak but

Joss Ackland's Captain Hook is as dastardly as his Mr. Darling is Pompous—a splendid double....Jane Carr's bossy little Wendy is a triumph.

Miles Anderson, both adult and a male, is an intelligent young actor, and he touches in both cockiness, the self-containment and even the tragedy of the fairy boy. But he does not seem to be of a different flesh from the others. Perhaps Peter should be the only genuine child in the cast.

Just as in Barrie's time, there were critics who were not impressed with the play. Robert Cushman of the *Observer* wrote:

The traditional dilapidated productions have left *Peter Pan* looking like a relic. Now the Barbican takes it over, in a careful and occasionally

Katy Behean as Wendy
with Mark Rylance as
Peter in the 1983 RSC
production. Photo: Sophie
Baker.

brilliant production...and it still looks like a relic; a fascinating one,
but appealing more as a guide to the author's psyche than as a play or
adventure story in its own right.

Cushman goes on to say

But the middle episodes are diminished! The fact of the children's
escaping to Never-land is more important than what happens to them
there....The flying is thrillingly done, up to the full height of the
monstrous stage; though if ever a play cried out to be turned into a
musical it is this one at the moment of lift-off.

On December 22, 1983, the RSC repeated their success with
Stephen Moore swapping his part of the Story Teller for the more
challenging Captain Hook, a new Wendy in Katy Behean, and a
replacement for Peter, too. Moore and Behean received good
notices, but it was Peter whom the critics really noticed. John Barber
in the *Daily Telegraph* wrote:

A too-mature Miles Anderson turned in a decent professional job as
Peter before. But Mark Rylance with his faun-like face is a capering
sprite—young, slim, lithe and, as Barrie wanted, more than impish.
There is a devil in him. Dancing with Wendy, he almost whirls her into

perdition. Something of the mystery and melancholy of the actor's Ariel still clings to him.

In the *Tribune* Barney Bardsley agreed:

I must congratulate Mark Rylance on a beautiful performance—one of the best all year. His mixture of clench-fisted petulance and surefooted grace suited Pan's character exactly. No sweet-faced boychild this, but an angry Puck who damn well would not grow up—or do as he was told.

For a third year the RSC repeated their success. This time Peter was played by John McAndrew, previously Michael Darling. His reviews were also good. Keith Nurse of the *Daily Telegraph* felt that McAndrew's Pan

...is as healthy and refreshing as they come: athletic, spring-heeled and displaying all the giddy talents of an airborne gymnast.

Carole Woodis of the *City Limits* used just a few words to describe this special episode in the life of the RSC.

Wonderfully realized by designer John Napier and Andreanne Neofitou...the Nunn/Caird partnership have done for Barrie what they did for *Nickleby*. It's the kind of experience of which legends are made.

The Darling Family in 1983, from left: John, kneeling (David Parfitt), Mrs. Darling (Frances Tomelty), Michael, seated (John McAndrew), Mr. Darling (Stephen Moore), and Wendy (Katy Behean). In 1984 John McAndrew played Peter. Photo: Sophie Baker.

Welcome Back, Mary!

I was just so happy to have been a part of Peter Pan *and will always think of myself as Peter Pan.*

—*Mary Martin, 1989*

"*T*he clapping worked," read the cover of *People* magazine in 1989. "Peter Pan Is Back!" It was hard to believe, but the perennial favorite had not been telecast in sixteen years. The videotape had been aired only three times since its 1960 debut—1963, 1966, and 1973—yet for a generation growing up during this period it seemed as if it had become an annual event. The original cast album went away to college with many students along with their Beatles and Rolling Stones records, but by the 1980s Mary Martin's *Peter Pan* was added to the collection of childhood memories.

At the University of Wisconsin, a production of *Peter Pan* made the news for its unorthodox staging. The pirates were brutal policemen, six coeds danced in the nude, Tinker Bell died, and Peter Pan left Never Never Land and became an adult. An Off-Broadway review, *Forbidden Broadway,* humorously poked fun at the reverence many feel about the play, and in particular, Mary Martin as its star.

Mary did not exactly sit back and reflect on her laurels. Following *The Sound of Music* she starred in *Jenny* with its Howard Dietz–Arthur Schwartz score. "She has the star quality that transcends marquees and animates legends." said *Time* magazine. "In her bearing, timing, suppleness, versatility, she is a flawless professional." Not the success as anticipated, Mary "played it safe" with her next show in 1965 by touring the world with an established hit, *Hello, Dolly!,* that is if you consider performing for the soldiers in Vietnam safe! In 1966 *Dolly* producer David Merrick starred her in a Broadway musical that boasted a cast of two— Mary and Robert Preston. *I Do! I Do!* was a lively adaptation of *The Fourposter* by Jan de Hartog, a narrative covering fifty years of marriage. With only one set—a bedroom—it earned another Tony nomination for Mary for her portrayal of Agnes in the musical written by Tom Jones and Harvey Schmidt, creators of *The Fantasticks.* The 560 performances began to take their toll and the tour was cut short due to the poor health of both stars. The Hallidays retired to Brazil on property that they had purchased some years earlier to be near their good friends, the legendary designer Adrian, who had since passed away, and his wife, Janet

Gaynor, who remarried and moved away. When Richard Halliday died in 1973, Mary moved to California and began to act again.

During the next few years she tried new plays such as *Do You Turn Somersaults* (a failure) and her own talk show (a moderate success), but it was her son Larry Hagman who provided her with professional and personal joy. Hagman had already established himself in the long-running television series *I Dream of Jeannie*, but it was his portrayal of dastardly J. R. Ewing on *Dallas* that made him a household name.

In 1982, Mary was badly hurt in a San Francisco car accident that immediately killed her manager, Ben Washer, and claimed the life later of Janet Gaynor. A punctured lung, a broken pelvis, and two fractured ribs caused concern over whether Mary would walk again. Yet a year later she was flying through San Francisco's Symphony Hall for a charity benefit. She wore her original *Peter Pan* costume, which was borrowed from the Museum of the City of New York.

In 1985 Mary was anxious to act in a play again. Unfortunately, she and Carol Channing were ill-advised to accept the leads in *Legends!*—a great title in need of a great play. Playwright James Kirkwood, who already won praise and prizes for his novels and plays, which included *P.S. Your Cat Is Dead*, *Some Kind of Hero*, and *A Chorus Line*, begged Mary to costar. It became apparent on the road that *Legends!* would never reach the status of his other work, but the real shame arrived in 1989 when Kirkwood's

PAGE 244: Mary promoting *Peter Pan* in 1989. (Author's collection); RIGHT: Mary and Robert Preston in *I Do! I Do!*, 1966. Photo: Friedman–Abeles (Courtesy of Harvey Schmidt)

Diary of a Mad Playwright was posthumously published. With chapters like "Chasing Peter Pan," "Meeting Peter Pan," and "Hello, Dolly." Kirkwood's book, valid or not, seemed bent on humiliating his stars.

Suddenly, in 1989, Mary Martin and *Peter Pan* were making news again. On March 24, NBC reran its property after many years but it was not that easy to get Peter back on television. For years rumors persisted that the original tapes were lost, destroyed by a warehouse fire, or accidentally erased. To everyone's surprise, on June 13, 1988, a refurbished version of the show was presented at the Museum of Broadcasting in New York. The initial screening was introduced by Mary and just her appearance caused cheers from the audience. Sondra Lee was there and remembers, "...what was thrilling was sitting in the audience, seeing this show with Danny DeVito and his kids. The audience went crazy screaming! They called me up from the audience.... You would have thought I was a baseball player coming home from a great game or something!"

Sondra Lee was not the only person impressed by the reception of this long-lost gem. " I had always loved the property," Richard Riesenberg later told reporters. "I went, bringing my wife and my son, and we came out exhilarated." Riesenberg was a director of program development for an advertising firm. One of its clients was the Campbell Soup Company and he suggested that Campbell sponsor the return of *Peter Pan*. When NBC learned of a potential buyer, the network's West Coast vice president, Carl Meyer, was asked to see if the tapes from its "New Jersey mystery warehouse" were usable. Meanwhile, Riesenberg began negotiating with the many parties responsible for the musical, including the songwriters, the director, the star, and the estate of Richard Halliday. The Children's Hospital in London was also involved, for even though NBC owned the tape, it did not own the rights to televise it again.

Technician Edward Ancona found many problems with the condition of the tapes. A master tape no longer existed and the first-generation tapes had a lot of scratches, not to mention that they were shedding iron oxide. Two of the best copies were brought to Image Transform, a videotape post-production house, so that they could be edited on to one tape. The new tape then went to another company to digitalize the optical signal and reduce the visual noise, which appears as snow in a weak picture. Color quality also had to be improved for the original had bluish shadows instead of neutral. Then the improved picture was matched to the original sound recordings from a two-inch tape.

Ancona credits NBC for "taking the time to do it. There was no pressure to do it as there was no air date at this point. *Peter Pan* was saved in the nick of time!" When the new tape was completed, the network was still reluctant to offer it to a sponsor, their concern being that the production values would not meet today's standards. Sandy Duncan's successful Broadway run was another reason why the television special could not be aired, but the main concern was public interest. Brandon Tartikoff stated, "A 1970s version with Mia Farrow did not perform very well, and there was no impetus to show *Peter Pan* again at that time. But now we're at the end of the eighties and we realize what a nugget we have in the Mary Martin production." Miraculously, all the legalities were worked out, and an Easter weekend date was set. In January 1989, Brandon Tartikoff told reporters that *Peter Pan* would again be shown on television. *Peter Pan* had become the pet project for the peacock network, and everyone held their breath. If this beloved relic did not command respectable ratings, it would be unlikely that it would be aired again, much less made available on video.

The announcement of the airing was greeted with much enthusiasm by the press and public. Every paper and magazine seemed to feature the story. Across the country parties were organized at private residences to watch the show, and countless VCRs were set to record the musical for keeps. "And it is my thinking that Yuppies will station their puppies in front of the tube to enjoy the magic they remember," wrote critic Steve Sonsky of the *Miami Herald*. The ratings were the best that NBC had seen in several months. A few minutes of the tape were omitted for commercial time, including Liza's entrance to Never Never Land and her dance, making it a bit strange to see her later sing "I've Gotta Crow" with Peter.

The uncut version was released on home video in 1990 at about the same time Disney was marketing its animated version. The only problem with the tape was the packaging, which falsely labeled the classic as "live" television. In any case, the tape has been selling very well. There is a reason for the renewed interest in the taped classic. The "baby-boom" generation had grown up and now had children of their own. With the advent of videotapes and laser discs, the boomers were collecting films and programs that delighted them in their childhood to share with their offspring.

RCA tried to cash in on the video's success by changing the cover of its CD release of the Broadway cast recording to the same package design as the videotape. When I first spotted the disc, I thought that the television sound track had been released, but further inspection revealed it to be the Broadway version. Misleading!

Tragically, as *Peter Pan* was being welcomed back, Mary Martin left us. The actress died of cancer on November 3, 1990. A year before, she had been planning to star in *Grover's Corners*, Tom

"I'm Flying." Kathleen Nolan, Joseph Stafford (Michael), and Robert Harrington (John) fly to Never Never Land with Mary Martin. (Photofest)

Jones's and Harvey Schmidt's musical adaptation of Thornton Wilder's *Our Town*. If only…still, she provided so many wonderful moments that theatre goers will never forget. There was a Mary Martin. There still is her *Peter Pan*.

"The very important aspect of that production of *Peter Pan* was her presence, her absolute belief in the show, and her insistence that she was going to do it," reflected Mary Hunter at the *Peter Pan* symposium. "I remember very well indeed when a New York delegation made up of her very dear friends, each of whom had a special project that he or she wanted Mary to do, came out to visit the show in San Francisco. She and Richard suffered their presence, while each of that group, one after the other, said 'This is terrible. It'll ruin your career. What are you doing in this?'" Hunter continued, "It was one of the most extraordinary and devastating experiences that could happen to a person who is responsible, as a star must be, to the success and final result of the show. Mary and Richard smiled sweetly, took those people out to dinner, got them plastered, and put them back on the train. And that was that."

Hunter summed up: "Mary's contribution, as a creative person and as a performer, at a point in her career when she was subject to all kinds of pressures, was that she never wavered. She even survived being dropped from the wire in a terrible, horrible accident, which could have been fatal. And it never stopped her from performing."

Hook

Never Land is not a cartoon world. It is the real place.
—Steven Spielberg, 1991

*I*n 1979, Howard Kissel ended his *Women's Wear Daily* review of the latest *Peter Pan* with the following thought:

Some time ago Michael Bennett wanted to rethink *Peter Pan* completely—with Peter as a boy really faced with the problem of growing up. Bennett said he gave up the idea because he resolved the issues the play presented to him in analysis. Seeing this enjoyable but not really satisfying revival made me wish he had a less skillful analyst.

Twelve years later Steven Spielberg filmed a variation of the same theme.

The idea of a live-action film of *Peter Pan* has occurred to more than one producer since Disney unveiled his animated adaptation. In 1962, Leonard Key, president of Berkeley Films, purchased the rights for £35,714 for a projected movie starring Audrey Hepburn as Peter, Hayley Mills as Wendy, and Peter Sellers as Captain Hook. Two years later, it was announced that George Cukor would direct a film version of *Pan* following *My Fair Lady,* and again Hepburn was mentioned for Peter.

In 1967, Mel Ferrer planned on making the film with Mia Farrow, but he sold the rights to Universal in 1968. With a new screenplay that he had written, Ferrer again bought the film rights from the Great Ormand Street Hospital for Sick Children with hopes of producing the films at Pinewood Studios in England. Nothing materialized.

For several years in the eighties it was rumored that rock star Michael Jackson was going to star in a Steven Spielberg film, but the producer-director denied this in 1984. "Michael is a very close friend of mine," Spielberg told *Variety,* "but he never was and never will be, Peter Pan." Spielberg planned to have the film ready for a 1986 Easter release. Plans fell through, and by 1989 he was saying that he would never film the play.

Dustin Hoffman's name also began surfacing in the late eighties as a leading contender for the part of Captain Hook, even though no definite film was in the works. In 1987, Jerry

PAGE 250: Robin Williams as Peter Pan Banning with his son, Jack, played by Charlie Korsmo. RIGHT: Williams as Peter Pan. (Copyright © 1991 TriStar Pictures, Inc.)

Robin Williams as Mork in the late seventies.

Weintraub Entertainment said that Hoffman would be in their version, which was to be directed by Lasse Hallstöm, and Hoffman's name came up again in 1990 for a film to be produced by Dodi Fayed. For a while it looked as if Hoffman would have as much luck with the material as Michael Jackson.

In 1989, TriStar bought the rights to an original screenplay entitled *Hook*. Developed by screenwriter Jim Hart, it was initially presented as a package by producers Gary Adelson and Craig Baumgarten with Nick Castle as director. The script was shown to Spielberg, who became very excited over the prospects only to find out that Castle was part of the package. At this point, TriStar chairman Mike Medavoy decided that such an expensive venture could only succeed under Spielberg's direction. Castle was disappointed, but he was promised another TriStar film and a handsome settlement for his contribution to the story. Finally, Steven Spielberg was going to work on the film that he seemed destined to create.

Spielberg's imagination and love of filmmaking has become obvious to all, it seems, except to his own industry. Everyone wants to work with him or be involved in one of his projects, but he has yet to be recognized by his own industry as one of the major "artistic" directors of our time. Which brings us to *Hook,* an ambitious film that succeeds and fails on many different levels.

Hook must not be considered a sequel to *Peter Pan*, for Barrie made it clear that Peter would not grow up. Screenwriter Jim Hart derived the idea from a family dinner game, "What if…" "What if Peter Pan grew up?" asked his son. Together with Hart and screenwriter Malia Scotch Marmo, Spielberg envisioned a fantasy film that had a very important message to the materialistic "yuppie" generation; don't forget your priority—the family!

The writers respected the idea that Peter continued to visit the Darling nursery—until he gazed on the beauty of Wendy Moira Angela Darling's granddaughter, Moira. He fell in love with her and could not leave. The film opens with Peter "Banning," now an adult, married to Moira with two children of his own. More shocking, he has become a pirate of the 1990s, a lawyer! He hardly has any time for his family, and he is warned by his wife to spend time with them now while they want to be with him, because in a few years he will be chasing them to spend time with him.

A visit to London opens his eyes when his children are kidnapped by Captain Hook, who managed to escape that crocodile after all. What follows is an adventure fantasy as Tinker Bell aids Peter in returning to Never Land to rescue them. Slowly, Peter is able to recapture the spirit of his youth, and eventually he relearns how to fly.

Julia Roberts, Steven Speilberg, and Robin Williams watch the day's *Hook* rushes. (Copyright © 1991 TriStar Pictures, Inc.)

The tale is subtly sprinkled with authentic lines and characters from the original sources. Wendy, played by Maggie Smith, herself a Peter Pan at the London Colliseum in 1973, is a woman of about ninety, just the age Wendy would be if we consider Barrie's 1911 novel instead of the play as her origin. Living in her home is one of the last survivors of the original lost boys, Tootles (veteran actor Arthur Malet), who symbolically lost his youth when he "lost his marbles," toy marbles. There is also a housekeeper named Liza, but she is much too young to be the same servant employed by Wendy's parents, unless she enjoyed a couple of extended holidays in Never Land.

Robin Williams is the stuffy Peter Banning, who transforms back to Peter Pan with all the impish qualities of Mork, a character Williams made popular on television in the 1970s. Even his ears become Spock-like, closer to Disney's conception.

Jack Mathews of *Newsday* found that "ultimately, *Hook* is Robin Williams's film and it's at its best when he's being Robin Williams, tossing out lines that only he could have conjured up." Critic David Ansen of *Newsweek* also enjoyed Williams's performance, stating that "he gives us just enough hint of the lost waif in Peter Banning to redeem this '90s cliche of the soulless corporate grind, and his transition to Pan is built with lovely comic steps."

As for Dustin Hoffman's Hook, the critics felt that it was not one of his best performances. "He's perfectly amusing," wrote

The Lost Boys led by Dante Basco (center). (Copyright © 1991 TriStar Pictures, Inc.)

Dustin Hoffman as
Captain Hook. (Copyright
© 1991 TriStar Pictures,
Inc.)

Kathleen Carroll of the *Daily News,* "but not terrifying enough to
have the reputation as 'the sleaziest sleaze of the high seas.'" David
Ansen found his portrayal agreeable but added that Hoffman "never
becomes the dominating figure the title promises."

Good performances also came from thirteen-year-old Charlie
Korsmo as Peter's son and Bob Hoskins. Carroll found the lost boys'
antics monotonous and the boys themselves as "'Our Gang' look-
alikes, the multi-racial band of rambunctious urchins."

Julia Roberts plays Tinker Bell who, despite all the hype, could
have easily been replaced by the traditional flickering stage light.
Not that Roberts was bad, her role just was not interesting.

The film's most satisfying aspects were the stunning sets by
John Napier, who also greatly enhanced the musical *Miss Saigon*
with his helicopter scene and was also responsible for the highly
praised decor of the RSC's production of *Peter Pan* a decade earlier.
Never Land cost some $8 million and looked it. Napier designed a
magnificent seventy-foot *Jolly Roger* pirate ship docked at a fantastic wharf made of other vessels that Captain Hook had blown out of
the water. Unfortunately, when all you hear about are the sets of a
film and how much it all costs, the final product has to compete with
its own publicity. The film reportedly ran, incredibly, between $60
to $70 million.

The originality of *Hook* and what was borrowed from Barrie
was a clever concept not totally realized. The major problem is that
it is not a great film. It settles for blandness in small areas that
together harm the whole. Why would Spielberg hire Leslie Bricusse
to write the lyrics for the quasi–"I Won't Grow Up" tune, "We

RIGHT: Bob Hoskins as Smee. BELOW: Julia Roberts as Tinker Bell. (Copyright © 1991 TriStar Pictures, Inc.)

Don't Wanna Grow Up"? Perhaps the rights to the original song were impossible to get, but was the lyricist paid to create a mediocre version of a recognized anthem of youth? Even the Toys "R" Us commercials song is better, yet salaries paid for such ineffectiveness are partly responsible for the ever-soaring costs of making a film. "When You're Alone" is the other nondistinguished contribution offered by Bricusse, which, amazingly, was nominated for an Oscar! Is this the same man who wrote the wonderful song lyrics for *Victor/Victoria* a decade earlier?

John Williams composed another of his soaring Spielbergian scores, making the music of *Hook* sound like his work for *E.T.*, *Superman,* and *Close Encounters of the Third Kind.*

In his review in the *New York Times,* Vincent Canby found *Hook* to be

overwhelmed by a screenplay heavy with complicated exposition, but what are, in effect, big busy nonsinging, nondancing production numbers and some contemporary cant about rearing children and the high price paid for success. The acute difficulty of having it all may be of greater urgency to Mr. Spielberg than to most of the people who will see the movie.

Canby also considered that

it's probably not the writers' fault that one keeps hearing what sound like song cues, if only because the 1954 *Peter Pan* remains so fresh....Perhaps one day Mr. Hoffman will get a chance to sing that show's classic "Captain Hook's Waltz"....In the meantime he does very well just acting the role with brilliance, a cappella.

Interestingly, the last line in the film, my favorite, is most appropriate in a decade of increased teen-age suicide. As a boy Peter declares, "To die will be an awfully big adventure." As a man he reflects, "To live will be an awfully big adventure." With *Hook,* Steven Spielberg gives an important message to parents and children. Unfortunately, the medium in which he chose to sell it falls short of expectations from the master filmmaker. "After seeing what he and $70 million can do with sets and flying cameras," wrote Jack Mathews, "we recognize that the film almost certainly would have become the Peter Pan for generations to come—all over the world.

"But Spielberg chose to make Hook instead," concluded Mathews, "and the match made in heaven turned out to be just another deal made in Hollywood."

Still, the picture made lots of money. Who knows? Perhaps Steven Spielberg will someday get together with James M. Barrie's original concept. And what an adventure that would be!

Cathy Rigby

*It is a show that is just magical. I always wanted to go back and do it. I didn't think
about it for a long time, and then I was offered the part in 1986 and jumped at the
chance to do it. It's one of those shows when you know a part is so right for you.*
—*Cathy Rigby, 1990*

For *Peter Pan*, 1990 was certainly the year. Not only were the Disney and Mary Martin
versions of *Pan* made available on videotapes and discs, another version of the tiny character
was brought to the small screen by Fox Television. *Peter Pan and the Pirates* was presented to
the afterschool crowd every weekday. The beautifully executed drawings and dazzling colors
became a delightful diversion from the run-of-the-mill cartoons offered during this time.
Wendy, John, and Michael were once again caught up in Peter's adventures with Captain
Hook in the Never Never Land. With all of this, one might have thought that parents were up
to their ears with *Peter Pan* and would not tolerate any more of the mischievous boy. This
proved not to be the case.

On December 13, 1990, amid the videos and television series, *Peter Pan* once more flew
on Broadway to the delight of children and their parents. Producers Thomas P. McCoy and
Keith Stava booked a cross-country tour that was doing fantastic business since beginning
nearly a year earlier. Though the Broadway run was limited to only six weeks, it generated an
enthusiasm that has been rare this time of year. Perhaps what surprised the critics and
audiences most was the performance given by a little waif named Cathy Rigby.

Cathy was already a household name thanks to her spectacular performances as a
gymnast in the summer Olympics of 1968 and 1972. Her position as sports commentator for
ABC furthered her appeal to mass audiences. In 1973 Cathy was offered the part of Peter in
the NBC Arena Touring Production of *Peter Pan*. The physical combination of Cathy and
Peter Pan seemed a natural. Her gymnastic experience would add another dimension to the
character that should be portrayed with much bravado. The voices for this show, however,
were all prerecorded and did not necessarily belong to the performers seen on stage. This
experience hooked Cathy on acting. Tom Adair joined Jule Styne to create two new songs for
this production, "Hook's Hook" and "Youth, Joy and Freedom."

Aided by her strict sense of discipline, Cathy began acting and singing lessons, and in

PAGE 258: Cathy Rigby listens to Tinker Bell's plea. Photo: Martha Swope Associates, Carol Rosegg. RIGHT: Fifteen-year-old Cathy Rigby, a young gymnast preparing for the Olympics. Her discipline was an asset when she decided to become an actress. (Courtesy of Cathy Rigby)

PAGE 258: Cathy Rigby listens to Tinker Bell's plea. Photo: Martha Swope Associates, Carol Rosegg. RIGHT: Fifteen-year-old Cathy Rigby, a young gymnast preparing for the Olympics. Her discipline was an asset when she decided to become an actress. (Courtesy of Cathy Rigby)

1981 she appeared as Dorothy in *The Wizard of Oz*, for which she received excellent reviews. From there she went on to *Meet Me in St. Louis*, *Paint Your Wagon*, and *They're Playing Our Song*.

In 1986, Cathy once again was cast in *Peter Pan*, this time in a live West Coast production. Surprisingly, Cathy managed to rise above the obvious casting gimmick to put her own stamp on *Pan*. In 1986 she received the DramaLogue Award on the West Coast for her starring performance in *Peter Pan*, but playing to Broadway audiences is a much different story.

During her interview, Cathy presented an analogy between herself and Peter Pan:

"...I grew up very much like him. On one hand I was full of adventure and taking risks, being very daring and throwing caution to the wind with my gymnastics. There was also another part of my situation [where] I had a coach who wanted to keep me a child, didn't want me to grow up, didn't want me to take responsibility. I didn't deal with feelings very well."

She continued, "I was very much like Peter....I'd put my fingers in my ears if I couldn't deal with something...a lot of bravado, toughening-everything act. And that's exactly what [he] does. I also grew up very tomboyish. There are many parallels in my life to that of Peter Pan. I felt like I was at home with the part."

This writer felt like Scrooge as he shelled out ninety-seven dollars for two tickets to see a December 26 performance of the musical. I had never seen Cathy Rigby in a play and I wasn't too keen on spending that kind of money for an introduction. Further-more, on that special evening I was introducing my six-year-old son, Drew, to Broadway, and while it seemed fitting that *Peter Pan* should be offered during the Christmas season as it has been in England for so many years, I wanted his first Broadway experience to be a memorable one. In addition, I realized that it would be inevitable that Drew would compare this Peter either to perfor-mances he had seen on video or even to an excellent production at the Staten Island Civic Theatre. For my part, I merely expected a serviceable performance by a top-class gymnast.

Surprise! Cathy Rigby gave an enchanting and poignant per-formance that captured the hearts of the audience immediately. Rather than saturate her portrayal with her renowned acrobatic talent, she was beautifully restrained. Her Peter had the physical ability to do what he wanted, but only when he wanted. Her natural athletic prowess was seen to great advantage in "I've Gotta Crow," where Peter can actually impress Wendy in ways that a real little boy would try. No more theatricality in a finger-shadow puppet show or a trick shadow with a life of its own. Just a little boy running about showing all of his special tricks. But wait a minute! This kid can also sing! Her voice is strong, clear, and a bit husky, providing another asset to her portrayal of the boy who wouldn't grow up.

"I think one of the things that we tried to do in this particular version is to go back and make it as much of the straight play as we could," Cathy reflected. "The show has been so commercialized over the years that it lost some of the integrity of the story." Director Fran Soeder omitted the "Oh My Mysterious Lady" number and reverted to Barrie's original "Marooner's Rock," which, according to Rigby, "is crucial to the show."

Since Cathy has played the musical with and without "Oh My Mysterious Lady," it was interesting to hear her comments about the number:

"It totally took away from the fact that this is a boy. All of a sudden he becomes this woman singing this aria and it becomes about slapstick and shtick. I think as a vehicle for Mary and Cyril Ritchard, it worked! It was lovely and funny. It fit the style of the show they were doing. But I felt it would really not fit." She explained further, "If we were going to make this play with music and go back to the book, we needed to take it out. The writing is clever enough. It's funny, it's endearing, you don't need to add that stuff to it. It holds itself without it and we want people to get lost in the story."

The addition of Marooner's Rock lets audiences experience the vulnerability of Peter as well as hear a classic line in literature, "To die will be an awfully big adventure." It also provides Rigby with an opportunity to show her range as an actress. This segment is the most touching in the play and a welcome addition for audiences who have not been exposed to this scene.

Stephen Hanan brought a sinister quality to Hook that generations of audiences had not encountered. Even his makeup resembled that of the early portrayals in England. When he threatened to blow up the ship creating a holocaust of children, you better believe that he would do it. Hanan combined his excellent voice and poise to create a villain straight out of an operetta, reminiscent at times of Barnaby from *Babes in Toyland*. He was fully capable of torturing his victims before murdering them, but not before he entertained them with a song. Altogether, this Hook was a demented character who could easily scare young children who are accustomed to such villains from films and television.

Cindy Robinson was delightful and humorous as Wendy with her sharp delivery in that odd little voice. Lauren Thompson brought a fresh interpretation to Mrs. Darling, a woman who now tolerates her husband's behavior. Finally, Don Potter was as memo-

Cathy Rigby and Cindy Robinson as Wendy, "Flying." Photo: Martha Swope Associates, Carol Rosegg

Cathy from a 1975 production of *Peter Pan* aboard Captain Hook's ship. (Courtesy NBC Touring Productions)

rable a Smee as any before him, only his costume was quite more ornate.

So how did the critics react? Linda Winer of *New York Newsday* was impressed with Rigby's gymnastic abilities but

more important, she creates a character—believably boyish, a little gruff, a little fragile—who knows his way around Neverland [sic] like a long-term resident....When someone comes too close to touching Peter's heart, she hunches her shoulders and stiffens up like a scared tough kid. With her solid little body and her round face, she has the pug quality of the young James Cagney.

Daily News critic Howard Kissel said:

When Cathy Rigby, who plays Peter in this revival, whooshes in through the window of the Darling's London townhouse, flying with an abandon, a carefree spirit few have equaled, the musical seems utterly fresh and enchanting....Chunky, tomboyish, uncomplicated, Rigby is youthful energy itself. She crows jubilantly. She has a hearty singing voice, fine for most of the music, not agile or high enough for the operatic duet written for Peter and Hook, which has been cut.

Kissel also felt that Rigby

acts with great conviction, especially when she makes her impassioned plea for us to clap to save Tinker Bell's life. She is at her most persuasive when she's in the air: No one has made flying look more exhilarating.

Edwin Wilson of the *Wall Street Journal* was equally impressed with the flying scenes. He went on to write:

But Ms. Rigby has other assets. She is a true tomboy, which is just right for Peter, and she has a quite acceptable singing voice—certainly good enough for the score of *Peter Pan*. All in all, this remains an ideal introduction for the youngsters to the joys of the theatre. The older folk who take them won't have a bad time either.

The *Boston Globe*'s Kevin Kelly said:

Cathy Rigby is remarkably talented...she sings wonderfully, with precision, with range, with style....She is irresistible. Rigby will lift you out of your seat.

Among those unimpressed with the revival was Clive Barnes of the *New York Post* who wrote that

this musical version of *Peter Pan*...has only two things wrong with it: the play upon which it is based and the music which has been added to it.

He found the production mediocre, at best.

Finally, Mel Gussow of the *New York Times* praised Rigby's stage presence, pleasant singing voice, and flying ability, but he was not impressed with the total production. Almost all of the critics agreed that the sound system was overamplified, giving the feeling that occasionally the singing was not "live."

Cathy was nominated for a Tony Award for Best Actress in a Musical. Following the Broadway run, she took the show back on the road, returning to the Great White Way again in 1991, just in time for Christmas. The so-called Thirty-Fifth Anniversary Production of *Peter Pan* was produced by McCoy/Rigby Entertainment, a company formed by Cathy and her husband, producer Tom McCoy. Together they package musical plays that properly showcase Cathy's talents. In 1992, she began touring in a new version of Irving Berlin's *Annie Get Your Gun*, which premiered at the Houston Grand Opera.

Wouldn't it be nice if Peter made regular visits to Broadway during the year-end holidays? Barrie's invitation for audience participation was ahead of its time in 1904. Today the play remains a delightful introduction for children to theatre, while for adults it conjures up precious memories of youth.

It has been over fifty years since Broadway audiences have seen the "straight" version of *Peter Pan*. For many, the musical treatment of James M. Barrie's play by Moose Charlap, Carolyn Leigh, Jule

Styne, Betty Comden, Adolph Green, and Jerome Robbins remains the definitive *Pan*. Ironically, like the original source, there have been several changes with each new production of the musical. Songs are removed or added, while the libretto moves unconsciously between the material provided by Comden and Green, the original play, *Peter Pan, or The Boy Who Wouldn't Grow Up,* and the book, *Peter and Wendy*. I believe that there is no pure *Peter Pan* and there never was.

Cathy Rigby in the premiere of her 1986 *Peter Pan* and in the two Broadway versions of her touring production, in 1990 and 1991. Note the slightly altered art work on the *Playbill* cover of the second engagement.

"Peter Pan holds a peculiar position. His is the only story of recent centuries to escape from literature into folklore," wrote author Roger Lancelyn Green in 1960. "For every one person who has seen the play or read the story there are hundreds who know perfectly well who and what Peter Pan is. Besides being a fairy-tale character, he is also a symbol—of what, precisely, even Barrie could not find words to describe: 'I'm youth, I'm joy! I'm a little bird that has broken out of the egg!'" Like folklore," Peter Pan belongs temporarily to the teller and the listener, the actor and the audience. Barrie's original play went through many revisions during the author's lifetime, even after the script was published. The musical, which is almost forty years old, cannot escape the same destiny.

History does have a funny way of repeating itself.

Appendix A

A Selected Discography

There are many recorded readings of *Peter Pan* as well as several musical adaptations made for very young children. Included here are only those recordings, in their most recent pressings, directly related to the stage and screen productions.

Marilyn Miller Version

The only recordings were of a song dedicated to the actress by songwriters Robert King and Ray Henderson.

Victor
Released: 1924
19570
    "All Alone"—International Novelty Orchestra
    "Peter Pan (I Love You)"—Waring's Pennsylvanians
19651
    "Peter Pan (I Love You)"—Henry Burr
    "West of the Great Divide"—Henry Burr

Cameo 630
Released: 1924
    "Peter Pan (I Love You)"—Bob Haring and his Orchestra
    "Oh! Flo"—Dixie Daisies

Gennett 5609
Released: 1924
    "Peter Pan" (from *Peter Pan*)—Westchester Biltmore Country Club Orchestra
    "Nobody Loves You Like I Do"—Willie Creager's Orchestra

Oriole 367
Released: 1924
    "Peter Pan (I Love You)"—Irving Post

Perfect 14331
Released: 1924
    "Dear One"—Mike Speciale and His Carton Terrace Orchestra
    "Peter Pan (I Love You)"—Max Terr and His Orchestra

Jean Forbes-Robertson Version

His Master's Voice #10
Released: 1939, England
Scenes, Songs, and Music. Music and lyrics by James Crook and J. M. Barrie. Jean Forbes-Robertson (Peter), Dinah Sheridan (Wendy), Gordon Harker (Captain Hook), George Baker (Hook's songs), Nancy Evans (Mrs. Darling), Orchestra conducted by Clifford Greenwood

B 9117
    Excerpts from Act I—The Nursery Scene
    Excerpts from Act I—The Nursery Scene—Part Two

B 9118
    Scene: The Home Under the Ground.
    Captain Hook's Song—George Baker; "Lullaby"—Nancy Evans; Song of the Lost Boys, "We'll Build a House for Wendy"—The Italia Conti Children

B 9119
   Jolly Tunes from the Incidental Music
   "Hook's Monologue"—Gordon Harker; "The Pirate's Song"—George Baker

Glynis Johns

Caedmon CAE (CS) CPN-1395
Released: 1970
This is not a cast recording but rather a reading by the actress who appeared as Pan in 1943. The music for this record was composed by Dick Hyman.

Jean Arthur Version

Columbia ML/OL-4312 LP (mono)
Released: 1950

Columbia MJV-92 78 rpm
Released: 1950
In this special recording edited for children, the Bernstein songs have been omitted.

Columbia AOL-4312 reissue.
Released: 1973

Columbia CK 4312 Compact Disc.
Released: 1988
Peter Pan Broadway cast. Songs and lyrics by Leonard Bernstein. (This recording omits the incidental music by Trude Rittman and substitutes the music of Alec Wilder.) Jean Arthur, Boris Karloff, Marcia Henderson, Peg Hillias, Joe E. Marks, Orchestra conducted by Ben Steinberg.

Painted Smiles PS-1377 (stereo)
Ben Bagley's Leonard Bernstein Revisited. Jo Sullivan sings "Dream With Me," which was cut from final production.

Etcetera ETC-1037
Roberta Alexander Sings Bernstein. Includes "Never-Land."

Disney Animated Film

Disneyland 1206 (mono)
Released: 1953
Peter Pan. Film sound track. Songs by Sammy Cahn and Sammy Fain, Oliver Wallace, Ed Penner, Ted Sears, and Winston Hibler. Bobby Driscoll, Kathryn Beaumont, Hans Conreid, Bill Thompson, and Candy Candido.

Ovation 5000 (stereo)
Released: 1978
The Magical Music of Walt Disney. Includes five songs from the film sound track.

RCA 10" LPM-3101 (mono)
Released: 1953
Peter Pan. Songs from the film. Conducted by Hugo Winterhalter. Vocals: Stuart Foster and Judy Valentine. Includes "Never Smile at a Crocodile," which was deleted from the film.

Columbia (EP) B-1590
Released: 1953
"Peter Pan"—Doris Day

Mary Martin Version

RCA LOC-1019-LP (mono)
EYA-48 45 rpm (mono)
Released: 1954
   LSO-1019 (Rechanneled stereo), reissued in 1959

AYL1-3762e (Rechanneled stereo), reissued in 1981.
3762-2-RG Compact Disc (mono).
Songs by Mark Charlap, Carolyn Leigh, Jule Styne, Betty Comden, and Adolph Green. Incidental music by Trude Rittman and Elmer Bernstein. "Tinker Bell" by Jaye Rubanoff. Orchestra conducted by Louis Adrian.

Dolphin 1- 10″ LP (mono)
Released: 1955
Cyril Ritchard: Odd Songs and a Poem. Includes "The Old Gavotte" by Nancy Hamilton and Morgan Lewis.

Heritage 0057 (mono)
Released: 1954
Reissued in 1984 by DRG Records.
Comden and Green. The songwriters perform their own material that includes "Distant Melody," "Hook's Waltz," "Never, Never land," and "Oh My Mysterious Lady."

Capitol WAO 1197 (mono), SWAO 1197 (stereo)
Released: 1958
A Party with Betty Comden and Adolph Green. A live performance of the Theatre Guild production. Includes "Oh My Mysterious Lady."

Stet S2L-5177 (stereo)
Released: 1977
A Party with Betty Comden and Adolph Green. A new production recorded live on May 1 in Washington, D.C. Includes "Hook's Waltz," "Never, Never Land," and "Oh My Mysterious Lady."

Private 45 PP 1/2
Released: 1973

"Youth, Joy, and Freedom"—a song by Jule Styne and Tom Adair which was added to the 1954 score for the 1973 NBC Arena Touring Production of *Peter Pan,* sung by Yvonne Green.
"I've Gotta Crow"—Yvonne Green

Anita Harris

Golden Hour GH-590
Released: 1974
Anita Harris is Peter. Includes "Nobody" and "Build A House" by John Taylor. The rest of the album contains songs that are not from this production.

Sandy Duncan

Dove Books on Tape
Released: 1989
Sandy Duncan Reads Peter Pan. Not the Broadway musical but a straight reading of the play.

"Casino de Paris" Version

Carrere Music (A Time Warner Company) 9031-76251-2
Released: 1991, France
Songs by Mark Charlap, Carolyn Leigh, Jule Styne, Betty Comden, and Adolph Green. Incidental music by Trude Rittman and Elmer Bernstein. In French, with Fabienne Guyon (Peter), Nathalie Lhermitte (Wendy), Sophie Tellier (Tiger Lily), and Bernard Alane (Captain Hook).

Hook

Epic 48888
Released: 1991
Sound track. Music composed and conducted by John Williams. Includes "We Don't Wanna Grow Up" and "When You're Alone" with lyrics by Leslie Bricusse.

Appendix B

Cast Lists

Actors and actresses who have played Peter, Wendy, and Captain Hook in productions of *Peter Pan*. Asterisk (*) indicates dual role of Captain Hook/Mr. Darling.

LONDON

Year	Peter Pan	Wendy	Captain Hook
1904–05	Nina Boucicault	Hilda Trevelyan	* Gerald du Maurier
1905–06	Cecilia Loftus	Hilda Trevelyan	Gerald du Maurier
1906–07	Pauline Chase	Hilda Trevelyan	* Gerald du Maurier
1907–08	Pauline Chase	Hilda Trevelyan	Robb Harwood
1908–09	Pauline Chase	Gertrude Lang	Robb Harwood
1909–10	Pauline Chase	Hilda Trevelyan	Robb Harwood
1910–11	Pauline Chase	Gertrude Lang	E. Holman Clark
1911–12	Pauline Chase	Hilda Trevelyan	E. Holman Clark
1912–13	Pauline Chase	Mary Glynne	E. Holman Clark
1912–13	Pauline Chase	Mary Glynne	E. Holman Clark
1913–14	Pauline Chase	Mary Glynne	Godfrey Tearle
1914–15	Madge Titheradge	Hilda Trevelyan	E. Holman Clark
1915–16	Unity More	Dot Temple	Arthur Wontner
1916–17	Unity More	Dot Temple	E. Holman Clark
1917–18	Fay Compton	Isobel Elsom	E. Holman Clark
1918–19	Faith Celli	Isobel Elsom	Julian Royce
1919–20	Georgette Cohan	Rennee Mayer	Allan Jeayes
1920–21	Edna Best	Freda Godfrey	* Henry Ainley
1921–22	Joan Maclean	Sylvia Oakley	Ernest Thesiger
1922–23	Edna Best	Sylvia Oakley	Lyn Harding
1923–24	Gladys Cooper	Lila Maraven	Franklyn Dyall
1924–25	Gladys Cooper	Angela du Maurier	* Ian Hunter
1925–26	Dorothy Dickson	Angela du Maurier	Lyn Harding
1926–27	Dorothy Dickson	Annie Kasmir	Alfred Drayton
1927–28	Jean Forbes-Robertson	Mary Casson	William Luff
1928–29	Jean Forbes-Robertson	Mary Casson	Malcolm Keen
1929–30	Jean Forbes-Robertson	Mary Casson	* Gerald du Maurier
1930–31	Jean Forbes-Robertson	Mary Casson	* George Curzon
1931–32	Jean Forbes-Robertson	Mary Casson	* George Curzon
1932–33	Jean Forbes-Robertson	Mary Casson	* George Curzon
1933–34	Jean Forbes-Robertson	Daphne Courtney	* Ralph Richardson
1934–35	Jean Forbes-Robertson	Pamela Stanley	* George Curzon
1935–36	Nova Pilbeam	Violet Loxley	* George Hayes
1936–37	Elsa Lanchester	Pamela Standish	Charles Laughton
1937–38	Anna Neagle	Pamela Standish	* George Curzon
1938–39	Jean Forbes-Robertson	Pamela Standish	Seymour Hicks
1939–40	No West End London production due to the war.		
1940–41	No London or touring companies due to the war.		
1941–42	Barbara Mullen	Joan Greenwood	Alastair Sim
1942–43	Ann Todd	Joyce Redman	* Alastair Sim
1943–44	Glynis Johns	Diana Deare	* Baliol Holloway
1944–45	Frances Day	Angela Wyndham-Lewis	* Walter Fitzgerald
1945–46	Celia Lipton	June Holden	* George Curzon

Year	Peter Pan	Wendy	Captain Hook
1946–47	Mary Morris	Diana Calderwood	Alastair Sim
1947–48	Phyllis Calvert	Christina Forest	* Peter Murray Hill
1948–49	Joan Hopkins	Judith Stott	* George Cuzon
1949–50	Margaret Lockwood	Christina Forest	* John Justin
1950–51	Margaret Lockwood	Shirley Lorimer	* Alan Judd
1951–52	Joan Greenwood	Shirley Lorimer	* George Curzon
1952–53	Brenda Bruce	Hilary Rennie	* James Donald
1953–54	Pat Kirkwood	Norah Gorsen	Donald Wolfit
1954–55	Barbara Kelly	Dorothy Bromiley	* Richard Wordsworth
1955–56	Peggy Cummins	Roberta Woolley	* Frank Thring
1956–57	Janette Scott	Francis Guthrie	* John McCallum
1957–58	Margaret Lockwood	Julia Lockwood	* Michael Warre
1958–59	Sarah Churchill	Julia Lockwood	* John Justin
1959–60	Julia Lockwood	Patricia Garwood	* Richard Wordsworth
1960–61	Julia Lockwood	Juliet Mills	* Donald Sinden
1961–62	Anne Heywood	Jane Asher	* John Gregson
1962–63	No London production.		
1963–64	Julia Lockwood	April Wilding	Alastair Sim
1964–65	Dawn Addams	Alison Frazer	Alastair Sim (evening); Robert Eddison (matinees)
1965–66	Sylvia Syms	Alison Frazer	* Ronald Lewis
1966–67	Julia Lockwood	Mia Martin	* Ron Moody
1967–68	Millicent Martin	Mia Martin	* Paul Daneman
1968–69	Wendy Craig	Caroline Delavigne	Alastair Sim (evening); Richard Wordsworth (matinees)
1969–70	Hayley Mills	Louise Rush	* Bill Travers
1970–71	No London production.		
1971–72	Dorothy Tutin	Wendy Padbury	* Ron Moody
1972–73	Dorothy Tutin	Belinda Carroll	* Eric Porter
1973–74	Maggie Smith	Gail Harrison	* Dave Allen
1974–75	Susan Hampshire	Stacy Dorning	* Michael Denison
1975–76	Lulu	Tessa Wyatt	* Ron Moody
1976–77	No London production.		
1977–78	Susannah York	Astrid Clifford	* Ron Moody
1978–79	Jane Asher	Andrea Kealy	* Nigel Patrick
1979–80	Gayle Hunnicut	Briony McRoberts	* James Villiers
1980–81	No London production.		
1981–82	No London production.		
1982–83	Miles Anderson	Jane Carr	* Joss Ackland
1983–84	Mark Rylance	Katy Behean	* Stephen Moore
1984–85	John McAndrew	Jane Carr	* Stephen Moore
1985–86	Bonnie Langford	Annabelle Lanyon	* Joss Ackland
1986–87	No London production.		
1987–88	No London production.		
1988–89	Lulu	Michelle Thorneycroft	* Christopher Timothy
1989–90	Tina Doyle	Debbie Wall	* George Sewell

NOTE: The John Crook score was used exclusively until 1959 when additional music by Alan Abbott was added. In 1967, Donald Elliott and Neil Feiling contributed to the Crook-Abbott score, which continued to be used until 1971. That year Grant Foster supplied new music, although in the years following a few John Crook songs were put back in the show. The RSC commissioned Stephen Oliver to write an entire new score in 1982. The Mary Martin musical version was presented in 1985 and 1988. A new musical version with music and lyrics by Piers Chater-Robinson premiered in 1989.

NEW YORK PRODUCTIONS

Year	Peter Pan	Wendy	Captain Hook
1905–06	Maude Adams	Mildred Morris	* Ernest Lawford
1912	Maude Adams	Dorothy Dunn	* R.P. Carter
1915	Maude Adams	Gladys Gillan	* R.P. Carter
1924–25	Marilyn Miller	Dorothy Hope	Leslie Banks
1928–29	Eva Le Gallienne	Josephine Hutchinson	Walter Beck–Egon Brecker
1929–30	Eva Le Gallienne	Josephine Hutchinson	Walter Beck
1930–31	Eva Le Gallienne	Josephine Hutchinson	Water Beck
1931–32	Eva Le Gallienne	Josephine Hutchinson	Walter Beck
1932–33	Eva Le Gallienne	Josephine Hutchinson	Walter Beck
1946	Anne Edgar	Pamela Coppen	Sam Payne
1950–51	Jean Arthur	Marcia Henderson	* Boris Karloff
1954	Mary Martin	Kathy Nolan	* Cyril Ritchard
1979–80	Sandy Duncan	Marsha Kramer	* George Rose (replaced in touring company by Christopher Hewett)
1990–91	Cathy Rigby	Cindy Robinson	* Stephen Hanan

SELECT BRITISH TOURING COMPANIES

Not included are touring companies that basically featured the same cast as in the London productions.

Year	Peter Pan	Wendy	Captain Hook
1906 (1st)	Cecilia Loftus	Hilda Trevelyan	* Loring Fernie
1906–07	Zena Dare	Ela Q. May	* Lionel Mackinder
1913–14	Majorie Manners	Alice Hatton	Lionel Gadsen
1914–15	Gladys Gaynor	Alice Hatton	Lionel Gadsen
1916	Eva Embury	Dot Temple	J. Scott-Leighton
	Stephanie Stephens	Alice Hatton	Lionel Gadsen
1919	Molly Terraine	Ethel Ward	* Edward MacLean
1920	Lila Maravan	Ethel Ward	* Talbot Homewood
1920–21	Irene Arnold	Marguerite Morgan	Lionel Gadsen
1922	Maisie Darrell	Marguerite Morgan	* Lionel Gadsen
1922–23	Doris Littell	Marguerite Morgan	Lionel Gadsen
1925–26	Kathleen Vaughan	Miriam Adams	Alfred Drayton
1928–29	Sheila Moloney	Judy Hallat	Lionel Gadsen
1931–32	Doris Hilditch	Daphne Courtney	Lionel Gadsen
1933–34	Moira Lynd	Rosemary Bambe	Lionel Gadsen
1934–35	Betty Marsden	Dinah Sheridan	Lionel Gadsen
1935–36	Ena Moon	Diana Sinclair Hill	Harry Welchman
1936–37	Dinah Sheridan	Diana Sinclair Hill	* George Hayes
1937–38	Anona Winn	Diana Sinclair Hill	Leo Sheffield
1938–39	Joan Shipman	Diana Deare	Leo Sheffield
1939–40	Margaret Cooper	Hilda Schroder	* Raf de la Torre
1944	Celia Lipton	Barbara White	* Baliol Halloway
1945	Nova Pilbeam	Angela Wyndham-Lewis	* Walter Fitzgerald

SELECT U.S. TOURING COMPANIES

Year	Peter Pan	Wendy	Captain Hook
1907	Vivian Martin	Violet Hemming	* John MacFarlane
1910	Eva Lang	Ethel Valentine	Frank Denithorne
1912	Beverly West	Isoldi Illian	* Eric Blind
1938	Leslie C. Gorall	Jewel Morse	John Ireland

Year	Peter Pan	Wendy	Captain Hook
1951	Jean Arthur/Joan McCracken	Jennifer Bunker	* Boris Karloff
1951	Veronica Lake	Peggy O'Hara	* Lawrence Tibbett
1959	Rosemary Harris	Chase Crosley	* Eric Portman
1966	Betsy Palmer	Sandy Duncan	* George S. Irving

CINEMA

Year	Peter Pan	Wendy	Captain Hook
1924	Betty Bronson	Mary Brian	Ernest Torrence
1953 (voices)	Bobby Driscoll	Kathryn Beaumont	Hans Conreid
1992	Robin Williams	Maggie Smith	Dustin Hoffman

TELEVISION

Year	Peter Pan	Wendy	Captain Hook
1955	Mary Martin	Kathy Nolan	* Cyril Ritchard
1956	Mary Martin	Kathy Nolan	* Cyril Ritchard
1960	Mary Martin	Maureen Baily	* Cyril Ritchard
1976	Mia Farrow	Briony McRoberts	* Danny Kaye

SPECIAL PERFORMANCES OF SCENES BY THE JUVENILE MEMBERS OF THE LONDON COMPANY

Year	Peter Pan	Wendy	Captain Hook
Jan. 26, 1906	Winifred Geoghegan	Ela Q. May	[No Hook]
Feb. 19, 1907	Winifred Geoghegan	Dorothy Le Marchand	* George Hersee
Feb. 9, 1909	Tessie Parke	Beryl St. Leger	Herbert Hollom
Feb. 8, 1910	Herbert Hollom	Tessie Parke	Harry Duff
Feb. 3, 1911	Mary Glynne	Stephanie Bell	Herbert Hollom

Bibliography

BARRIE'S WORKS

Published

Barrie, James M. *Margaret Ogilvy*. New York: Charles Scribner's Sons, 1886.
_____. *Sentimental Tommy*. New York: Charles Scribner's Sons, 1896.
_____. *The Little Minister*. New York: Grosset and Dunlap, 1897.
_____. *Tommy and Grizel*. New York: Charles Scribner's Sons, 1900.
_____. *The Little White Bird*. New York: Charles Scribner's Sons, 1902.
_____. *Peter Pan in Kensington Gardens*. New York: Charles Scribner's Sons, 1906.
_____. *Peter and Wendy*. New York: Charles Scribner's Sons, 1911.
_____. *Peter and Wendy* (Photoplay edition entitled *Peter Pan*). New York: Grosset and Dunlap, 1924.
_____. *Peter Pan or, The Boy Who Wouldn't Grow Up*. New York: Charles Scribner's Sons, 1928.
_____. *When Wendy Grew Up: An Afterthought*. London: Nelson, 1957 (published posthumously).

Unpublished

Barrie, James M. "The Boy Castaways of Black Lake Island." The only existing copy is part of the Barrie collection at the Beinecke Library at Yale University.
_____. "A Play." This original draft of *Peter Pan* dated November 23, 1903, is in the collection of the Lillie Library at the University of Indiana.
_____. "Peter Pan or, The Boy Who Wouldn't Grow Up." A script from the 1910 edition with Pauline Chase is in the collection of the Museum of the City of New York.
_____. "Peter Pan...Grow Up." A script from the Civic Repertory Theatre is in the collection of the Beineke Library at Yale University.

WORKS ABOUT BARRIE
Published

In particular, Andrew Birkin's beautifully written and researched biography, *J. M. Barrie and the Lost Boys* was of great help and should be of interest to anyone even remotely interested in Barrie. *Fifty Years of Peter Pan* by Roger Lancelyn Green, which documents the early British productions, is also an important and valuable work. Finally, *The Story of J. M. B.*, Denis Mackail's exhaustive biography, remains a work of art itself fifty years after its first publication.

Asquith, Cynthia. *Portrait of Barrie*. London: Robert Cunningham and Sons Ltd., 1954.
Birkin, Andrew. *J. M. Barrie and the Lost Boys*. London: Constable, 1979.
Dunbar, Janet. *J. M. Barrie, The Man Behind the Image*. Boston: Houghton Mifflin Company, 1970.
Green, Roger Lancelyn. *Fifty Years of Peter Pan*. London: Davis, 1953.
_____. *J. M. Barrie*. New York: Henry Z. Walck, Inc., 1960.
Haill, Catherine, and Nanette Newman. *Dear Peter Pan....* London: Victoria and Albert Museum, 1983.
Hammerton, Sir John Alexander. *J. M. Barrie and His Books* (reprint of 1900 edition). New York: Haskell House Publishers Ltd., 1974.
Mackail, Denis. *Barrie—The Story of J. M. B.* New York: Scribner's, 1941.
Meynell, Viola. *Letters of James M. Barrie*. New York: Scribner's, 1947.

WORKS ABOUT THE ARTISTS WHO HAVE WORKED ON *PETER PAN*
Published

Bodeen, DeWitt. "Betty Bronson." *Films in Review,* December 1974.
Boucicault, Nina. "When I Was Peter Pan." *The Strand Magazine,* January 1923.
Chase, Pauline. *Peter Pan's Postbag.* London: Heinemann, 1909.
———. "My Reminiscences of Peter Pan." *The Strand Magazine,* January 1913.
Davies, Action. *Maude Adams.* New York: Frederick A. Stokes Company, 1901.
Du Maurier, Angela. *It's Only the Sister.* London: Peter Davies, 1949.
Du Maurier, Daphne. *Gerald: A Portrait.* New York: Doubleday, 1935.
Gordon, Ruth. *My Side.* New York: Harper and Row, 1976.
Harris, Warren G. *The Other Marilyn.* New York: Arbor House, 1985.
Kirkwood, James. *Diary of a Mad Playwright.* New York: E. P. Dutton, 1989.
Lanchester, Elsa. *Elsa Lanchester, Herself.* New York: St. Martin's Press, 1983.
Le Gallienne, Eva. *At 33.* New York: Longmans, Green, 1934.
———. *With a Quiet Heart.* New York: Viking Press, 1953.
Lesley, Cole. *Remembered Laughter: The Life of Noël Coward.* New York: Knopf, 1976.
Maltin, Leonard. *The Disney Films.* New York: Crown, 1973.
Mank, Gregory. "Josephine Hutchinson." *Films in Review,* November 1980.
Marcosson, Isaac F., and Daniel Frohman. *Charles Frohman—Manager and Man.* New York: Harper and Brothers, 1916.
Martin, Mary. *My Heart Belongs.* New York: William Morrow, 1976.
Maxwell, Perriton. *The Stage Story of Maude Adams,* Pamphlet. No source, 1908.
Newman, Shirlee P. *Mary Martin on Stage.* Philadelphia: Westminister Press, 1969.
Patterson, Ada. *Maude Adams.* New York: Meyer and Bros., 1907.
Ralston, Esther. *Someday We'll Laugh.* Metuchen, New Jersey: Scarecrow Press, 1985.
Robbins, Phyllis. *Maude Adams—An Intimate Portrait.* New York: G. P. Putnam's Sons, 1956.
———. *The Young Maude Adams.* New Hampshire: Marshall Jones, 1959.
Rose, Jacqueline. "Writing as Auto-Visualisation: Notes on a Scenario and Film of *Peter Pan* c. 1924." *Screen 16* (Autumn 1975).
Shelton, George. *It's Smee.* London: Ernest Benn, 1928.
"On Peter Pan," *The Journal,* the Society of Stage Directors and Choreographers, June 1982. This excellent resource is a transcription of the Round Table panel that consisted of Betty Comden, Adolph Green, Carolyn Leigh, Jerome Robbins, Jule Styne, and Mary Hunter as moderator. An Afterword was written by Mary Martin. The S.D.C. Foundation is the only organization in the United States devoted to fostering, promoting, and developing the creativity and craft of professional stage directors and choreographers.

Many newspapers and magazines were used and are cited in the chapters.

Unpublished

Barrie, James M. "Peter Pan." Joan McCracken's April 24, 1950, script from the Imperial Theatre is part of the Billy Rose Collection at the New York Public Library of Performing Arts. Also in that collection are several scripts from the 1954 musical, including the stage manager's prompt book and the abridged television script.
Bronson, Betty. The Betty Bronson Papers—a collection of personal scrapbooks, memoirs, and diaries in the Arts Special Collection at U.C.L.A.
Christie, Edith. "Peter Pan Pictures, and Other Pictures of Miss Adams." Scrapbook from Stephens College in Columbia, Missouri, where Maude Adams taught. 1908.
Le Gallienne, Eva. "On Playing Peter Pan." Courtesy of Eloise Armen of the Eva Le Gallienne Estate and biographer Helen Sheehy. 1992.
Leigh, Carolyn. All of her unused lyrics are collected with the original drafts of the 1954 musical of *Peter Pan* in the Museum of the City of New York.
Trevelyan, Hilda. A letter describing Barrie's *An Afterthought* dated December 10, 1957. At the Beinecke Library at Yale University.

GENERAL REFERENCES

Darton, F. J. Harvey. *Children's Books in England.* London: Cambridge University Press, 1966.

Green, Stanley. *Broadway Musicals.* Milwaukee, Wisconsin: Hal Leonard Books, 1987.

Hummel, David. *The Collector's Guide to the American Musical Theatre.* Metuchen, New Jersey: Scarecrow Press, 1984.

Jablonski, Edward. *The Encyclopedia of American Music.* New York: Doubleday, 1981.

Knight, Arthur. *The New York Times Directory of the Film.* New York: Arno Press/Random House, 1971.

Leonard, William Torbert. *Theatre: Stage to Screen to Television.* Metuchen, New Jersey: Scarecrow Press, 1981.

Mordden, Ethan. *Better Foot Forward:* A History of American Musical Theatre. New York: Grossman Publishers, 1976.

Suskin, Steven. *Show Tunes—1905–1991, 2nd edition.* New York: Limelight, 1991.

Acknowledgments

*I*t is my pleasure to thank the following people who have worked on various productions of *Peter Pan* and who have generously shared their memories for this book.

Mary Brian, Betty Comden, Sandy Duncan, Charles Eaton, Adolph Green, Mary Hunter, Josephine Hutchinson, Sondra Lee, the late Mary Martin, Kathleen Nolan, Esther Ralston, Cathy Rigby, Jerome Robbins, Norman Shelly, Jule Styne.

I would also like to express my gratitude to the following people for their invaluable help:

Michael Allerti, Sheela Amembal, Eloise Armen, Edward Ancona, Tim Bagley, Larry Baker, Sophie Baker, Ben Bagley, Donna Benz, Andrew Birkin, Andreas Brown, Elizabeth Charlap, Paul Charlap, Dom Crincoli, Dorothy Decker and Ira Shapiro of Jule Styne's office, Diane Deigman, Doris Eaton Travis, Aaron T. Farr, John Falocco, Susan Fletcher, Dr. Thomas Finnegan, Jack Gottlieb of Amberson Music, Susan Grushken, Barbara Heffernan, Charlie Heidecker, Peggy Hilton, Anne Kaufman Schnieder, Henry Klingler, Jan Kreher-Policastro of NBC, Ken Mandelbaum, Carl Meyer of NBC, Merle Murphy, Terry Pickett of Qualex, Robert Reisenberg, Dana Rich, Nancy Richter, Sharron and Eddie Rossi, "Joanio" Russo, Abram Samuels, Helen Sheehy, June Silver, Beatrice Smith, Sherry Shokriah, Steven Suskin, Melanie Tromba, Mary Umhoefer, Anke Wandell, Valerie Wodjat, and my friends at North Hunterdon who have been so supportive.

The following were also very helpful:

The Larry Edmunds Book Shop, Morris Everett, Jr., of The Last Moving Picture Company, De Stan Video, David Drummond, Howard and Ron Mandelbaum of Photofest, Gayla Rauh of Film Favorites, Margarita Reeve, Ph.D., Morton J. Savada of Records Revisited, Richard Stoddard, and Bob Willoughby for his generosity and beautiful photographs.

My gratitude to:

Richard Bagehot, Esq., of Field Fischer Waterhouse Limited for aiding me in securing permission to use unpublished and rare Barrie material.

The helpful and patient staff of the Billy Rose Collection and the Rodgers and Hammerstein Archives of Recorded Sound of the Performing Arts Research Center at the New York Public Library at Lincoln Center.

David Bogart and Joseph Weiss of Edwin H. Morris and Company.

Melanie T. Christoudia and Barry Norman of the Theatre Museum, a branch of the Victoria and Albert Museum in London.

Mitch Douglas of I.C.M. for bringing Eva Le Gallienne's "Playing Peter Pan" to my attention and for his good advice.

Aria Edry, development director of Stage Directors and Choreographers Foundation Inc.

Karen Gilmour, representative of Barrie's Birthplace—the National Trust for Scotland.

Vincent Girourd, curator of the Barrie Collection, and Patricia Willis, curator of American Literature, both at Yale Beinecke Library.

Edith Golub of Charles Scribner's Sons.

The Great Ormand St. Hospital for Sick Children for allowing me to reprint the unpublished Peter Pan material.

Dr. Jan-Christopher Horak, senior curator of film collections, and Kay McRae, administrative assistant of film collections, the George Eastman House, Rochester, New York.

David Hummel, Archives of the American Musical Theatre.

The Library at Indiana University.

Brigitte Kueppers, head of the Arts Special Collection at UCLA.

Edwin M. Matthias, reference librarian at the Library of Congress.

The Brooklyn Public Library Information.

The Metropolitan Post Card Collectors' Club.

Sylvia Morris, assistant librarian, the Shakespeare Birthplace Trust, the Shakespeare Centre, Stratford-Upon-Avon.

Dr. Jeanne Newlin, curator of the Harvard Theatre Collection of Pusey Library at Harvard.

Hillary Ray of the Museum of the City of New York.

Lynn Pearson, assistant vice president, and Elizabeth Wright, editorial assistant of publications department at Sotheby's.

Joanna Todd, director of Reader's Services at Hugh Stephen's Library.

Henry Wallengren of Samuel French, Inc.

The Ziegfeld Club, Inc.

I will always remember my students from the Florence M. Gaudineer School who influenced me more than they know to take on this project: Leslie (Wendy), Aaron (John), Nick (Michael), Jessica (Nana), Seth (Mr. Darling), Kelly (Mrs. Darling), Vincent (Peter Pan), Julie (Tiger Lily), Billy (Captain Hook), Kelly A. (Liza), Anita, Greg, and all those wonderful lost boys and pirates.

A special note of thanks to:

Emily R. Coleman for being so helpful with her solid advice.
Karl Michael Emyrs for sharing his insight and expertise on Peter Pan.
Dr. Judith Gaines for her editorial assistance during the early stage of the manuscript and for allowing me to adopt her computer for two years.
Harriet Goldberg, my New Dorp High School English teacher.
Joseph T. McMahon for the use of his photographs.
Marianne Simmonetti, a good friend who also acted as my personnel secretary during the interview stages of research for this book.
Harvey Schmidt for the many beautiful photographic contributions to this book. Thank you for your enthusiasm and support.

Miles Kreuger, Institute of the American Musical.

This book could not have been made possible without the aid of my good friend, Robert Gable. For your photographs, ideas, advice, and contacts, thank you, Mr. Gable.

I must also thank my family:

Allen and Sonia Buckwald, Lettario and Helene Laspada, Mark and Sharon Hanson, and my son, Drew Tobias, who always kept me in touch with the latest promotional items for Peter Pan—including toys! I am most grateful to Allan J. Wilson for this confidence in this project and in an unknown writer. His artistic influence can be seen throughout his book. He is also a gentleman. I also appreciate the hard work Alvin H. Marill encountered while editing the manuscript and his excellent suggestions.

Thank you Carol Siegel for your editorial comments.
Thanks to Paula Scher for her beautiful cover and Stephanie Bart-Horvath for the design of the book.

Finally, thank you Donna, for showing your support in this project as well as in all of my other areas of interest. Your thoughts are always backed by your deeds.

Credits

Index